LEE CHILD
TRIPWIRE

PENGUIN BOOKS

The Jack Reacher series

For more information see www.JackReacher.com

Lee Child is one of the world's leading thriller writers. He was born in Coventry, raised in Birmingham, and now lives in New York. It is said one of his novels featuring his hero Jack Reacher is sold somewhere in the world every nine seconds. His books consistently achieve the number-one slot on bestseller lists around the world and have sold over one hundred million copies. Lee is the recipient of many awards, including Author of the Year at the 2019 British Book Awards. He was appointed CBE in the 2019 Queen's Birthday Honours.

TRANSWORLD PUBLISHERS
Penguin Random House, One Embassy Gardens,
8 Viaduct Gardens, London SW11 7BW
www.penguin.co.uk

Transworld is part of the Penguin Random House group of comanies whose
addresses can be found at global.penguinrandomhouse.com

Penguin
Random House
UK

First published in Great Britain in 1999 by Bantam Press
an imprint of Transworld Publishers
Bantam edition published 2000
Bantam edition reissued 2011
Penguin paperback edition reissued 2024

A CIP catalogue record for this book
is available from the British Library.

ISBN
9781804993644

Typeset in Times New Roman by Phoenix Tyepsetting,
Auldgirth, Dumfriesshire.
Printed and bound in Great Britain by Clays Ltd, Elcograf S.p.A.

The authorized representative in the EEA is Penguin Random House Ireland,
Morrison Chambers, 32 Nassau Street, Dublin D02 YH68.

Penguin Random House is committed to a sustainable future for
our business, our readers and our planet. This book is made from
Forest Stewardship Council® certified paper.

MIX
Paper | Supporting
responsible forestry
FSC® C018179

For my daughter, Ruth.
Once the world's greatest kid,
now a woman I'm proud to call my friend.

Foreword by Karin Slaughter

From the beginning, Jack Reacher has always felt like a thrilling amalgamation of some of the great British classics: a dash of Arthur Conan Doyle's Sherlockian skills of deduction, a hint of Agatha Christie's class consciousness, a pinch of John le Carré's moral ambiguity, and a heaping dose of James Bond's thuggery. He's clever, capable, intuitive, observant and brutal. This last adjective gets a lot of attention, and clearly gives Reacher his ability to be the physical embodiment of justice. Readers know that no matter what happens, Reacher is going to be there to kick some ass and restore the world to justice – even if that justice goes against the technical letter of the law. We all know that vigilantes operate in grey areas, but we all are equally accepting of the fact that Jack Reacher will always do the right thing. The continuing story of justice in an unjust world is why presidents and rock stars and all types of readers in between flock to the bookstore every time there's a new Jack Reacher on the shelves.

But as with every Reacher novel, there's more to the story. At six-five, weighing upwards to 250 pounds, with a chest measurement of fifty inches and hands the size of dinner plates, Reacher is the type of man who commands attention, particularly from the type of men who are used to being the toughest guy in the room. But that discounts the other parts of the character that are in some ways more important to the legend that is Jack Reacher. Yes, he's a lethal weapon, but Reacher's ability to think before reacting, his guiding moral compass, and his mathematical ability to puzzle out the mystery, take him from being the vigilante people root for to the character that readers love.

As an author, I've often tried to figure out why Jack Reacher is such a compelling character, and why no matter what I'm doing, everything stops when a new book comes out. I think Lee would likely agree that the plots are uncomplicated by design. With a few exceptions, like a side-trip to Paris or a glimpse at Reacher's early years, the set-up follows a tried-and-true pattern: Reacher, a drifter, finds himself in a small American town where some bad guys are up to bad things. Instead of doing what most of us would do – hitching on to the next town – he sticks around and puts things right. Usually, Reacher meets a woman along the way. Usually, there's gonna be some guys getting shot in the kneecaps. Usually, there's going to be some math. Each new book does not reinvent the wheel, so why is it that every Reacher feels fresh and exciting?

One of the reasons is because there are so many interesting layers to the character. Yes, Reacher is a loner, but he somehow manages to become part of whatever community he's traversing through. In one story, he's digging pools by hand, in another, he's cleaning bars of gold while keeping an eye on a couple of embezzlers on a military base. There are a lot of military bases in Reacher novels, because he was raised in a military family and cut his investigative teeth working as a military police officer for much of his career. That military training is likely why Reacher's brain works like a tactical machine, but, as we find out, his heart is guided by a sense of fairness that was instilled in him by his French mother. Not to be trite, but Reacher's mom made sure that he understood his great strength carried with it a great responsibility. This is why a cunning, towering man like Jack Reacher, who could've easily ended up running a criminal enterprise, instead ended up using his skills to protect others from criminal acts.

For me, the primary reason I am so drawn to Jack Reacher is that he is, much as Lee Child, his creator, a man who listens to women. It seems like such a simple thing to say, but as someone who constantly reads crime novels, who is immersed in the business of writing crime, and who adores nothing more than a good crime story, it's very rare to read a novel by a man about a male hero where women play an equal role in finding justice. Generally, they are there to be saved or screwed. Generally, they are used as objects to make the hero seem more heroic. Not so with Jack Reacher.

For me, a scene that sticks out the most of any Reacher novel has him speaking to a rag-tag group of locals who are gearing up to take on the bad guys. This happens often in Reacher novels, because, while he is a loner, he's never going to say no to a little help when justice is on the line. In the scene, Reacher has a plan because he always has a plan. It's thoughtful. It makes sense. It seems like it will get the job done.

Then, one of the group speaks up. She has an alternate plan. Reacher thinks about it, then he says two words that women seldom hear from men: 'You're right.' This, to me, is the ultimate show of strength, and it embodies everything I love about Reacher (and Lee). He has no problem admitting someone might have a better idea. He isn't intimidated by intelligent women; in fact, he admires them. His sense of self, his masculinity, doesn't flow from making other people feel lesser than. It comes from his security in himself and his ability to appreciate that characteristic in other people. Even if they're women.

The evolution of this dynamic comes to play in *Tripwire*, when Reacher is reunited with Jodie, whose late father, General Leon Garber, was Reacher's former commanding officer, mentor and friend. Garber's guiding voice still fills Reacher's thoughts, but it's Jodie who catches his eye. She is a highly successful attorney who is smart, independent, capable and beautiful. She's also recently single. She's a good match for Reacher, though long-term readers know they shouldn't get their hopes up.

In the book, Jodie and Reacher team up to complete Garber's last project: a military family has lost their life savings to a scam artist who has promised to reveal the location of their fallen son. From the start, there is a palpable sexual chemistry between Jodie and Reacher, but for all of his assertiveness in the other areas of his life, he is reserved with Jodie. He feels protective, like he owes Garber the duty of looking out for his daughter. Instinctively, he wants to keep her safe. Reacher knows how awful the world can be and he is willing to put himself firmly between her and that awfulness. What he comes to realize is that Jodie is driven by the same sense of justice as her father, as Reacher himself, and that, more importantly, Jodie doesn't need his protection. She's quite capable of going shoulder-to-shoulder with him against the world.

Which is exactly what they do.

The villain of the story is more than made for the match. When you have an outsized hero, you need an outsized villain. With *Tripwire*, we find the perfect Moriarty to Reacher's Sherlock. He's smart and ruthless and willing to sacrifice whatever it takes. In that Christie fashion, the villain's wealth has given him a certain arrogance and greed. He is adept at pulling the levers of power and influence to his advantage. As with a le Carré character, the bad guy is comfortable living outside of the law. Then there's the dash of the Bond villain with his scarred and mutilated body, which gives him a backstory that might bring one to empathy but for the deplorable crimes he's committed against innocent, grieving families.

Reacher and Jodie's quest to find justice for the family isn't about the stolen money. It's about finding the location of their missing son, a helicopter pilot who served in Vietnam. Reacher wants to give them answers. He wants them to have a resolution. It's the sort of fight that we know Reacher will never back down from. And he isn't above seeking Jodie's help to get here.

But there's a twist.

Of all the books in the series, *Tripwire* shows something that we don't often see in Reacher: a crisis in confidence. When he realizes that he's misjudged someone entirely, his belief in his own intuition cracks. Any other character might be overwhelmed by this vulnerability, but Jack Reacher isn't one to stare into his navel and question the ways of the world. In true Reacher form, there is more going on behind the scenes. Not to give anything away but if the final pages of this story don't make your heart race, then you might want to make sure your heart is still working.

Tripwire is, in many ways, one of my very favourite Jack Reacher novels. As always, the plotting is fast paced. The twists are so good and so unexpected and so completely satisfying. The romance is believable and engaging. The mystery kaleidoscopes in a way that is utterly enjoyable. It's clear to me as a fellow writer that Lee was hitting his stride when he wrote this, his third in the series, and every subsequent novel has shown a man who, much like Reacher, knows exactly what he is doing.

Karin Slaughter

PROLOGUE

Hook Hobie owed the whole of his life to a secret nearly thirty years old. His liberty, his status, his money, everything. And like any cautious guy in his particular situation, he was ready to do what was necessary to protect his secret. Because he had a lot to lose. The whole of his life.

The protection he relied on for nearly thirty years was based on just two things. The same two things anybody uses to protect against any danger. The same way a nation protects itself against an enemy missile, the same way an apartment dweller protects himself against a burglar, the same way a boxer guards against a knockout blow. Detection and response. Stage one, stage two. First you spot the threat, and then you react.

Stage one was the early-warning system. It had changed over the years, as other circumstances had changed. Now it was well rehearsed and simplified. It was made up of two layers, like two concentric tripwires. The first tripwire was eleven thousand miles from home. It was an early-early warning. A wake-up call. It would tell him they were getting close. The second tripwire was five thousand miles nearer, but still six

15

thousand miles from home. A call from the second location would tell him they were about to get very close. It would tell him stage one was over, and stage two was about to begin.

Stage two was the response. He was very clear on what the response had to be. He had spent nearly thirty years thinking about it, but there was only ever one viable answer. The response would be to run. To disappear. He was a realistic guy. The whole of his life he had been proud of his courage and his cunning, his toughness and his fortitude. He had always done what was necessary, without a second thought. But he knew that when he heard the warning sounds from those distant tripwires, he had to get out. Because no man could survive what was coming after him. No man. Not even a man as ruthless as he was.

The danger had ebbed and flowed like a tide for years. He had spent long periods certain it was about to wash over him at any time. And then long periods certain it would never reach him at all. Sometimes the deadening sensation of time made him feel safe, because thirty years is an eternity. But other times it felt like the blink of an eye. Sometimes he waited for the first call on an hourly basis. Planning, sweating, but always knowing he could be forced to run at any moment.

He had played it through his head a million times. The way he expected it, the first call would come in maybe a month before the second call. He would use that month to prepare. He would tie up the loose ends, close things down, cash in, transfer assets, settle scores. Then, when the second call came in, he would take off. Immediately. No hesitation. Just get the hell out, and stay the hell out.

But the way it happened, the two calls came in on the same day. The second call came first. The nearer trip-wire was breached an hour before the farther one. And Hook Hobie didn't run. He abandoned thirty years of careful planning and stayed to fight it out.

ONE

Jack Reacher saw the guy step in through the door. Actually, there was no door. The guy just stepped in through the part of the front wall that wasn't there. The bar opened straight out on to the sidewalk. There were tables and chairs out there under a dried-up old vine that gave some kind of nominal shade. It was an inside-outside room, passing through a wall that wasn't there. Reacher guessed there must be some kind of an iron grille they could padlock across the opening when the bar closed. If it closed. Certainly Reacher had never seen it closed, and he was keeping some pretty radical hours.

The guy stood a yard inside the dark room and waited, blinking, letting his eyes adjust to the gloom after the hot whiteness of the Key West sun. It was June, dead-on four o'clock in the afternoon, the southernmost part of the United States. Way farther south than most of the Bahamas. A hot white sun and a fierce temperature. Reacher sat at his table in back and sipped water from a plastic bottle and waited.

The guy was looking around. The bar was a low room built from old boards dried to a dark colour. They looked like they had come from old broken-up sailing ships. Random pieces of nautical junk were nailed to them. There were old brass things and green glass globes. Stretches of old nets. Fishing equipment, Reacher guessed, although he had never caught a fish in his life. Or sailed a boat. Overlaying everything were ten thousand business cards, tacked up over every spare square inch, including the ceiling. Some of them were new, some of them were old and curled, representing ventures that had folded decades ago.

The guy stepped farther into the gloom and headed for the bar. He was old. Maybe sixty, medium height, bulky. A doctor would have called him overweight, but Reacher just saw a fit man some way down the wrong side of the hill. A man yielding gracefully to the passage of time without getting all stirred up about it. He was dressed like a northern city guy on a short-notice trip to somewhere hot. Light grey pants, wide at the top, narrow at the bottom, a thin crumpled beige jacket, a white shirt with the collar spread wide open, blue-white skin showing at his throat, dark socks, city shoes. New York or Chicago, Reacher guessed, maybe Boston, spent most of his summer in air-conditioned buildings or cars, had these pants and this jacket stashed away in the back of his closet ever since he bought them twenty years ago, brought them out occasionally and used them as appropriate.

The guy reached the bar and went into his jacket and pulled a wallet. It was a small overloaded old item in fine black leather. The sort of wallet that moulds itself tight around the stuff crammed inside. Reacher saw the guy open it with a practised flick and show it to the bartender and ask a quiet question. The bartender glanced away like he'd been insulted. The guy put the wallet away and smoothed his wisps of grey hair into the sweat on his scalp. He muttered something else and the bartender came up with a beer from a chest of ice. The old guy held the cold bottle against his face for a moment and then took a long pull. Belched discreetly behind his hand and smiled like a small disappointment had been assuaged.

Reacher matched his pull with a long drink of water. The fittest guy he had ever known was a Belgian soldier who swore the key to fitness was to do whatever the hell you liked as long as you drank five litres of mineral water every day. Reacher figured five litres was about a gallon, and since the Belgian was a small whippy guy half his size, he should make it two gallons a day. Ten full-size bottles. Since arriving in the heat of the Keys, he had followed that regimen. It was working for him. He had never felt better. Every day at four o'clock he sat at this dark table and drank three bottles of still water, room temperature. Now he was as addicted to the water as he had once been to coffee.

The old guy was side-on to the bar, busy with his beer. Scanning the room. Reacher was the only person in it apart from the bartender. The old guy pushed off with his hip and stepped over. Waved his beer in a vague gesture that said *may I?* Reacher nodded to the opposite chair and broke the plastic seal on his third bottle. The guy sat heavily. He overwhelmed the chair. He was the sort of guy who keeps keys and money and handkerchiefs in his pants pockets so that the natural width of his hips is way exaggerated.

'Are you Jack Reacher?' he asked across the table.

Not Chicago or Boston. New York, for sure. The voice sounded exactly like a guy Reacher had known, spent the first twenty years of his life never more than a hundred yards from Fulton Street.

'Jack Reacher?' the old guy asked again.

Up close, he had small wise eyes under an over-hanging brow. Reacher drank and glanced across at him through the clear water in his bottle.

'Are you Jack Reacher?' the guy asked for the third time.

Reacher set his bottle on the table and shook his head.

'No,' he lied.

The old guy's shoulders slumped a fraction in disappointment. He shot his cuff and checked his watch. Moved his bulk forward on the chair like he was about to get up, but then sat back, like suddenly there was time to spare.

'Five after four,' he said.

Reacher nodded. The guy waved his empty beer bottle at the bartender who ducked around with a fresh one.

'Heat,' he said. 'Gets to me.'

Reacher nodded again and sipped water.

'You know a Jack Reacher around here?' the guy asked.

Reacher shrugged.

'You got a description?' he asked back.

The guy was into a long pull on the second bottle. He wiped his lips with the back of his hand and used the gesture to hide a second discreet belch.

'Not really,' he said. 'Big guy, is all I know. That's why I asked you.'

Reacher nodded.

'There are lots of big guys here,' he said. 'Lots of big guys everywhere.'

'But you don't know the name?'

'Should I?' Reacher asked. 'And who wants to know?'

The guy grinned and nodded, like an apology for a lapse in manners.

'Costello,' he said. 'Pleased to meet you.'

Reacher nodded back, and raised his bottle a fraction in response.

'Skip tracer?' he asked.

'Private detective,' Costello said.

'Looking for a guy called Reacher?' Reacher asked. 'What's he done?'

Costello shrugged. 'Nothing, far as I know. I just got asked to find him.'

'And you figure he's down here?'

'Last week he was,' Costello said. 'He's got a bank account in Virginia and he's been wiring money to it.'

'From down here in Key West?'

Costello nodded.

'Every week,' he said. 'For three months.'

'So?'

'So he's working down here,' Costello said. 'Has been, for three months. You'd think somebody would know him.'

'But nobody does,' Reacher said.

Costello shook his head. 'I asked all up and down Duval, which seems to be where the action is in this town. Nearest I got was a titty bar upstairs someplace, girl in there said there was a big guy been here exactly three months, drinks water every day at four o'clock in here.'

He lapsed into silence, looking hard at Reacher, like he was issuing a direct challenge. Reacher sipped water and shrugged back at him.

'Coincidence,' he said.

Costello nodded.

'I guess,' he said quietly.

23

He raised the beer bottle to his lips and drank, keeping his wise old eyes focused tight on Reacher's face.

'Big transient population here,' Reacher said to him. 'People drift in and out, all the time.'

'I guess,' Costello said again.

'But I'll keep my ears open,' Reacher said.

Costello nodded.

'I'd appreciate it,' he said ambiguously.

'Who wants him?' Reacher asked.

'My client,' Costello said. 'Lady called Mrs Jacob.'

Reacher sipped water. The name meant nothing to him. Jacob? Never heard of any such person.

'OK, if I see him around, I'll tell him, but don't hold your breath. I don't see too many people.'

'You working?'

Reacher nodded.

'I dig swimming pools,' he said.

Costello pondered, like he knew what swimming pools were, but like he had never considered how they got there.

'Digger operator?'

Reacher smiled and shook his head.

'Not down here,' he said. 'We dig them by hand.'

'By hand?' Costello repeated. 'What, like with shovels?'

'The lots are too small for machinery,' Reacher said. 'Streets are too narrow, trees are too low. Get off Duval, and you'll see for yourself.'

Costello nodded again. Suddenly looked very satisfied.

'Then you probably won't know this Reacher guy,' he said. 'According to Mrs Jacob, he was an Army officer. So I checked, and she was right. He was a major. Medals and all. Military police bigshot, is what they said. Guy like that, you won't find him digging swimming pools with a damn shovel.'

Reacher took a long pull on his water, to hide his expression.

'So what would you find him doing?'

'Down here?' Costello said. 'I'm not sure. Hotel security? Running some kind of a business? Maybe he's got a cruiser, charters it out.'

'Why would he be down here at all?'

Costello nodded, like he was agreeing with an opinion.

'Right,' he said. 'Hell of a place. But he's here, that's for certain. He left the Army two years ago, put his money in the nearest bank to the Pentagon and disappeared. Bank account shows money wiring out all over the damn place, then for three months money wiring back in from here. So he drifted for a spell, then he settled down here, making some dough. I'll find him.'

Reacher nodded.

'You still want me to ask around?'

Costello shook his head. Already planning his next move.

'Don't you worry about it,' he said.

He eased his bulk up out of the chair and pulled a crumpled roll from his pants pocket. Dropped a five on the table and moved away.

'Nice meeting you,' he called, without looking back.

He walked out through the missing wall into the glare of the afternoon. Reacher drained the last of his water and watched him go. Ten after four in the afternoon.

* * *

An hour later Reacher was drifting down Duval Street, thinking about new banking arrangements, choosing a place to eat an early dinner, and wondering why he had lied to Costello. His first conclusion was he would cash up and stick with a roll of bills in his pants pocket. His second conclusion was he would follow his Belgian friend's advice and eat a big steak and ice cream with another two bottles of water. His third conclusion was that he had lied because there had been no reason not to.

There was no reason why a private investigator from New York should have been looking for him. He had never lived in New York. Or any big northern city. He had never really lived anywhere. That was the defining feature of his life. It made him what he was. He had been born the son of a serving Marine Corps officer, and he had been dragged all over the world from the very day his mother carried him out of the maternity ward of a Berlin infirmary. He had lived nowhere except in an endless blur of different military bases, most of them in distant and inhospitable parts of the globe. Then he had joined the Army himself, military police investigator, and lived and served in those same bases all over again until the peace dividend had closed his unit down and cut him loose. Then he had come home to the United States and drifted around like a cheap tourist until he had washed up on the extreme tip of the nation with his savings running out. He had taken a couple of days' work digging holes in the ground, and the couple of days had stretched into a couple of weeks, and the weeks had stretched into months, and he was still there.

He had no living relatives anywhere capable of leaving him a fortune in a will. He owed no money. He had never stolen anything, never cheated anybody. Never fathered any children. He was on as few pieces of paper as it was possible for a human being to be. He was just about invisible. And he had never known anybody called Jacob. He was sure of that. So whatever Costello wanted, he wasn't interested in it. Certainly not interested enough to come out from under and get involved with anything.

Because being invisible had become a habit. In the front part of his brain, he knew it was some kind of a complex, alienated response to his situation. Two years ago, everything had turned upside down. He had gone from being a big fish in a small pond to being nobody. From being a senior and valued member of a highly structured community to being just one of 270 million anonymous civilians. From being necessary and wanted to being one person too many. From being where someone told him to be every minute of every day to being confronted with three million square miles and maybe forty more years and no map and no schedule. The front part of his brain told him his response was understandable, but defensive, the response of a man who liked solitude but was worried by loneliness. It told him it was an extremist response, and he should take care with it.

But the lizard part of his brain buried behind the frontal lobes told him he liked it. He liked the anonymity. He liked his secrecy. It felt warm and comfortable and reassuring. He guarded it. He was friendly and gregarious on the surface, without ever saying much about himself. He liked to pay cash and travel by road. He was never on any passenger manifests or credit card carbons. He told nobody his name. In Key West, he had checked into a cheap motel under the name Harry S Truman. Scanning back through the register, he had seen he wasn't unique. Most of the forty-one presidents had stayed there, even the ones nobody had heard of, like John Tyler and Franklin Pierce. He had found names did not mean much in the Keys. People just waved and smiled and said hello. They all assumed everybody had something to be private about. He was comfortable there. Too comfortable to be in any hurry to leave.

He strolled for an hour in the noisy warmth and then ducked off Duval towards a hidden courtyard restaurant where they knew him by sight and had his favourite brand of water and would give him a steak that hung off both sides of the plate at once.

The steak came with an egg and fries and a complicated mix of some sort of warm-weather vegetables, and the ice cream came with hot chocolate sauce and nuts. He drank another quart of water and followed it with two cups of strong black coffee. Pushed back from the table and sat there, satisfied.

'OK now?' The waitress smiled.

Reacher grinned back at her and nodded.

'It hit the spot,' he said.

'And it looks good on you.'

'It feels good on me.'

It was true. His next birthday was going to be his thirty-ninth, but he felt better than ever. He had always been fit and strong, but the last three months had brought him to a new peak. He was six foot five, and he had weighed 220 when he left the Army. A month after joining the swimming pool gang, the work and the heat had burned him down to 210. Then the next two months, he had built back all the way to about 250, all of it pure hard muscle. His workload was prodigious. He figured to shift about four tons of earth and rock and sand every day. He had developed a technique of digging and scooping and twisting and throwing the dirt with his shovel so that every part of his body was working out all day long. The result was spectacular. He was burned a deep brown by the sun and he was in the best shape of his life. Like a condom crammed with walnuts, is what some girl had said. He figured he needed to eat about ten thousand calories a day just to stay level, as well as the two gallons of water he needed to drink.

'So you working tonight?' the waitress asked.

Reacher laughed. He was earning money for doing a fitness regime most people would pay a fortune for at any shiny city gymnasium, and now he was headed for his evening job, which was something else he got paid for that most men would gladly do for free. He was the bouncer in the nude bar Costello had mentioned. On Duval. He sat in there all night with no shirt on, looking tough, drinking free drinks and making sure the naked women didn't get hassled. Then somebody gave him fifty bucks for it.

'It's a chore,' he said. 'But somebody's got to do it, I guess.'

The girl laughed with him, and he paid his check and headed back to the street.

Fifteen hundred miles to the north, just below Wall Street in New York City, the chief executive officer took the elevator down two floors to the finance director's suite. The two men went into the inner office together and sat side by side behind the desk. It was the kind of expensive office and expensive desk that

29

get specified and paid for when times are good and then sit there like a sullen reproach when times turn bad. It was a high-floor office, dark rosewood all over the place, cream linen window blinds, brass accents, a huge slab of a desk, an Italian table light, a big computer that had cost more than it needed to. The computer was glowing and waiting for a password. The CEO typed it in and hit ENTER and the screen redrew into a spreadsheet. It was the only spreadsheet that told the truth about the company. Which was why it was protected by a password.

'Are we going to make it?' the CEO asked.

That day had been D-Day. D stood for *downsizing*. Their human resources manager out at the manufacturing plant on Long Island had been busy since eight o'clock that morning. His secretary had rustled up a long line of chairs in the corridor outside his office, and the chairs had been filled with a long line of people. The people had waited most of the day, shuffling up one place every five minutes, then shuffling off the end of the line into the human resources manager's office for a five-minute interview that terminated their livelihoods, thank you and goodbye.

'Are we going to make it?' the CEO asked again.

The finance director was copying large numbers on to a sheet of paper. He subtracted one from another and looked at a calendar. He shrugged.

'In theory, yes,' he said. 'In practice, no.'

'No?' the CEO repeated.

'It's the time factor,' the finance director said. 'We did the right thing out at the plant, no doubt about that. Eighty per cent of the people gone, saves us ninety-one per cent of the payroll, because we only kept the cheap ones. But we paid them all up to the end of next month. So the cash-flow enhancement doesn't hit us for six weeks. And in fact right now the cash flow gets much worse, because the little bastards are all out there cashing a six-week pay cheque.'

The CEO sighed and nodded.

'So how much do we need?'

The finance director used the mouse and expanded a window.

'One-point-one million dollars,' he said. 'For six weeks.'

'Bank?'

'Forget it,' the finance director said. 'I'm over there every day kissing ass just to keep what we already owe them. I ask for more, they'll laugh in my face.'

'Worse things could happen to you,' the CEO said.

'That's not the point,' the finance director said. 'The point is they get a sniff we're still not healthy, they'll call those loans. In a heartbeat.'

The CEO drummed his fingers on the rosewood and shrugged.

'I'll sell some stock,' he said.

The finance director shook his head.

'You can't,' he said, patiently. 'You put stock in the market, the price will go through the floor. Our existing borrowing is secured on stock, and if it gets any more worthless, they'll close us down tomorrow.'

'Shit,' the CEO said. 'We're six weeks away. I'm not going to lose all this for six lousy weeks. Not for a lousy million bucks. It's a trivial amount.'

'A trivial amount we haven't got.'

'Got to be somewhere we can get it.'

The finance director made no reply to that. But he was sitting there like he had something more to say.

'What?' the CEO asked him.

'I heard some talk,' he said. 'Guys I know, gossiping. There's maybe somewhere we can go. For six weeks, it might be worth it. There's an outfit I heard about. A lender-of-last-resort type of thing.'

'On the level?'

'Apparently,' the finance director said. 'Looks very respectable. Big office over in the World Trade Center. He specializes in cases like this.'

The CEO glared at the screen.

'Cases like what?'

'Like this,' the finance director repeated. 'Where you're almost home and dry, but the banks are too tight-assed to see it.'

The CEO nodded and gazed around the office. It was a beautiful place. And his own office was two floors higher, on a corner, and even more beautiful.

'OK,' he said. 'Do it.'

'I can't do it,' the finance director said. 'This guy won't deal below CEO level. You'll have to do it.'

It started out a quiet night in the nude bar. A midweek evening in June, way too late for the snowbirds and the spring breakers, too early for the summer vacationers who came down to roast. Not more than maybe forty people in all night, two girls behind the bar, three girls out there dancing. Reacher was watching a woman called Crystal. He assumed that was not her real name, but he had never asked. She was the best. She earned a lot more than Reacher had ever earned as a major in the military police. She spent a percentage of her income running an old black Porsche. Reacher sometimes heard it in the early afternoons, rumbling and blatting around the blocks where he was working.

The bar was a long narrow upstairs room with a

catwalk and a small circular stage with a shiny chrome pole. Snaking around the catwalk and the stage was a line of chairs. There were mirrors everywhere, and where there weren't, the walls were painted flat black. The whole place pulsed and pounded to loud music coming out of half-a-dozen speakers serious enough to drown out the roar of the air-conditioning.

Reacher was at the bar, his back to it, a third of the way into the room. Near enough the door to be seen straight away, far enough into the room that people wouldn't forget he was there. The woman called Crystal had finished her third spot and was hauling a harmless guy backstage for a twenty-buck private show when Reacher saw two men emerge at the top of the stairs. Strangers, from the north. Maybe thirty years old, bulky, pale. Menacing. Northern tough guys, in thousand-dollar suits and shined shoes. Down here in some kind of a big hurry, still dressed for their city office. They were standing at the desk, arguing about the three-buck cover charge. The girl at the desk glanced anxiously at Reacher. He slid off his stool. Walked over.

'Problem, guys?' he asked.

He had used what he called his college-kid walk. He had noticed that college boys walk with a curious tensed-up, limping motion. Especially on the beach, in their shorts. As if they were so tremendously muscle-bound they couldn't quite make their limbs operate in the normal way. He thought it made 130-pound teenagers look pretty comical. But he had learned it made a 250-pound six-foot-five guy look pretty scary. The college-kid walk was a tool of his new trade. A tool that worked. Certainly the two guys in their thousand-dollar suits looked reasonably impressed by it.

'Problem?' he asked again.

That one word was usually enough. Most guys backed off at that point. But these two didn't. Up close, he felt something coming off them. Some kind of a blend of menace and confidence. Some arrogance in there, maybe. A suggestion they normally got their own way. But they were far from home. Far enough south of their own turf to act a little circumspect.

'No problem, Tarzan,' the left-hand guy said.

Reacher smiled. He had been called a lot of things, but that was a new one.

'Three bucks to come in,' he said. 'Or it's free to go back downstairs.'

'We just want to speak with somebody,' the right-hand guy said.

Accents, from both of them. From somewhere in New York. Reacher shrugged.

'We don't do too much speaking in here,' he said. 'Music's too loud.'

'What's your name?' the left-hand guy asked.

Reacher smiled again.

'Tarzan,' he said.

'We're looking for a guy called Reacher,' the guy said back. 'Jack Reacher. You know him?'

Reacher shook his head.

'Never heard of him,' he said.

'So we need to talk to the girls,' the guy said. 'We were told they might know him.'

Reacher shook his head again.

'They don't,' he said.

The right-hand guy was looking past Reacher's shoulder into the long narrow room. He was glancing at the girls behind the bar. He was figuring Reacher for the only security on duty.

'OK, Tarzan, step aside,' he said. 'We're coming in now.'

'Can you read?' Reacher asked him. 'Big words and all?'

He pointed up at a sign hanging above the desk. Big Day-Glo letters on a black background. It said Management Reserves the Right to Refuse Admission.

'I'm management,' Reacher said. 'I'm refusing you admission.'

The guy glanced between the sign and Reacher's face.

'You want a translation?' Reacher asked him. 'Words of one syllable? It means I'm the boss and you can't come in.'

'Save it, Tarzan,' the guy said.

Reacher let him get level, shoulder to shoulder on his way past. Then he raised his left hand and caught the guy's elbow. He straightened the joint with his palm and dug his fingers into the soft nerves at the bottom of the guy's tricep. It's like getting a continuous pounding on the funny bone. The guy was jumping around like he was getting flooded with electricity.

'Downstairs,' Reacher said softly.

The other guy was busy calculating the odds. Reacher saw him doing it and figured full and fair disclosure was called for. He held his right hand up, eye level, to confirm it was free and ready for activity. It was a huge hand, brown, calloused from the shovel handle, and the guy got the message. He shrugged and started down the stairs. Reacher straight-armed his pal after him.

'We'll see you again,' the guy said.

'Bring all your friends,' Reacher called down. 'Three bucks each to get in.'

He started back into the room. The dancer called Crystal was standing right there behind him.

'What did they want?' she asked.

He shrugged.

'Looking for somebody.'

'Somebody called Reacher?'

He nodded.

'Second time today,' she said. 'There was an old guy in here before. He paid the three bucks. You want to go after them? Check them out?'

He hesitated. She swept his shirt off the barstool and handed it to him.

'Go for it,' she said. 'We're OK in here for a spell. Quiet night.'

He took the shirt. Pulled the sleeves right side out.

'Thanks, Crystal,' he said.

He put the shirt on and buttoned it. Headed for the stairs.

'You're welcome, Reacher,' she called after him.

He spun around, but she was already walking back towards the stage. He looked blankly at the desk girl and headed down to the street.

Key West at eleven in the evening is about as lively as it gets. Some people are halfway through their night, others are just starting out. Duval is the main street, running the length of the island east to west, bathed in light and noise. Reacher wasn't worried about the guys waiting for him on Duval. Too crowded. If they had revenge on their minds, they'd pick a quieter location. Of which there was a fair choice. Off Duval, especially to the north, it gets quiet quickly. The town

36

is miniature. The blocks are tiny. A short stroll takes you twenty blocks up into what Reacher thought of as the suburbs, where he dug pools into the tiny yards behind the small houses. The street lighting gets haphazard and the bar noise fades into the heavy buzz of night-time insects. The smell of beer and smoke is replaced by the heavy stink of tropical plants blooming and rotting in the gardens.

He walked a sort of spiral through the darkness. Turning random corners and quartering the quiet areas. Nobody around. He walked in the middle of the road. Anybody hiding in a doorway, he wanted to give them ten or fifteen feet of open space to cover. He wasn't worried about getting shot at. The guys had no guns. Their suits proved it. Too tight to conceal weapons. And the suits meant they'd come south in a hurry. Flown down. No easy way to get on a plane with a gun in your pocket.

He gave it up after a mile or so. A tiny town, but still big enough for a couple of guys to lose themselves in. He turned left along the edge of the graveyard and headed back towards the noise. There was a guy on the sidewalk against the chain-link fence. Sprawled out and inert. Not an unusual sight in Key West, but there was something wrong. And something familiar. The wrong thing was the guy's arm. It was trapped under his body. The shoulder nerves would be shrieking hard enough to cut through however drunk or stoned the guy was. The familiar thing was the pale gleam of an old beige jacket. The top half of the guy was light, the bottom half was dark. Beige jacket, grey pants. Reacher paused and glanced around. Stepped near. Crouched down.

It was Costello. His face was pounded to pulp.

Masked in blood. There were crusty brown rivulets all over the triangle of blue-white city skin showing through at the neck of his shirt. Reacher felt for the pulse behind the ear. Nothing. He touched the skin with the back of his hand. Cool. No rigor, but then it was a hot night. The guy was dead maybe an hour.

He checked inside the jacket. The overloaded wallet was gone. Then he saw the hands. The fingertips had been sliced off. All ten of them. Quick efficient angled cuts, with something neat and sharp. Not a scalpel. A broader blade. Maybe a linoleum knife.

TWO

'It's my fault,' Reacher said.

Crystal shook her head.

'You didn't kill the guy,' she said.

Then she looked up at him sharply. 'Did you?'

'I got him killed,' Reacher said. 'Is there a difference?'

The bar had closed at one o'clock and they were side by side on two chairs next to the empty stage. The lights were off and there was no music. No sound at all, except the hum of the air-conditioning running at quarter speed, sucking the stale smoke and sweat out into the still night air of the Keys.

'I should have told him,' Reacher said. 'I should have just told him, sure, I'm Jack Reacher. Then he'd have told me whatever he had to tell me, and he'd be back home by now, and I could have just ignored it all anyway. I'd be no worse off, and he'd still be alive.'

Crystal was dressed in a white T-shirt. Nothing else. It was a long T-shirt, but not quite long enough. Reacher was not looking at her.

'Why do you care?' she asked.

It was a Keys question. Not callous, just mystified at his concern about a stranger down from another country. He looked at her.

'I feel responsible,' he said.

'No, you feel guilty,' she said.

He nodded.

'Well, you shouldn't,' she said. 'You didn't kill him.'

'Is there a difference?' he asked again.

'Of course there is,' she said. 'Who was he?'

'A private detective,' he said. 'Looking for me.'

'Why?'

He shook his head.

'No idea,' he said.

'Were those other guys with him?'

He shook his head again.

'No,' he said. 'Those other guys killed him.'

She looked at him, startled. 'They did?'

'That's my guess,' he said. 'They weren't with him, that's for sure. They were younger and richer than he was. Dressed like that? Those suits? Didn't look like his subordinates. Anyway, he struck me as a loner. So the two of them were working for somebody else. Probably told to follow him down here, find out what the hell he was doing. He must have stepped on some toes up north, given somebody a problem. So he was tailed down here. They caught up with him, beat out of him who he was looking for. So then they came looking, too.'

'They killed him to get your name?'

'Looks that way,' he said.

'Are you going to tell the cops?'

Another Keys question. Involving the cops with anything was a matter for long and serious debate. He shook his head for the third time.

'No,' he said.

'They'll trace him, then they'll be looking for you, too.'

'Not right away,' he said. 'There's no ID on the body. And no fingerprints, either. Could be weeks before they even find out who he was.'

'So what are you going to do?'

'I'm going to find Mrs Jacob,' he said. 'The client. She's looking for me.'

'You know her?'

'No, but I want to find her.'

'Why?'

He shrugged.

'I need to know what's going on,' he said.

'Why?' she asked again.

He stood up and looked at her in a mirror on the wall. He was suddenly very restless. Suddenly more than ready to get right back to reality.

'You know why,' he said to her. 'The guy was killed because of something to do with me, so that makes me involved, OK?'

She stretched a long bare leg on to the chair he had just vacated. Pondered his feeling of involvement like it was some kind of an obscure hobby. Legitimate, but strange, like folk dancing.

'OK, so how?' she asked.

'I'll go to his office,' he said. 'Maybe he had a secretary. At least there'll be records there. Phone numbers, addresses, client agreements. This Mrs Jacob was probably his latest case. She'll probably be top of the pile.'

'So where's his office?'

'I don't know,' he said. 'New York somewhere, according to the way he sounded. I know his name, I know he was an ex-cop. An ex-cop called Costello, about sixty years old. Can't be too hard to find.'

'He was an ex-cop?' she asked. 'Why?'

'Most private dicks are, right?' he said. 'They retire early and poor, they hang out a sign, they set up as one-man bands, divorce and missing persons. And that thing about my bank? He knew all the details. No way to do that, except through a favour from an old buddy still in the job.'

She smiled, slightly interested. Stepped over and joined him near the bar. Stood next to him, close, her hip against his thigh.

'How do you know all this complicated stuff?'

He listened to the rush of the air through the extractors.

'I was an investigator myself,' he said. 'Military police. Thirteen years. I was pretty good at it. I'm not just a pretty face.'

'You're not *even* a pretty face,' she said back. 'Don't flatter yourself. When do you start?'

He looked around in the darkness.

'Right now, I guess. Certain to be an early flight out of Miami.'

She smiled again. This time, warily.

'And how are you going to get to Miami?' she asked. 'This time of night?'

He smiled back at her. Confidently.

'You're going to drive me,' he said.

'Do I have time to get dressed?'

'Just shoes,' he said.

He walked her around to the garage where her old Porsche was hidden. He rolled the door open and she slid into the car and fired it up. She drove him the half-mile north to his motel, taking it slowly, waiting until the oil warmed through. The big tyres banged on broken pavement and thumped into potholes. She eased to a stop opposite his neon lobby and waited, the motor running fast against the choke. He opened his door, and then he closed it again, gently.

'Let's just go,' he said. 'Nothing in there I want to take with me.'

She nodded in the glow from the dash.

'OK, buckle up,' she said.

She snicked it into first and took off through the town. Cruised up North Roosevelt Drive. Checked the gauges and hung a left on to the causeway. Switched on the radar detectors. Mashed the pedal into the carpet and the rear end dug in hard. Reacher was pressed backward into the leather like he was leaving Key West on board a fighter plane.

She kept the Porsche above three figures all the way north to Key Largo. Reacher was enjoying the ride. She was a great driver. Smooth, economical in her movements, flicking up and down the gearbox, keeping the motor wailing, keeping the tiny car in the centre of her lane, using the cornering forces to catapult herself out into the straightaways. She was smiling, her flawless face illuminated by the red dials. Not an easy car to drive fast. The heavy motor is slung out way behind the rear axle, ready to swing like a vicious pendulum, ready to trap the driver who gets it wrong for longer than a split second. But she was getting it right. Mile for mile, she was covering the ground as fast as a light plane.

Then the radar detectors started screaming and the lights of Key Largo appeared a mile ahead. She braked hard and rumbled through the town, and floored it again and blasted north towards the dark horizon. A tight curving left, over the bridge, on to the mainland of America, and north towards the town called Homestead on a flat straight road cut through the swamp. Then a tight right on to the highway, high speed all the way, radar detectors on maximum, and they were at Miami departures just before five o'clock in the morning. She eased to a stop in the drop-off lane and waited, motor running.

'Well, thanks for the ride,' Reacher said to her.

She smiled.

'Pleasure,' she said. 'Believe me.'

He opened the door and sat there, staring forward.

'OK,' he said. 'See you later, I guess.'

She shook her head.

'No you won't,' she said. 'Guys like you never come back. You leave, and you don't come back.'

He sat in the warmth of her car. The motor popped and burbled. The silencers ticked as they cooled. She leaned towards him. Dipped the clutch and shoved the gearshift into first so that she had room to get close. Threaded an arm behind his head and kissed him hard on the lips.

'Goodbye, Reacher,' she said. 'I'm glad I got to know your name, at least.'

He kissed her back, hard and long.

'So what's your name?' he asked.

'Crystal,' she said, and laughed.

He laughed with her and lifted himself up and out of the car. She leaned across and pulled the door behind him. Gunned the motor and drove away. He stood by himself on the kerb and watched her go. She turned in front of a hotel bus and was lost to sight. Three months of his life disappeared with her like the haze of her exhaust.

Five o'clock in the morning, fifty miles north of New York City, the CEO was lying in bed, wide awake, staring at the ceiling. It had just been painted. The whole house had just been painted. He had paid the decorators more than most of his employees earned in a year. Actually, he hadn't paid them. He had fudged their invoice through his office and his company had paid them. The expense was hidden somewhere in the secret spreadsheet, part of a seven-figure total for buildings maintenance. A seven-figure total on the debit side of the accounts, pulling his business down like heavy cargo sinks a listing ship. Like a straw breaks a camel's back.

His name was Chester Stone. His father's name had been Chester Stone, and his grandfather's. His grandfather had established the business, back when a spreadsheet was called a ledger and written by hand with a pen. His grandfather's ledger had been heavy on the credit side. He had been a clock maker who spotted the coming appeal of the cinema very early. He had used his expertise with gearwheels and intricate little mechanisms to build a projector. He had taken on board a partner who could get big lenses ground in Germany. Together they had dominated the market and made a fortune. The partner had died young with no heirs. Cinema had boomed from coast to coast. Hundreds of movie theatres. Hundreds of projectors. Then thousands. Then tens of thousands. Then sound. Then CinemaScope. Big, big entries on the credit side of the ledger.

Then television. Cinemas closing down, and the ones that stayed open hanging on to their old equipment until it fell apart. His father, Chester Stone II, taking control. Diversifying. Looking at the appeal of home movies. Eight-millimetre projectors. Clockwork cameras. The vivid era of Kodachrome.

Zapruder. The new manufacturing plant. Big profits ticking up on the slow wide tape of an early IBM mainframe.

Then the movies coming back. His father dying, the young Chester Stone III at the helm, multiplexes everywhere. Four projectors, six, twelve, sixteen, where there had been just one before. Then stereo. Five-channel, Dolby, Dolby Digital. Wealth and success. Marriage. The move to the mansion. The cars.

Then video. Eight-millimetre home movies deader than the deadest thing that ever died. Then competition. Cutthroat bidding from new outfits in Germany and Japan and Korea and Taiwan, taking the multiplex business out from underneath him. The desperate search for anything to make out of small pieces of sheet metal and precision-cut gears. Anything at all. The ghastly realization that mechanical things were yesterday's things. The explosion of solid-state microchips, RAM, games consoles. Huge profits being made from things he had no idea how to manufacture. Big deficits piling up inside the silent software on his desktop machine.

His wife stirred at his side. She blinked open her eyes and turned her head left and right, first to check the clock and then to look at her husband. She saw his stare, fixed on the ceiling.

'Not sleeping?' she asked quietly.

He made no reply. She looked away. Her name was Marilyn. Marilyn Stone. She had been married to Chester for a long time. Long enough to know. She knew it all. She had no real details, no real proof, no inclusion, but she knew it all anyway. How could she not know? She had eyes and a brain. It was a long time since she had seen her husband's products proudly displayed in any store. It was a long time since any multiplex owner had dined them in celebration of a big new order. And it was a long time since Chester had slept a whole night through. So she knew.

But she didn't care. For richer, for poorer was what she had said, and it was what she had meant. Rich had been good, but poor could be good, too. Not that they would ever be poor, like some people are poor. Sell the damn house, liquidate the whole sorry mess, and they would still be way more comfortable than she had ever expected to be. They were still young. Well, not young, but not old, either. Healthy. They had interests. They had each other. Chester was worth having. Grey, but still trim and firm and vigorous. She loved him. He loved her. And she was still worth having, she knew that. Forty-something, but twenty-nine in her head. Still slim, still blonde, still exciting. Adventurous. Still worth having, in any old sense of the phrase. It was all going to be OK. Marilyn Stone breathed deeply and rolled over. Pressed herself into the mattress. Fell back to sleep, five thirty in the morning, while her husband lay quietly beside her and stared at the ceiling.

Reacher stood inside the departures terminal, breathing the canned air, his tan turning yellow in the fluorescence, listening to a dozen conversations in Spanish, checking a television monitor. New York was at the top of the list, as he had thought it would be. First flight of the day was Delta to LaGuardia, via Atlanta, in half an hour. Second was Mexicana heading south, third was United, also to LaGuardia, but direct, leaving in an hour. He headed to the United ticket desk. Asked about the price of a one-way ticket. Nodded and walked away.

He walked to the bathroom, and stood in front of the mirror. Pulled his cash roll from his pocket and assembled the price he had just been quoted from the smallest bills he had. Then he buttoned his shirt all the way up and smoothed his hair down with his palm. Walked back out and over to the Delta counter.

The ticket price was the same as United's. He knew it would be. It always is, somehow. He counted the money out, ones and tens and fives, and the counter girl took it all and straightened the bills and shuffled them into denominations.

'Your name, sir?' she asked.

'Truman,' Reacher said. 'Like the president.'

The girl looked blank. She was probably born overseas during Nixon's final days. Maybe during Carter's first year. Reacher didn't care. He had been born overseas at the start of Kennedy's term. He wasn't about to say anything. Truman was ancient history to him, too. The girl typed the name into her console and the ticket printed out. She put it in a folder with a red-and-blue world on it, then she tore it straight back out.

'I can check you in right now,' she said.

Reacher nodded. The problem with paying cash for an airline ticket, especially at Miami International, is the war on drugs. If he had swaggered up to the desk and pulled his roll of hundreds, the girl would have been obliged to tread on a small secret button on the floor under her counter. Then she would have fiddled with her keyboard until the police came in, left and right. The police would have seen a big rough guy with a tan and a big wad of cash and figured him for a courier, straight off the bat. Their strategy is to chase the drugs, for sure, but to chase the money, too. They won't let you put it in the bank, they won't let you

48

spend it without getting all concerned about it. They assume normal citizens use plastic cards for big purchases. Especially for travel. Especially at the airport desk twenty minutes before takeoff. And that assumption would lead to delay and hassle and paperwork, which were three things Reacher was always keen to avoid. So he had evolved a careful act. He made himself look like a guy who couldn't even get a credit card if he wanted one, like a down-on-his-luck insolvent roughneck. Buttoning the shirt and carefully fingering the small bills were what did it. It gave him a shy, embarrassed look. It put the counter clerks on his side. They were all underpaid and struggling with their own maxed-out plastic. So they looked up and saw a guy just a little farther down the road than they were, and sympathy was their instinctive reaction, not suspicion.

'Gate B Six, sir,' the girl said. 'I've given you a window.'

'Thanks,' Reacher said.

He walked to the gate and fifteen minutes later was accelerating down the runway with pretty much the same feeling as being back in Crystal's Porsche, except he had a lot less leg room and the seat next to him was empty.

Chester Stone gave it up at six o'clock. He shut off the alarm half an hour before it was due to sound and slid out of bed, quietly, so as not to wake Marilyn. He took his robe from the hook and padded out of the bedroom and downstairs to the kitchen. His stomach was too acid to contemplate breakfast, so he made do with coffee and headed for the shower in the guest suite where it didn't matter if he made a noise. He wanted to let Marilyn sleep, and he didn't want her to know that he couldn't. Every night she woke and made some comment about him lying there, but she never followed up on it, so he figured she didn't remember it by the morning, or else she put it down to some kind of a dream. He was pretty sure she didn't know anything. And he was happy to keep it that way, because it was bad enough dealing with the problems, without worrying about her worrying about them as well.

He shaved and spent his shower time thinking about what to wear and how to act. Truth was he would be approaching this guy practically on his knees. A lender of last resort. His last hope, his last chance. Somebody who held the whole of his future in the palm of his hand. So how to approach such a guy? Not on his knees. That was not how the game of business is played. If you look like you really need a loan, you don't get it. You only get it if you look like you don't really need it. Like it's a matter of very little consequence to you. Like it's a fifty-fifty decision whether you even allow the guy to climb on board with you and share a little wedge of the big exciting profits just around the next corner. Like your biggest problem is deciding exactly whose loan offer you're even going to consider.

A white shirt, for sure, and a quiet tie. But which suit? The Italians were maybe too flashy. Not the Armani. He had to look like a serious man. Rich enough to buy a dozen Armanis, for sure, but somehow too serious to consider doing that. Too serious and too preoccupied with weighty affairs to spend time shopping on Madison Avenue. He decided heritage was the feature to promote. An unbroken three-generation heritage of business success, maybe reflected in a dynastic approach to dressing. Like his grandfather had taken his father to his tailor and introduced him, then his father had taken him in turn. Then he thought about his Brooks Brothers suit. Old, but nice, a quiet check, vented, slightly warm for June. Would Brooks Brothers be a clever double bluff? Like saying, I'm so rich and successful it really doesn't matter to me what I wear? Or would he look like a loser?

He pulled it off the rack and held it against his body. Classic, but dowdy. He looked like a loser. He put it back. Tried the grey Savile Row from London. Perfect. It made him look like a gentleman of substance. Wise, tasteful, infinitely trustworthy. He selected a tie with just a hint of pattern and a pair of solid black shoes. Put it all on and twisted left and right in front of the mirror. Couldn't be better. Looking like that, he might almost trust himself. He finished his coffee, dabbed his lips, and slipped through to the garage. Fired up the Benz and was on an uncongested Merritt Parkway by six forty-five.

Reacher spent fifty minutes on the ground in Atlanta, then took off again and swung east and north towards New York. The sun was up out over the Atlantic and was coming in through the right-hand windows with the freezing brightness of high-altitude dawn. He was drinking coffee. The stewardess had offered him water, but he'd taken the coffee instead. It was thick and strong, and he was drinking it black. He was using it to fuel his brain. Trying to figure out who the hell Mrs Jacob could be. And why she had paid Costello to scour the country for him.

They stacked up over LaGuardia. Reacher loved that. Low lazy circles over Manhattan in the bright morning sun. Like a million movies, without the soundtrack. The plane rocking and tilting. The tall buildings sliding by under them, tinted gold by the sun. The Twin Towers. The Empire State Building. The Chrysler, his favourite. Citicorp. Then they were looping around and diving for the north shore of Queens, and landing. The buildings of Midtown across the river raked past the tiny windows as they turned to taxi in to the terminal.

His appointment was for nine o'clock. He hated that. Not because of the time. Nine o'clock was halfway through the morning for most of the Manhattan business community. The hour was not upsetting him. It was the fact that he had an appointment at all. It was a very long time indeed since Chester Stone had made an appointment to see anybody. In fact he couldn't accurately recall ever making an appointment to see anybody. Maybe his grandfather had, in the very early days. Since then it had always worked the other way around. All three Chester Stones, be it first, second or third, had secretaries who graciously tried to fit supplicants into a busy schedule. Many times people had waited days for a provisional window, and then hours in an anteroom. But now it was different. And it was burning him up.

He was early, because he was anxious. He had spent forty minutes in his office reviewing his options. He had none. Whichever way he cut it, he was one-point-one million dollars and six weeks short of success. And that was choking him, too. Because it wasn't a spectacular crash and burn. Not a total disaster. It was a measured and realistic response to the market that was almost all the way there, but not quite. Like a heroic drive off the tee that lands an inch short of the green. Very, very close, but not close enough.

Nine o'clock in the morning, the World Trade Center on its own is the sixth largest city in New York State. Bigger than Albany. Only sixteen acres of land, but a daytime population of 130,000 people. Chester Stone felt like most of them were swirling around him as he stood in the plaza. His grandfather would have been standing in the Hudson River. Chester himself had watched from his own office window as the land-fill inched out into the water and the giant towers had risen from the dry riverbed. He checked his watch and went inside. Took an elevator to the eighty-eighth floor and stepped out into a quiet deserted corridor. The ceiling was low and the space was narrow. There were locked doors leading into offices. They had small rectangular wired-glass portholes set off-centre. He found the right door and glanced through the glass and pressed the buzzer. The lock clicked back and he went inside to a reception area. It looked like a normal office suite. Surprisingly ordinary. There was a brass-and-oak counter, an attempt at opulence, and a male receptionist sitting behind it. He paused and straightened his back and stepped over towards him.

'Chester Stone,' he said firmly. 'I've got a nine o'clock with Mr Hobie.'

The male receptionist was the first surprise. He had expected a woman. The second surprise was that he was shown straight in. He was not kept waiting. He had expected to sit for a spell, out there in reception in an uncomfortable chair. That's how he would have done it. If some desperate person was coming to him for a last-ditch loan, he'd have let him sweat for twenty minutes. Surely that was an elementary psychological move?

The inner office was very large. Walls had been removed. It was dark. One wall was all windows, but they were covered with vertical blinds, open no more than narrow slits. There was a big desk. Facing it were three sofas completing a square. There were lamp tables at each end of each sofa. A huge square coffee table in the middle, brass and glass, standing on a rug. The whole thing looked like a living-room display in a store window.

There was a man behind the desk. Stone started the long walk in towards him. He dodged between the sofas and crabbed around the coffee table. Approached the desk. Stuck out his right hand.

'Mr Hobie?' he said. 'I'm Chester Stone.'

The man behind the desk was burned. He had scar tissue all the way down one side of his face. It was scaly, like a reptile's skin. Stone stared away from it in horror, but he was still seeing it in the corner of his eye. It was textured like an overcooked chicken's foot, but it was unnaturally pink. There was no hair growing where it ran up over the scalp. Then there were crude tufts, shading into proper hair on the other side. The hair was grey. The scars were hard and lumpy, but the skin on the unburned side was soft and lined. The guy was maybe fifty or fifty-five. He was sitting there, his chair pushed in close to the desk, his hands down in his lap. Stone was standing, forcing himself not to look away, his right hand stuck out over the desk.

It was a very awkward moment. There is nothing more awkward than standing there ready to shake hands while the gesture is ignored. Foolish to keep standing there like that, but somehow worse to pull your hand back. So he kept it extended, waiting. Then the man moved. He used his left hand to push back from the desk. Brought his right hand up to meet Stone's. But it wasn't a hand. It was a glittering metal hook. It started way up under his cuff. Not an artificial hand, not a clever prosthetic device, just a simple hook, the shape of a capital letter J, forged from shiny stainless steel and polished like a sculpture. Stone nearly went to grasp it anyway, but then he pulled back and froze. The man smiled a brief generous smile with the mobile half of his face. Like it meant nothing to him at all.

'They call me Hook Hobie,' he said.

He sat there with his face rigid and the hook held up like an object for examination. Stone swallowed and tried to recover his composure. Wondered if he should offer his left hand instead. He knew some people did that. His great-uncle had had a stroke. The last ten years of his life, he always shook left-handed.

'Take a seat,' Hook Hobie said.

Stone nodded gratefully and backed away. Sat on the end of the sofa. It put him sideways on, but he was happy just to be doing something. Hobie looked at him and laid his arm on the desktop. The hook hit the wood with a quiet metallic sound.

'You want to borrow money,' he said.

The burned side of his face did not move at all. It was thick and hard like a crocodile's back. Stone felt his stomach going acid and he looked straight down at the coffee table. Then he nodded and ran his palms over the knees of his trousers. Nodded again, and tried to remember his script.

'I need to bridge a gap,' he said. 'Six weeks, one-point-one million.'

'Bank?' Hobie asked.

Stone stared at the floor. The tabletop was glass, and there was a patterned rug under it. He shrugged wisely, as if he was including a hundred fine points of arcane business strategy in a single gesture, communicating with a man he wouldn't dream of insulting by suggesting he was in any way ignorant of any of them.

'I prefer not to,' he said. 'We have an existing loan package, of course, but I beat them down to a hell of a favourable rate based on the premise that it was all fixed-amount, fixed-term stuff, with no rolling component. You'll appreciate that I don't want to upset those arrangements for such a trivial amount.'

Hobie moved his right arm. The hook dragged over the wood.

'Bullshit, Mr Stone,' he said quietly.

Stone made no reply. He was listening to the hook.

'Were you in the service?' Hobie asked him.

'Excuse me?'

'Were you drafted? Vietnam?'

Stone swallowed. The burns, and the hook.

'I missed out,' he said. 'Deferred, for college. I was very keen to go, of course, but the war was over by the time I graduated.'

Hobie nodded, slowly.

'I went,' he said. 'And one of the things I learned over there was the value of intelligence gathering. It's a lesson I apply in my business.'

There was silence in the dark office. Stone nodded. Moved his head and stared at the edge of the desk. Changed the script.

'OK,' he said. 'Can't blame me for trying to put a brave face on it, right?'

'You're in relatively deep shit,' Hobie said. 'You're actually paying your bank top points, and they'll say no to any further funds. But you're doing a reasonably good job of digging yourself out from under. You're nearly out of the woods.'

'Nearly,' Stone agreed. 'Six weeks and one-point-one million away, is all.'

'I specialize,' Hobie said. 'Everybody specializes. My arena is cases exactly like yours. Fundamentally sound enterprises, with temporary and limited exposure problems. Problems that can't be solved by the banks, because they specialize too, in other arenas, such as being dumb and unimaginative as shit.'

He moved the hook again, scraping it across the oak.

'My charges are reasonable,' he said. 'I'm not a loan shark. We're not talking about hundreds of per cent interest here. I could see my way to advancing you one-point-one, say six per cent to cover the six weeks.'

Stone ran his palms over his thighs again. Six per cent for six weeks? Equivalent to an annual rate of what? Nearly 52 per cent. Borrow one-point-one million now, pay it all back plus sixty-six thousand dollars in interest six weeks from now. Eleven thousand dollars a week. Not quite a loan shark's terms. Not too far away, either. But at least the guy was saying yes.

'What about security?' Stone asked.

'I'll take an equity position,' Hobie said.

Stone forced himself to raise his head and look at him. He figured this was some kind of a test. He swallowed hard. Figured he was so close, honesty was the best policy.

'The stock's worth nothing,' he said quietly.

Hobie nodded his terrible head, like he was pleased with the reply.

'Right now it isn't,' he said. 'But it will be worth something soon, right?'

'Only after your exposure is terminated,' Stone said. 'Catch-22, right? The stock only goes back up after I repay you. When I'm out of the woods.'

'So I'll benefit then,' Hobie said. 'I'm not talking about a temporary transfer. I'm going to take an equity position, and I'm going to keep it.'

'Keep it?' Stone said. He couldn't keep the surprise out of his voice. Fifty-two per cent interest and a gift of stock?

'I always do,' Hobie said. 'It's a sentimental thing. I like to have a little part of all the businesses I help. Most people are glad to make the arrangement.'

Stone swallowed. Looked away. Examined his options. Shrugged.

'Sure,' he said. 'I guess that's OK.'

Hobie reached to his left and rolled open a drawer. Pulled out a printed form. Slid it across to the front of the desk.

'I prepared this,' he said.

Stone crouched forward off the sofa and picked it up. It was a loan agreement, one-point-one million, six weeks, 6 per cent, and a standard stock-transfer protocol. For a chunk that was worth a million dollars not long ago, and might be again, very soon. He blinked.

'Can't do it any other way,' Hobie said. 'Like I told you, I specialize. I know this corner of the market. You won't get better anyplace else. Fact is, you won't get a damn thing anyplace else.'

Hobie was six feet away behind the desk, but Stone felt he was right next to him on the sofa with his awful face jammed in his and the glittering hook ripping through his guts. He nodded, just a faint silent movement of his head, and went into his coat for his fat Mont Blanc fountain pen. Stretched forward and signed in both places against the cold hard glass of the coffee table. Hobie watched him, and nodded in turn.

'I assume you want the money in your operating account?' he asked. 'Where the other banks won't see it?'

Stone nodded again, in a daze.

'That would be good,' he said.

Hobie made a note. 'It'll be there in an hour.'

'Thank you,' Stone said. It seemed appropriate.

'So now I'm the one who's exposed,' Hobie said. 'Six weeks, no real security. Not a nice feeling at all.'

'There won't be a problem,' Stone said, looking down.

Hobie nodded.

'I'm sure there won't,' he said. He leaned forward and pressed the intercom in front of him. Stone heard a buzzer sounding faintly outside in the anteroom.

'The Stone dossier, please,' Hobie said into the microphone.

There was silence for a moment, and then the door opened. The male receptionist walked over to the desk. He was carrying a thin green file. He bent and placed it in front of Hobie. Walked back out and closed the door quietly. Hobie used his hook to push the file over to the front edge of the desk.

'Take a look,' he said.

Stone crouched forward and took the file. Opened it up. There were photographs in it. Several big eight-by-tens, in glossy black and white. The first photograph was of his house. Clearly taken from inside a car stopped at the end of his driveway. The second was of his wife. Marilyn. Shot with a long lens as she walked in the flower garden. The third was of Marilyn coming out of her beauty parlour in town. A grainy, long-lens image. Covert, like a surveillance photograph. The fourth picture was a close-up of the licence plate of her BMW.

The fifth photograph was also of Marilyn. Taken at night through their bedroom window. She was dressed in a bathrobe. Her hair was down, and it looked damp. Stone stared at it. To get that picture, the photographer had been standing on their back lawn. His vision blurred and his ears hummed with silence. Then he shuffled the pictures together and closed the file. Put it back on the desk, slowly. Hobie leaned forward and pressed the tip of his hook into the thick green paper. He used it to pull the file back towards him. The hook rasped across the wood, loudly in the silence.

'That's my security, Mr Stone,' he said. 'But like you just told me, I'm sure there won't be a problem.'

Chester Stone said nothing. Just stood up and threaded his way through all the furniture and over to the door. Through the reception area and into the corridor and into the elevator. Down eighty-eight floors and back outside, where the bright morning sun hit him in the face like a blow.

THREE

That same sun was on the back of Reacher's neck as he made his way into Manhattan in the rear seat of a mini cab. He preferred to use unlicensed operators, given the choice. It suited his covert habit. No reason at all why anyone should ever want to trace his movements by checking with cab drivers, but a cab driver who couldn't admit to being one was the safest kind there was. And it gave the opportunity for a little negotiation about the fare. Not much negotiating to be done with the meter in a yellow taxi.

They came in over the Triborough Bridge and entered Manhattan on 125th Street. Drove west through traffic as far as Roosevelt Square. Reacher had the guy pull over there while he scanned around and thought for a moment. He was thinking about a cheap hotel, but he wanted one with working phones. And intact phone books. His judgement was he couldn't meet all three requirements in that neighbourhood. But he got out anyway, and paid the guy off. Wherever he was going, he'd walk the last part. A cut-out period, on his own. It suited his habit.

*   *   *

The two young men in the crumpled thousand-dollar suits waited until Chester Stone was well clear. Then they went into the inner office and threaded through the furniture and stood quietly in front of the desk. Hobie looked up at them and rolled open a drawer. Put the signed agreements away with the photographs and took out a new pad of yellow paper. Then he laid his hook on the desktop and turned in his chair so the dim light from the window caught the good side of his face.

'Well?'

'We just got back,' the first guy said.

'You get the information I asked for?'

The second guy nodded. Sat down on the sofa.

'He was looking for a guy called Jack Reacher.'

Hobie made a note of the name on the yellow pad. 'Who's he?'

There was a short silence.

'We don't know,' the first guy said.

Hobie nodded, slowly. 'Who was Costello's client?'

Another short silence.

'We don't know that either,' the guy said.

'Those are fairly basic questions,' Hobie said.

The guy just looked at him through the silence, uneasy.

'You didn't think to ask those fairly basic questions?'

The second guy nodded. 'We asked them. We were asking them like crazy.'

'But Costello wouldn't answer?'

'He was going to,' the first guy said.

'But?'

'He died on us,' the second guy said. 'He just upped and died. He was old, overweight. It was maybe a heart attack, I think. I'm very sorry, sir. We both are.'

Hobie nodded again, slowly. 'Exposure?'

'Nil,' the first guy said. 'He's unidentifiable.'

Hobie glanced down at the fingertips of his left hand. 'Where's the knife?'

'In the sea,' the second guy said.

Hobie moved his arm and tapped a little rhythm on the desktop with the point of his hook. Thought hard, and nodded again, decisively.

'OK, not your fault, I guess. Weak heart, what can you do?'

The first guy relaxed and joined his partner on the sofa. They were off the hook, and that had a special meaning in this office.

'We need to find the client,' Hobie said into the silence.

The two guys nodded and waited.

'Costello must have had a secretary, right?' Hobie said. 'She'll know who the client was. Bring her to me.'

The two guys stayed on the sofa.

'What?'

'This Jack Reacher,' the first guy said. 'Supposed to be a big guy, three months in the Keys. Costello told us people were talking about a big guy, been there three months, worked nights in a bar. We went to see him. Big tough guy, but he said he wasn't Jack Reacher.'

'So?'

'Miami airport,' the second guy said. 'We took United because it was direct. But there was an earlier flight just leaving, Delta to Atlanta and New York.'

'And?'

'The big guy from the bar? We saw him, heading down to the gate.'

'You sure?'

The first guy nodded. 'Ninety-nine per cent certain. He was a long way ahead, but he's a real big guy. Difficult to miss.'

Hobie started tapping his hook on the desk again. Lost in thought.

'OK, he's Reacher,' he said. 'Has to be, right? Costello asking around, then you guys asking on the same day, it spooks him and he runs. But where? Here?'

The second guy nodded. 'If he stayed on the plane in Atlanta, he's here.'

'But why?' Hobie asked. 'Who the hell is he?'

He thought for a moment and answered his own question.

'The secretary will tell me who the client is, right?'

Then he smiled.

'And the client will tell me who this Reacher guy is.'

The two guys in the smart suits nodded quietly and stood up. Threaded their way around the furniture and walked out of the office.

Reacher was walking south through Central Park. Trying to get a grip on the size of the task he had set himself. He was confident he was in the right city. The three accents had been definitive. But there was a huge population to wade through. Seven and a half million people spread out over the five boroughs, maybe altogether eighteen million in the metropolitan area. Eighteen million people close enough to focus inward when they want a specialized urban service like a fast and efficient private detective. His gut assumption was Costello may have been located in Manhattan, but it was entirely possible that Mrs Jacob was suburban. If you're a woman living somewhere in the suburbs and you want a private detective, where do you look for one? Not next to the supermarket or the video rental. Not in the mall next to the dress shops. You pick up the Yellow Pages for the nearest major city and you start calling. You have an initial conversation and maybe the guy drives out to you, or you get on the train and come in to him. From anywhere in a big dense area that stretches hundreds of square miles.

He had given up on hotels. He didn't necessarily need to invest a lot of time. Could be he'd be in and out within an hour. And he could use more information than hotels had to offer. He needed phone books for all five boroughs and the suburbs. Hotels wouldn't have all of those. And he didn't need to pay the kind of rates hotels like to charge for phone calls. Digging swimming pools had not made him rich.

So he was heading for the public library. Forty-second Street and Fifth. The biggest in the world? He couldn't remember. Maybe, maybe not. But certainly big enough to have all the phone books he needed, and big wide tables and comfortable chairs. Four miles from Roosevelt Square, an hour's brisk walk, interrupted only by traffic on the cross streets and a quick diversion into an office-supply store to buy a note-book and a pencil.

The next guy into Hobie's inner office was the receptionist. He stepped inside and locked the door behind him. Walked over and sat down on the end of the sofa nearest the desk. Looked at Hobie, long and hard, and silently.

'What?' Hobie asked him, although he knew what.

'You should get out,' the receptionist said. 'It's risky now.'

Hobie made no reply. Just held his hook in his left hand and traced its wicked metal curve with his remaining fingers.

'You planned,' the receptionist said. 'You promised. No point planning and promising if you don't do what you're supposed to do.'

Hobie shrugged. Said nothing.

'We heard from Hawaii, right?' the receptionist said. 'You planned to run as soon as we heard from Hawaii.'

'Costello never went to Hawaii,' Hobie said. 'We checked.'

'So that just makes it worse. Somebody else went to Hawaii. Somebody we don't know.'

'Routine,' Hobie said. 'Had to be. Think about it. No reason for anybody to go to Hawaii until we've heard from the other end. It's a sequence, you know that. We hear from the other end, we hear from Hawaii, step one, step two, and then it's time to go. Not before.'

'You promised,' the guy said again.

'Too early,' Hobie said. 'It's not logical. Think about it. You see somebody buy a gun and a box of bullets, they point the gun at you, are you scared?'

'Sure I am.'

'I'm not,' Hobie said. 'Because they didn't load it. Step one is buy the gun and the bullets, step two is load it. Until we hear from the other end, Hawaii is an empty gun.'

The receptionist laid his head back and stared up at the ceiling.

'Why are you doing this?'

Hobie rolled open his drawer and pulled out the Stone dossier. Took out the signed agreement.

Tilted the paper until the dim light from the window caught the bright blue ink of his twin signatures.

'Six weeks,' he said. 'Maybe less. That's all I need.'

The receptionist craned his head up again and squinted over.

'Need for what?'

'The biggest score of my life,' Hobie said.

He squared the paper on the desk and trapped it under his hook.

'Stone just handed me his whole company. Three generations of sweat and toil, and the stupid asshole just handed me the whole thing on a plate.'

'No, he handed you shit on a plate. You're out one-point-one million dollars in exchange for some worthless paper.'

Hobie smiled.

'Relax, let me do the thinking, OK? I'm the one who's good at it, right?'

'OK, so how?' the guy asked.

'You know what he owns? Big factory out on Long Island and a big mansion up in Pound Ridge. Five hundred houses all clustered around the factory. Must be three thousand acres all told, prime Long Island real estate, near the shore, crying out for development.'

'The houses aren't his,' the guy objected.

Hobie nodded. 'No, they're mostly mortgaged to some little bank in Brooklyn.'

'OK, so how?' the guy asked again.

'Just think about it,' Hobie said. 'Suppose I put this stock in the market?'

'You'll get shit for it,' the guy said back. 'It's totally worthless.'

'Exactly, it's totally worthless. But his bankers don't really know that yet. He's lied to them. He's kept his problems away from them. Why else would he come to me? So his bankers will have it rammed under their noses exactly how worthless their security is. A valuation, straight from the Exchange. They'll be told: this stock is worth exactly less than shit. Then what?'

'They panic,' the guy said.

'Correct,' Hobie said. 'They panic. They're exposed, with worthless security. They shit themselves until Hook Hobie comes along and offers them twenty cents on the dollar for Stone's debt.'

'They'd take that? Twenty cents on the dollar?'

Hobie smiled. His scar tissue wrinkled.

'They'll take it,' he said. 'They'll bite my other hand off to get it. And they'll include all the stock they hold, part of the deal.'

'OK, then what? What about the houses?'

'Same thing,' Hobie said. 'I own the stock, I own the factory out there, I close it down. No jobs, five hundred defaulted mortgages. The Brooklyn bank will get real shaky over that. I'll buy those mortgages for ten cents on the dollar, foreclose everybody and sling them out. Hire a couple of bulldozers, and I've got three thousand acres of prime Long Island real estate, right near the shore. Plus a big mansion up in Pound Ridge. Total cost to me, somewhere around eight-point-one million dollars. The mansion alone is worth two. That leaves me down six-point-one for a package I can market for a hundred million, if I pitch it right.'

The receptionist was staring at him.

'That's why I need six weeks,' Hobie said.

Then the receptionist was shaking his head.

'It won't work,' he said. 'It's an old family business. Stone still holds most of the stock himself. It's not all

68

traded. His bank's only got some of it. You'd only be a minority partner. He wouldn't let you do all that stuff.'

Hobie shook his head in turn.

'He'll sell out to me. All of it. The whole nine yards.'

'He won't.'

'He will.'

There was good news and bad news at the public library. Plenty of people called Jacob listed in the phone books for Manhattan, the Bronx, Brooklyn, Queens, Staten Island, Long Island, Westchester, the Jersey shore, Connecticut. Reacher gave it an hour's radius from the city. People an hour away turn instinctively to the city when they need something. Farther out than that, maybe they don't. He made marks with his pencil in his notebook and counted 129 potential candidates for the anxious Mrs Jacob.

But the Yellow Pages showed no private investigators called Costello. Plenty of private Costellos in the white pages, but no professional listings under that name. Reacher sighed. He was disappointed, but not surprised. It would have been too good to be true to open up the book and see Costello Investigations – We Specialize in Finding Ex-MPs Down in the Keys.

Plenty of the agencies had generic names, a lot of them competing for the head of the alphabetical listings with a capital A as their first letter. Ace, Acme, A-One, AA Investigators. Others had plain geographical connotations, like Manhattan or Bronx. Some were heading upmarket by using the words 'paralegal services'. One was claiming the heritage trade by calling itself Gumshoe. Two were staffed only by women, working only for women.

He pulled the white pages back and turned the page in his notebook and copied fifteen numbers for the NYPD. Sat for a while, weighing his options. Then he walked outside, past the giant crouching lions and over to a pay phone on the sidewalk. He propped his notebook on top of the phone with all the quarters he had in his pocket and started down his list of precinct houses. Each one, he asked for administration. He figured he would get some grizzled old desk sergeant who would know everything worth knowing.

He got the hit on his fourth call. The first three precincts were unable to help, without sounding any too regretful about it. The fourth call started the same way, a ring tone, a quick transfer, a long pause, then a wheezing acknowledgement as the phone was answered deep in the bowels of some grimy file room.

'I'm looking for a guy called Costello,' he said. 'Retired from the job and set up private, maybe on his own, maybe for somebody else. Probably about sixty.'

'Yeah, who are you?' a voice replied. Identical accent. Could have been Costello himself on the line.

'Name's Carter,' Reacher said. 'Like the president.'

'So what you want with Costello, Mr Carter?'

'I got something for him, but I lost his card,' Reacher said. 'Can't find his number in the book.'

'That's because Costello ain't in the book. He only works for lawyers. He don't work for the general public.'

'So you know him?'

'Know him? Of course I know him. He worked detective out of this building fifteen years. Not surprising I would know him.'

'You know where his office is?'

'Down in the Village someplace,' the voice said, and stopped.

Reacher sighed away from the phone. Like pulling teeth.

'You know where in the Village?'

'Greenwich Avenue, if I recall.'

'You got a street number?'

'No.'

'Phone number?'

'No.'

'You know a woman called Jacob?'

'No, should I?'

'Just a long shot,' Reacher said. 'She was his client.'

'Never heard of her.'

'OK, thanks for your help,' Reacher said.

'Yeah,' the voice said.

Reacher hung up and walked back up the steps and inside. Checked the Manhattan white pages again for a Costello on Greenwich Avenue. No listing. He put the books back on the shelf and went back out into the sun, and started walking.

Greenwich Avenue is a long straight street running diagonally south-east from Fourteenth Street and Eighth to Eighth Street and Sixth. It is lined on both sides with pleasant low-rise Village buildings, some of them with scooped-out semi-basement floors in use as small stores and galleries. Reacher walked the northern side first, and found nothing. Dodged the traffic at the bottom and came back on the other side and found a small brass plaque exactly halfway up the street, fixed to the stone frame of a doorway. The plaque was a well-polished rectangle, one of a cluster, and it said *Costello*. The door was black, and it was

71

open. Inside was a small lobby with a noticeboard of ridged felt and press-in white plastic letters, indicating the building was subdivided into ten small office suites. Suite five was marked *Costello*. Beyond the lobby was a glass door, locked. Reacher pressed the buzzer for five. No reply. He used his knuckle and leaned on it, but it got him nowhere. So he pressed six. A voice came back, distorted.

'Yes?'

'UPS,' he said, and the glass door buzzed and clicked open.

It was a three-floor building, four if you counted the separate basement. Suites one, two and three were on the first floor. He went up the stairs and found suite four on his left, six on his right, and five right at the back of the building with its door tucked under the angle of the staircase as it wound up to the third storey.

The door was a polished mahogany affair, and it was standing open. Not wide open, but open enough to be obvious. Reacher pushed it with his toe, and it swung on its hinges to reveal a small, quiet reception area the size of a motel room. It was decorated in a pastel colour somewhere between light grey and light blue. Thick carpet on the floor. A secretary's desk in the shape of a letter L, with a complicated telephone and a sleek computer. A filing cabinet and a sofa. There was a window with pebbled glass and another door leading straight ahead to an inner office.

The reception area was empty, and it was quiet. Reacher stepped inside and closed the door behind him with his heel. The lock was latched back, like the office had been opened up for business. He padded across the carpet to the inner door. Wrapped his hand in his shirt-tail and turned the knob. Stepped through into a second room of equal size. Costello's room. There were framed black-and-white photographs of younger versions of the man he had met in the Keys standing with police commissioners and captains and local politicians Reacher did not recognize. Costello had been a thin man, many years ago. The pictures showed him getting fatter as he got older, like a diet advertisement in reverse. The photographs were grouped on a wall to the right of a desk. The desk held a blotter and an old-fashioned inkwell and a telephone, and behind it was a leather chair, crushed into the shape of a heavy man. The left-hand wall held a window with more obscure glass and a line of locked cabinets. In front of the desk was a pair of client chairs, neatly arranged at a comfortable and symmetrical angle.

Reacher stepped back to the outer office. There was a smell of perfume in the air. He threaded around the secretary's desk and found a woman's bag, open, neatly stowed against the vanity panel to the left of the chair. The flap was folded back, revealing a soft leather wallet and a plastic pack of tissues. He took out his pencil and used the eraser end to poke the tissues aside. Underneath them was a clutter of cosmetics and a bunch of keys and the soft aroma of expensive cologne.

The computer monitor was swirling with a watery screensaver. He used the pencil to nudge the mouse. The screen crackled and cleared and revealed a half-finished letter. The cursor was blinking patiently in the middle of an uncompleted word. That morning's date sat underneath a letterhead. Reacher thought about Costello's body, sprawled out on the sidewalk next to the Key West graveyard, and he glanced between the tidy placement of the absent woman's bag, the open door, the uncompleted word, and he shivered.

Then he used the pencil to exit the word processor. A window opened and asked him if he wanted to save the changes to the letter. He paused and hit NO. Opened the file manager screen and checked the directories. He was looking for an invoice. It was clear from looking around that Costello ran a neat operation. Neat enough to invoice for a retainer before he went looking for Jack Reacher. But when did that search start? It must have followed a clear sequence. Mrs Jacob's instructions coming at the outset, nothing except a name, a vague description about his size, his Army service. Costello must then have called the military's central storage facility, a carefully guarded complex in St Louis that holds every piece of paper relating to every man and woman who has ever served in uniform. Carefully guarded in two ways, physically with gates and wire, and bureaucratically with a thick layer of obstruction designed to discourage frivolous access. After patient enquiries he would have discovered the honourable discharge. Then a puzzled pause, staring at a dead end. Then the long shot with the bank account. A call to an old buddy, favours called in, strings pulled. Maybe a blurry faxed printout from Virginia, maybe a blow-by-blow narrative of credits and debits over the telephone. Then the hurried flight south, the questions up and down Duval, the two guys, the fists, the linoleum knife.

A reasonably short sequence, but St Louis and Virginia would have been major delays. Reacher's guess was getting good information out of the records office would take three days, maybe four, for a citizen like Costello. The Virginia bank might not have been any quicker. Favours aren't necessarily granted immediately. The timing has got to be right. Call it a total of seven days' bureaucratic fudge, separated by a day's thinking time, plus a day at the start and a day at the end. Maybe altogether ten days since Mrs Jacob set the whole thing in motion.

He clicked on a subdirectory labelled INVOICES. The right-hand side of the screen came up with a long field of file names, stacked alphabetically. He ran the cursor down the list and spooled them up from the bottom. No Jacob in the Js. Mostly they were just initials, long acronyms maybe standing for law firm names. He checked the dates. Nothing from exactly ten days ago. But there was one nine days old. Maybe Costello was faster than he thought, or maybe his secretary was slower. It was labelled SGR&T-09. He clicked on it and the hard drive chattered and the screen came up with a thousand-dollar retainer against a missing persons enquiry, billed to a Wall Street firm called Spencer Gutman Ricker and Talbot. There was a billing address, but no phone number.

He quit file manager and entered the database. Searched for SGR&T again and came up with a page showing the same address, but this time with numbers for phone, fax, telex and e-mail. He leaned down and used his fingers and thumb to pull a couple of tissues from the secretary's pack. Wrapped one around the telephone receiver and opened the other flat and laid it across the keypad. Dialled the number by pressing through it. There was ring tone for a second, and then the connection was made.

75

'Spencer Gutman,' a bright voice said. 'How may we help you?'

'Mrs Jacob, please,' Reacher said, busily.

'One moment,' the voice said.

There was tinny music and then a man's voice. He sounded quick, but deferential. Maybe an assistant.

'Mrs Jacob, please,' Reacher said again.

The guy sounded busy and harassed. 'She already left for Garrison, and I really don't know when she'll be in the office again, I'm afraid.'

'Do you have her address in Garrison?'

'Hers?' the guy said, surprised. 'Or his?'

Reacher paused and listened to the surprise and took a chance.

'His, I mean. I seem to have lost it.'

'Just as well you did,' the voice said back. 'It was misprinted, I'm afraid. I must have redirected at least fifty people this morning.'

He recited an address, apparently from memory. Garrison, New York, a town about sixty miles up the Hudson River, more or less exactly opposite West Point, where Reacher had spent four long years.

'I think you'll have to hurry,' the guy said.

'Yes, I will,' Reacher said, and hung up, confused.

He closed the database and left the screen blank. Took one more glance at the missing secretary's abandoned bag and caught one more breath of her perfume as he left the room.

The secretary died five minutes after she gave up Mrs Jacob's identity, which was about five minutes after Hobie started in on her with his hook. They were in the executive bathroom inside the office suite on the eighty-eighth floor. It was an ideal location. Spacious, sixteen feet square, way too big for a bathroom. Some expensive decorator had put shiny grey granite tiling over all six surfaces, walls and floor and ceiling. There was a big shower stall, with a clear plastic curtain on a stainless-steel rail. The rail was Italian, grossly over-specified for the task of holding up a clear plastic curtain. Hobie had discovered it could take the weight of an unconscious human, handcuffed to it by the wrists. Time to time, heavier people than the secretary had hung there, while he asked them urgent questions or persuaded them as to the wisdom of some particular course of action.

The only problem was soundproofing. He was pretty sure it was OK. It was a solid building. Each of the Twin Towers weighs more than half a million tons. Plenty of steel and concrete, good thick walls. And he had no inquisitive neighbours. Most of the suites on eighty-eight were leased by trade missions from small obscure foreign nations, and their skeleton staffs spent most of their time up at the UN. Same situation on eighty-seven and eighty-nine. That was why he was where he was. But Hobie was a man who never took an extra risk if he could avoid it. Hence the duct tape. Before starting, he always lined up some six-inch strips, stuck temporarily to the tiling. One of them would go over the mouth. When whoever it was started nodding wildly, eyes bulging, he would tear off the strip and wait for the answer. Any screaming, he would slam the next strip on and go to work again. Normally he got the answer he wanted after the second strip came off.

Then the tiled floor allowed a simple sluicing operation. Set the shower running hard, throw a few bucketfuls of water around, get busy with a mop, and the place was safe again as fast as water drains down eighty-eight floors and away into the sewers. Not that Hobie ever did the mopping himself. A mop needs two hands. The second young guy was doing the mopping, with his expensive pants rolled up and his socks and shoes off. Hobie was outside at his desk, talking to the first young guy.

'I'll get Mrs Jacob's address, you'll bring her to me, OK?'

'Sure,' the guy said. 'What about this one?'

He nodded towards the bathroom door. Hobie followed his glance.

'Wait until tonight,' he said. 'Put some of her clothes back on, take her down to the boat. Dump her a couple of miles out in the bay.'

'She's likely to wash back in,' the guy said. 'Couple of days.'

Hobie shrugged.

'I don't care,' he said. 'Couple of days, she'll be all bloated up. They'll figure she fell off a motorboat. Injuries like that, they'll put it down to propeller damage.'

The covert habit had advantages, but it also had problems. Best way to get up to Garrison in a hurry would be to grab a rental car and head straight out. But a guy who chooses not to use credit cards and won't carry a driver's licence loses that option. So Reacher was back in a cab, heading for Grand Central. He was pretty sure the Hudson Line ran a train up there. He guessed commuters sometimes lived as far north as that. If not, the big Amtraks that ran up to Albany and Canada might stop there.

He paid off the cab and pushed through the crowd

78

to the doors. Down the long ramp and out into the giant concourse. He glanced around and craned his head to read the departures screen. Tried to recall the geography. Croton-Harmon trains were no good. They terminated way too far south. He needed Poughkeepsie at the minimum. He scanned down the list. Nothing doing. No trains out of there inside the next hour and a half that would get him to Garrison.

They did it the usual way. One of them rode ninety floors down to the underground loading bay and found an empty carton in the trash pile. Refrigerator cartons were best, or soda machines, but once he'd done it with the box from a thirty-five-inch colour television. This time, he found a filing cabinet carton. He used a janitor's trolley from the loading ramp and wheeled it into the freight elevator. Rode with it back up to the eighty-eighth floor.

The other guy was zipping her into a body bag in the bathroom. They folded it into the carton and used the remaining duct tape to secure the carton shut. Then they hefted it back on the trolley and headed for the elevator once more. This time, they rode down to the parking garage. Wheeled the box over to the black Suburban. Counted to three and heaved it into the back. Slammed the tailgate shut and clicked the lock. Walked away and glanced back. Deep tints on the windows, dark garage, no problem.

'You know what?' the first guy said. 'We fold the seat down, we'll get Mrs Jacob in there along with her. Do it all in one trip, tonight. I don't like going on that boat any more times than I have to.'

'OK,' the second guy said. 'Were there more boxes?'

'That was the best one. Depends if Mrs Jacob is big or small, I guess.'

'Depends if she's finished by tonight.'

'You got any doubts on that score? The mood he's in today?'

They strolled together to a different slot and unlocked a black Chevy Tahoe. Little brother to the Suburban, but still a giant vehicle.

'So where is she?' the second guy asked.

'A town called Garrison,' the first guy said. 'Straight up the Hudson, a ways past Sing Sing. An hour, hour and a half.'

The Tahoe backed out of the slot and squealed its tyres on its way around the garage. Bumped up the ramp into the sunshine and headed out to West Street, where it made a right and accelerated north.

FOUR

West Street becomes Eleventh Avenue right opposite Pier 56, where the westbound traffic spills out of Fourteenth Street and turns north. The big black Tahoe was caught in the congestion and added its horn to the frustrated blasts cannoning off the high buildings and echoing out over the river. It crawled nine blocks and made a left at Twenty-third Street, then swung north again on Twelfth. It got above walking speed until it passed the back of the Javits Convention Center, and then it got jammed up again in the traffic pouring out of West Forty-second. Twelfth became the Miller Highway and it was still solid, all the way over the top of the huge messy acreage of the old rail yards. Then the Miller became the Henry Hudson Parkway. Still a slow road, but the Henry Hudson was technically Route 9A, which would become Route 9 up in Crotonville and take them all the way north to Garrison. A straight line, no turns anywhere, but they were still in Manhattan, stuck in Riverside Park, a whole half-hour after setting out.

It was the word processor that meant the most. The cursor, patiently blinking in the middle of a word.

The open door and the abandoned bag were persuasive, but not critical. Office workers usually take their stuff and close their doors, but not always. The secretary might have just stepped across the hall and got involved in something, a quest for bond paper or a plea for help with somebody's copying machine, leading to a cup of coffee and a juicy story about last night's date. A person expecting to be absent two minutes might leave her bag behind and her door open and end up being gone a half-hour. But nobody leaves computer work unsaved. Not even for a minute. And this woman had. The machine had asked him DO YOU WANT TO SAVE THE CHANGES? Which meant she had got up from her desk without clicking on the SAVE icon, which is a habit just about as regular as breathing for people who spend their days fighting with software.

Which put a very bad complexion on the whole thing. Reacher was through in Grand Central's other big hall, with a twenty-ounce cup of black coffee he had bought from a vendor. He jammed the lid down tight and squeezed the cash roll in his pocket. It was thick enough for what he was going to have to do. He ran back and around to the track where the next Croton train was waiting to leave.

The Henry Hudson Parkway splits into a tangle of curling ramps around 170th Street and the north lanes come out again labelled Riverside Drive. Same road, same direction, no turn, but the complex dynamic of heavy traffic means that if one driver slows down more than the average, then the highway can back up dramatically, with hundreds of people stalled way behind, all because some out-of-towner a mile ahead became momentarily confused. The big black Tahoe was brought to a complete halt opposite Fort Washington and was reduced to a lurching stop–start crawl all the way under the George Washington Bridge. Then Riverside Drive broadens out and it got itself up into third gear before the label changed back to the Henry Hudson and the traffic in the toll plaza stopped it again. It waited in line to pay the money that let it off the island of Manhattan and away north through the Bronx.

There are two types of train running up and down the Hudson River between Grand Central and Croton-Harmon: locals and expresses. The expresses do not run any faster in terms of speed, but they stop less often. They make the journey last somewhere between forty-nine and fifty-two minutes. The locals stop everywhere, and the repeated braking and waiting and accelerating spin the trip out to anywhere between sixty-five and seventy-three minutes. A maximum advantage for the express of up to twenty-four minutes.

Reacher was on a local. He had given the trainman five and a half bucks for an off-peak one-way and was sitting sideways on an empty three-person bench, wired from too much coffee, his head resting on the window, wondering exactly where the hell he was going, and why, and what he was going to do when he got there. And whether he would get there in time to do it, anyway, whatever it was.

Route 9A became 9 and curved gracefully away from the river to run behind Camp Smith. Up in Westchester, it was a fast enough road. Not exactly a racetrack, because it curved and bounced around too much for sustained high speed, but it was clear and empty, a patchwork of old sections and new stretches carved through the woods. There were housing developments here and there, with high timber fencing and neat painted siding and optimistic names carved into imposing boulders flanking the entrance gates. The Tahoe hustled along, one guy driving and the other with a map across his knees.

They passed Peekskill and started hunting a left turn. They found it and swung head-on towards the river, which they sensed ahead of them, an empty break in the landscape. They entered the township of Garrison, and started hunting the address. Not easy to find. The residential areas were scattered. You could have a Garrison zip code and live way in the back of beyond. That was clear. But they found the right road and made all the correct turns and found the right street. Slowed and cruised through the thinning woods above the river, watching the mailboxes. The road curved and opened out. They cruised on. Then they spotted the right house up ahead and slowed abruptly and pulled in at the kerb.

Reacher got out of the train at Croton, seventy-one minutes after getting in. He ran up the stairs and across and down to the taxi rank. There were four operators lined up, all nose-in to the station entrance, all of them using old-model Caprice wagons with fake wood on the sides. First driver to react was a stout woman who tilted her head up like she was ready to pay attention.

'You know Garrison?' Reacher asked her.

'Garrison?' she said. 'That's a long way, mister, twenty miles.'

'I know where it is,' he said.

'Could be forty bucks.'

'I'll give you fifty,' he said. 'But I need to be there right now.'

He sat in front, next to her. The car stank like old taxis do, sweet cloying air-freshener and upholstery cleaner. There were a million miles on the clock and it rode like a boat on a swell as the woman hustled through the parking lot and up on to Route 9 and headed north.

'You got an address for me?' she asked, watching the road.

Reacher repeated what the assistant in the law firm had told him. The woman nodded and settled to a fast cruise.

'Overlooks the river,' she said.

She cruised for a quarter of an hour, passed by Peekskill and then slowed, looking for a particular left. Hauled the huge boat around and headed west. Reacher could feel the river up ahead, a mile-wide trench in the forest. The woman knew where she was going. She went all the way to the river and turned north on a country road. The rail tracks ran parallel between them and the water. No trains on them. The land fell away and Reacher could see West Point ahead and on his left, a mile away across the blue water.

'Should be along here someplace,' she said.

It was a narrow country road, domesticated with ranch fencing in rough timber and tamed with mowed shoulders and specimen plantings. There were mail-boxes a hundred yards apart and poles that hung cables through the treetops.

'Whoa,' the woman said, surprised. 'I guess this is it.'

85

The road was already narrow, and now it became just about impassable. There was a long line of cars parked up on the shoulder. Maybe forty automobiles, many of them black or dark blue. All neat late-model sedans or big sport-utilities. The woman eased the taxi into the driveway. The line of parked cars stretched nose-to-tail all the way to the house. Another ten or twelve cars were parked together on the apron in front of the garage. Two of them were plain Detroit sedans, in flat green. Army vehicles. Reacher could spot Defense Department issue a mile away.

'OK?' the woman asked him.

'I guess,' he said, cautiously.

He peeled a fifty off his roll and handed it to her. Got out and stood in the driveway, unsure. He heard the taxi whine away in reverse. He walked back up to the road. Looked at the long line of cars. Looked at the mailbox. There was a name spelled out in little aluminium letters along the top of it. The name was Garber. A name he knew as well as his own.

The house was set in a large lot, casually land-scaped, placed somewhere comfortable in the region between natural and neglected. The house itself was low and sprawling, dark cedar siding, dark screens at the windows, big stone chimney, somewhere between suburban modest and cosy cottage. It was very quiet. The air smelled hot and damp and fecund. He could hear insects massing in the undergrowth. He could sense the river beyond the house, a mile-wide void dragging stray sounds away to the south.

He walked closer and heard muted conversation behind the house. People talking low, maybe a lot of people. He walked down towards the sound and came out around the side of the garage. He was at the top of a flight of cement steps, looking west across the back-yard to the river, blue and blinding in the sun. A mile away in the haze, slightly north-west to his right, was West Point, low and grey in the distance.

The backyard was a flat area cleared out of the woods on the top of the bluff. It was covered in coarse grass, mowed short, and there was a solemn crowd of a hundred people standing in it. They were all dressed in black, men and women alike, black suits and ties and blouses and shoes, except for half a dozen Army officers in full dress uniform. They were all talking quietly, soberly, juggling paper buffet plates and glasses of wine, sadness in the slope of their shoulders.

A funeral. He was gate-crashing a funeral. He stood there awkwardly, looming against the skyline in the gear he had thrown on yesterday in the Keys, faded chinos, creased pale yellow shirt, no socks, scuffed shoes, sun-bleached hair sticking out all over the place, a day's beard on his face. He gazed down at the group of mourners and as if he had suddenly clapped his hands they all fell silent and turned to look up at him. He froze. They all stared at him, quietly, enquiringly, and he looked back at them, blankly. There was silence. Stillness. Then a woman moved. She handed her paper plate and her glass to the nearest bystander and stepped forward.

She was a young woman, maybe thirty, dressed like the others in a severe black suit. She was pale and strained, but very beautiful. Achingly beautiful. Very slim, tall in her heels, long legs in sheer dark nylon. Fine blonde hair, long and unstyled, blue eyes, fine bones. She moved delicately across the lawn and stopped at the bottom of the cement steps, like she was waiting for him to come down to her.

'Hello, Reacher,' she said, softly.

He looked down at her. She knew who he was. And he knew who she was. It came to him suddenly like a stop-motion film blasting through fifteen years in a single glance. A teenage girl grew up and blossomed into a beautiful woman right in front of his eyes, all in a split second. Garber, the name on the mailbox. Leon Garber, for many years his commanding officer. He recalled their early acquaintance, getting to know each other at backyard barbecues on hot wet evenings in the Philippines. A slender girl gliding in and out of the shadows around the bleak base house, enough of a woman at fifteen to be utterly captivating but enough of a girl to be totally forbidden. Jodie, Garber's daughter. His only child. The light of his life. This was Jodie Garber, fifteen years later, all grown up and beautiful and waiting for him at the bottom of a set of cement steps.

He glanced at the crowd and went down the steps to the lawn.

'Hello, Reacher,' she said again.

Her voice was low and strained. Sad, like the scene around her.

'Hello, Jodie,' he said.

Then he wanted to ask *who died?* But he couldn't frame it in any way that wasn't going to sound callous, or stupid. She saw him struggling, and nodded.

'Dad,' she said simply.

'When?' he asked.

'Five days ago,' she said. 'He was sick the last few months, but it was sudden at the end. A surprise, I guess.'

He nodded slowly.

'I'm very sorry,' he said.

He glanced at the river and the hundred faces in front of him became a hundred faces of Leon Garber. A short, squat, tough man. A wide smile he always used whether he was happy or annoyed or in danger. A brave man, physically and mentally. A great leader. Honest as the day is long, fair, perceptive. Reacher's role model during his vital formative years. His mentor and his sponsor. His protector. He had gone way out on a limb and promoted him twice in an eighteen-month span which made Reacher the youngest peacetime major anybody could remember. Then he had spread his blunt hands wide and smiled and disclaimed any credit for his ensuing successes.

'I'm very sorry, Jodie,' he said again.

She nodded silently.

'I can't believe it,' he said. 'I can't take it in. I saw him less than a year ago. He was in good shape then. He got sick?'

She nodded again, still silent.

'But he was always so tough,' he said.

She nodded, sadly. 'He was, wasn't he? Always so tough.'

'And not old,' he said.

'Sixty-four.'

'So what happened?'

'His heart,' she said. 'It got him in the end. Remember how he always liked to pretend he didn't have one?'

Reacher shook his head. 'Biggest heart you ever saw.'

'I found that out,' she said. 'When Mom died, we were best friends for ten years. I loved him.'

'I loved him too,' Reacher said. 'Like he was my dad, not yours.'

She nodded again. 'He still talked about you all the time.'

Reacher looked away. Stared out at the unfocused shape of the West Point buildings, grey in the haze. He was numb. He was in that age zone where people he knew died. His father was dead, his mother was dead, his brother was dead. Now the nearest thing to a substitute relative was dead, too.

'He had a heart attack six months ago,' Jodie said. Her eyes clouded and she hooked her long straight hair behind her ear. 'He sort of recovered for a spell, looked pretty good, but really he was failing fast. They were considering a bypass, but he took a turn for the worse and went down too quickly. He wouldn't have survived the surgery.'

'I'm very sorry,' he said, for the third time.

She turned alongside him and threaded her arm through his.

'Don't be,' she said. 'He was always a very contented guy. Better for him to go fast. I couldn't see him being happy lingering on.'

Reacher had a flash in his mind of the old Garber, bustling and raging, a fireball of energy, and he understood how desperate it would have made him to become an invalid. Understood too how that overloaded old heart had finally given up the struggle. He nodded, unhappily.

'Come and meet some people,' Jodie said. 'Maybe you know some of them.'

'I'm not dressed for this,' he said. 'I feel bad. I should go.'

'Doesn't matter,' she said. 'You think Dad would care?'

He saw Garber in his old creased khaki and his

battered hat. He was the worst-dressed officer in the US Army, all thirteen years Reacher had served under him. He smiled, briefly.

'I guess he wouldn't mind,' he said.

She walked him on to the lawn. There were maybe six people out of the hundred he recognized. A couple of the guys in uniform were familiar. A handful in suits were men he'd worked with here and there in another lifetime. He shook hands with dozens of people and tried to listen to the names, but they went in one ear and out the other. Then the quiet chatter and the eating and the drinking started up again, the crowd closed around him, and the sensation of his untidy arrival was smoothed over and forgotten. Jodie still had hold of his arm. Her hand was cool on his skin.

'I'm looking for somebody,' he said. 'That's why I'm here, really.'

'I know,' she said. 'Mrs Jacob, right?'

He nodded.

'Is she here?' he asked.

'I'm Mrs Jacob,' she said.

The two guys in the black Tahoe backed it out of the line of cars, out from under the power lines so the car phone would work without interference. The driver dialled a number and the ring tone filled the quiet vehicle. Then the call was answered sixty miles south and eighty-eight floors up.

'Problems, boss,' the driver said. 'There's some sort of a wake going on here, a funeral or something. Must be a hundred people milling around. We got no chance of grabbing this Mrs Jacob. We can't even tell which one she is. There are dozens of women here, she could be any one of them.'

The speaker relayed a grunt from Hobie. 'And?'

'The guy from the bar down in the Keys? He just showed up here in a damn taxi. Got here about ten minutes after we did, strolled right in.'

The speaker crackled. No discernible reply.

'So what do we do?' the driver asked.

'Stick with it,' Hobie's voice said. 'Maybe hide the vehicle and lay up someplace. Wait until everybody leaves. It's her house, as far as I can tell. Maybe the family home or a weekend place. So everybody else will leave, and she'll be the one who stays. Don't you come back here without her, OK?'

'What about the big guy?'

'If he leaves, let him go. If he doesn't, waste him. But bring me this Jacob woman.'

'You're Mrs Jacob?' Reacher asked.

Jodie Garber nodded.

'Am, was,' she said. 'I'm divorced, but I keep the name for work.'

'Who was he?'

She shrugged.

'A lawyer, like me. It seemed like a good idea at the time.'

'How long?'

'Three years, beginning to end. We met at law school, got married when we got jobs. I stayed on Wall Street, but he went to a firm in DC, couple of years ago. The marriage didn't go with him, just kind of petered out. The papers came through last fall. I could hardly remember who he was. Just a name, Alan Jacob.'

Reacher stood in the sunny yard and looked at her. He realized he was upset that she had been married.

She had been a skinny kid but totally gorgeous at fifteen, self-confident and innocent and a little shy about it all at the same time. He had watched the battle between her shyness and her curiosity as she sat and worked up the courage to talk to him about death and life and good and evil. Then she would fidget and tuck her bony knees up under her and work the conversation around to love and sex and men and women. Then she would blush and disappear. He would be left alone, icy inside, captivated by her and angry at himself for it. Days later he would see her somewhere around the base, still blushing furiously. And now fifteen years later she was a grown woman, college and law school, married and divorced, beautiful and composed and elegant, standing there in her dead father's yard with her arm linked through his.

'Are you married?' she asked him.

He shook his head. 'No.'

'But are you happy?'

'I'm always happy,' he said. 'Always was, always will be.'

'Doing what?'

He shrugged.

'Nothing much,' he said.

He glanced over the top of her head and scanned the faces in the crowd. Subdued busy people, substantial lives, big careers, all of them moving steadily from A to Z. He looked at them and wondered if they were the fools, or if he was. He recalled the expression on Costello's face.

'I was just in the Keys,' he said. 'Digging swimming pools with a shovel.'

Her face didn't change. She tried to squeeze his forearm with her hand, but her hand was too small and his arm was too big. It came out as a gentle pressure from her palm.

'Costello find you down there?' she asked.

He didn't find me to invite me to a funeral, he thought.

'We need to talk about Costello,' he said.

'He's good, isn't he?'

Not good enough, he thought. She moved away to circulate through the crowd. People were waiting to offer their second-layer condolences. They were getting loose from the wine, and the buzz of talk was getting louder and more sentimental. Reacher drifted over to a patio, where a long table with a white cloth held food. He loaded a paper plate with cold chicken and rice and took a glass of water. There was an ancient patio furniture set, ignored by the others because it was all spotted with little grey-green botanical droppings from the trees. The sun umbrella was stiff and faded white. Reacher ducked under it and sat quietly in a dirty chair on his own.

He watched the crowd as he ate. People were reluctant to leave. The affection for old Leon Garber was palpable. A guy like that generates affection in others, maybe too much to express to his face, so it has to all come out later. Jodie was moving through the crowd, nodding, clasping hands, smiling sadly. Everybody had a tale to tell her, an anecdote about witnessing Garber's heart of gold peeping out from under his gruff and irascible exterior. He could add a few stories. But he wouldn't, because Jodie didn't need it explained to her that her father had been one of the good guys. She knew. She was moving with the serenity of a person who had loved the old guy all her life, and had been loved back. There was nothing she

94

had neglected to tell him, nothing he had neglected to tell her. People live, and then they die, and as long as they do both things properly, there's nothing much to regret.

They found a place on the same road that was obviously a weekend cottage, closed up tight and unoccupied. They backed the Tahoe around behind the garage where it was hidden from the street, but ready for pursuit. They took the nine-millimetres out of the glove box and stowed them in their jacket pockets. Walked back down to the road and ducked into the undergrowth.

It was hard going. They were just sixty miles north of Manhattan, but they might as well have been in the jungles of Borneo. There were ragged vines tangled everywhere, grabbing at them, tripping them, whipping their faces and hands. The trees were second-growth native broadleafs, growing wild, basically weeds, and their branches came out of them at crazy low angles. They took to walking backwards, forcing their way through. When they got level with the Garber driveway, they were panting and gasping and smeared with moss and green pollen dust. They pushed through on to the property and found a depression in the ground where they were concealed. They ducked left and right to get a view of the pathway leading up from the backyard. People were heading out, getting ready to leave.

It was becoming obvious which one was Mrs Jacob. If Hobie was right and this was her place, then she was the thin blonde shaking hands and saying goodbye like all these departing people had been her guests. They were leaving, she was staying. She was Mrs

Jacob. They watched her, the centre of attention, smiling bravely, embracing, waving. People filed up the driveway, ones and twos, then larger groups. Cars were starting. Blue exhaust haze was drifting. They could hear the hiss and groan of power steering as people eased out of the tight line. The rub of tyres on pavement. The burble of motors accelerating away down the road. This was going to be easy. Pretty soon she was going to be standing there all by herself, all choked up and sad. Then she was going to get a couple of extra visitors. Maybe she would see them coming and take them for a couple of mourners arriving late. After all, they were dressed in dark suits and ties. What fits in down in Manhattan's financial district looks just about right for a funeral.

Reacher followed the last two guests up the cement steps and out of the yard. One was a colonel and the other was a two-star general, both in immaculate dress uniform. It was what he had expected. A place with free food and drink, the soldiers will always be the last to leave. He didn't know the colonel, but he thought he vaguely recognized the general. He thought the general recognized him, too, but neither of them pursued it. No desire on either part to get into long and complicated so-what-are-you-doing-now explanations.

The brass shook hands quite formally with Jodie and then they snapped to attention and saluted. Crisp parade-ground moves, gleaming boots smashing into the tarmac, eyes rigidly to the front, thousand-yard stares, all quite bizarre in the green stillness of a suburban driveway. They got into the last car left on the garage forecourt, one of the flat green saloons parked nearest to the house. First to arrive, last to leave. Peacetime, no Cold War, nothing to do all day. It was why Reacher had been happy when they cut him loose, and as he watched the green car turn and head out, he knew he was right to be happy.

Jodie stepped sideways to him and linked her arm through his again.

'So,' she said quietly. 'That's that.'

Then there was just building silence as the noise from the green car faded and died along the road.

'Where's he buried?' Reacher asked.

'The town cemetery,' she said. 'He could have chosen Arlington, of course, but he didn't want that. You want to go up there?'

He shook his head.

'No, I don't do stuff like that. Makes no difference to him now, does it? He knew I'd miss him, because I told him so, a long time ago.'

She nodded. Held his arm.

'We need to talk about Costello,' he said again.

'Why?' she asked. 'He gave you the message, right?'

He shook his head.

'No, he found me, but I was wary. I said I wasn't Jack Reacher.'

She looked up at him, astonished. 'But why?'

He shrugged.

'Habit, I guess. I don't go around looking for involvement. I didn't recognize the name Jacob, so I just ignored him. I was happy, living quiet down there.'

She was still looking at him.

'I guess I should have used Garber,' she said. 'It was Dad's business anyway, not mine. But I did it through the firm, and I never even thought about it. You'd have listened to him if he'd said Garber, right?'

'Of course,' he said.

'And you needn't have worried, because it was no kind of a big deal.'

'Can we go inside?' he asked.

She was surprised again. 'Why?'

'Because it was some kind of a very big deal.'

They saw her lead him in through the front door. She pulled the screen and he held it while she turned the knob and opened up. Some kind of a big front door, dull brown wood. They went inside and the door closed behind them. Ten seconds later a dim light came on in a window, way off to the left. Some kind of a sitting room or den, they guessed, so shaded by the runaway plantings outside that it needed lights on even in the middle of the day. They crouched in their damp hollow and waited. Insects were drifting through the sunbeams all around them. They glanced at each other and listened hard. No sound.

They eased off the ground and pushed through to the driveway. Ran crouched to the corner of the garage. Pressed up against the siding and slid around to the front. Across the front towards the house. They went into their jackets for the pistols. Held them pointed at the ground and went one at a time for the front porch. They regrouped and eased slowly over the old timbers. Ended up squatting on the floor, backs pressed against the house, one on either side of the front door, pistols out and ready. She'd gone in this way. She'd come back out. Just a matter of time.

'Somebody killed him?' Jodie repeated.

'And his secretary, probably,' Reacher said.

'I don't believe it,' she said. 'Why?'

She had led him through a dark hallway to a small den in the far corner of the house. A tiny window and dark wood panelling and heavy brown leather furniture made it gloomy, so she switched on a desk lamp, which changed it into a cosy man's space like the pre-war bars Reacher had seen in Europe. There were shelves of books, cheap editions bought by subscription decades ago, and curled faded photographs thumbtacked to the front edges of the shelves. There was a plain desk, the sort of place where an old under-employed man does his bills and taxes in imitation of how he used to work when he had a job.

'I don't know why,' Reacher said. 'I don't know anything. I don't even know why you sent him looking for me.'

'Dad wanted you,' she said. 'He never really told me why. I was busy, I had a trial, complex thing, lasted months. I was preoccupied. All I know is, after he got sick he was going to the cardiologist, right? He met somebody there and got involved with something. He was worried about it. Seemed to me he felt he was under some kind of a big obligation. Then later when he got worse, he knew he would have to drop it, and he started saying he should find you and let you take a look at it, because you were a person who could maybe do something about it. He was getting all agitated, which was really not a good idea, so I said I'd get Costello to locate you. We use him all the time at the firm, and it felt like the least I should do.'

It made some kind of sense, but Reacher's first thought was *why me?* He could see Garber's problem. In the middle of something, health failing, unwilling to abandon an obligation, needing help. But a guy like

Garber could get help anywhere. The Manhattan Yellow Pages were full of investigators. And if it was something too arcane or too personal for a city investigator, then all he had to do was pick up the phone and a dozen of his friends from the military police would come running. Two dozen. A hundred. All of them willing and anxious to repay his many kindnesses and favours which stretched right back through their whole careers. So Reacher was sitting there asking himself *why me in particular?*

'Who was the person he met at the cardiologist's?'

She shrugged, unhappily.

'I don't know. I was preoccupied. We never really went into it.'

'Did Costello come up here? Discuss it directly with him?'

She nodded. 'I called him and told him we'd pay him through the firm, but he was to come here and get the details. He called me back a day or two later, said he'd discussed it with Dad and it all boiled down to finding you. He wanted me to retain him officially, on paper, because it could get expensive. So naturally I did that, because I didn't want Dad worrying about the cost or anything.'

'Which is why he told me his client was Mrs Jacob,' Reacher said. 'Not Leon Garber. Which is why I ignored him. Which is how I got him killed.'

She shook her head and looked at him sharply, like he was some kind of a new associate who had just done a piece of sloppy drafting. It took him by surprise. He was still thinking of her as a fifteen-year-old girl, not a thirty-year-old lawyer who spent her time getting preoccupied with long and complex trials.

'Non sequitur,' she said. 'It's clear what happened,

100

right? Dad told Costello the story, Costello tried some kind of a shortcut before he went looking for you, whereby he turned over the wrong stone and got somebody alerted. That somebody killed him to find out who was looking, and why. Makes no difference if you'd played ball right away. They'd still have got to Costello to ask him exactly who put him on the trail. So it's me who got him killed, ultimately.'

Reacher shook his head. 'It was Leon. Through you.'

She shook her head in turn. 'It was the person at the cardiology clinic. Him, through Dad, through me.'

'I need to find that person,' he said.

'Does it matter now?'

'I think it does,' he said. 'If Leon was worried about something, then I'm worried about it, too. That's how it worked for us.'

Jodie nodded quietly. Stood up quickly and stepped over to the bookshelves. Pincered her fingernails and levered the thumbtack out of one of the photographs. Looked hard at the photograph and then passed it across to him.

'Remember that?' she asked.

The photograph must have been fifteen years old, the colours fading to pale pastels the way old Kodak does with age and sunlight. It had the harsh bright sky of Manila above a dirt yard. Leon Garber was on the left, about fifty, dressed in creased olive fatigues. Reacher himself was on the right, twenty-four years old, a lieutenant, a foot taller than Garber, smiling with all the blazing vigour of youth. Between the two of them was Jodie, fifteen, in a sundress, one bare arm around her father's shoulders, the other around Reacher's waist. She was squinting in the sun, smiling,

101

leaning towards Reacher like she was hugging his waist with all the strength in her skinny brown frame.

'Remember? He'd just bought the Nikon in the PX? With the self-timer? Borrowed a tripod and couldn't wait to try it out?'

Reacher nodded. He remembered. He remembered the smell of her hair that day, in the hot Pacific sun. Clean, young hair. He remembered the feel of her body against his. He remembered the feel of her long thin arm around his waist. He remembered screaming at himself *hold on, pal, she's only fifteen and she's your CO's daughter.*

'He called that his family picture,' she said. 'Always did.'

He nodded again. 'That's why. That's how it worked for us.'

She gazed at the photograph for a long moment, something in her face.

'And there's the secretary,' he said to her. 'They'll have asked her who the client was. She'll have told them. And even if she didn't, they'll find out anyway. Took me thirty seconds and one phone call. So now they're going to come looking for you, to ask you who's behind all of this.'

She looked blank and put the old photograph on the desk.

'But I don't know who.'

'You think they're going to believe that?'

She nodded vaguely and glanced towards the window.

'OK, so what do I do?'

'You get out of here,' he said. 'That's for damn sure. Too lonely, too isolated. You got a place in the city?'

'Sure,' she said. 'A loft on lower Broadway.'

'You got a car here?'

She nodded. 'Sure, in the garage. But I was going to stay here tonight. I've got to find his will, do the paperwork, close things down. I was going to leave tomorrow morning, early.'

'Do all that stuff now,' he said. 'As fast as you can, and get out. I mean it, Jodie. Whoever these people are, they're not playing games.'

The look on his face told her more than the words. She nodded quickly and stood up.

'OK, the desk. You can give me a hand.'

From his high school ROTC until his ill-health demobilization Leon Garber had done almost fifty years of military service of one sort or another. It showed right there in his desk. The upper drawers contained pens and pencils and rulers, all in neat rows. The lower drawers were double height, with concertina files hanging on neat rods. Each was labelled in careful handwriting. Taxes, phone, electricity, heating oil, yard work, appliance warranties. There was a label with newer handwriting in a different colour: LAST WILL AND TESTAMENT. Jodie flicked through the files and ended up lifting the whole concertina out of each drawer. Reacher found a battered leather suitcase in the den closet and they loaded the concertinas straight into it. Forced the lid down tight and snapped it shut. Reacher picked up the old photograph from the desk and looked at it again.

'Did you resent it?' he asked. 'The way he thought about me? Family?'

She paused in the doorway and nodded.

'I resented it like crazy,' she said. 'And one day I'll tell you exactly why.'

He just looked at her and she turned and disappeared down the hallway.

'I'll get my things,' she called. 'Five minutes, OK?'

He stepped over to the bookshelf and tacked the old picture back in its original position. Then he snapped the light off and carried the suitcase out of the room. Stood in the quiet hallway and looked around. It was a pleasant house. It had been expanded in size at some stage in its history. That was clear. There was a central core of rooms that made some kind of sense in terms of layout, and then there were more rooms off the doglegged hallway he was standing in. They branched out from arbitrary little inner lobbies. Too small to be called a warren, too big to be predictable. He wandered through to the living room. The windows overlooked the yard and the river, with the West Point buildings visible at an angle from the fireplace end. The air was still and smelled of old polish. The decor was faded, and had been plain to start with. Neutral wood floors, cream walls, heavy furniture. An ancient TV, no video. Books, pictures, more photographs. Nothing matched. It was an undesigned place, evolved, comfortable. It had been lived in.

Garber must have bought it thirty years ago. Probably when Jodie's mother got pregnant. It was a common move. Married officers with a family often bought a place, generally near their first service base or near some other location they imagined was going to be central to their lives, like West Point. They bought the place and usually left it empty while they lived overseas. The point was to have an anchor, somewhere identifiable they knew they would come back to when it was all over. Or somewhere their families could live if the overseas posting was

104

unsuitable, or if their children's education demanded consistency.

Reacher's parents had not taken that route. They had never bought a place. Reacher had never lived in a house. Grim service bungalows and army bunkhouses were where he had lived, and since then, cheap motels. And he was pretty sure he never wanted anything different. He was pretty sure he didn't want to live in a house. The desire just passed him by. The necessary involvement intimidated him. It was a physical weight, exactly like the suitcase in his hand. The bills, the property taxes, the insurance, the warranties, the repairs, the maintenance, the decisions, new roof or new stove, carpeting or rugs, the budgets. The yard work. He stepped over and looked out of the window at the lawn. Yard work summed up the whole futile procedure. First you spend a lot of time and money making the grass grow, just so you can spend a lot of time and money cutting it down again a little while later. You curse about it getting too long, and then you worry about it staying too short and you sprinkle expensive water on it all summer, and expensive chemicals all fall.

Crazy. But if any house could change his mind, maybe Garber's house might do it. It was so casual, so undemanding. It looked like it had prospered on benign neglect. He could just about imagine living in it. And the view was powerful. The wide Hudson rolling by, reassuring and physical. That old river was going to keep on rolling by, whatever anybody did about the houses and the yards that dotted its banks.

'OK, I'm ready, I guess,' Jodie called.

She appeared in the living-room doorway. She was carrying a leather garment bag and she had changed

105

out of her black funeral suit. Now she was in a pair of faded Levi's and a powder-blue sweatshirt with a small logo Reacher couldn't decipher. She had brushed her hair, and the static had kicked a couple of strands outward. She was smoothing them back with her hand, hooking them behind her ear. The powder-blue shirt picked up her eyes and emphasized the pale honey of her skin. The last fifteen years had done her no harm at all.

They walked through to the kitchen and bolted the door to the yard. Turned off all the appliances they could see and screwed the taps tight shut. Came back out into the hallway and opened the front door.

FIVE

Reacher was first out through the door, for a number of reasons. Normally he might have let Jodie go out ahead of him, because his generation still carried with it the last vestiges of American good manners, but he had learned to be wary about displaying chivalry until he knew exactly how the woman he was with was going to react. And it was her house, not his, which altered the dynamic anyway, and she would need to use the key to lock the door behind them. So for all those reasons he was the first person to step out to the porch, and so he was the first person the two guys saw.

Waste the big guy and bring me Mrs Jacob, Hobie had told them. The guy on the left went for a snapshot from a sitting position. He was tensed up and ready, so it took his brain a lot less than a second to process what his optic nerve was feeding it. He felt the front door open, he saw the screen swing out, he saw somebody stepping onto the porch, he saw it was the big guy coming first, and he fired.

The guy on the right was in a dumb position. The screen creaked open right in his face. In itself it was no kind of an obstacle, because tight nylon gauze designed to stop insects is not going to do a lot about

107

stopping bullets, but he was a right-handed guy and the frame of the screen was moving on a direct collision course with his gun hand as it swung around into position. That made him hesitate fractionally and then scramble up and forward around the arc of the frame. He grabbed it backhanded with his left and pulled it into his body and folded himself around it with his right hand swinging up and into position.

By then Reacher was operating unconsciously and instinctively. He was nearly thirty-nine years old, and his memory stretched back through maybe thirty-five of those years to the dimmest early fragments of his childhood, and that memory was filled with absolutely nothing except military service, his father's, his friends' fathers', his own, his friends'. He had never known stability, he had never completed a year in the same school, he had never worked nine to five Monday to Friday, he had never counted on anything at all except surprise and unpredictability. There was a portion of his brain developed way out of all proportion, like a grotesquely overtrained muscle, which made it seem to him entirely reasonable that he should step out of a door in a quiet New York suburban town and glance down at two men he had last seen two thousand miles away in the Keys crouching and swinging nine-millimetre pistols up in his direction. No shock, no surprise, no gasping freezing fear or panic. No pausing, no hesitation, no inhibitions. Just instant reaction to a purely mechanical problem laid out in front of him like a geometric diagram involving time and space and angles and hard bullets and soft flesh.

The heavy suitcase was in his left hand, swinging forward as he laboured with it over the threshold. He did two things at once. First he kept the swing going,

108

using all the new strength in his left shoulder to kick the case onward and outward. Second he windmilled his right arm backward and shoved Jodie in the chest, smashing her back inside the hallway. She staggered back a step and the moving suitcase caught the first bullet. Reacher felt it kick in his hand. He jerked it right to the end of its swing, leaning out into the porch like a hesitant diver over a cold pool, and it hit the left-hand guy a glancing blow in the face. He was half up and half down, crouching, unstable, and the blow from the case rolled him over and backward and out of the picture.

But Reacher didn't see him go down, because his eyes were already on the other guy looping around the screen with his gun about fifteen degrees away from ready. Reacher used the momentum of the swinging suitcase to hurl himself forward. He let the handle pull out through his hooked fingertips and flip him into a dive with his right arm accelerating back past him straight out across the porch. The gun swung around and smacked him flat on his chest. He heard it fire and felt the muzzle blast sear his skin. The bullet launched sideways under his raised left arm and hit the distant garage about the same time his right elbow hit the guy in the face.

An elbow moving fast ahead of 250 pounds of diving body weight does a lot of damage. It glanced off the frame of the screen and caught the guy in the chin. The shock wave went back and up through the hinge of the jaw, which is a sturdy enough joint that the force was carried undiminished up into the guy's brain. Reacher could tell from the rubbery way he fell across his back that he was out for a spell. Then the screen door was creaking shut against its spring and the left-hand guy was scrabbling sideways across the porch floorboards for his gun, which was skittering away from him. Jodie was framed in the doorway, bent double, hands clasped to her chest, gasping for breath. The old suitcase was toppling end over end out on to the front lawn.

Jodie was the problem. He was separated from her by about eight feet, and the left-hand guy was between the two of them. If he grabbed the skittering gun and lined it up to his right, he would be lined up on her. Reacher heaved the unconscious guy out of the way and threw himself at the door. Batted the screen back and fell inside. Dragged Jodie a yard into the hallway and slammed the door shut. It kicked and banged three times as the guy fired after him and dust and wood splinters blasted out into the air. He clicked the lock and pulled Jodie across the floor to the kitchen.

'Can we get to the garage?'

'Through the breezeway,' she gasped.

It was June, so the storm windows were down and the breezeway was nothing but a wide passage with floor-to-ceiling screens on both sides. The left-hand guy was using an M9 Beretta, which would have started the day with fifteen rounds in the box. He'd fired four, one into the suitcase and three into the door. Eleven left, which was not a comforting thought when all that stood between you and him was a few square yards of nylon mesh.

'Car keys?'

She fumbled them out of her bag. He took them and closed them into his fist. The kitchen door had a glass panel with a view straight through the breezeway to an identical door exactly opposite, which led into the garage.

'Is that door locked?'

She nodded breathlessly. 'The green one. Green for garage.'

He looked at the bunch of keys. There was an old Yale, dotted with a smear of green paint. He eased the kitchen door open and knelt and eased his head out, lower than would be expected. He craned around, both ways. No sign of the guy waiting outside. Then he selected the green key and held it pointed out in front of him like a tiny lance. Pushed to his feet and sprinted. Checked and slammed the key into the hole and turned it and yanked it back out. Pushed the door open and waved Jodie across after him. She fell into the garage and he slammed the door behind her. Locked it and listened. No sound.

The garage was a large dark space, open rafters, open framing, smelling of old motor oil and creosote. It was full of garage things, mowers and hoses and lawn chairs, but they were all old things, the belongings of a man who stopped buying new gizmos twenty years ago. So the main doors were just manual rollers that ran upward in curving metal tracks. No mechanism. No electric opener. The floor was smooth poured concrete, aged and swept to a shine. Jodie's car was a new Oldsmobile Bravada, dark green, gold accents. It was crouched there in the dark, nose-in to the back wall. Badges on the tailgate, boasting about four-wheel drive and a V-6 engine. The four-wheel drive would be useful, but how fast that V-6 started would be crucial.

'Get in the back,' he whispered. 'Down on the floor, OK?'

She crawled in head first, and lay down across the gearbox. He crossed the garage and found the key to

111

the door out to the yard. Opened it up and peered out and listened. No movement, no sound. Then he came back to the car and slid the key in and switched on the ignition so he could rack the electric seat all the way back to the end of its runners.

'I'll be there in a minute,' he whispered.

Garber's tool area was as tidy as his desk had been. There was an eight-by-four pegboard with a full set of household tools neatly arranged on it. Reacher selected a heavy carpenter's hammer and lifted it down. Stepped out of the door to the yard and threw the hammer overarm, diagonally right over the house, to send it crashing into the undergrowth he had seen at the front. He counted to five to give the guy time to hear it and react to it and run towards it from wherever he was currently hiding. Then he ducked back inside to the car. Stood alongside the open door and turned the key, arm's length. Fired it up. The engine started instantly. He dodged backward and flung the roller door up. It crashed along its metal track. He threw himself into the driver's seat and smashed the selector into reverse and stamped on the pedal. All four tyres howled and then bit on the smooth concrete and the vehicle shot backward out of the garage. Reacher glimpsed the guy with the Beretta, way off to his left on the front lawn, spinning to look at them. He accelerated all the way up the driveway and lurched backward into the road. Braked fiercely and spun the wheel and found drive and took off in a haze of blue tyre smoke.

He accelerated hard for fifty yards and then lifted off the gas. Coasted to a gentle stop just beyond the neighbour's driveway. Selected reverse again and idled backward into it and down into the plantings.

Straightened up and killed the motor. Behind him, Jodie struggled up off the floor and stared.

'Hell are we doing *here*?' she said.

'Waiting.'

'For what?'

'For them to get out of there.'

She gasped, halfway between outrage and astonishment.

'We're not *waiting*, Reacher, we're going straight to the police with this.'

He turned the key again to give him power to operate the window. Buzzed it all the way down, so he could listen to the sounds outside.

'I can't go to the police with this,' he said, not looking at her.

'Why the hell can't you?'

'Because they'll start looking at me for Costello.'

'You didn't kill Costello.'

'You think they'll be ready and willing to believe that?'

'They'll have to believe it, because it wasn't you, simple as that.'

'Could take them time to find somebody looks better for it.'

She paused. 'So what are you saying?'

'I'm saying it's all-around advantageous I stay away from the police.'

She shook her head. He saw it in the mirror.

'No, Reacher, we *need* the police for this.'

He kept his eyes on hers, in the mirror.

'Remember what Leon used to say? He used to say hell, I *am* the police.'

'Well, he was, and you were. But that was a long time ago.'

113

'Not so long ago, for either of us.'

She went quiet. Sat forward. Leaned towards him. 'You don't *want* to go to the police, right? That's it, isn't it? Not that you *can't*, you just damn well don't *want* to.'

He half turned in the driver's seat so he could look straight at her. He saw her eyes drop to the burn on his shirt. There was a long teardrop shape there, a black sooty stain, gunpowder particles tattooed into the cotton. He undid the buttons and pulled the shirt open. Squinted down. The same teardrop shape was burned into his skin, the hairs frizzed and curled, a blister already puffing up, getting red and angry. He licked his thumb and pressed it on the blister and grimaced.

'They mess with me, they answer to me.'

She stared at him. 'You're totally unbelievable, you know that? You're just as bad as my father was. We should go to the police, Reacher.'

'Can't do it,' he said. 'They'll throw me in jail.'

'We should,' she said again.

But she said it weakly. He shook his head and said nothing back. Watched her closely. She was a lawyer, but she was also Leon's daughter, and she knew how things worked outside in the real world. She was quiet for a long spell, and then she shrugged helplessly and put her hand on her breastbone, like it was tender.

'You OK?' he asked her.

'You hit me kind of hard,' she said.

I could rub it better, he thought.

'Who were those guys?' she asked.

'The two who killed Costello,' he said.

She nodded. Then she sighed. Her blue eyes glanced left and right.

'So where *are* we going?'

He relaxed. Then he smiled. 'Where's the last place they'll look for us?'

She shrugged. Took her hand off her chest and used it to smooth her hair.

'Manhattan?' she said.

'The house,' he said. 'They saw us run, they won't expect us to double back.'

'You're crazy, you know that?'

'We need the suitcase. Leon might have made notes.'

She shook her head, dazed.

'And we need to close the place up again. We can't leave the garage open. It'll end up full of raccoons. Whole families of the bastards.'

Then he held up his hand. Put his finger to his lips. There was the sound of a motor starting up. Maybe a big V-8, maybe two hundred yards away. There was the rattle of big tyres on a distant stony driveway. The burble of acceleration. Then a black shape flashed across their view. A big black jeep, aluminium wheels. A Yukon or a Tahoe, depending on whether it said GMC on the back, or Chevrolet. Two guys in it, dark suits, one of them driving and the other slumped back in his seat. Reacher stuck his head all the way out of the window and listened to the sound as it died to silence in the direction of town.

Chester Stone waited in his own office suite more than an hour, and then he called downstairs and had the finance director contact the bank and check on the operating account. It showed a one-point-one-million-dollar credit, wired in fifty minutes ago from the Cayman office of a Bahamas-owned trust company.

'It's there,' the finance guy said. 'You did the trick, chief.'

Stone gripped the phone and wondered exactly what trick he had done.

'I'm coming down,' he said. 'I want to go over the figures.'

'The figures are good,' the finance guy said. 'Don't worry about it.'

'I'm coming down anyway,' Stone said.

He rode the elevator two floors down and joined the finance guy in his plush inner office. Entered the password and called up the secret spreadsheet. Then the finance guy took over and typed in the new balance available in the operating account. The software ran the calculation and came up exactly level, six weeks into the future.

'See?' the guy said. 'Bingo.'

'What about the interest payment?' Stone asked.

'Eleven grand a week, six weeks? Kind of steep, isn't it?'

'Can we pay it?'

The guy nodded confidently. 'Sure we can. We owe two suppliers seventy-three grand. We got it, ready to go. If we lose the invoices, get them to re-submit, we free that cash up for a spell.'

He tapped the screen and indicated a provision against received invoices.

'Seventy-three grand, minus eleven a week for six weeks, gives us seven grand spare. We should go out to dinner a couple of times.'

'Run it again, OK?' Stone said. 'Double check.'

The guy gave him a look, but he ran it again. He took out the one-point-one, ended up in the red, put it back in again, and ended up balanced. He cancelled the provision against the invoices, subtracted eleven thousand every seven days, and ended the six-week period with an operating surplus of seven thousand dollars.

'Close,' he said. 'But the right side of close.'

'How do we repay the principal?' Stone asked. 'We need one-point-one million available at the end of the six weeks.'

'No problem,' the guy said. 'I've got it all figured. We'll have it in time.'

'Show me, OK?'

'OK, see here?' He was tapping the screen on a different line, where payments due in from customers were listed. 'These two wholesalers owe us exactly one-point-one-seven-three, which exactly matches the principal plus the lost invoices, and it's due exactly six weeks from now.'

'Will they pay on time?'

The guy shrugged. 'Well, they always have.'

Stone stared at the screen. His eyes moved up and down, left and right.

'Run it all again. Triple-check.'

'Don't sweat it, chief. It adds up.'

'Just do it, OK?'

The guy nodded. It was Stone's company, after all. He ran it again, the whole calculation, beginning to end, and it came out just the same. Hobie's one-point-one disappeared as the blizzard of pay checks cleared, the two suppliers went hungry, the interest got paid, the payments came in from the wholesalers, Hobie got his one-point-one back, the suppliers got paid late, and the sheet ended up showing the same trivial seven-thousand-dollar surplus in their favour.

'Don't sweat it,' the guy said again. 'It works out.'

Stone was staring at the screen, wondering if that spare seven grand would buy Marilyn a trip to Europe. Probably not. Not a six-week trip, anyway. And it would alert her. It would worry her. She'd ask him why he was making her go. And he'd have to tell her. She was very smart. Smart enough to get it out of him, one way or another. And then she would refuse to go to Europe, and she would end up lying awake every night for six weeks, too.

The suitcase was still there, lying on the front lawn. There was a bullet hole punched in one end. No exit hole. The bullet must have gone through the leather, through the sturdy plywood carcass, and burned to a stop against the packed paper inside. Reacher smiled and carried it back to join Jodie over at the garage.

They left the jeep on the tarmac forecourt and went in the same way they had come out. Closed up the roller door and walked through to the breezeway. Locked the inside door behind them with the green key and walked through to the kitchen. Locked that door behind them and stepped past Jodie's abandoned garment bag in the hallway. Reacher carried the suitcase into the living room. More space and more light there than in the den.

He opened the case and lifted the concertina files out on to the floor. The bullet fell out with them and bounced on the rug. It was a standard nine-millimetre Parabellum, full copper jacket. Slightly flattened on the nose from the impact with the old plywood, but otherwise unmarked. The paper had slowed it to a complete stop in the space of about eighteen inches. He could see the hole punched all the way through half the files. He weighed the bullet in his palm, and then he saw Jodie at the door, watching him. He tossed the bullet to her. She caught it, one-handed.

'Souvenir,' he said.

She juggled it like it was hot and dropped it in the fireplace. Joined him on the rug, kneeling hip to hip beside him in front of the mass of paper. He caught her perfume, something he did not recognize, but something subtle and intensely feminine. The sweatshirt was too big on her, large and shapeless, but somehow it emphasized her figure. The sleeves finished halfway down the backs of her hands, almost at her fingers. Her Levi's were cinched in tight around her tiny waist with a belt, and her legs left them slightly empty. She looked fragile, but he could remember the strength in her arms. Thin, but wiry. She bent to look at the files, and her hair fell forward, and he caught the same soft smell he recalled from fifteen years previously.

'What are we looking for?' she asked.

He shrugged. 'We'll know when we find it, I guess.'

They looked hard, but they found nothing. There was nothing there. Nothing current, nothing significant. Just a mass of household paper, looking suddenly old and pathetic as it charted its way through a domestic life that was now over. The most recent item was the will, on its own in a separate slot, sealed into an envelope with neat writing on it. Neat, but slightly slow and shaky, the writing of a man just back from the hospital after his first heart attack. Jodie took it out to the hallway and slipped it into the pocket of her garment bag.

'Any unpaid bills?' she called.

There was a slot marked PENDING. It was empty.

'Can't see any,' he called back. 'There'll be a few coming in, I guess, right? Do they come in monthly?'

She gave him a look from the doorway and smiled. 'Yes, they do,' she said. 'Monthly, every month.'

There was a slot marked MEDICAL. It was over-stuffed with receipted bills from the hospital and the clinic and sheaves of efficient correspondence from the insurance provider. Reacher leafed through it all.

'Christ, is that what this stuff costs?'

Jodie came back and bent to look.

'Sure it is,' she said. 'Have you got insurance?'

He looked at her, blankly.

'I think maybe the VA gives it to me, at least for a period.'

'You should check it out,' she said. 'Make sure.'

He shrugged. 'I feel OK.'

'So did Dad,' she said. 'For sixty-three and a half straight years.'

She knelt beside him again, and he saw her eyes cloud over. He laid his hand on her arm, gently.

'Hell of a day, right?' he said.

She nodded and blinked. Then she came up with a small, wry smile.

'Unbelievable,' she said. 'I bury the old man, I get shot at by a couple of murderers, I break the law by failing to report so many felonies I can't even count them, and then I get talked into hooking up with some wild man aiming to run some kind of a vigilante deal. You know what Dad would have said to me?'

'What?'

She pursed her lips and lowered her voice into a close imitation of Garber's good-natured growl. '*All in a day's work, girl, all in a day's work*. That's what he would have said to me.'

Reacher grinned back at her and squeezed her arm

again. Then he leafed through the medical junk and picked out a letterhead.

'Let's go find this clinic,' he said.

There was a lot of debate going on inside the Tahoe about whether they should go back at all. Failure was not a popular word in Hobie's vocabulary. It might be better just to take off and disappear. Just get the hell out. It was an attractive prospect. But they were pretty sure Hobie would find them. Maybe not soon, but he would find them. And that was not an attractive prospect.

So they turned their attention to damage limitation. It was clear what they had to do. They made the necessary stops and wasted a plausible amount of time in a diner just off the southbound side of Route 9. By the time they had battled the traffic back down to the southern tip of Manhattan, they had their whole story straight.

'It was a no-brainer,' the first guy said. 'We waited for hours, which is why we're so late back. Problem was there was a whole bunch of soldiers there, kind of ceremonial, but they had rifles all over the place.'

'How many?' Hobie asked.

'Soldiers?' the second guy said. 'At least a dozen. Maybe fifteen. They were all milling around, so it was hard to count them exactly. Some kind of honour guard.'

'She left with them,' the first guy said. 'They must have escorted her down from the cemetery, and then she went back somewhere with them afterward.'

'You didn't think to follow?'

'No way we could,' the second guy said. 'They were driving slow, a long line of cars. Like a funeral

121

procession? They'd have made us in a second. We couldn't just tag on the end of a funeral procession, right?'

'What about the big guy from the Keys?'

'He left real early. We just let him go. We were watching for Mrs Jacob. It was pretty clear by then which one she was. She stayed around, then she left, all surrounded by this bunch of military.'

'So what did you do then?'

'We checked the house,' the first guy said. 'Locked up tight. So we went into the town and checked the property title. Everything's listed in the public library. The place was registered to a guy called Leon Garber. We asked the librarian what she knew, and she just handed us the local newspaper. Page three, there was a story about the guy. Just died, heart trouble. Widower, only surviving relative is his daughter Jodie, the former Mrs Jacob, who is a young but very eminent financial attorney with Spencer Gutman Ricker and Talbot of Wall Street, and who lives on Lower Broadway right here in New York City.'

Hobie nodded slowly, and tapped the sharp end of his hook on the desk, with a jittery little rhythm.

'And who was this Leon Garber, exactly? Why all the soldiers at his wake?'

'Military policeman,' the first guy said.

The second guy nodded. 'Mustered out with three stars and more medals than you can count, served forty years, Korea, Vietnam, everywhere.'

Hobie stopped tapping. He sat still and the colour drained out of his face, leaving his skin dead white, all except for the shiny pink burn scars that glowed vivid in the gloom.

'Military policeman,' he repeated quietly.

He sat for a long time with those words on his lips. He just sat and stared into space, and then he lifted his hook off the desk and rotated it in front of his eyes, slowly, examining it, allowing the thin beams of light from the blinds to catch its curves and contours. It was trembling, so he took it in his left hand and held it still.

'Military policeman,' he said again, staring at the hook. Then he transferred his gaze to the two men on the sofas.

'Leave the room,' he said to the second guy.

The guy glanced once at his partner and went out and closed the door softly behind him. Hobie pushed back in his chair and stood up. Came out from behind the desk and stepped over and stopped still, directly behind the first guy, who just sat there on his sofa, not moving, not daring to turn around and look.

He wore a size sixteen collar, which made his neck a fraction over five inches in diameter, assuming a human neck is more or less a uniform cylinder, which was an approximation Hobie had always been happy to make. Hobie's hook was a simple steel curve, like a capital letter J, generously sized. The inside diameter of the curve was four and three-quarter inches. He moved fast, darting the hook out and forcing it over the guy's throat from behind. He stepped back and pulled with all his strength. The guy threw himself upward and backward, his fingers scrabbling under the cold metal to relieve the gagging pressure. Hobie smiled and pulled harder. The hook was riveted to a heavy leather cup and a matching shaped corset, the cup over the remains of his forearm, the corset buckled tight over his bicep above his elbow. The forearm assembly was just a stabilizer. It was the upper corset, smaller than the bulge of his elbow joint, that took all the strain and made it impossible for the hook to be separated from the stump. He pulled until the gagging turned to fractured wheezing and the redness in the guy's face began to turn blue. Then he eased off an inch and bent close to the guy's ear.

'He had a big bruise on his face. What the hell was that about?'

The guy was wheezing and gesturing wildly. Hobie twisted the hook, which relieved the pressure on the guy's voice box, but brought the tip up into the soft area under his ear.

'What the hell was that about?' he asked again.

The guy knew that with the hook at that angle any extra rearward pressure was going to put the tip right through his skin into that vulnerable triangle behind the jaw. He didn't know much about anatomy, but he knew he was half an inch away from dying.

'I'll tell you,' he wheezed. 'I'll tell you.'

Hobie kept the hook in position, twisting it every time the guy hesitated, so that the whole true story took no longer than three minutes, beginning to end.

'You failed me,' Hobie said.

'Yes, we did,' the guy gasped. 'But it was his fault. He got all tangled up behind the screen door. He was useless.'

Hobie jerked the hook.

'As opposed to what? Like he's useless and you're useful?'

'It was his fault,' the guy gasped again. 'I'm still useful.'

'You're going to have to prove that to me.'

'How?' the guy wheezed. 'Please, how? Just tell me.'

'Easy. You can do something for me.'

'Yes,' the guy gasped. 'Yes, anything, please.'

124

'Bring me Mrs Jacob,' Hobie screamed at him.

'Yes,' the guy screamed back.

'And don't screw up again,' Hobie screamed.

'No,' the guy gasped. 'No, we won't, I promise.'

Hobie jerked the hook again, twice, in time with his words.

'Not *we*. Just *you*. Because you can do something else for me.'

'What?' the guy wheezed. 'Yes, what? Anything.'

'Get rid of your useless partner,' Hobie whispered. 'Tonight, on the boat.'

The guy nodded as vigorously as the hook would allow his head to move. Hobie leaned forward and slipped the hook away. The guy collapsed sideways, gasping and retching into the fabric on the sofa.

'And bring me his right hand,' Hobie whispered. 'To prove it.'

They found that the clinic Leon had been attending was not really a place in its own right, but just an administrative unit within a giant private hospital facility serving the whole of lower Putnam County. There was a ten-storey white building set in parkland, with medical practices of every description clustered around its base. Small roads snaked through tasteful landscaping and led to little culs-de-sac ringed with low offices for the doctors and the dentists. Anything the professions couldn't handle in the offices got transferred to rented beds inside the main building. Thus the cardiology clinic was a notional entity, made up of a changing population of doctors and patients depending on who was sick and how bad they were. Leon's own correspondence showed he had been seen in several different physical locations, ranging from the ICU at the outset, to the recovery ward, then to one of the outpatient offices, then back to the ICU for his final visit.

The name of the supervising cardiologist was the only constant feature throughout the paperwork, a Dr McBannerman, who Reacher pictured in his mind as a kindly old guy, white hair, erudite, wise and sympathetic, maybe of ancient Scottish extraction, until Jodie told him she had met with her several times and she was a woman from Baltimore aged about thirty-five. He was driving Jodie's jeep around the small curving roads, while she was scanning left and right for the correct office. She recognized it at the end of a cul-de-sac, a low brick structure, white trim, somehow glowing with an antiseptic halo like medical buildings do. There were half a dozen cars parked outside, with one spare slot which Reacher backed into.

The receptionist was a heavy old busybody who welcomed Jodie with a measure of sympathy. She invited them to wait in McBannerman's inner office, which earned them glares from the other patients in the waiting room. The inner office was an inoffensive place, pale and sterile and silent, with a token examination table and a large coloured cutaway diagram of the human heart on the wall behind the desk. Jodie was staring up at it like she was asking *so which part finally failed?* Reacher could feel his own heart, huge and muscular and thumping gently in his chest. He could feel the blood pumping and the pulses ticking in his wrists and his neck.

They waited like that for ten minutes, and then the inner door opened and Dr McBannerman stepped in, a plain dark-haired woman in a white coat, a

126

stethoscope around her neck like a badge of office, and concern in her face.

'Jodie,' she said. 'I'm terribly sorry about Leon.'

It was 99 per cent genuine, but there was a stray edge of worry there, too. *She's worried about a malpractice suit*, Reacher thought. The patient's daughter was a lawyer, and she was right there in her office straight from the funeral ceremony. Jodie caught it too, and she nodded, a reassuring little gesture.

'I just came to say thank you. You were absolutely wonderful, every step of the way. He couldn't have had better care.'

McBannerman relaxed. The 1 per cent of worry washed away. She smiled and Jodie glanced up at the big diagram again.

'So which part finally failed?' she asked.

McBannerman followed her gaze and shrugged gently.

'Well, all of it, really, I'm afraid. It's a big complex muscle, it beats and it beats, thirty million times a year. If it lasts twenty-seven hundred million beats, which is ninety years, we call it old age. If it lasts only eighteen hundred million beats, sixty years, we call it premature heart disease. We call it America's biggest health problem, but really all we're saying is sooner or later it just stops going.'

She paused and looked directly at Reacher. For a second he thought she had spotted some symptom he was displaying. Then he realized she was waiting for an introduction.

'Jack Reacher,' he said. 'I was an old friend of Leon's.'

She nodded slowly, like a puzzle had just been solved.

'The famous Major Reacher. He spoke about you, often.'

She sat and looked at him, openly interested. She scanned his face, and then her eyes settled on his chest. He wasn't sure if that was because of her professional speciality, or if she was looking at the scorch mark from the muzzle blast.

'Did he speak about anything else?' Jodie asked. 'I got the impression he was concerned about something.'

McBannerman turned to her, puzzled, like she was thinking *well, all of my patients are concerned about something, like life and death.*

'What sort of thing?'

'I don't really know,' Jodie said. 'Maybe something one of the other patients might have involved him with?'

McBannerman shrugged and looked blank, like she was about to dismiss it, but then they saw her remember.

'Well, he did mention something. He told me he had a new task.'

'Did he say what it was?'

McBannerman shook her head.

'He mentioned no details. Initially, it seemed to bore him. He was reluctant about it, at first. Like somebody had landed him with something tedious. But then he got a lot more interested, later. It got to where it was overstimulating him. His ECGs were way up, and I wasn't at all happy about it.'

'Was it connected to another patient?' Reacher asked her.

She shook her head again.

'I really don't know. It's possible, I guess. They

spend a lot of time together, out there in reception. They talk to each other. They're old people, often bored and lonely, I'm afraid.'

It sounded like a rebuke. Jodie blushed.

'When did he first mention it?' Reacher asked, quickly.

'March?' McBannerman said. 'April? Soon after he became an outpatient, anyway. Not long before he went to Hawaii.'

Jodie stared at her, surprised. 'He went to Hawaii? I didn't know that.'

McBannerman nodded. 'He missed an appointment and I asked him what had happened, and he said he'd been to Hawaii, just a couple of days.'

'Hawaii? Why would he go to Hawaii without telling me?'

'I don't know why he went,' McBannerman said.

'Was he well enough to travel?' Reacher asked her.

She shook her head.

'No, and I think he knew it was silly. Maybe that's why he didn't mention it.'

'When did he become an outpatient?' Reacher asked.

'Beginning of March,' she said.

'And when did he go to Hawaii?'

'Middle of April, I think.'

'OK,' he said. 'Can you give us a list of your other patients during that period? March and April? People he might have talked to?'

McBannerman was already shaking her head.

'No, I'm sorry, I really can't do that. It's a confidentiality issue.'

She appealed to Jodie with her eyes, doctor to lawyer, woman to woman, a you-know-how-it-is sort of a look. Jodie nodded, sympathetically.

'Maybe you could just ask your receptionist? You know, see if she saw Dad talking with one of the others out there? That would just be conversational, third-party, no confidentiality issues involved. In my opinion, certainly.'

McBannerman recognized an impasse when she saw one. She buzzed the intercom and asked the receptionist to step inside. The woman was asked the question, and she started nodding busily and answering before it was even finished.

'Yes, of course, Mr Garber was always talking to that nice elderly couple, you know, the man with the dodgy valve? Upper right ventricle? Can't drive any more so his wife brings him in every time? In that awful old car? Mr Garber was doing something for them, I'm absolutely sure of it. They were always showing him old photographs and pieces of paper.'

'The Hobies?' McBannerman asked her.

'That's right, they all got to be thick as thieves together, the three of them, Mr Garber and old Mr and Mrs Hobie.'

SIX

Hook Hobie was alone in his inner office, eighty-eight floors up, listening to the quiet background sounds of the giant building, thinking hard, changing his mind. He was not an inflexible guy. He prided himself on that. He admired the way he could change and adapt and listen and learn. He felt it gave him his edge, made him distinctive.

He had gone to Vietnam more or less completely unaware of his capabilities. More or less completely unaware of everything, because he had been very young. And not just very young, but also straight out of a background that was repressed and conducted in a quiet suburban vacuum that held no scope for anything much in the way of experience.

Vietnam changed him. It could have broken him. It broke plenty of other guys. All around him, there were guys going to pieces. Not just the kids like him, but the older guys too, the long-service professionals who had been in the Army for years. Vietnam fell on people like a weight, and some of them cracked, and some of them didn't.

He didn't. He just looked around, and changed and adapted. Listened and learned. Killing was easy. He was a guy who had never seen anything dead before apart from roadkill, the chipmunks and the rabbits and the occasional stinking skunk on the leafy lanes near his home. First day in-country in 'Nam he saw eight American corpses. It was a foot patrol neatly triangulated by mortar fire. Eight men, twenty-nine pieces, some of them large. A defining moment. His buddies were going quiet and throwing up and groaning in sheer abject miserable disbelief. He was unmoved.

He started out as a trader. Everybody wanted something. Everybody was moaning about what they didn't have. It was absurdly easy. All it took was a little listening. Here was a guy who smoked but didn't drink. There was a guy who loved beer but didn't smoke. Take the cigarettes from the one guy and exchange them for the other guy's beer. Broker the deal. Keep a small percentage back for yourself. It was so easy and so obvious he couldn't believe they weren't doing it for themselves. He didn't take it seriously, because he was sure it couldn't last. It wasn't going to take long for them all to catch on, and cut him out as middleman.

But they never caught on. It was his first lesson. He could do things other people couldn't. He could spot things they couldn't. So he listened harder. What else did they want? Lots of things. Girls, food, penicillin, records, duty at base camp, but not latrine duty. Boots, bug repellent, side arms plated with chromium, dried ears from VC corpses for souvenirs. Marijuana, aspirin, heroin, clean needles, safe duty for the last hundred days of a tour. He listened and learned and searched and skimmed.

Then he made his big breakthrough. It was a

conceptual leap he always looked back on with tremendous pride. It served as a pattern for the other giant strides he made later. It came as a response to a couple of problems he was facing. First problem was the sheer hard work everything was causing him. Finding specific physical things was sometimes tricky. Finding undiseased girls became very difficult, and finding virgins became impossible. Getting hold of a steady supply of drugs was risky. Other things were tedious. Fancy weapons, VC souvenirs, even decent boots all took time to obtain. Fresh new officers on rotation were screwing up his sweetheart deals in the safe non-combat zones.

The second problem was competition. It was coming to his attention that he wasn't unique. Rare, but not unique. Other guys were getting in the game. A free market was developing. His deals were occasionally rejected. People walked away, claiming a better trade was available elsewhere. It shocked him.

Change and adapt. He thought it through. He spent an evening on his own, lying in his narrow cot in his hooch, thinking hard. He made the breakthrough. Why chase down specific physical things that were already hard to find, and could only get harder? Why trek on out to some medic and ask what he wanted in exchange for a boiled and stripped Charlie skull? Why then go out and barter for whatever damn thing it was and bring it back in and pick up the skull? Why deal in all that stuff? Why not just deal in the commonest and most freely available commodity in the whole of Vietnam?

American dollars. He became a moneylender. He smiled about it later, ruefully, when he was convalescing and had time to read. It was an absolutely classic progression. Primitive societies start out with barter, and then they progress to a cash economy. The American presence in Vietnam had started out as a primitive society. That was for damn sure. Primitive, improvised, disorganized, just crouching there on the muddy surface of that awful country. Then as time passed it became bigger, more settled, more mature. It grew up, and he was the first of his kind to grow up with it. The first, and for a very long time the only. It was a source of huge pride to him. It proved he was better than the rest. Smarter, more imaginative, better able to change and adapt and prosper.

Cash money was the key to everything. Somebody wanted boots or heroin or a girl some lying gook swore was twelve and a virgin, he could go buy it with money borrowed from Hobie. He could gratify his desire today, and pay for it next week, plus a few per cent in interest. Hobie could just sit there, like a fat lazy spider in the centre of a web. No legwork. No hassle. He put a lot of thought into it. Realized early the psychological power of numbers. Little numbers like *nine* sounded small and friendly. Nine per cent was his favourite rate. It sounded like nothing at all. Nine, just a little squiggle on a piece of paper. A single figure. Less than ten. Really nothing at all. That's how the other grunts looked at it. But 9 per cent a week was 468 per cent a year. Somebody let the debt slip for a week, and compound interest kicked in. That 468 per cent ramped up to 1,000 per cent pretty damn quickly. But nobody looked at that. Nobody except Hobie. They all saw the number *nine*, single figure, small and friendly.

The first defaulter was a big guy, savage, ferocious, pretty much subnormal in the head. Hobie smiled.

Forgave him his debt and wrote it off. Suggested that he might repay this generosity by getting alongside him and taking on the role of enforcer. There were no more defaulters after that. The exact method of deterrence was tricky to establish. A broken arm or leg just sent the guy way back behind the lines to the field hospital, where he was safe and surrounded by white nurses who would probably put out if he came up with some kind of heroic description about how he got the injury. A bad break might even get him invalided out of the service altogether and returned Stateside. No kind of deterrence in that. No kind of deterrence at all. So Hobie had his enforcer use punji spikes. They were a VC invention, a small sharp wooden spike like a meat skewer, coated with buffalo dung, which is poisonous. The VC concealed them in shallow holes, so GIs would step on them and get septic crippling wounds in the feet. Hobie's enforcer aimed to use them through the defaulter's testicles. The feeling among Hobie's clientele was the long-term medical consequences were not worth risking, even in exchange for escaping the debt and getting out of uniform.

By the time he got burned and lost his arm, Hobie was a seriously rich man. His next coup was to get the whole of his fortune home, undetected and complete. Not everybody could have done it. Not in the particular set of circumstances he found himself in. It was further proof of his greatness. As was his subsequent history. He arrived in New York after a circuitous journey, crippled and disfigured, and immediately felt at home. Manhattan was a jungle, no different from the jungles of Indochina. So there was no reason for him to start acting any different. No reason to change his line of business. And this time, he was starting out

135

with a massive capital reserve. He wasn't starting out with nothing.

He loan-sharked for years. He built it up huge. He had the capital, and he had the image. The burn scars and the hook meant a lot, visually. He attracted a raft of helpers. He fed off whole identifiable waves and generations of immigrants and poor people. He fought off the Italians to stay in business. He paid off whole squads of cops and prosecutors to stay invisible.

Then he made his second great breakthrough. Similar to the first. It was a process of deep radical thought. A response to a problem. The problem was the sheer insane scale. He had millions on the street, but it was all nickel-and-dime. Thousands of separate deals, a hundred bucks here, a hundred and fifty there, 9 or 10 per cent a week, 500 or 1,000 per cent a year. Big paperwork, big hassles, running fast all the time just to keep up. Then he suddenly realized *less could be more*. It came to him in a flash. Five per cent of some corporation's million bucks was worth more in a week than 500 per cent of street-level shit. He got in a fever about it. He froze all new lending and turned the screws to get back everything he was owed. He bought suits and rented office space. Overnight he became a corporate lender.

It was an act of pure genius. He had sniffed out that grey margin that lies just to the left of conventional commercial practice. He had found a huge constituency of borrowers who were just slipping off the edge of what the banks called acceptable. A huge constituency. A desperate constituency. Above all, a soft constituency. Soft targets. Civilized men in suits coming to him for a million bucks, posing much less of a risk than somebody in a dirty undershirt wanting a hundred in a filthy tenement block with a rabid dog behind the door. Soft targets, easy to intimidate. Unaccustomed to the harsh realities of life. He let his enforcers go, and sat back and watched as his clientele shrank to a handful, his average loan increased a millionfold, his interest rates dropped back into the stratosphere, and his profits grew bigger than he could ever imagine. *Less is more*.

It was a wonderful new business to be in. There were occasional problems, of course. But they were manageable. He changed his deterrence tactic. These civilized new borrowers were vulnerable through their families. Wives, daughters, sons. Usually, the threat was enough. Occasionally, action had to be taken. Often, it was fun. Soft suburban wives and daughters could be amusing. An added bonus. A wonderful business. Achieved through a constant willingness to change and adapt. Deep down, he knew his talent for flexibility was his greatest strength. He had promised himself never ever to forget that fact. Which was why he was alone in his inner office, up there on the eighty-eighth floor, listening to the quiet background sounds of the giant building, thinking hard, and changing his mind.

Fifty miles away to the north, in Pound Ridge, Marilyn Stone was changing her mind, too. She was a smart woman. She knew Chester was in financial trouble. It couldn't be anything else. He wasn't having an affair. She knew that. There are signs husbands give out when they're having affairs, and Chester wasn't giving them out. There was nothing else he could be worried about. So it was financial trouble.

Her original intention had been to wait. Just to sit

tight and wait until the day he finally needed to get it off his chest and told her all about it. She had planned to wait for that day and then step in. She could manage the situation from there on in, however far it went exactly, debt, insolvency, even bankruptcy. Women are good at managing situations. Better than men. She could take the practical steps, she could offer whatever consolation was needed, she could pick her way through the ruins without the ego-driven hopelessness Chester was going to be feeling.

But now she was changing her mind. She couldn't wait any longer. Chester was killing himself with worry. So she was going to have to go ahead and do something about it. No use talking to him. His instinct was to conceal problems. He didn't want to upset her. He would deny everything and the situation would keep on getting worse. So she had to go ahead and act alone. For his sake, as well as hers.

The obvious first step was to place the house with a realtor. Whatever the exact degree of trouble they were in, selling the house might be necessary. Whether it would be enough, she had no way of telling. It might solve the problem on its own, or it might not. But it was the obvious place to start.

A rich woman living in Pound Ridge like Marilyn has many contacts in the real estate business. One step down the status ladder, where the women are comfortable without being rich, a lot of them work for realtors. They keep it part-time and try to make it look like a hobby, like it was more connected with an enthusiasm for interior decoration than mere commerce. Marilyn could immediately list four good friends she could call. Her hand was resting on the phone as she tried to choose between them. In the end, she chose a

138

woman called Sheryl, who she knew the least well of the four, but who she suspected was the most capable. She was taking this seriously, and her realtor needed to, as well. She dialled the number.

'Marilyn,' Sheryl answered. 'How nice to talk to you. Can I help?'

Marilyn took a deep breath.

'We might be selling the house,' she said.

'And you've come to me? Marilyn, thank you. But why on earth are you guys thinking of selling? It's so lovely where you are. Are you moving out of state?'

Marilyn took another deep breath. 'I think Chester's going broke. I don't really want to talk about it, but I figure we need to start making contingency plans.'

There was no pause. No hesitation, no embarrassment.

'I think you're very wise,' Sheryl said. 'Most people hang on way too long, then they have to sell in a hurry, and they lose out.'

'Most people? This happens a lot?'

'Are you kidding? We see this all the time. Better to face it early and pick up the true value. You're doing the right thing, believe me. But then women usually do, Marilyn, because we can handle this stuff better than men, can't we?'

Marilyn breathed out and smiled into the phone. Felt like she was doing exactly the right thing, and like this was exactly the right person to be doing it with.

'I'll list it right away,' Sheryl said. 'I suggest an asking price a dollar short of two million, and a target of one-point-nine. That's achievable, and it should spark something pretty quickly.'

'How quickly?'

'Today's market?' Sheryl said. 'With your location? Six weeks? Yes, I think we can pretty much guarantee an offer inside six weeks.'

Dr McBannerman was still pretty uptight about confidentiality issues, so although she gave up old Mr and Mrs Hobie's address, she wouldn't accompany it with a phone number. Jodie saw no legal logic in that, but it seemed to keep the doctor happy, so she didn't bother arguing about it. She just shook hands and hustled back through the waiting area and outside to the car, with Reacher following behind her.

'Bizarre,' she said to him. 'Did you see those people? In reception?'

'Exactly,' Reacher replied. 'Old people, half dead.'

'That's what Dad looked like, towards the end. Just like that, I'm afraid. And I guess this old Mr Hobie won't look any different. So what were they up to together that people are getting killed over it?'

They got into the Bravada together and she leaned over from the passenger seat and unhooked her car phone. Reacher started the motor to run the air. She dialled information. The Hobies lived north of Garrison, up past Brighton, the next town on the railroad. She wrote their number in pencil on a scrap of paper from her pocketbook and then dialled it immediately. It rang for a long time, and then a woman's voice answered.

'Yes?' the voice said, hesitantly.

'Mrs Hobie?' Jodie asked.

'Yes?' the voice said again, wavering. Jodie pictured her, an old, infirm woman, grey, thin, probably wearing a flowery housecoat, gripping an ancient receiver in an old dark house smelling of stale food and furniture wax.

'Mrs Hobie, I'm Jodie Garber, Leon Garber's daughter.'

'Yes?' the woman said again.

'He died, I'm afraid, five days ago.'

'Yes, I know,' the old woman said. She sounded sad about it. 'Dr McBannerman's receptionist told us at yesterday's appointment. I was very sorry to hear about it. He was a good man. He was very nice to us. He was helping us. And he told us about you. You're a lawyer. I'm very sorry for your loss.'

'Thank you,' Jodie said. 'But can you tell me about whatever it was he was helping you with?'

'Well, it doesn't matter now, does it?'

'Doesn't it? Why not?'

'Well, because your father died,' the woman said. 'You see, I'm afraid he was really our last hope.'

The way she said it, it sounded like she meant it. Her voice was low. There was a resigned fall at the end of the sentence, a sort of tragic cadence, like she'd given up on something long cherished and anticipated. Jodie pictured her, a bony hand holding the phone up to her face, a wet tear on a thin, pale cheek.

'Maybe he wasn't,' she said. 'Maybe I could help you.'

There was a silence on the line. Just a faint hiss.

'Well, I don't think so,' the woman said. 'I'm not sure it's the kind of thing a lawyer would normally deal with, you see.'

'What kind of thing is it?'

'I don't think it matters now,' the woman said again.

'Can't you give me some idea?'

'No, I think it's all over now,' the woman said, like her old heart was breaking.

Then there was silence again. Jodie glanced out through the windshield at McBannerman's office. 'But how was my father able to help you? Was it something he especially knew about? Was it because he was in the Army? Is that what it was? Something connected with the Army?'

'Well, yes it was. That's why I'm afraid you wouldn't be able to help us, as a lawyer. We've tried lawyers, you see. We need somebody connected with the Army, I think. But thank you very much for offering. It was very generous of you.'

'There's somebody else here,' Jodie said. 'He's with me, right now. He used to work with my father, in the Army. He'd be willing to help you out, if he can.'

There was silence on the line again. Just the same faint hiss, and breathing. Like the old woman was thinking. Like she needed time to adjust to some new considerations.

'His name is Major Reacher,' Jodie said into the silence. 'Maybe my father mentioned him? They served together for a long time. My father sent for him, when he realized he wouldn't be able to carry on any longer.'

'He sent for him?' the woman repeated.

'Yes, I think he thought he would be able to come and take over for him, you know, keep on with helping you out.'

'Was this new person in the military police, too?'

'Yes, he was. Is that important?'

'I'm really not sure,' the woman said.

She went quiet again. She was breathing close to the phone.

'Can he come here to our house?' she asked suddenly.

'We'll both come,' Jodie said. 'Would you like us to come right away?'

There was silence again. Breathing, thinking.

'My husband's just had his medication,' the woman said. 'He's sleeping now. He's very sick, you know.'

Jodie nodded in the car. Opened and closed her spare hand in frustration.

'Mrs Hobie, can't you tell us what this is about?'

Silence. Breathing, thinking.

'I should let my husband tell you. I think he can explain it better than me. It's a long story, and I sometimes get confused.'

'OK, when will he wake up?' Jodie asked. 'Should we come by a little later?'

There was another pause.

'He usually sleeps right through, after his medication,' the old woman said. 'It's a blessing, really, I think. Can your father's friend come first thing in the morning?'

Hobie used the tip of his hook to press the intercom buzzer on his desk. Leaned forward and called through to his receptionist. He used the guy's name, which was an unusual intimacy for Hobie, generally caused by stress.

'Tony?' he said. 'We need to talk.'

Tony came in from his brass-and-oak reception counter in the lobby and threaded his way around the coffee table to the sofa.

'It was Garber who went to Hawaii,' he said.

'You sure?' Hobie asked him.

Tony nodded. 'On American, White Plains to Chicago, Chicago to Honolulu, April fifteenth. Returned the next day, April sixteenth, same route. Paid by Amex. It's all in their computer.'

'But what did he do there?' Hobie said, more or less to himself.

'We don't know,' Tony muttered. 'But we can guess, can't we?'

There was an ominous silence in the office. Tony watched the unburned side of Hobie's face, waiting for a response.

'I heard from Hanoi,' Hobie said, into the silence.

'Christ, when?'

'Ten minutes ago.'

'Jesus, Hanoi?' Tony said. 'Shit, shit, shit.'

'Thirty years,' Hobie said. 'And now it's happened.'

Tony stood up and walked around behind the desk. Used his fingers to push two slats of the window blind apart. A bar of afternoon sunlight fell across the room.

'So you should get out now. Now it's way, way too dangerous.'

Hobie said nothing. He clasped his hook in the fingers of his left hand.

'You promised,' Tony said urgently. 'Step one, step two. And they've happened. Both steps have happened now, for God's sake.'

'It'll still take them some time,' Hobie said. 'Won't it? Right now, they still don't know anything.'

Tony shook his head. 'Garber was no fool. He knew something. If he went to Hawaii, there was a good reason for it.'

Hobie used the muscle in his left arm to guide the

hook up to his face. He ran the smooth, cold steel over the scar tissue there. Time to time, pressure from the hard curve could relieve the itching.

'What about this Reacher guy?' he asked. 'Any progress on that?'

Tony squinted out through the gap in the blind, eighty-eight floors up.

'I called St Louis,' he said. 'He was a military policeman too, served with Garber the best part of thirteen years. They'd had another enquiry on the same subject, ten days ago. I'm guessing that was Costello.'

'So why?' Hobie asked. 'The Garber family pays Costello to chase down some old Army buddy? Why? What the hell for?'

'No idea,' Tony said. 'The guy's a drifter. He was digging swimming pools down where Costello was.'

Hobie nodded, vaguely. He was thinking hard.

'A military cop,' he said to himself. 'Who's now a drifter.'

'You should get out,' Tony said again.

'I don't like the military police,' Hobie said.

'I know you don't.'

'So what's the interfering bastard doing here?'

'You should get out,' Tony said for the third time.

Hobie nodded.

'I'm a flexible guy,' he said. 'You know that.'

Tony let the blind fall back into place. The room went dark. 'I'm not asking you to be flexible. I'm asking you to stick to what you planned all along.'

'I changed the plan. I want the Stone score.'

Tony came back around the desk and took his place on the sofa. 'Too risky to stick around for it. Both calls are in now. Vietnam and Hawaii, for Christ's sake.'

'I know that,' Hobie said. 'So I changed the plan again.'

'Back to what it was?'

Hobie shrugged and shook his head. 'A combination. We get out, for sure, but only after I nail Stone.'

Tony sighed and laid his hands palm-up on the upholstery. 'Six weeks is way, way too long. Garber already went to Hawaii, for Christ's sake. He was some kind of a hot-shot general. And obviously he knew stuff, or why would he go out there?'

Hobie was nodding. His head was moving in and out of a thin shaft of light that picked up the crude grey tufts of his hair. 'He knew stuff, I accept that. But he took sick and died. The stuff he knew died with him. Otherwise why would his daughter resort to some half-assed private dick and some unemployed drifter?'

'So what are you saying?'

Hobie slipped his hook below the level of the desktop and cupped his chin with his good hand. He let the fingers spread upward, over the scars. It was a pose he used subconsciously, when he was aiming to look accommodating and unthreatening.

'I can't give up on the Stone score,' he said. 'You can see that, right? It's just sitting there, begging to be eaten up. I give up on that, I couldn't live with myself the whole rest of my life. It would be cowardice. Running is smart, I agree with you, but running too early, earlier than you really need to, that's cowardice. And I'm not a coward, Tony, you know that, right?'

'So what are you saying?' Tony asked again.

'We do both things together, but accelerated. Because I agree with you, six weeks is way too long. We need to get out before six weeks. But we aren't going without the Stone score, so we speed things up.'

'OK, how?'

'I put the stock in the market today,' Hobie said. 'It'll hit the floor ninety minutes before the closing bell. That should be long enough to get the message through to the banks. Tomorrow morning, Stone will be coming here all steamed up. I won't be here tomorrow, so you'll tell him what we want, and what we'll do if we don't get it. We'll have the whole nine yards within a couple of days, tops. I'll pre-sell the Long Island assets so we don't hit any delay out there. Meanwhile, you'll close things down here.'

'OK, how?' Tony asked again.

Hobie looked around the dim office, all four corners.

'We'll just walk away from this place. Wastes six months of lease, but what the hell. Those two assholes playing at being my enforcers will be no problem. One of them is wasting the other tonight, and you'll work with him until he gets hold of this Mrs Jacob for me, whereupon you'll waste her and him together. Sell the boat, sell the vehicles, and we're out of here, no loose ends. Call it a week. Just a week. I think we can give ourselves a week, right?'

Tony nodded. Leaned forward, relieved at the prospect of action.

'What about this Reacher guy? He's still a loose end.'

Hobie shrugged in his chair. 'I've got a separate plan for him.'

'We won't find him,' Tony said. 'Not just the two of us. Not within a week. We don't have the time to go out searching around for him.'

'We don't need to.'

147

Tony stared at him. 'We do, boss. He's a loose end, right?'

Hobie shook his head. Then he dropped his hand away from his face and came out from under the desktop with his hook. 'I'll do this the efficient way. No reason to waste my energy finding him. I'll let him find me. And he will. I know what military cops are like.'

'And then what?'

Hobie smiled.

'Then he leads a long and happy life,' he said. 'Thirty more years at least.'

'So what now?' Reacher asked.

They were still in the lot outside McBannerman's long low office, engine idling, air roaring to combat the sun beating down on the Bravada's dark green paint. The vents were angled all over the place, and he was catching Jodie's subtle perfume mixed in with the Freon blast. Right at that moment, he was a happy guy, living an old fantasy. Many times in the past he'd speculated about how it would feel to be within touching distance of her when she was all grown up. It was something he had never expected to experience. He had assumed he would lose track of her and never see her again. He had assumed his feelings would just die away, over time. But there he was, sitting right next to her, breathing in her fragrance, taking sideways glances at her long legs sprawling down into the foot well. He had always assumed she would grow up pretty spectacular. Now he was feeling a little guilty for underestimating how beautiful she would become. His fantasies had not done her justice.

'It's a problem,' she said. 'I can't go up there

tomorrow. I can't take more time out. We're very busy right now, and I've got to keep on billing the hours.'

Fifteen years. Was that a long time or a short time? Does it change a person? It felt like a short time to him. He didn't feel radically different from the person he had been fifteen years before. He was the same person, thinking the same way, capable of the same things. He had acquired a thick gloss of experience during those years, he was older, more burnished, but he was the same person. He felt she had to be different. Had to be, surely. Her fifteen years had been a greater leap, through bigger transitions. High school, college, law school, marriage, divorce, the partnership track, hours to bill. So now he felt he was in uncharted waters, unsure of how to relate to her, because he was dealing with three separate things, all competing in his head: the reality of her as a kid, fifteen years ago, and then the way he had imagined she would turn out, and then the way she really had turned out. He knew all about two of those things, but not the third. He knew the kid. He knew the adult he'd invented inside his head. But he didn't know the reality, and it was making him unsure, because suddenly he wanted to avoid making any stupid mistakes with her.

'You'll have to go by yourself,' she said. 'Is that OK?'

'Sure,' he said. 'But that's not the issue here. You need to take care.'

She nodded. Pulled her hands up inside her sleeves, and hugged herself. He didn't know why.

'I'll be OK, I guess,' she said.

'Where's your office?'

'Wall Street and Lower Broadway.'

'That's where you live, right? Lower Broadway?'

She nodded. 'Thirteen blocks. I usually walk.'

'Not tomorrow,' he said. 'I'll drive you.'

She looked surprised. 'You will?'

'Damn right I will,' he said. 'Thirteen blocks on foot? Forget about it, Jodie. You'll be safe enough at home, but they could grab you on the street. What about your office? Is it secure?'

She nodded again. 'Nobody gets in, not without an appointment and ID.'

'OK,' he said. 'So I'll be in your apartment all night, and I'll drive you door to door in the morning. Then I'll come back up here and see these Hobie people, and you can stay right there in the office until I come get you out again, OK?'

She was silent. He tracked back and reviewed what he'd said.

'I mean, you got a spare room, right?'

'Sure,' she said. 'There's a spare room.'

'So is that OK?'

She nodded, quietly.

'So what now?' he asked her. She turned sideways on her seat. The blast of air from the centre vents caught her hair and blew it over her face. She smoothed it back behind her ear and her eyes flicked him up and down. Then she smiled.

'We should go shopping,' she said.

'Shopping? What for? What do you need?'

'Not what I need,' she said. 'What you need.'

He looked at her, worried. 'What do I need?'

'Clothes,' she said. 'You can't go visiting with those old folks looking like a cross between a beach bum and the wild man of Borneo, can you?'

Then she leaned sideways and touched the mark on his shirt with her fingertip.

'And we should find a pharmacy. You need something to put on that burn.'

'What the hell are you doing?' the finance director screamed.

He was in Chester Stone's office doorway, two floors above his own, gripping the frame with both hands, panting with exertion and fury. He hadn't waited for the elevator. He had raced up the fire stairs. Stone was staring at him, blankly.

'You idiot,' he screamed. 'I told you not to do this.'

'Do what?' Stone said back.

'Put stock in the market,' the finance guy yelled. 'I told you not to do that.'

'I didn't,' Stone said. 'There's no stock in the market.'

'There damn well is,' the guy said. 'A great big slice, sitting there doing absolutely nothing at all. You got people shying away from it like it's radioactive or something.'

'What?'

The finance guy breathed in. Stared at his employer. Saw a small, crumpled man in a ridiculous British suit sitting at a desk that alone was now worth a hundred times the corporation's entire net assets.

'You asshole, I told you not to do this. Why not just take a page in the *Wall Street Journal* and say, hey, people, my company's worth exactly less than jack shit?'

'What are you talking about?' Stone asked.

'I've got the banks on the phone,' the guy said. 'They're watching the ticker. Stone stock popped up an hour ago, and the price is unwinding faster than the damn computers can track it. It's unsaleable. You've

151

sent them a message, for God's sake. You've told them you're insolvent. You've told them you owe them sixteen million dollars against security that isn't worth sixteen damn cents.'

'I didn't put stock in the market,' Stone said again.

The finance guy nodded sarcastically.

'So who the hell did? The tooth fairy?'

'Hobie,' Stone said. 'Has to be. Jesus, why?'

'Hobie?' the guy repeated.

Stone nodded.

'Hobie?' the guy said again, incredulous. 'Shit, you gave him stock?'

'I had to,' Stone said. 'No other way.'

'Shit,' the guy said again, panting. 'You see what he's doing here?'

Stone looked blank, and then he nodded, scared. 'What can we do?'

The finance director dropped his hands off the door frame and turned his back.

'Forget *we*. There's no *we* here any more. I'm resigning. I'm out of here. You can fix it yourself.'

'But you recommended the guy,' Stone yelled.

'I didn't recommend giving him stock, you asshole,' the guy yelled back. 'What are you? A moron? If I recommended you visit the aquarium to see the piranha fish, would you stick your damn finger in the tank?'

'You've got to help me,' Stone said.

The guy just shook his head. 'You're on your own. I'm resigning. Right now my recommendation is you go down to what was my office and get started. There's a line of phones on what was my desk, all ringing. My recommendation is you start with whichever one is ringing the loudest.'

152

'Wait up,' Stone yelled. 'I need your help here.'

'Against Hobie?' the guy yelled back. 'Dream on, pal.'

Then he was gone. He just turned and strode out through the secretarial pen and disappeared. Stone came out from behind his desk and stood in the doorway, and watched him go. The suite was silent. His secretary had left. Earlier than she should have. He walked out into the corridor. The sales department on the right was deserted. The marketing suite on the left was empty. The photocopiers were silent. He called the elevator and the mechanism sounded very loud in the hush. He rode down two floors, alone. The finance director's suite was empty. Drawers were standing open. Personal belongings had been taken away. He wandered through to the inner office. The Italian desk light was glowing. The computer was turned off. The phones were off their hooks, lying on the rosewood desktop. He picked one of them up.

'Hello?' he said into it. 'This is Chester Stone.'

He repeated it twice into the electronic silence. Then a woman came on and asked him to hold. There were clicks and buzzes. A moment of soothing music.

'Mr Stone?' a new voice said. 'This is the Insolvency Unit.'

Stone closed his eyes and gripped the phone.

'Please hold for the director,' the voice said.

There was more music. Fierce baroque violins, scraping away, relentlessly.

'Mr Stone?' a deep voice said. 'This is the director.'

'Hello,' Stone said. It was all he could think of to say.

'We're taking steps,' the voice said. 'I'm sure you understand our position.'

153

'OK,' Stone said. He was thinking *what steps? Lawsuits? Prison?*

'We should be out of the woods, start of business tomorrow,' the voice said.

'Out of the woods? How?'

'We're selling the debt, obviously.'

'Selling it?' Stone repeated. 'I don't understand.'

'We don't want it any more,' the voice said. 'I'm sure you can understand that. It's moved itself way outside of the parameters that we feel happy with. So we're selling it. That's what people do, right? They got something they don't want any more, they sell it, best price they can get.'

'Who are you selling it to?' Stone asked, dazed.

'A trust company in the Caymans. They made an offer.'

'So where does that leave us?'

'Us?' the voice repeated, puzzled. 'It leaves us nowhere. Your obligation to us is terminated. There is no *us*. Our relationship is over. My only advice is that you never try to resurrect it. We would tend to regard that as insult added to injury.'

'So who do I owe now?'

'The trust company in the Caymans,' the voice said patiently. 'I'm sure whoever's behind it will be contacting you very soon, with their repayment proposals.'

Jodie drove. Reacher got out and walked around the hood and got back in on the passenger side. She slid over the centre console and buzzed the seat forward. Cruised south through the sunny Croton reservoirs, down towards the city of White Plains. Reacher was twisting around, scanning behind them. No pursuers.

154

Nothing suspicious. Just a perfect lazy June afternoon in the suburbs. He had to touch the blister through his shirt to remind himself that anything had happened at all.

She headed for a big mall. It was a serious building the size of a stadium, crowding proudly against office towers its own height, standing inside a knot of busy roads. She drifted left and right across the traffic lanes and followed a curved ramp underground to the parking garage. It was dark down there, dusty oil-stained concrete, but there was a brass-and-glass doorway in the distance, leading directly into a store and blazing with white light like a promise. Jodie found a slot fifty yards from it. She eased in and went away to do something with a machine. Came back and laid a small ticket on the dash, where it could be read through the windshield.

'OK,' she said. 'Where to first?'

Reacher shrugged. This was not his area of expertise. He had bought plenty of clothes in the last two years, because he had developed a habit of buying new stuff instead of washing the old stuff. It was a defensive habit. It defended him against carrying any kind of a big valise, and it defended him against having to learn the exact techniques of laundering. He knew about laundromats and dry cleaners, but he was vaguely worried about being alone in a laundromat and finding himself unsure of the correct procedures. And giving stuff to a dry cleaner implied a commitment to be back in the same physical location at some future time, which was a commitment he was reluctant to make. The most straightforward practice was to buy new and junk the old. So he had bought clothes, but exactly where he had bought them was hard for him to pin down. Generally he just saw clothes in a store window, went in and bought them, and came out again without really being sure of the identity of the establishment he had visited.

'There was a place I went in Chicago,' he said. 'I think it was a chain store, short little name. Hole? Gap? Something like that. They had the right sizes.'

Jodie laughed. Linked her arm through his.

'The Gap,' she said. 'There's one right in here.'

The brass-and-glass doorway led straight into a department store. The air was cold and stank of soap and perfume. They passed through the cosmetics into an area with tables piled high with summer clothes in pastel cottons. Then out into the main thoroughfare of the mall. It was oval like a racetrack, ringed with small stores, the whole arrangement repeated on two more levels above them. The walks were carpeted and music was playing and people were swarming everywhere.

'I think the Gap's upstairs,' Jodie said.

Reacher smelled coffee. One of the units opposite was done out as a coffee bar, like a street place in Italy. The inside walls were painted like outside walls, and the ceiling was flat black, so it would disappear like the sky. An inside place looking like an outside place, in an inside mall that was trying to look like an outside shopping street, except it had carpets.

'You want to get coffee?' he asked.

Jodie smiled and shook her head. 'First we shop, then we get coffee.'

She led him towards an escalator. He smiled. He knew how she was feeling. He had felt the same, fifteen years before. She had come with him, nervous and tentative, on a routine visit to the glass house in

156

Manila. Familiar territory to him, just routine, really nothing at all. But new and strange to her. He had felt busy and happy, and somehow educational. It had been fun being with her, showing her around. Now she was feeling the same thing. All this mall stuff was nothing to her. She had come home to America a long time ago and learned its details. Now he was the stranger in her territory.

'What about this place?' she called to him.

It wasn't the Gap. It was some one-off store, heavily designed with weathered shingles and timbers rescued from some old barn. The clothes were made from heavy cottons and dyed in subdued colours, and they were artfully displayed in the beds of old farm carts with iron-banded wheels.

He shrugged. 'Looks OK to me.'

She took his hand. Her palm felt cool and slim against his. She led him inside and put her hair behind her ears and bent and started looking through the displays. She did it the way he'd seen other women do it. She used little flicks of her wrist to put together assemblages of different items. A pair of pants, still folded, laid over the bottom half of a shirt. A jacket laid sideways over both of them, with the shirt peeping out at the top, and the pants showing at the bottom. Half-closed eyes, pursed lips. A shake of the head. A different shirt. A nod. Real shopping.

'What do you think?' she asked.

She had put together a pair of pants, khaki, but a little darker than most chinos. A shirt in a quiet check, greens and browns. A thin jacket in dark brown which seemed to match the rest pretty well. He nodded.

'Looks OK to me,' he said again.

The prices were handwritten on small tickets

157

attached to the garments with string. He flicked one over with his fingernail.

'Christ,' he said. 'Forget about it.'

'It's worth it,' she said. 'Quality's good.'

'I can't afford it, Jodie.'

The shirt on its own was twice what he had ever paid for a whole outfit. To dress in that stuff was going to cost him what he had earned in a day, digging pools. Ten hours, four tons of sand and rock and earth.

'I'll buy them for you.'

He stood there with the shirt in his hands, uncertain.

'Remember the necklace?' she asked.

He nodded. He remembered. She had developed a passion for a particular necklace in a Manila jeweller's. It was a plain gold thing, like a rope, vaguely Egyptian. Not really expensive, but out of her league. Leon was into some self-discipline thing with her and wouldn't spring for it. So Reacher had bought it for her. Not for her birthday or anything, just because he liked her and she liked it.

'I was so happy,' she said. 'I thought I was going to burst. I've still got it, I still wear it. So let me pay you back, OK?'

He thought about it. Nodded.

'OK,' he said.

She could afford it. She was a lawyer. Probably made a fortune. And it was a fair trade, looking at it in proportion, cost-versus-income, fifteen years of inflation.

'OK,' he said again. 'Thanks, Jodie.'

'You need socks and things, right?'

They picked out a pair of khaki socks and a pair of white boxers. She went to a till and used a gold card. He took the stuff into a changing cubicle and tore off

158

the price tickets and put everything on. He transferred his cash from his pants pocket and left the old clothes in the trash can. The new stuff felt stiff, but it looked pretty good in the mirror, against his tan. He came back out.

'Nice,' Jodie said. 'Pharmacy next.'

'Then coffee,' he said.

He bought a razor and a can of foam and a toothbrush and toothpaste. And a small tube of burn ointment. Paid for it all himself and carried it in a brown paper bag. The walk to the pharmacy had taken them near a food court. He could see a rib place that smelled good.

'Let's have dinner,' he said. 'Not just coffee. My treat.'

'OK,' she said, and linked her arm through his again.

The dinner for two cost him the price of the new shirt, which he thought was not outrageous. They had dessert and coffee, and then some of the smaller stores were closing up for the day.

'OK, home,' he said. 'And we play it real cautious from here.'

They walked through the department store, through the displays in reverse, first the pastel summer cottons and then the fierce smell of the cosmetics. He stopped her inside the brass-and-glass doors and scanned ahead out in the garage, where the air was warm and damp. A million-to-one possibility, but worth taking into account. Nobody there, just people hustling back to their cars with bulging bags. They walked together to the Bravada and she slid into the driver's seat. He got in beside her.

'Which way would you normally go?'

159

'From here? FDR Drive, I guess.'

'OK,' he said. 'Head out for LaGuardia, and we'll come in down through Brooklyn. Over the Brooklyn Bridge.'

She looked at him. 'You sure? You want to do the tourist thing, there are better places to go than the Bronx and Brooklyn.'

'First rule,' he said. 'Predictability is unsafe. If you've got a route you'd normally take, today we take a different one.'

'You serious?'

'You bet your ass. I used to do VIP protection for a living.'

'I'm a VIP now?'

'You bet your ass,' he said again.

An hour later it was dark, which is the best condition for using the Brooklyn Bridge. Reacher felt like a tourist as they swooped around the ramp and up over the hump of the span and Lower Manhattan was suddenly there in front of them with a billion bright lights everywhere. One of the world's great sights, he thought, and he had inspected most of the competition.

'Go a few blocks north,' he said. 'We'll come in from a distance. They'll be expecting us to come straight home.'

She swung wide to the right and headed north on Lafayette. Hung a tight left and another and came back travelling south on Broadway. The light at Leonard was red. Reacher scanned ahead in the neon wash.

'Three blocks,' Jodie said.

'Where do you park?'

160

'Garage under the building.'

'OK, turn off a block short,' he said. 'I'll check it out. Come around again and pick me up. If I'm not waiting on the sidewalk, go to the cops.'

She made the right on Thomas. Stopped and let him out. He slapped lightly on the roof and she took off again. He walked around the corner and found her building. It was a big square place, renovated lobby with heavy glass doors, big lock, a vertical row of fifteen buzzers with names printed behind little plastic windows. Apartment twelve had *Jacob/Garber*, like there were two people living there. There were people on the street, some of them loitering in knots, some of them walking, but none of them interesting. The parking garage entrance was farther on down the sidewalk. It was an abrupt slope into darkness. He walked down. It was quiet and badly lit. There were two rows of eight spaces, fifteen altogether because the ramp up to the street was where the sixteenth would be. Eleven cars parked up. He checked the full length of the place. Nobody hiding out. He came back up the ramp and ran back to Thomas. Dodged the traffic and crossed the street and waited. She was coming south through the light towards him. She saw him and pulled over and he got back in alongside her.

'All clear,' he said.

She made it back out into the traffic and then pulled right and bumped down the ramp. Her headlights bounced and swung. She stopped in the centre aisle and backed into her space. Killed the motor and the lights.

'How do we get upstairs?' he asked.

She pointed. 'Door to the lobby.'

There was a flight of metal steps up to a big industrial door, which had a steel sheet riveted over it. The door had a big lock, same as on the glass doors to the street. They got out and locked the car. He carried her garment bag. They walked to the steps and up to the door. She worked the lock and he swung it open. The lobby was empty. A single elevator opposite them.

'I'm on four,' she said.

He pressed five.

'We'll come down the stairs from above,' he said. 'Just in case.'

They used the fire stairs and came back down to four. He had her wait on the landing and peered out. A deserted hallway. Tall and narrow. Apartment ten to the left, eleven to the right, and twelve straight ahead.

'Let's go,' he said.

Her door was black and thick. Spy hole at eye level, two locks. She used the keys and they went inside. She locked up again and dropped an old hinged bar into place, right across the whole doorway. Reacher pressed it down in its brackets. It was iron, and as long as it was there, nobody else was going to get in. He put her garment bag against a wall. She flicked switches and the lights came on. She waited by the door while Reacher walked ahead. Hallway, living room, kitchen, bedroom, bathroom, bedroom, bathroom, closets. Big rooms, very high. Nobody in them. He came back to the living room and shrugged off his new jacket and threw it on a chair and turned back to her and relaxed.

But she wasn't relaxed. He could see that. She was looking directly away from him, more tense than she'd been all day. She was just standing there with her sweatshirt cuffs way down over her hands, in the doorway to her living room, fidgeting. He had no idea what was wrong with her.

'You OK?' he asked.

She ducked her head forward and back in a figure eight to drop her hair behind her shoulders.

'I guess I'll take a shower,' she said. 'You know, hit the sack.'

'Hell of day, right?'

'Unbelievable.'

She crabbed right around him on her way through the room, keeping her distance. She gave him a sort of shy wave, just her fingers peeping out from the sweat-shirt sleeve.

'What time tomorrow?' he asked.

'Seven-thirty will do it,' she said.

'OK,' he said. 'Good night, Jodie.'

She nodded and disappeared down the inner hallway. He heard her bedroom door open and close. He stared after her for a long moment, surprised. Then he sat on the sofa and took off his shoes. Too restless to sleep right away. He padded around in his new socks, looking at the apartment.

It wasn't really a loft, as such. It was an old building with very high ceilings, was all. The shell was original. It had probably been industrial. The outside walls were sandblasted brick, and the inner walls were smooth clean plaster. The windows were huge. Probably put there to illuminate the sewing-machine operation or whatever was there a hundred years ago.

The parts of the walls that were brick were a warm natural brick colour, but everything else was white, except for the floor, which was pale maple strips. The decor was cool and neutral, like a gallery. There was no sign that more than one person had ever lived there.

No sign of two tastes competing. The whole place was very unified. White sofas, white chairs, bookshelves built in simple cubic sections, painted with the same white paint that had been used on the walls. Big steam pipes and ugly radiators, all painted white. The only definite colour in the living room was a life-size Mondrian copy on the wall above the largest sofa. It was a proper copy, done by hand in oil on canvas, with the proper colours. Not garish reds and blues and yellows, but the correct dulled tones, with authentic little cracks and crazings in the white, which was nearer a grey. He stood and looked at it for a long time, totally astonished. Piet Mondrian was his favourite painter of all time, and this exact picture was his favourite work of all time. The title was *Composition with Red, Yellow and Blue*. Mondrian had painted the original in 1930 and Reacher had seen it in Zürich, Switzerland.

There was a tall cabinet opposite the smallest sofa, painted the same white as everything else. There was a small TV in it, a video, a cable box, a CD player with a pair of large headphones plugged into the jack. A small stack of CDs, mostly fifties jazz, stuff he liked without really being crazy about.

The windows gave out over Lower Broadway. There was a constant wash of traffic hum, neon blaze from up and down the street, an occasional siren wailing and booping and blasting loud as it came out through the gaps between blocks. He tilted the blind with a clear plastic wand and looked down at the sidewalk. There were still the same knots of people hanging around. Nothing to make him nervous. He tilted the blind back and closed it up tight.

The kitchen was huge and tall. All the cupboards

were wood, painted white, and the appliances were industrial sizes in stainless steel, like pizza ovens. He had lived in places smaller than the refrigerator. He pulled it open and saw a dozen bottles of his favourite water, the same stuff he had grown to love in the Keys. He took the seal off one of them and carried it into the guest bedroom.

The bedroom was white, like everything else. The furniture was wood, which had started out with a different finish, but which was now white like the walls. He put the water on the night table and used the bathroom. White tiles, white sink, white tub, all old enamel and tiling. He closed the blinds and stripped and folded his new clothes on to the closet shelf. Threw back the cover and slid into bed and fell to thinking.

Illusion and reality. What was nine years, anyway? A lot, he guessed, when she was fifteen and he was twenty-four, but what was it now? He was thirty-eight, and she was either twenty-nine or thirty, he wasn't exactly sure which. Where was the problem with that? *Why wasn't he doing something?* Maybe it wasn't the age thing. Maybe it was Leon. She was his daughter, and always would be. It gave him the guilty illusion she was somewhere between his kid sister and his niece. That obviously gave him a very inhibiting feeling, but it was just an illusion, right? She was the relative of an old friend, was all. An old friend who was now dead. So why the hell did he feel so bad about looking at her and seeing himself peeling off her sweat-shirt and undoing the belt from around her waist? *Why wasn't he just doing it?* Why the hell was he in the guest room instead of on the other side of the wall in bed with her? Like he'd ached to be through countless

165

forgotten nights in the past, some of them shameful, some of them wistful?

Because presumably her realities were rooted in the same kind of illusions. For kid sister and niece, call it big brother and uncle. Favourite uncle, for sure, because he knew she liked him. There was a lot of affection there. But that just made it worse. Affection for favourite uncles was a specific type of affection. Favourite uncles were there for specific types of things. Family things, like shopping and spoiling, one way or the other. Favourite uncles were not there to put the moves on you. That would come out of the blue like some kind of a shattering betrayal. Horrifying, unwelcome, incestuous, psychologically damaging.

She was on the other side of the wall. But there was nothing he could do about it. Nothing. It was never going to happen. He knew it was going to drive him crazy, so he forced his mind away from her and started thinking about other things. Things that were realities for sure, not just illusions. The two guys, whoever they were. They would have her address by now. There were a dozen ways of discovering where a person lives. They could be outside the building right at that moment. He scanned through the apartment building in his head. The lobby door, locked. The door from the parking garage, locked. The door to the apartment, locked and barred. The windows, all closed up, the blinds all drawn. So tonight, they were safe. But tomorrow morning was going to be dangerous. Maybe very dangerous. He concentrated on fixing the two guys in his mind as he fell asleep. Their vehicle, their suits, their build, their faces.

*　　*　　*

166

But at that exact moment, only one of the two guys had a face. They had sailed together ten miles south of where Reacher lay, out into the black waters of lower New York Harbor. They had worked together to unzip the rubber bodybag and lower the secretary's cold corpse down into the oily Atlantic swell. One guy had turned to the other with some cheap joke on his lips and was shot full in the face with a silenced Beretta. Then again, and again. The slow fall of his body put the three bullets all in different places. His face was all one big fatal wound, black in the darkness. His arm was levered up across the mahogany rail and his right hand was severed at the wrist with a stolen restaurant cleaver. Five blows were required. It was messy and brutal work. The hand went into a plastic bag and the body slipped into the water without a sound, less than twenty yards from the spot where the secretary was already sinking.

SEVEN

Jodie woke early that morning, which was unusual for her. Normally she slept soundly right up to the point when her alarm went off and she had to drag herself out of bed and into the bathroom, sleepy and slow. But that morning, she was awake an hour before she had to be, alert, breathing lightly, heart racing gently in her chest.

Her bedroom was white, like all her rooms, and her bed was a king with a white wood frame, set with the head against the wall opposite her window. The guest room was back to back with her room, laid out in exactly the same way, symmetrically, but in reverse, because it faced in the opposite direction. Which meant that his head was about eighteen inches away from hers. Just through the wall.

She knew what the walls were made of. She had bought the apartment before it was finished. She had been in and out for months, watching over the conversion. The wall between the two bedrooms was an original wall, a hundred years old. There was a great baulk of timber lying crossways on the floor, with bricks built up on top of it, all the way to the ceiling. The builders had simply patched the bricks where they were weak, and then plastered over them the way the Europeans do it, giving a solid hard stucco finish. The architect felt it was the right way to do it. It added solidity to the shell, and it gave better fire-proofing and better soundproofing. But it also gave a foot-thick sandwich of stucco and brick and stucco between her and Reacher.

She loved him. She was in no doubt about that. No doubt at all. She always had, right from the start. But was that OK? Was it OK to love him the way she did? She had agonized over that question before. She had lain awake nights about it, many years ago. She had burned with shame about her feelings. The nine-year age gap was obscene. Shameful. She knew that. A fifteen-year-old should not feel that way about her own father's fellow officer. Army protocol had made it practically incestuous. It was like feeling that way about an uncle. Almost like feeling that way about her father himself. But she loved him. There was no doubt about it.

She was with him whenever she could. Talking with him whenever she could, touching him whenever she could. She had her own print of the self-timer photo-graph from Manila, her arm around his waist. She had kept it pressed in a book for fifteen years. Looked at it countless times. For years, she had fed off the feeling of touching him, hugging him hard for the camera. She still remembered the exact feel of him, his broad hard frame, his smell.

The feelings had never really gone away. She had wanted them to. She had wanted it just to be an adoles-cent thing, a teenage crush. But it wasn't. She knew that from the way the feelings endured. He had disap-peared, she had grown up and moved on, but the feelings were always there. They had never receded, but they had eventually moved parallel to the main flow of her life. Always there, always real, always strong, but not necessarily connected with her day-to-day reality any more. Like people she knew, lawyers or bankers, who had really wanted to be dancers or ballplayers. A dream from the past, unconnected with reality, but absolutely defining the identity of the person involved. A lawyer, who had wanted to be a dancer. A banker, who had wanted to be a ballplayer. A divorced thirty-year-old woman, who had wanted to be with Jack Reacher all along.

Yesterday should have been the worst day of her life. She had buried her father, her last relative on earth. She had been attacked by men with guns. People she knew were in therapy for much less. She should be prostrate with misery and shock. But she wasn't. Yesterday had been the best day of her life. He had appeared like a vision on the steps, behind the garage, above the yard. The noon sun directly over his head, illuminating him. Her heart had thumped and the old feelings had swarmed back into the centre of her life, fiercer and stronger than ever, like a drug howling through her veins, like claps of thunder.

But it was all a waste of time. She knew it. She had to face it. He looked at her like a niece or a kid sister. Like the nine-year gap still counted for something. Which it no longer did. A couple aged fifteen and twenty-four would certainly have been a problem. But thirty and thirty-nine was perfectly OK. There were thousands of couples with gaps bigger than that. Millions of couples. There were guys aged seventy with twenty-year-old wives. But it still counted for something with him. Or maybe he was just too used to seeing her as Leon's kid. Like a niece. Like the CO's daughter. The rules of society or the protocol of the Army had blinded him to the possibility of seeing her any other way. She had always burned with resentment about that. She still did. Leon's affection for him, his claiming of him as his own, had taken him away from her. It had made it impossible from the start.

They had spent the day like brother and sister, like uncle and niece. Then he had turned all serious, like a bodyguard, like she was his professional responsibility. They had had fun, and he cared about her physical safety, but nothing more. There never would be anything more. And there was nothing she could do about it. Nothing. She had asked guys out. All women her age had. It was permissible. Accepted, even normal. But what could she say to him? What? What can a sister say to a brother or a niece to an uncle without causing outrage and shock and disgust? So it wasn't going to happen, and there was absolutely nothing she could do about it.

She stretched out in her bed and brought her hands up above her head. Laid her palms gently against the dividing wall and held them there. At least he was in her apartment, and at least she could dream.

The guy got less than three hours in the sack, by the time he sailed the boat single-handed back to the slip and closed it down and got back across town to bed. He was up again at six and back on the street by six-twenty, with a quick shower and no breakfast. The hand was wrapped in the plastic, parcelled up in yesterday's *Post* and carried in a Zabar's bag he had from the last time he bought ingredients and made his own dinner at home.

171

He used the black Tahoe and made quick time past all the early morning delivery people. He parked underground and rode up to the eighty-eighth floor. Tony the receptionist was already at the brass-and-oak counter. But he could tell from the stillness that nobody else was in. He held up the Zabar's bag, like a trophy.

'I've got this for the Hook,' he said.

'The Hook's not here today,' Tony said.

'Great,' the guy said, sourly.

'Stick it in the refrigerator,' Tony said.

There was a small office kitchen off the reception lobby. It was cramped and messy, like office kitchens are. Coffee rings on the counters, mugs with stains on the inside. The refrigerator was a miniature item under the counter. The guy shoved milk and a six-pack aside and folded the bag into what space was left.

'Target for today is Mrs Jacob,' Tony said. He was now in the kitchen doorway. 'We know where she lives. Lower Broadway, north of City Hall. Eight blocks from here. Neighbours say she always leaves at seven-twenty, walks to work.'

'Which is where exactly?' the guy asked.

'Wall Street and Broadway,' Tony said. 'I'll drive, you grab her.'

Chester Stone had driven home at the normal time and said nothing to Marilyn. There was nothing he could say. The speed of the collapse had left him bewildered. His whole world had turned inside out in a single twenty-four-hour period. He just couldn't get a handle on it. He planned to ignore it until the morning and then go see Hobie and try to talk some sense. In his heart he didn't believe he couldn't save himself.

The corporation was ninety years old, for God's sake. Three generations of Chester Stones. There was too much *there* for it all to disappear overnight. So he said nothing and got through the evening in a daze.

Marilyn Stone said nothing to Chester, either. Too early for him to know she had taken charge. The circumstances had to be right for that discussion. It was an ego thing. She just bustled about, doing her normal evening things, and then tried to sleep while he lay awake beside her, staring at the ceiling.

When Jodie placed her palms flat on the dividing wall, Reacher was in the shower. He had three distinct routines worked out for showering, and every morning he made a choice about which one to use. The first was a straight shower, nothing more. It took eleven minutes. The second was a shave and a shower, twenty-two minutes. The third was a special procedure, rarely used. It involved showering once, then getting out and shaving, and then showering all over again. It took more than a half-hour, but the advantage was moisturization. Some girl had explained the shave was better if the skin was already thoroughly moisturized. And she had said it can't hurt any to shampoo twice.

He was using the special procedure. Shower, shave, shower. It felt good. Jodie's guest bathroom was big and tall, and the shower head was set high enough for him to stand upright under it, which was unusual. There were bottles of shampoo, neatly lined up. He suspected they were brands she had tried and hadn't liked, relegated to the guest room. But he didn't care. He found one which claimed to be aimed at dry, sun-damaged hair. He figured that was exactly what he needed. He ladled it on and lathered up. Scrubbed his body all over with some kind of yellow soap and rinsed. Dripped all over the floor as he shaved at the sink. He did it carefully, right up from his collarbones, around the bottom of his nose, sideways, backward, forward. Then back into the shower all over again.

He spent five minutes on his teeth with the new toothbrush. The bristles were hard, and it felt like they were doing some good in there. Then he dried off and shook the creases out of his new clothes. Put the pants on without the shirt and wandered through to the kitchen for something to eat.

Jodie was in there. She was fresh from the shower, too. Her hair was dark with water and hanging straight down. She was wearing an oversize white T-shirt that finished an inch above her knees. The material was thin. Her legs were long and smooth. Her feet were bare. She was very slender, except where she shouldn't be. He caught his breath.

'Morning, Reacher,' she said.

'Morning, Jodie,' he said back.

She was looking at him. Her eyes were all over him. Something in her face.

'That blister,' she said. 'Looks worse.'

He squinted down. It was still red and angry. Spreading slightly, and puffy.

'You put the ointment on?' she asked.

He shook his head.

'Forgot,' he said.

'Get it,' she said.

He went back to his bathroom and found it in the brown bag. Brought it back to the kitchen. She took it from him and unscrewed the cap. Pierced the metal seal with the plastic spike and squeezed a dot of the

174

salve onto the pad of her index finger. She was concentrating on it, tongue between her teeth. She stepped in front of him and raised her hand. Touched the blister gently and rubbed with her fingertip. He stared rigidly over her head. She was a foot away from him. Naked under her shirt. Rubbing his bare chest with her fingertip. He wanted to take her in his arms. He wanted to lift her off her feet and crush her close. Kiss her gently, starting with her neck. He wanted to turn her face up to his and kiss her mouth. She was rubbing small gentle circles on his chest. He could smell her hair, damp and glossy. He could smell her skin. She was tracing her finger the length of the burn. A foot away from him, naked under her shirt. He gasped and clenched his hands. She stepped away.

'Hurting?' she asked.

'What?'

'Was I hurting you?'

He saw her fingertip, shiny from the grease.

'A little,' he said.

She nodded.

'I'm sorry,' she said. 'But you needed it.'

He nodded back.

'I guess,' he said.

Then the crisis was past. She screwed the cap back on the tube and he moved away, just to be moving. He pulled the refrigerator door and took a bottle of water. Found a banana in a bowl on the counter. She put the tube of ointment on the table.

'I'll go get dressed,' she said. 'We should get moving.'

'OK,' he said. 'I'll be ready.'

She disappeared back into her bedroom and he drank the water and ate the fruit. Wandered back to his bedroom and shrugged the shirt on and tucked it in. Found his socks and shoes and jacket. Strolled through to the living room to wait. He pulled the blind all the way up and unlocked the window and pushed it up. Leaned right out and scanned the street four floors below.

Very different in the early daylight. The shiny neon wash was gone, and the sun was coming over the buildings opposite and bouncing around in the street. The lazy night-time knots of people were gone, too, replaced by purposeful striding workers heading north and south with paper cups of coffee and muffins clutched in napkins. Cabs were grinding down through the traffic and honking at the lights to make them change. There was a gentle breeze and he could smell the river.

The building was on the west side of Lower Broadway. Traffic was one-way, to the south, running left to right under the window. Jodie's normal walk to work would give her a right turn out of her lobby, walking with the traffic. She would keep to the right-hand sidewalk, to stay in the sun. She would cross Broadway at a light maybe six or seven blocks down. Walk the last couple of blocks on the left-hand side-walk and then make the left turn, east down Wall Street to her office.

So how would they aim to grab her up? Think like the enemy. Think like the two guys. Physical, unsub-tle, favouring a direct approach, willing and dangerous, but not really schooled beyond the point of amateur enthusiasm. It was pretty clear what they would do. They would have a four-door vehicle waiting in a side street maybe three blocks south, parked in the right lane, facing east, ready to swoop out and hang the right on Broadway. They would be waiting together in the front seats, silent. They would be scanning left to right through the windshield, watching the crosswalk in front of them. They would expect to see her hurrying across, or pausing and waiting for the signal. They would wait a beat and ease out and make the right turn. Driving slow. They would fall in behind her. Pull level. Pull ahead. Then the guy in the passenger seat would be out, grabbing her, opening the rear door, forcing her inside, cramming himself in after her. One smooth brutal movement. A crude tactic, but not difficult. Not difficult at all. More or less guaranteed to succeed, depending on the target and the level of awareness. Reacher had done the same thing, many times, with targets bigger and stronger and more aware than Jodie. Once, he had done it with Leon himself at the wheel.

He bent forward from the waist and put his whole upper body out through the window. Craned his head around to the right and gazed down the street. Looked hard at the corners, two and three and four blocks south. It would be one of those.

'Ready,' Jodie called to him.

They rode down ninety floors together to the underground garage. Walked through to the right zone and over to the bays leased along with Hobie's office suite.

'We should take the Suburban,' the enforcer said. 'Bigger.'

'OK,' Tony said. He unlocked it and slid into the driver's seat. The enforcer hoisted himself into the passenger seat. Glanced back at the empty load bed. Tony fired it up and eased out towards the ramp to the street.

177

'So how do we do this?' Tony asked.

The guy smiled confidently. 'Easy enough. She'll be walking south on Broadway. We'll wait around a corner until we see her. Couple of blocks south of her building. We see her pass by on the crosswalk, we pull around the corner, get alongside her, and that's that, right?'

'Wrong,' Tony said. 'We'll do it different.'

The guy looked across at him. 'Why?'

Tony squealed the big car up and out into the sunlight.

'Because you're not very smart,' he said. 'If that's how you'd do it, there's got to be a better way, right? You screwed up in Garrison. You'll screw up here. She's probably got this Reacher guy with her. He beat you there, he'll beat you here. So whatever you figure is the best way to do it, that's the last thing we're going to do.'

'So how are we going to do it?'

'I'll explain it to you real careful,' Tony said. 'I'll try to keep it real simple.'

Reacher slid the window back down. Clicked the lock and rattled the blind down into position. She was standing just inside the doorway, hair still darkened by the shower, dressed in a simple sleeveless linen dress, bare legs, plain shoes. The dress was the same colour as her wet hair, but would end up darker as her hair dried. She was carrying a purse and a large leather briefcase, the size he had seen commercial pilots using. It was clearly heavy. She put it down and ducked away to her garment bag, which was on the floor against a wall, where he had dumped it the previous night. She slid the envelope containing Leon's will out of the pocket and unclicked the lid of the briefcase and stowed it inside.

'Want me to carry that?' he asked.

She smiled and shook her head.

'Union town,' she said. 'Bodyguarding doesn't include holding around here.'

'It looks pretty heavy,' he said.

'I'm a big girl now,' she replied, looking at him.

He nodded. Lifted the old iron bar out of its brackets and left it upright. She leaned past him and turned the locks. The same perfume, subtle and feminine. Her shoulders in the dress were slim, almost thin. Small muscles in her left arm were bunching to balance the heavy case.

'What sort of law you got in there?' he asked.

'Financial,' she said.

He eased the door open. Glanced out. The hallway was empty. The elevator indicator was showing somebody heading down to the street from three.

'What sort of financial?'

They stepped across and called the elevator.

'Debt rescheduling, mostly,' she said. 'I'm more of a negotiator than a lawyer, really. More like a counsellor or a mediator, you know?'

He didn't know. He had never been in debt. Not out of any innate virtue, but simply because he had never had the opportunity. All the basics had been provided for him by the Army. A roof over his head, food on his plate. He had never gotten into the habit of wanting much more. But he'd known guys who had run into trouble. They bought houses with mortgages and cars on time payment plans. Sometimes they got behind. The company clerk would sort it out. Talk to the bank, deduct the necessary provision straight from the guy's

179

paycheck. But he guessed that was small-time, compared to what she must deal with.

'Millions of dollars?' he asked.

The elevator arrived. The doors slid open.

'At least,' she said. 'Usually tens of millions, sometimes hundreds.'

The elevator was empty. They stepped inside.

'Enjoy it?' he asked.

The elevator whined downward.

'Sure,' she said. 'A person needs a job, it's as good as she's going to get.'

The elevator settled with a bump.

'You good at it?'

She nodded.

'Yes,' she said simply. 'Best there is on Wall Street, no doubt about that.'

He smiled. She was Leon's daughter, that was for damn sure.

The elevator doors slid open. An empty lobby, the street door sucking shut, a broad woman heading slowly down the steps to the sidewalk.

'Car keys?' he said.

She had them in her hand. A big bunch of keys on a brass ring.

'Wait here,' he said. 'I'll back it up to the stairs. One minute.'

The door from the lobby to the garage opened from the inside with a push bar. He went through and down the metal steps and scanned ahead into the gloom as he walked. Nobody there. At least, nobody visible. He walked confidently to the wrong car, a big dark Chrysler something, two spaces from Jodie's jeep. He dropped flat to the floor and looked across, under the intervening vehicles. Nothing there.

180

Nobody hiding on the floor. He got up again and squeezed around the Chrysler's hood. Around the next car. He dropped to the floor again, jammed up in the space between the Oldsmobile's tailgate and the wall. Craned his head down and looked for wires where there shouldn't be wires. All clear. No booby traps.

He unlocked the door and slid in. Fired it up and eased into the aisle. Backed up level with the bottom of the stairs. Leaned across inside and sprang the passenger door as she came through from the lobby behind him. She skipped down the steps and climbed straight in the car, all one smooth fluid movement. She slammed the door and he took off forward and made the right up the ramp and the right on the street.

The morning sun in the east flashed once in his eyes, and then he was through it, heading south. The first corner was thirty yards ahead. Traffic was slow. Not stopped, just slow. The light caught him three cars back from the turn. He was in the right lane, and he had no angle to see into the mouth of the cross street. Traffic poured right to left out of it, ahead of him, three cars away. He could see the far stream was slowed, spilling around some kind of obstacle. Maybe a parked vehicle. Maybe a parked four-door, just waiting there for something. Then the sideways flow stopped, and the light on Broadway went green.

He drove across the intersection with his head turned, half an eye ahead, and the rest of his attention focused sideways. Nothing there. No parked four-door. The obstruction was a striped sawhorse placed against an open manhole. There was a power company truck ten yards farther down the street. A gaggle of workmen on the sidewalk, drinking soda from cans. The traffic ground on. Stopped again, for the next light. He was four cars back.

This was not the street. The traffic pattern was wrong. It was flowing west, left to right in front of him. He had a good view out to his left. He could see fifty yards down the street. Nothing there. Not this one. It was going to be the next one.

Ideally he would have liked to do more than just drive straight by the two guys. A better idea would be to track around the block and come up behind them. Ditch the jeep a hundred yards away and stroll up on them from the rear. They would be craning forward, watching the crosswalk through the windshield. He could take a good look at them, as long as he wanted. He could even get right in their car with them. The rear doors would be unlocked, for sure. The guys would be staring straight ahead. He could slip in behind them and plant a hand on the side of each head and bang them together like a bandsman letting rip with the cymbals. Then he could do it again, and again, and again, until they started answering some basic questions.

But he wasn't going to do that. *Concentrate on the job in hand* was his rule. The job in hand was getting Jodie to her office, safe and secure. Bodyguarding was about defence. Start mixing offence in with it, and neither thing gets done properly. Like he had told her, he used to do this for a living. He was trained in it. Very well trained, and very experienced. So he was going to stay defensive, and he was going to count it a major victory to see her walking in through her office door, all safe and secure. And he was going to stay quiet about how much trouble she was in. He didn't want her worrying about it. No reason why whatever Leon had started should end up giving her any kind of anguish. Leon would not have wanted that. Leon would have just wanted him to handle everything. So that was how he was going to do it. Deliver her to the office door, no long explanations, no gloomy warnings.

The light went green. The first car took off, then the second. Then the third. He eased forward. Checked the gap ahead of him and craned his head right. Were they there? The cross street was narrow. Two lanes of stopped traffic, waiting at the light. Nothing parked up in the right lane. Nothing waiting. They weren't there. He moved slowly through the whole width of the intersection, scanning right. Nobody there. He breathed out and relaxed and faced forward. There was a huge metallic bang. A tremendous loud metallic punch in his back. Tearing sheet metal, instant violent acceleration. The jeep was hurled forward and smashed into the vehicle ahead and stopped dead. The airbags exploded. He saw Jodie bouncing off her seat and crashing against the tension of her belt, her body stopping abruptly, her head still cannoning forward. Then it was bouncing backward off the airbag and whipping and smashing into the headrest behind her. He noticed her face was fixed in space exactly alongside his, with the inside of the car blurring and whirling and spinning past it, because his head was doing exactly the same things as hers.

The twin impacts had torn his hands off the wheel. The airbag was collapsing in front of him. He dragged his eyes to the mirror and saw a giant black bonnet buried in the back of the jeep. The top of a shiny chrome grille, bent out of shape. Some huge four-wheel-drive truck. One guy in it, visible behind the tinted screen. Not a guy he knew. Cars were honking behind them and traffic was pulling left and steering around the obstruction. Faces were turning to stare. There was a loud hissing somewhere. Steam from his radiator, or maybe ringing from his ears after the enormous sudden sounds. The guy behind was getting out of the four-wheel drive. Hands held up in apology, worry and fright in his face. He was folding himself around his door, out there in the slow traffic stream, walking up towards Reacher's window, glancing sideways at the tangle of sheet metal as he passed. A woman was getting out of the sedan in front, looking dazed and angry. The traffic was snarling around them. The air was shimmering from overheated motors and loud with horns blasting. Jodie was upright in her seat, feeling the back of her neck with her fingers.

'You OK?' he asked her.

She thought about it for a long moment, and then she nodded.

'I'm OK,' she said. 'You?'

'Fine,' he said.

She poked at the collapsed airbag with her finger, fascinated.

'These things really work, you know that?'

'First time I ever saw one deploy,' he said.

'Me too.'

Then there was rapping on the driver's side window. The guy from behind was standing there, knocking urgently with his knuckles. Reacher stared out at him. The guy was gesturing for him to open up, urgently, like he was anxious about something.

'Shit,' Reacher yelled.

He stamped on the gas. The jeep struggled forward, pushing against the woman's wrecked saloon. It made a yard, slewing to the left, sheet metal screeching.

'Hell are you doing?' Jodie screamed.

The guy had his hand on the door handle. His other hand in his pocket.

'Get down,' Reacher shouted.

He found reverse and howled back the yard he'd made and smashed into the four-wheel drive behind. The new impact won him another foot. He shoved the gear into drive and spun the wheel and barged left. Smashed into the rear quarter of the saloon in a new shower of glass. Traffic behind was swerving and slewing all over again. He glanced right and one of the guys he'd seen in Key West and Garrison was at the window with his hand on Jodie's door. He stamped on the gas and hurled the jeep backward, spinning the wheel. The guy kept a tight hold, jerked backward by his arm, flung off his feet by the violent motion. Reacher smashed all the way backward into the black truck and bounced off again forward, screaming the motor, spinning the wheel. The guy was up again, still gripping the door handle, jerking and hauling, spare arm and legs flailing, like he was a wrangler and the jeep was a wild young steer in a desperate fight out of a trap. Reacher mashed the pedal and angled out forward close to the rear corner of the woman's wrecked saloon and scraped the guy off against the trunk. The wing took him at the knees and he somersaulted and his head came down on the rear glass. In the mirror Reacher saw a blur of flailing arms and legs as his momentum carried him up over the roof. Then he was gone, sprawling back to the sidewalk.

'Watch out!' Jodie screamed.

The guy from the truck was still there at the driver's window. Reacher was out in the traffic stream, but the traffic stream was slow and the guy was just running fast beside him, struggling to free something from his pocket. Reacher swerved left and came in parallel to a panel truck in the next lane. The guy was still running, skipping sideways, holding the door handle, coming out with something from his pocket. Reacher jammed left again and thumped him hard against the side of the truck. He heard a dull boom as the guy's head hit the metal and then he was gone. The truck jammed to a panic stop and Reacher hauled left and got in front of it. Broadway was a solid mass of traffic. Ahead of him was a shimmering patchwork of metallic colours, saloon roofs winking in the sun, dodging left, dodging right, crawling forward, fumes rising, horns blasting. He hauled left again and turned and went through a pedestrian crossing against the light, a crowd of jostling people skittering out of his way. The jeep was juddering and bouncing and pulling hard to the right. The temperature gauge was off the scale. Steam was boiling up through the gaps around the buckled hood. The collapsed airbag was hanging down to his knees. He jerked forward and hauled left again and jammed into an alley full of restaurant waste. Boxes, empty drums of cooking oil, rough wooden trays piled with spoiled vegetables. He buried the nose in a pile of cartons. They spilled down on the wrecked hood and bounced off the windshield. He killed the motor and pulled the keys.

He had put it too close to the wall for Jodie's door to open. He grabbed her briefcase and her purse and threw them out through his door. Squeezed out after them and turned back for her. She was scrambling across the seats behind him. Her dress was riding up. He grabbed her around the waist and she ducked her head to his shoulder and he lifted her through the gap. She clung on hard, bare legs around his waist. He turned and ran her six feet away. She weighed nothing at all. He set her on her feet and ducked back for her bags. She was smoothing her dress over her thighs. Breathing hard. Damp hair all over the place.

'How did you know?' she gasped. 'That it wasn't an accident?'

He gave her the purse and carried the heavy brief-case himself. Led her by the hand back down the alley to the street, panting with adrenaline rush.

'Talk while we walk,' he said.

They turned left and headed east for Lafayette. The morning sun was in their eyes, the river breeze in their faces. Behind them, they could hear the traffic snarl on Broadway. They walked together fifty yards, breathing hard, calming down.

'How did you know?'

'Statistics. I guess. What were the chances we'd be in an accident on the exact same morning we figured there were guys out looking for us? Million to one, at best.'

She nodded. A slight smile on her face. Head up, shoulders back, recovering fast. No trace of shock. She was Leon's daughter, that was for damn sure.

'You were great,' she said. 'You reacted so fast.'

He shook his head as he walked.

'No, I was shit,' he said. 'Dumb as hell. One mistake after another. They changed personnel. Some new guy in charge. I never even thought about that. I was figuring what the original pair of assholes might do, never even thought about them putting in somebody smarter. And whoever that guy was, he was pretty smart. It was a good plan, almost worked. I never saw

187

it coming. Then when it happened, I still wasted a shit-load of time talking to you about the damn airbags deploying.'

'Don't feel bad,' she said.

'I do feel bad. Leon had a basic rule: do it right. Thank God he wasn't there to see that screw-up. He'd have been ashamed of me.'

He saw her face cloud over. Realized what he'd said.

'I'm sorry. I just can't make myself believe he's dead.'

They came out on Lafayette. Jodie was at the kerb, scanning for a cab.

'Well, he is,' she said, gently. 'We'll get used to it, I guess.'

He nodded. 'And I'm sorry about your car. I should have seen it coming.'

She shrugged. 'It's only leased. I'll get them to send another one just like it. Now I know it stands up in a collision, right? Maybe a red one.'

'You should report it stolen,' he said. 'Call the cops and say it wasn't there in the garage when you went for it this morning.'

'That's fraud,' she said.

'No, that's smart. Remember I can't afford for the cops to be asking me questions about this. I don't even carry a driver's licence.'

She thought about it. Then she smiled. *Like a kid sister smiles when she's forgiving her big brother for some kind of waywardness*, he thought.

'OK,' she said. 'I'll call them from the office.'

'The office? You're not going to the damn office.'

'Why not?' she said, surprised.

He waved vaguely west, back towards Broadway. 'After what happened there? I want you where I can see you, Jodie.'

188

'I need to go to work, Reacher,' she said. 'And be logical. The office hasn't become unsafe just because of what happened over there. It's a completely separate proposition, right? The office is still as safe now as it always was. And you were happy for me to go there before, so what's changed?'

He looked at her. He wanted to say *everything's changed*. Because whatever Leon started with some old couple from a cardiology clinic has now got halfway-competent professionals mixed in with it. Halfway-competent professionals who were about half a second away from winning this morning. And he wanted to say: I love you and you're in danger and I don't want you anyplace I can't be looking out for you. But he couldn't say any of that. Because he had committed himself to keeping it all away from her. All of it, the love and the danger. So he just shrugged, lamely.

'You should come with me,' he said.

'Why? To help?'

He nodded. 'Yes, help me with these old folks. They'll talk to you, because you're Leon's daughter.'

'You want me with you because I'm Leon's daughter?'

He nodded again. She spotted a cab and waved it down.

'Wrong answer, Reacher,' she said.

He argued with her, but he got nowhere. Her mind was made up, and she wouldn't change it. The best he could do was to get her to solve his immediate problem and rent him a car, with her gold card and her licence. They took the cab up to Midtown and found a Hertz office. He waited outside in the sun for quarter of an

189

hour and then she came around the block in a brand-new Taurus and picked him up. She drove all the way back Downtown on Broadway. They passed by her building and passed by the scene of the ambush three blocks south. The damaged vehicles were gone. There were shards of glass in the gutter and oil stains on the tarmac, but that was all. She drove on south and parked on a hydrant opposite her office door. Left the motor running and racked the seat all the way back, ready for the change of driver.

'OK,' she said. 'You'll pick me up here, about seven o'clock?'

'That late?'

'I'm starting late,' she said. 'I'll have to finish late.'

'Don't leave the building, OK?'

He got out on the sidewalk and watched her all the way inside. There was a broad paved area in front of the building. She skipped across it, bare legs flashing and dancing under the dress. She turned and smiled and waved. Pushed sideways through the revolving door, swinging her heavy case. It was a tall building, maybe sixty storeys. Probably dozens of suites rented to dozens of separate firms, maybe hundreds. But the situation looked like it might be safe enough. There was a wide reception counter immediately inside the revolving door. A line of security guys sitting behind it, and behind them was a solid glass screen, wall to wall, floor to ceiling, with one opening in it, operated by a buzzer under their counter. Behind the screen were the elevators. No way in, unless the security guys saw fit to let you in. He nodded to himself. It might be safe enough. Maybe. It would depend on the diligence of the doormen. He saw her talking to one of them, head bent, blond hair falling forward. Then she was walking to the door in the screen, waiting, pushing it. She went through to the elevators. Hit a button. A door slid open. She backed in, levering her case over the threshold with both hands. The door slid shut.

He waited out on the paved area for a minute. Then he hurried across and shouldered in through the revolving door. Strode over to the counter like he did it every day of his life. Picked on the oldest security guy. The oldest ones are usually the most sloppy. The younger ones still entertain hopes of advancement.

'They want me up at Spencer Gutman,' he said, looking at his watch.

'Name?' the old guy asked.

'Lincoln,' Reacher said.

The guy was grizzled and tired, but he did what he was supposed to do. He picked a clipboard out of a slot and studied it.

'You got an appointment?'

'They just paged me,' Reacher said. 'Some kind of a big hurry, I guess.'

'Lincoln, like the car?'

'Like the president,' Reacher said.

The old guy nodded and ran a thick finger down a long list of names.

'You're not on the list,' he said. 'I can't let you in, without you're on the list.'

'I work for Costello,' Reacher said. 'They need me upstairs, like right now.'

'I could call them,' the guy said. 'Who paged you?'

Reacher shrugged. 'Mr Spencer, I guess. He's who I usually see.'

The guy looked offended. Placed the clipboard back in its slot.

'Mr Spencer died ten years ago,' he said. 'You want to come in, you get yourself a proper appointment, OK?'

Reacher nodded. The place was safe enough. He turned on his heel and headed back to the car.

Marilyn Stone waited until Chester's Mercedes was out of sight and then she ran back to the house and got to work. She was a serious woman, and she knew a possible six-week gap between listing and closing was going to need some serious input.

Her first call was to the cleaning service. The house was already perfectly clean, but she was going to move some furniture out. She took the view that presenting a house slightly empty of furniture created an impression of spaciousness. It made it seem even larger than it was. And it avoided trapping a potential buyer into preconceptions about what would look good, and what wouldn't. For instance, the Italian credenza in the hallway was the perfect piece for that hallway, but she didn't want a potential buyer to think the hallway wouldn't work any other way. Better to just have nothing there, and let the buyer's imagination fill the gap, maybe with a piece she already had.

So if she was going to move furniture out, she needed the cleaning service to attend to the spaces left behind. A slight lack of furniture created a spacious look, but obvious gaps created a sad look. So she called them, and she called the moving and storage people too, because she was going to have to put the displaced stuff somewhere. Then she called the pool service, and the gardeners. She wanted them there every morning until further notice, for an hour's work every day. She needed the yard looking its absolute best. Even at this end of the market, she knew kerb appeal was king.

Then she tried to remember other stuff she'd read, or things people had told her about. Flowers, of course, in vases, all over the place. She called the florist. She remembered somebody saying saucers of window cleaner neutralized all the little stray smells any house generates. Something to do with the ammonia. She remembered reading that putting a handful of coffee beans in a hot oven made a wonderful welcoming smell. So she put a new packet in her utensil drawer, ready. She figured if she put some in the oven each time Sheryl called to say she was on her way over with clients, that would be timing it about right, in terms of aroma.

EIGHT

Chester Stone's day started out in the normal way. He drove to work at the usual time. The Benz was as soothing as ever. The sun was shining, as it should be in June. The drive into the city was normal. Normal traffic, no more, no less. The usual rose vendors and paper sellers in the toll plazas. The slackening congestion down the length of Manhattan, proving he'd timed it just right, as he usually did. He parked in his normal leased slot under his building and rode the elevator up to his offices. Then his day stopped being normal.

The place was deserted. It was as if his company had vanished overnight. The staff had all disappeared, instinctively, like rats from a sinking ship. A single phone was trilling on a distant desk. Nobody was sitting there to answer it. The computers were all turned off. The monitor screens were dull grey squares, reflecting the strip lights in the ceiling. His own inner office was always quiet, but now there was a strange hush lying over it. He walked in and heard a sound like a tomb.

'I'm Chester Stone,' he said into the silence.

He said it just to be making some noise in the place,

194

but it came out like a croak. There was no echo, because the thick carpeting and the fibreboard walls soaked up the sound like a sponge. His voice just disappeared in the void.

'Shit,' he said.

He was angry. Mostly with his secretary. She had been with him a long time. She was the sort of employee he expected to stand up and be loyal, with a shy hand on his shoulder, a gleam in her eye, a promise to stay and beat the odds whatever the hell they were. But she'd done the same thing as all the others. She'd heard the rumours coming out of the finance department, the company was bust, the pay cheques would bounce, and she'd dumped some old files out of a carton and boxed up the photos of her damn nephews in their cheap brass frames and her ratty old spider plant from her desk and her junk from her drawers and carried it all home on the subway to her neat little apartment, wherever the hell that was. Her neat little apartment, decorated and furnished with his pay cheques from when the times were good. She would be sitting there now, in her bathrobe, drinking coffee slowly, an unexpected morning off, never to return to him, maybe leafing through the vacancies in the back of the newspaper, choosing her next port of call.

'Shit,' he said again.

He turned on his heel and barged out through the secretarial pen and back out all the way to the elevator. Rode down to the street and strode out into the sun. Turned west and set out walking fast, in a fury, with his heart thumping. The enormous glittering bulk of the Twin Towers loomed over him. He hurried across the plaza and inside to the elevators. He was sweating. The chill of the lobby air struck through his jacket. He rode the express up to eighty-eight. Stepped out and walked through the narrow corridor and into Hobie's brass-and-oak lobby for the second time in twenty-four hours.

The male receptionist was sitting behind his counter. On the other side of the lobby a thickset man in an expensive suit was coming out of a small kitchen, carrying two mugs in one hand. Stone could smell coffee. He could see steam rising and brown froth swirling in the mugs. He glanced between the two men.

'I want to see Hobie,' he said.

They ignored him. The thickset man walked over to the counter and set one of the mugs in front of the receptionist. Then he walked back behind Stone and put himself nearer the lobby door than Stone was. The receptionist leaned forward and rotated the coffee mug, carefully adjusting the angle of the handle until it was presented comfortably to his grasp.

'I want to see Hobie,' Stone said again, looking straight ahead.

'My name is Tony,' the receptionist said to him.

Stone just turned and stared at him, blankly. The guy had a red mark on his forehead, like a fresh bruise. The hair on his temple was newly combed but wet, like he'd pressed a cold cloth to his head.

'I want to see Hobie,' Stone said for the third time.

'Mr Hobie's not in the office today,' Tony said. 'I'll be dealing with your affairs for the time being. We have matters to discuss, don't we?'

'Yes, we do,' Stone said.

'So shall we go inside?' Tony said, and stood up.

He nodded to the other guy, who slid around the counter and took up position in the chair. Tony came out and stepped across to the inner door. Held it open and Stone walked through into the same gloom as the day before. The blinds were still closed. Tony padded ahead through the dark to the desk. He walked around it and sat down in Hobie's chair. The sprung base creaked once in the silence. Stone followed after him. Then he stopped and glanced left and right, wondering where he should sit.

'You'll remain standing,' Tony said to him.

'What?' Stone said back.

'You'll remain standing for the duration of the interview.'

'What?' Stone said again, astonished.

'Right in front of the desk.'

Stone just stood there, his mouth clamped shut.

'Arms by your sides,' Tony said. 'Stand straight and don't slump.'

He said it calmly, quietly, in a matter-of-fact voice, not moving at all. Then there was silence. Just faint background noises booming elsewhere in the building, and thumping in Stone's chest. His eyes were adjusting to the gloom. He could see the score marks on the desktop from Hobie's hook. They made an angry tracery, deep in the wood. The silence was unsettling him. He had absolutely no idea how to react to this. He glanced at the sofa to his left. It was humiliating to stand. Doubly so, when told to by a damn receptionist. He glanced at the sofa to his right. He knew he should fight back. He should just go ahead and sit down on one of the sofas. Just step left or right and sit down. Ignore the guy. *Just do it*. Just sit down, and show the guy who was boss. Like hitting a winning return or trumping an ace. *Sit down, for God's sake*, he told himself. But his legs would not move. It was like he was paralysed. He stood still, a yard in front of the desk, rigid with outrage and humiliation. And fear.

'You're wearing Mr Hobie's jacket,' Tony said. 'Would you take it off, please?'

Stone stared at him. Then he glanced down at his jacket. It was his Savile Row. He realized that for the first time in his life, he'd accidentally worn the same thing two days running.

'This is my jacket,' he said.

'No, it's Mr Hobie's.'

Stone shook his head. 'I bought it in London. It's definitely my jacket.'

Tony smiled in the dark.

'You don't understand, do you?' he said.

'Understand what?' Stone said, blankly.

'That Mr Hobie owns you now. You're his. And everything you have is his.'

Stone stared at him. There was silence in the room. Just the faint background noises from the building and the thumping in Stone's chest.

'So take Mr Hobie's jacket off,' Tony said, quietly.

Stone was just staring at him, his mouth opening and closing, no sound coming out of it.

'Take it off,' Tony said. 'It's not your property. You shouldn't be standing there wearing another man's jacket.'

His voice was quiet, but there was menace in it. Stone's face was rigid with shock, but then suddenly his arms were starting to move, like they were outside of his conscious control. He struggled off with the jacket and held it out by the collar, like he was in the menswear department, handing back a garment he'd tried and hadn't liked.

'On the desk, please,' Tony said.

Stone laid the jacket flat on the desk. He straightened it and felt the fine wool snagging over the rough surface. Tony pulled it closer and went into the pockets, one after the other. He assembled the contents in a small pile in front of him. Balled up the jacket and tossed it casually over the desk on to the left-hand sofa.

He picked up the Mont Blanc fountain pen. Made an appreciative little shape with his mouth and slipped it into his own pocket. Then he picked up the bunch of keys. Fanned them on the desktop and picked through them, one at a time. Selected the car key, and held it up between his finger and thumb.

'Mercedes?'

Stone nodded, blankly.

'Model?'

'500SEL,' Stone muttered.

'New?'

Stone shrugged. 'A year old.'

'Colour?'

'Dark blue.'

'Where?'

'At my office,' Stone muttered. 'In the lot.'

'We'll pick it up later,' Tony said.

He opened a drawer and dropped the keys into it. Pushed the drawer shut and turned his attention to the wallet. He held it upside down and shook it and raked the contents out with his finger. When it was empty, he tossed it under the desk. Stone heard it clang into a trash can. Tony glanced once at the picture of Marilyn and pitched it after the wallet. Stone heard a fainter clang as the stiff photographic paper hit the metal. Tony stacked the credit cards with three fingers and slid them to one side like a croupier.

'Guy we know will give us a hundred bucks for these,' he said.

Then he riffled the paper money together and sorted it by denomination. Counted it up and clipped it together with a paper clip. Dropped it into the same drawer as the keys.

'What do you guys want?' Stone asked.

Tony looked up at him.

'I want you to take Mr Hobie's tie off,' he said.

Stone shrugged, helplessly.

'No, seriously, what do you guys want from me?'

'Seventeen-point-one million dollars. That's what you owe us.'

Stone nodded. 'I know. I'll pay you.'

'When?' Tony asked.

'Well, I'll need a little time,' Stone said.

Tony nodded. 'OK, you've got an hour.'

Stone stared at him. 'No, I need more than an hour.'

'An hour is all you've got.'

'I can't do it in an hour.'

'I know you can't,' Tony said. 'You can't do it in an hour, or a day, or a week, or a month, or a year, because you're a useless piece of shit who couldn't manage his way out of a wet grocery sack, aren't you?'

'What?'

'You're a disgrace, Stone. You took a business your grandfather slaved over and your father built bigger and you flushed it all straight down the toilet, because you're totally stupid, aren't you?'

Stone shrugged, blankly. Then he swallowed.

'OK, so I took some hits,' he said. 'But what could I do?'

'Take the tie off,' Tony screamed at him.

Stone jumped and flung his hands up. Struggled with the knot.

'Get it off, you piece of shit,' Tony screamed.

He tore it off. Dropped it on the desk. It lay there in a tangle.

'Thank you, Mr Stone,' Tony said quietly.

'What do you guys want?' Stone whispered.

Tony opened a different drawer and came out with a handwritten sheet of paper. It was yellow and filled with a dense untidy scrawl. Some kind of a list, with figures totalled at the bottom of the page.

'We own thirty-nine per cent of your corporation,' he said. 'As of this morning. What we want is another twelve per cent.'

Stone stared at him. Did the maths in his head. 'A controlling interest?'

'Exactly,' Tony said. 'We hold thirty-nine per cent, another twelve gives us fifty-one, which would indeed represent a controlling interest.'

Stone swallowed again and shook his head.

'No,' he said. 'No, I won't do that.'

'OK, then we want seventeen-point-one million dollars within the hour.'

Stone just stood there, glancing wildly left and right. The door opened behind him and the thickset man in the expensive suit came in and padded soundlessly across the carpet and stood with his arms folded, behind Tony's left shoulder.

'The watch, please,' Tony said.

Stone glanced at his left wrist. It was a Rolex. It looked like steel, but it was platinum. He had bought it in Geneva. He unlatched it and handed it over. Tony nodded and dropped it in another drawer.

'Now take Mr Hobie's shirt off.'

'You can't make me give you more stock,' Stone said.

'I think we can. Take the shirt off, OK?'

'Look, I won't be intimidated,' Stone said, as confidently as he could.

'You're already intimidated,' Tony said back. 'Aren't you? You're about to make a mess in Mr Hobie's pants. Which would be a bad mistake, by the way, because we'd only make you clean them up.'

Stone said nothing. Just stared at a spot in the air between the two men.

'Twelve per cent of the equity,' Tony said gently. 'Why not? It's not worth anything. And you'd still have forty-nine per cent left.'

'I need to speak with my lawyers,' Stone said.

'OK, go ahead.'

Stone looked around the room, desperately. 'Where's the phone?'

'There's no phone in here,' Tony said. 'Mr Hobie doesn't like phones.'

'So how?'

'Shout,' Tony said. 'Shout real loud, and maybe your lawyers will hear you.'

'What?'

'Shout,' Tony said again. 'You're real slow, aren't you, Mr Stone? Put two and two together and draw a conclusion. There's no phone in here, you can't leave the room, you want to talk with your lawyers, so you'll have to shout.'

Stone stared blankly into space.

'Shout, you useless piece of shit,' Tony screamed at him.

'No, I can't,' Stone said helplessly. 'I don't know what you mean.'

'Take the shirt off,' Tony screamed.

Stone shook violently. Hesitated, with his arms halfway in the air.

'Get it off, you piece of shit,' Tony screamed.

Stone's hands leapt up and unbuttoned it, all the way down. He tore it off and stood there holding it, shaking in his undershirt.

'Fold it neatly, please,' Tony said. 'Mr Hobie likes his things neat.'

Stone did his best. He shook it out by the collar and folded it in half, and half again. He bent and laid it square on top of the jacket on the sofa.

'Give up the twelve per cent,' Tony said.

'No,' Stone said back, clenching his hands.

There was silence. Silence and darkness.

'Efficiency,' Tony said quietly. 'That's what we like here. You should have paid more attention to efficiency, Mr Stone. Then maybe your business wouldn't be in the toilet. So what's the most efficient way for us to do this?'

Stone shrugged, helplessly. 'I don't know what you're talking about.'

'Then I'll explain,' Tony said. 'We want you to comply. We want your signature on a piece of paper. So how do we get that?'

'You'll never get it, you bastard,' Stone said. 'I'll go bankrupt first, damn it. Chapter eleven. You won't get a damn thing from me. Not a thing. You'll be in court five years, minimum.'

Tony shook his head patiently, like a grade school teacher hearing the wrong answer for the hundredth time in a long career.

'Do whatever you want,' Stone said to him. 'I won't give you my company.'

'We could hurt you,' Tony said.

Stone's eyes dropped through the gloom to the desktop. His tie was still lying there, right on top of the rough gouges from the hook.

'Take Mr Hobie's pants off,' Tony screamed.

'No, I won't, damn it,' Stone screamed back.

The guy at Tony's shoulder reached under his arm. There was a squeak of leather. Stone stared at him, incredulous. The guy came out with a small black handgun. He used one arm and aimed it, eye level, straight out. He advanced around the desk towards Stone. Nearer and nearer. Stone's eyes were wide and staring. Fixed on the gun. It was aimed at his face. He was shaking and sweating. The guy was stepping quietly, and the gun was coming closer, and Stone's eyes were crossing, following it in. The gun came to rest with the muzzle on his forehead. The guy was pressing with it. The muzzle was hard and cold. Stone was shaking. Leaning backward against the pressure. Stumbling, trying to focus on the black blur that was the gun. He never saw the guy's other hand balling into a fist. Never saw the blow swinging in. It smashed hard into his gut and he went down like a sack, legs folding, squirming and gasping and retching.

'Take the pants off, you piece of shit,' Tony screamed down at him.

The other guy landed a savage kick and Stone yelped and rolled around and around on his back like a turtle, gasping, gagging, wrenching at his belt. He got it loose. Scrabbled for the buttons and the zip. He tore the pants down over his legs. They snagged on his shoes and he wrenched them free and pulled them off inside out.

'Get up, Mr Stone,' Tony said, quietly.

Stone staggered to his feet and stood, unsteadily, leaning forward, head down, panting, his hands on his knees, his stomach heaving, thin white hairless legs coming down out of his boxers, ludicrous dark socks and shoes on his feet.

'We could hurt you,' Tony said. 'You understand that now, right?'

Stone nodded and gasped. He was pressing both forearms into his gut. Heaving and gagging.

'You understand that, right?' Tony asked again.

Stone forced another nod.

'Say the words, Mr Stone,' Tony said. 'Say we could hurt you.'

'You could hurt me,' Stone gasped.

'But we won't. That's not how Mr Hobie likes things to be done.'

Stone raised a hand and swiped tears from his eyes and looked up, hopefully.

'Mr Hobie prefers to hurt the wives,' Tony said. 'Efficiency, you see? It gets faster results. So at this point, you really need to be thinking about Marilyn.'

The rented Taurus was much faster than the Bravada had been. On dry June roads, there was no contest. Maybe in the snows of January or the sleet of February he would have appreciated the full-time four-wheel drive, but for a fast trip up the Hudson in June, a regular sedan had it all over a jeep, that was for damn sure. It was low and stable, it rode well, it tracked through the bends like an automobile should. And it was quiet. He had its radio locked on to a powerful city station behind him, and a woman called Wynonna Judd was asking him *why not me?* He felt he shouldn't be liking Wynonna Judd as much as he was, because if somebody had asked him if he'd enjoy a country vocalist singing plaintively about love, he'd have probably said no he wouldn't, based on his preconceptions. But she had a hell of a voice, and the number had a hell of a guitar part. And the lyric was getting to him, because he was imagining it was Jodie singing to him, not Wynonna Judd. She was singing *why not me when you're growing old? Why not me?* He started singing along with it, his rough bass rumble underneath the soaring contralto, and by the time the number faded and the commercial started, he was figuring if he ever had a house and a stereo like other people did, he'd buy the record. *Why not me?*

He was heading north on Route 9, and he had a Hertz map open beside him which went up far enough to show him Brighton was halfway between Peekskill and Poughkeepsie, over to the west, right on the Hudson. He had the old couple's address beside it, written on a sheet from a medical pad from McBannerman's office. He had the Taurus moving at a steady sixty-five, fast enough to get him there, slow enough to get him there unmolested by the traffic cops, who he assumed were hiding out around every wooded corner, waiting to boost their municipal revenues with their radar guns and their books of blank tickets.

It took him an hour to get level with Garrison again, and he figured he would head on north to a big highway he remembered swinging away west over the river towards Newburgh. He should be able to come off that road just short of the Hudson and fall on Brighton from above. Then it was just a question of hunting down the address, which might not be easy.

But it was easy, because the road that dropped him

south into Brighton from the east–west highway was labelled with the same name as was in the second line of the old folks' address. He cruised south, watching for mailboxes and house numbers. Then it started to get harder. The mailboxes were grouped in sixes, clustered hundreds of yards apart, standing on their own, with no obvious connection to any particular houses. In fact, there were very few houses visible at all. It seemed like they were all up little rural tracks, gravel and patched tarmac, running off left and right into the woods like tunnels.

He found the right mailbox. It was set on a wooden post that the weather was rotting and the frost heave was canting forward. Vigorous green vines and thorny creepers were twisting up around it. It was a large-size box, dull green, with the house number painted on the side in faded but immaculate freehand script. The door was hanging open, because the box was completely stuffed with mail. He took it all out and squared it on the passenger seat beside him. Squeaked the door closed and saw a name painted on the front in the same faded neat hand: *Hobie*.

The mailboxes were all on the right side of the road, for the convenience of the mail carrier, but the tracks ran off in both directions. There were four of them visible from where he was stopped, two of them to the left and two to the right. He shrugged and headed down the first of them, leading to the right, over towards the river.

It was the wrong track. There were two houses down there, one north and one south. One of them had a duplicate nameplate on the gates: *Kozinsky*. The other had a bright red Pontiac Firebird parked under a new basketball hoop on the garage gable. Children's bicycles were sprawled on a lawn. Not persuasive evidence of aged and infirm people living there.

The first track on the left was wrong too. He found the right place on the second right-hand track. There was an overgrown driveway running away south, parallel with the river. There was an old rusted mailbox at the gate, back from when the postal service was prepared to come a little nearer your house. Same dull green colour, but even more faded. Same neat painted script, faded like a ghost: *Hobie*. There were power lines and a phone cable running in, swarming with vines that hung down like curtains. He swung the Taurus into the driveway, brushing vegetation on both sides, and came to a stop behind an old Chevy saloon, parked at an angle under a carport. The old car was a full-size, bonnet and trunk like flight decks, turning the same pitted dull brown that all old cars turn.

He killed the motor and got out in the silence. Ducked back in and grabbed the stack of mail and stood there, holding it. The house was a low one-storey, running away from him to the west towards the river. The house was the same brown as the car, ancient boards and shingles. The yard was a riot. It was what a tended garden becomes in fifteen untouched years of wet springs and hot summers. There had been a wide path running around from the carport to the front door, but it was narrowed like a gangplank with encroaching brush. He looked around and figured an infantry platoon equipped with flame-throwers would be more use there than gardeners.

He made it to the door, with the brush grabbing and snatching at his ankles. There was a doorbell, but it was rusted solid. He leaned forward and rapped on the wood with his knuckles. Then he waited. No response. He rapped again. He could hear the jungle seething behind him. Insect noise. He could hear the silencer ticking as it cooled underneath the Taurus over on the driveway. He knocked again. Waited. There was the creak of floorboards inside the house. The sound was carrying ahead of somebody's footsteps and spilling out to him. The footsteps halted on the other side of the door and he heard a woman's voice, thin and muffled by the wood.

'Who's there?' it called out.

'Reacher,' he called back. 'General Garber's friend.'

His voice was loud. Behind him, he heard panicked scurrying in the brush. Furtive animals were fleeing. In front of him, he heard a stiff lock turning and bolts easing back. The door creaked open. Darkness inside. He stepped forward into the shadow of the eaves and saw an old woman waiting. She was maybe eighty, stick thin, white hair, stooped, wearing a faded floral-print dress that flared right out from the waist over nylon petticoats. It was the sort of dress he'd seen in photographs of women at suburban garden parties in the fifties and the sixties. The sort of dress that was normally worn with long white gloves and a wide-brimmed hat and a contented bourgeois smile.

'We were expecting you,' she said.

She turned and stood aside. He nodded and went in. The radius of the skirt meant he had to push past its flare with a loud rustle of nylon.

'I brought your mail,' he said to her. 'Your box was full.'

He held up the thick stack of curled envelopes and waited.

'Thank you,' she said. 'You're very kind. It's a long walk out there, and we don't like to stop the car to get it, in case we get rear-ended. It's a very busy road. People drive terribly fast, you know. Faster than they should, I think.'

Reacher nodded. It was about the quietest road he had ever seen. A person could sleep the night out there right on the yellow line, with a good chance of surviving until morning. He was still holding the mail. The old lady showed no curiosity over it.

'Where would you like me to put it?'

'Would you put it in the kitchen?'

The hallway was a dark space, panelled in gloomy wood. The kitchen was worse. It had a tiny window, glassed in with yellow reeded glass. There was a collection of freestanding units in muddy dark veneer, and curious old enamel appliances, speckled in mint greens and greys, standing up on short legs. The whole room smelled of old food and a warm oven, but it was clean and tidy. A rag rug on worn linoleum. There was a chipped china mug with a pair of thick eyeglasses standing vertically in it. He put the stack of mail next to the mug. When her visitor was gone, she would use her eyeglasses to read her mail, right after she put her best frock back in the closet with the mothballs.

'May I offer you cake?' she asked.

He glanced at the stove top. There was a china plate there, covered over with a worn linen cloth. She'd baked something for him.

'And coffee?'

Next to the stove top was an ancient percolator, mint green enamel, green glass knob on the top,

210

connected to the outlet by a cord insulated with frayed fabric. He nodded.

'I love coffee and cake,' he said.

She nodded back, pleased. Bustled forward, crushing her skirt against the oven door. She used a thin trembling thumb and operated the switch on the percolator. It was already filled and ready to go.

'It takes a moment,' she said. Then she paused and listened. The old percolator started a loud gulping sound. 'So come and meet Mr Hobie. He's awake now, and very anxious to see you. While we're waiting for the machine.'

She led him through the hallway to a small parlour in the back. It was about twelve by twelve and heavily furnished with armchairs and sofas and glass-fronted chest-high cabinets filled with china ornaments. There was an old guy in one of the chairs. He was wearing a stiff serge suit, blue, worn and shiny in places, and at least three sizes too big for his shrunken body. The collar of his shirt was a wide stiff hoop around a pale scrawny neck. Random silky tufts of white were all that was left of his hair. His wrists were like pencils protruding from the cuffs of his suit. His hands were thin and bony, laid loosely on the arms of the chair. He had clear plastic tubes looped over his ears, running down under his nose. There was a bottle of oxygen on a wheeled cart, parked behind him. He looked up and took a long loud sniff of the gas to fuel the effort of lifting his hand.

'Major Reacher,' he said. 'I'm very pleased to meet you.'

Reacher stepped forward and grasped the hand and shook it. It was cold and dry, and it felt like a skeleton's hand wrapped in flannel. The old guy paused and sucked more oxygen and spoke again.

'I'm Tom Hobie, Major. And this lovely lady is my wife Mary.'

Reacher nodded.

'Pleased to meet you both,' he said. 'But I'm not a major any more.'

The old guy nodded back and sucked the gas through his nose.

'You served,' he said. 'Therefore I think you're entitled to your rank.'

There was a fieldstone fireplace, built low in the centre of one wall. The mantel was packed tight with photographs in ornate silver frames. Most of them were colour snaps showing the same subject, a young man in olive fatigues, in a variety of poses and situations. There was one older picture among them, airbrushed black-and-white, a different man in uniform, tall and straight and smiling, a private first class from a different generation of service. Possibly Mr Hobie himself, before his failing heart started killing him from the inside, although it was hard for Reacher to tell. There was no resemblance.

'That's me,' Hobie confirmed, following his gaze.

'World War Two?' Reacher asked.

The old man nodded. Sadness in his eyes.

'I never went overseas,' he said. 'I volunteered well ahead of the draft, but I had a weak heart, even back then. They wouldn't let me go. So I did my time in a storeroom in New Jersey.'

Reacher nodded. Hobie had his arm behind him, fiddling with the cylinder valve, increasing the oxygen flow.

'I'll bring the coffee now,' the old lady said. 'And the cake.'

'Can I help you with anything?' Reacher asked her.

'No, I'll be fine,' she said, and swished slowly out of the room.

'Sit down, Major, please,' Tom Hobie said.

Reacher nodded and sat down in the silence, in a small armchair near enough to catch the old guy's fading voice. He could hear the rattle of his breathing. Nothing else, just a faint hiss from the top of the oxygen bottle and the clink of china from the kitchen. Patient domestic sounds. The window had a venetian blind, lime-green plastic, tilted down against the light. The river was out there somewhere, presumably beyond an overgrown yard, maybe thirty miles upstream of Leon Garber's place.

'Here we are,' Mrs Hobie called from the hallway.

She was on her way back into the room with a wheeled cart. There was a matching china set stacked on it, cups and saucers and plates, with a small milk jug and a sugar bowl. The linen cover was off the platter, revealing a pound cake, drizzled with some kind of yellow icing. Maybe lemon. The old percolator was there, smelling of coffee.

'How do you like it?'

'No milk, no sugar,' Reacher said.

She poured coffee into a cup, her thin wrist quivering with the effort. The cup rattled in its saucer as she passed it across. She followed it with a quarter of the cake on a plate. The plate shook. The oxygen bottle hissed. The old man was rehearsing his story, dividing it up into bites, taking in enough oxygen to fuel each one of them.

'I was a printer,' he said suddenly. 'I ran my own shop. Mary worked for a big customer of mine. We met and were married in the spring of '47. Our son was born in the June of '48.'

He turned away and ran his glance along the line of photographs.

'Our son, Victor Truman Hobie.'

The parlour fell quiet, like an observance.

'I believed in duty,' the old man said. 'I was unfit for active service, and I regretted it. Regretted it bitterly, Major. But I was happy to serve my country any way I could, and I did. We brought our son up the same way, to love his country and to serve it. He volunteered for Vietnam.'

Old Mr Hobie closed his mouth and sucked oxygen through his nose, once, twice, and then he leaned down to the floor beside him and came up with a leather-bound folder. He spread it across his bony legs and opened it up. Took out a photograph and passed it across. Reacher juggled his cup and his plate and leaned forward to take it from the shaking hand. It was a faded colour print of a boy in a backyard. The boy was maybe nine or ten, stocky, toothy, freckled, grinning, wearing a metal bowl upside down on his head, with a toy rifle shouldered, his stiff denim trousers tucked into his socks to resemble the look of fatigues buckled into gaiters.

'He wanted to be a soldier,' Mr Hobie said. 'Always. It was his ambition. I approved of it at the time, of course. We were unable to have other children, so Victor was on his own, the light of our lives, and I thought that to be a soldier and to serve his country was a fine ambition for the only son of a patriotic father.'

There was silence again. A cough. A hiss of oxygen. Silence.

'Did you approve of Vietnam, Major?' Hobie asked suddenly.

Reacher shrugged.

'I was too young to have much of an opinion,' he said. 'But knowing what I know now, no, I wouldn't have approved of Vietnam.'

'Why not?'

'Wrong place,' Reacher said. 'Wrong time, wrong reasons, wrong methods, wrong approach, wrong leadership. No real backing, no real will to win, no coherent strategy.'

'Would you have gone?'

Reacher nodded.

'Yes, I would have gone,' he said. 'No choice. I was the son of a soldier, too. But I would have been jealous of my father's generation. Much easier to go to World War Two.'

'Victor wanted to fly helicopters,' Hobie said. 'He was passionate about it. My fault again, I'm afraid. I took him to a county fair, paid two bucks for him to have his first flight in one. It was an old Bell, a crop duster. After that, all he wanted to be was a helicopter pilot. And he decided the Army was the best place to learn how.'

He slid another photograph out of the folder. Passed it across. It showed the same boy, now twice the age, grown tall, still grinning, in new fatigues, standing in front of an Army helicopter. It was an H-23 Hiller, an old training machine.

'That's Fort Wolters,' Hobie said. 'All the way down in Texas. US Army Primary Helicopter School.'

Reacher nodded. 'He flew choppers in 'Nam?'

'He passed out second in his class,' Hobie said. 'That was no surprise to us. He was always an excellent student, all the way through high school. He was especially gifted in math. He understood accountancy. I imagined he'd go to college and then come into partnership with me, to do the book work. I looked forward to it. I struggled in school, Major. No reason to be coy about it now. I'm not an educated man. It was a constant delight for me to see Victor doing so well. He was a very smart boy. And a very good boy. Very smart, very kind, a good heart, a perfect son. Our only son.'

The old lady was silent. Not eating the cake, not drinking the coffee.

'His passing out was at Fort Rucker,' Hobie said. 'Down in Alabama. We made the trip to see it.'

He slid across the next photograph. It was a duplicate of one of the framed prints from the mantel. Faded pastel grass and sky, a tall boy in dress uniform, cap down over his eyes, his arm around an older woman in a print dress. The woman was slim and pretty. The photograph was slightly out of focus, the horizon slightly tilted. Taken by a fumbling husband and father, breathless with pride.

'That's Victor and Mary,' the old man said. 'She hasn't changed a bit, has she, that day to this?'

'Not a bit,' Reacher lied.

'We loved that boy,' the old woman said quietly. 'He was sent overseas two weeks after that photograph was taken.'

'July of '68,' Hobie said. 'He was twenty years old.'

'What happened?' Reacher asked.

'He served a full tour,' Hobie said. 'He was commended twice. He came home with a medal. I

216

could see right away the idea of keeping the books for a print shop was too small for him. I thought he would serve out his time and get a job flying helicopters for the oil rigs. Down in the Gulf, perhaps. They were paying big money then, for Army pilots. Or Navy, or Air Force, of course.'

'But he went over there again,' Mrs Hobie said. 'To Vietnam again.'

'He signed on for a second tour,' Hobie said. 'He didn't have to. But he said it was his duty. He said the war was still going on, and it was his duty to be a part of it. He said that's what patriotism meant.'

'And what happened?' Reacher asked.

There was a long moment of silence.

'He didn't come back,' Hobie said.

The silence was like a weight in the room. Somewhere a clock was ticking. It grew louder and louder until it was filling the air like blows from a hammer.

'It destroyed me,' Hobie said quietly.

The oxygen wheezed in and out, in and out, through a constricted throat.

'It just destroyed me. I used to say *I'll exchange the whole rest of my life, just for one more day with him.*'

'The rest of my life,' his wife echoed. 'For just one more day with him.'

'And I meant it,' Hobie said. 'And I still would. I still would, Major. Looking at me now, that's not much of a bargain, is it? I haven't got much life left in me. But I said it then, and I said it every day for thirty years, and as God is my witness, I meant it every single time I said it. The whole rest of my life, for one more day with him.'

'When was he killed?' Reacher asked, gently.

'He wasn't killed,' Hobie said. 'He was captured.'

'Taken prisoner?'

The old man nodded. 'At first, they told us he was missing. We assumed he was dead, but we clung on, hoping. He was posted missing, and he stayed missing. We never got official word he was killed.'

'So we waited,' Mrs Hobie said. 'We just kept on waiting, for years and years. Then we started asking. They told us Victor was missing, presumed killed. That was all they could say. His helicopter was shot down in the jungle, and they never found the wreckage.'

'We accepted that then,' Hobie said. 'We knew how it was. Plenty of boys died without a known grave. Plenty of boys always have, in war.'

'Then the memorial went up,' Mrs Hobie said. 'Have you seen it?'

'The Wall?' Reacher said. 'In DC? Yes, I've been there. I've seen it. I found it very moving.'

'They refused to put his name on it,' Hobie said.

'Why?'

'They never explained. We asked and we begged, but they never told us exactly why. They just said he's no longer considered a casualty.'

'So we asked them what he is considered as,' Mrs Hobie said. 'They just told us missing in action.'

'But the other MIAs are on the Wall,' Hobie said.

There was silence again. The clock hammered away in another room.

'What did General Garber say about this?' Reacher asked.

'He didn't understand it,' Hobie said. 'Didn't understand it at all. He was still checking for us when he died.'

There was silence again. The oxygen hissed and the clock hammered.

'But we know what happened,' Mrs Hobie said.

'You do?' Reacher asked her. 'What?'

'The only thing that fits,' she said. 'He was taken prisoner.'

'And never released,' Hobie said.

'That's why the Army is covering it up,' Mrs Hobie said. 'The government is embarrassed about it. The truth is some of our boys were never released. The Vietnamese held on to them, like hostages, to get foreign aid and trade recognition and credits from us, after the war. Like blackmail. The government held out for years, despite our boys still being prisoners over there. So they can't admit it. They hide it instead, and won't talk about it.'

'But we can prove it now,' Hobie said.

He slid another photograph from the folder. Passed it across. It was a newer print. Vivid glossy colours. It was a telephoto shot taken through tropical vegetation. There was barbed wire on bamboo fence posts. There was an Asian figure in a brown uniform, with a bandanna around his forehead. A rifle in his hands. It was clearly a Soviet AK-47. No doubt about it. And there was another figure in the picture. A tall Caucasian, looking about fifty, emaciated, gaunt, bent, grey, wearing pale rotted fatigues. Looking half away from the Asian soldier, flinching.

'That's Victor,' Mrs Hobie said. 'That's our son. That photograph was taken last year.'

'We spent thirty years asking about him,' Hobie said. 'Nobody would help us. We asked everybody. Then we found a man who told us about these secret camps. There aren't many. Just a few, with a handful of prisoners. Most of them have died by now. They've grown old and died, or been starved to death. This man went to Vietnam and checked for us. He got close enough to take this picture. He even spoke to one of the other prisoners through the wire. Secretly, at night. It was very dangerous for him. He asked for the name of the prisoner he'd just photographed. It was Vic Hobie, First Cavalry helicopter pilot.'

'The man had no money for a rescue,' Mrs Hobie said. 'And we'd already paid him everything we had for the first trip. We had no more left. So when we met General Garber at the hospital, we told him our story and asked him to try and get the government to pay.'

Reacher stared at the photograph. Stared at the gaunt man with the grey face.

'Who else has seen this picture?'

'Only General Garber,' Mrs Hobie answered. 'The man who took it told us to keep it a secret. Because it's very sensitive, politically. Very dangerous. It's a terrible thing, buried in the nation's history. But we had to show it to General Garber, because he was in a position to help us.'

'So what do you want me to do?' Reacher asked.

The oxygen hissed in the silence. In and out, in and out, through the clear plastic tubes. The old man's mouth was working.

'I just want him back,' he said. 'I just want to see him again, one more day before I die.'

After that, the old couple were done talking. They turned together and fixed misty gazes on the row of photographs on the mantel. Reacher was left sitting in the silence. Then the old man turned back and used both hands and lifted the leather-bound folder off his bony knees and held it out. Reacher leaned forward and took it. At first he assumed it was so he could put the three photographs back inside. Then he realized the baton had been passed to him. Like a ceremony. Their quest had become Leon's, and now it was his.

The folder was thin. Apart from the three photographs he had seen, it contained nothing more than infrequent letters home from their son and formal letters from the Department of the Army. And a sheaf of paperwork showing the liquidation of their life savings and the transfer by certified check of eighteen thousand dollars to an address in the Bronx, to fund a reconnaissance mission to Vietnam led by a man named Rutter.

The letters from the boy started with brief notes from various locations in the South, as he passed through Dix, and Polk, and Wolters, and Rucker, and Belvoir and Benning on his way through his training. Then there was a short note from Mobile in Alabama, as he boarded ship for the month-long voyage through the Panama Canal and across the Pacific to Indochina. Then there were flimsy Army Mailgrams from Vietnam itself, eight from the first tour, six from the second. The paper was thirty years old, and it was stiff and dry, like ancient papyrus. Like something discovered by archaeologists.

He hadn't been much of a correspondent. The letters were full of the usual banal phrases a young soldier writes home. There must have been a hundred million parents in the world with treasured old letters like these, different times, different wars, different languages, but the same messages: the food, the weather, the rumour of action, the reassurances.

The responses from the Department of the Army marched through thirty years of office technology. They started out typed on old manual machines, some letters misaligned, some wrongly spaced, some with red haloes above them where the ribbon had slipped. Then electric typewriters, crisper and more uniform. Then word processors, immaculately printed on better paper. But the messages were all the same. No information. Missing in action, presumed killed. Condolences. No further information.

The deal with the guy called Rutter had left them penniless. There had been some modest mutual funds and a little cash on deposit. There was a sheet written in a shaky hand Reacher guessed was the old woman's, totalling their monthly needs, working the figures again and again, paring them down until they matched the Social Security checks, freeing up their capital. The mutuals had been cashed in eighteen months ago and amalgamated with the cash holdings and the whole lot had been mailed to the Bronx. There was a receipt from Rutter, with the amount formally set off against the cost of the exploratory trip, due to leave imminently. There was a request for any and all information likely to prove helpful, including service number and history and any existing photographs. There was a letter dated three months subsequently, detailing the discovery of the remote camp, the risky clandestine photography, the whispered talk through the wire. There was a prospectus for a rescue mission, planned in great detail, at a projected cost to the Hobies of forty-five thousand dollars. Forty-five thousand dollars they didn't have.

'Will you help us?' the old woman asked through

the silence. 'Is it all clear? Is there anything you need to know?'

He glanced across at her and saw she had been following his progress through the dossier. He closed the folder and stared down at its worn leather cover. Right then the only thing he needed to know was *why the hell hadn't Leon told these people the truth?*

NINE

Marilyn Stone missed lunch because she was busy, but didn't mind because she was happy about the way the place was starting to look. She found herself regarding the whole business in a very dispassionate manner, which surprised her a little, because after all it was her home she was getting ready to sell, her own home, the place she'd chosen with care and thought and excitement not so many years ago. It had been the place of her dreams. Way bigger and better than anything she'd ever expected to have. It had been a physical thrill back then, just thinking about it. Moving in felt like she'd died and gone to heaven. Now she was just looking at the place like a showpiece, like a marketing proposition. She wasn't seeing rooms she'd decorated and lived in and thrilled to and enjoyed. There was no pain. No wistful glances at places where she and Chester had fooled around and laughed and ate and slept. Just a brisk and businesslike determination to bring it all up to a whole new peak of irresistibility.

The furniture movers had arrived first, just as she'd planned. She had them take the credenza out of the hallway, and then Chester's armchair out of the living room. Not because it was a bad piece, but because it was definitely an extra piece. It was his favourite chair, chosen in the way men choose things, for comfort and familiarity rather than for style and suitability. It was the only piece they'd brought from their last house. He'd put it next to the fireplace, at an angle. Day to day, she rather liked it. It gave the room a comfortable lived-in quality. It was the touch that changed the room from a magazine showpiece to a family home. Which was exactly why it had to go.

She had the movers carry out the butcher's block table from the kitchen, too. She had thought long and hard about that table. It certainly gave the kitchen a no-nonsense look. Like it was a proper workplace, speaking of serious meals planned and executed there. But without it, there was an uninterrupted thirty-foot expanse of tiled floor running all the way to the bay window. She knew that with fresh polish on the tiles, the light from the window would flood the whole thirty-foot span into a sea of space. She had put herself in a prospective buyer's shoes and asked herself *which would impress you more? A serious kitchen? Or a drop-dead spacious kitchen?* So the butcher's block was in the mover's truck.

The TV from the den was in there, too. Chester had a problem with television sets. Video had killed the home-movie side of his business and he had no enthusiasm for buying the latest and best of his competitors' products. So the TV was an obsolete RCA, not even a console model. It had shiny fake chrome around the screen, and it bulged out like a grey fishbowl. She had seen better sets junked on the side-walk, looking down from the train when it eased into the 125th Street station. So she'd had the movers clear it out of the den and bring the bookcase down from

225

the guest suite to fill its space. She thought the room looked much better for it. With just the bookcase and the leather couches and the dark lampshades, it looked like a cultured room. An intelligent room. It made it an aspirational space. Like a buyer would be buying a lifestyle, not just a house.

She spent some time choosing books for the coffee tables. Then the florist arrived with flat cardboard boxes full of blooms. She had the girl wash all her vases and then left her alone with a European magazine and told her to copy the arrangements. The guy from Sheryl's office brought the for-sale sign and she had him plant it in the shoulder next to the mailbox. Then the garden crew arrived at the same time the movers were leaving, which required some awkward manoeuvring out on the driveway. She led the crew chief around the garden, explaining what had to be done, and then she ducked back inside the house before the roar of the mowers started up. The pool boy came to the door at the same time as the cleaning service people arrived. She was caught glancing left and right between them, momentarily overcome and unsure of who to start first. But then she nodded firmly and told the cleaners to wait, and led the boy around to the pool and showed him what needed doing. Then she ran back to the house, feeling hungry, realizing she'd missed her lunch, but glowing with satisfaction at the progress she was making.

They both made it down the hallway to see him leave. The old man worked on the oxygen long enough to get himself up out of his chair, and then he wheeled the cylinder slowly ahead of him, partly leaning on it like a cane, partly pushing it like a golf trolley. His wife rustled along in front of him, her skirt brushing both door jambs and both sides of the narrow passageway. Reacher followed behind them, with the leather folder tucked up under his arm. The old lady worked the lock on the door and the old man stood panting and gripping the handle of the cart. The door opened and sweet fresh air blew in.

'Any of Victor's old friends still around here?' Reacher asked.

'Is that important, Major?'

Reacher shrugged. He had learned a long time ago the best way to prepare people for bad news was by looking very thorough, right from the start. People listened better if they thought you'd exhausted every possibility.

'I just need to build up some background,' he said.

They looked mystified, but like they were ready to think about it, because he was their last hope. He held their son's life in his hands, literally.

'Ed Steven, I guess, at the hardware store,' Mr Hobie said eventually. 'Thick as thieves with Victor, from kindergarten right through twelfth grade. But that was thirty-five years ago, Major. Don't see how it can matter now.'

Reacher nodded, because it didn't matter now.

'I've got your number,' he said. 'I'll call you, soon as I know anything.'

'We're relying on you,' the old lady said.

Reacher nodded again.

'It was a pleasure to meet you both,' he said. 'Thank you for the coffee and the cake. And I'm very sorry about your situation.'

They made no reply. It was a hopeless thing to say. Thirty years of agony, and he was sorry about their situation? He just turned and shook their frail hands and stepped back outside on to their overgrown path. Picked his way back to the Taurus, carrying the folder, looking firmly ahead.

He reversed down the driveway, catching the vegetation on both sides, and eased out of the track. Made the right and headed south on the quiet road he'd left to find the house. The town of Brighton firmed up ahead of him. The road widened and smoothed out. There was a gas station and a fire house. A small municipal park with a Little League diamond. A supermarket with a large parking lot, a bank, a row of small stores sharing a common frontage, set back from the street.

The supermarket's parking lot seemed to be the geographic centre of the town. He cruised slowly past it and saw a nursery, with lines of shrubs in pots under a sprinkler, which was making rainbows in the sun. Then a large shed, dull red paint, standing in its own lot: Steven's Hardware. He swung the Taurus in and parked next to a timber store in back.

The entrance was an insignificant door set in the end wall of the shed. It gave on to a maze of aisles, packed tight with every kind of thing he'd never had to buy. Screws, nails, bolts, hand tools, power tools, garbage cans, mailboxes, panes of glass, window units, doors, cans of paint. The maze led to a central core, where four shop counters were set in a square under bright fluorescent lighting. Inside the corral were a man and two boys, dressed in jeans and shirts and red canvas aprons. The man was lean and small, maybe fifty, and the boys were clearly his sons, younger versions of the same face and physique, maybe eighteen and twenty.

'Ed Steven?' Reacher asked.

The man nodded and set his head at an angle and raised his eyebrows, like a guy who has spent thirty years dealing with enquiries from salesmen and customers.

'Can I talk to you about Victor Hobie?'

The guy looked blank for a second, and then he glanced sideways at his boys, like he was spooling backward all the way through their lives and far beyond, back to when he last knew Victor Hobie.

'He died in 'Nam, right?' he said.

'I need some background.'

'Checking for his folks again?' He said it without surprise, and there was an edge of weariness in there, too. Like the Hobies' problems were well known in the town, and gladly tolerated, but no longer exciting any kind of urgent sympathy.

Reacher nodded. 'I need to get a feel for what sort of a guy he was. Story is you knew him pretty well.'

Steven looked blank again. 'Well, I did, I guess. But we were just kids. I only saw him once, after high school.'

'Want to tell me about him?'

'I'm pretty busy. I've got unloading to see to.'

'I could give you a hand. We could talk while we're doing it.'

Steven started to say a routine *no*, but then he glanced at Reacher, saw the size of him, and smiled like a labourer who's been offered the free use of a forklift.

'OK,' he said. 'Out back.'

He came out from the corral of counters and led Reacher through a rear door. There was a dusty pick-up parked in the sun next to an open shed with a tin roof. The pick-up was loaded with bags of cement.

The shelves in the open shed were empty. Reacher took his jacket off and laid it on the hood of the truck.

The bags were made of thick paper. He knew from his time with the pool gang that if he used two hands on the middle of the bags, they would fold themselves over and split. The way to do it was to clamp a palm on the corner and lift them one-handed. That would keep the dust off his new shirt, too. The bags weighed a hundred pounds, so he did them two at a time, one in each hand, holding them out, counterbalanced away from his body. Steven watched him, like he was a sideshow at the circus.

'So tell me about Victor Hobie,' Reacher grunted.

Steven shrugged. He was leaning on a post, under the tin roof, out of the sun.

'Long time ago,' he said. 'What can I tell you? We were just kids, you know? Our dads were in the chamber of commerce together. His was a printer. Mine ran this place, although it was just a lumberyard back then. We were together all the way through school. We started kindergarten on the same day, graduated high school on the same day. I only saw him once after that, when he was home from the Army. He'd been in Vietnam a year, and he was going back again.'

'So what sort of a guy was he?'

Steven shrugged again. 'I'm kind of wary about giving you an opinion.'

'Why? Some kind of bad news in there?'

'No, no, nothing like that,' Steven said. 'There's nothing to hide. He was a good kid. But I'd be giving you one kid's opinion about another kid from thirty-five years ago, right? Might not be a reliable opinion.'

Reacher paused, with a hundred-pound bag in each

hand. Glanced back at Steven. He was leaning on his post in his red apron, lean and fit, the exact picture of what Reacher assumed was a typical cautious small-town Yankee businessman. The sort of guy whose judgement might be reasonably solid. He nodded.

'OK, I can see that. I'll take it into account.'

Steven nodded back, like the ground rules were clear. 'How old are you?'

'Thirty-eight,' Reacher said.

'From around here?'

Reacher shook his head. 'Not really from around anywhere.'

'OK, couple of things you need to understand,' Steven said. 'This is a small, small suburban town, and Victor and I were born here in '48. We were already fifteen years old when Kennedy got shot, and sixteen before the Beatles arrived, and twenty when there was all that rioting in Chicago and LA. You know what I'm saying here?'

'Different world,' Reacher said.

'You bet your ass it was,' Steven said back. 'We grew up in a different world. Our whole childhood. To us, a real daring guy was one who put baseball cards in the wheels of his Schwinn. You need to bear that in mind, when you hear what I say.'

Reacher nodded. Lifted the ninth and tenth bag out of the pick-up bed. He was sweating lightly, and worrying about the state of his shirt when Jodie next saw it.

'Victor was a very straight kid,' Steven said. 'A very straight and normal kid. And like I say, for comparative purposes, that was back when the rest of us thought we were the bee's knees for staying out until half past nine on a Saturday night, drinking milk shakes.'

231

'What was he interested in?' Reacher asked.

Steven blew out his cheeks and shrugged. 'What can I tell you? Same things as all the rest of us, I guess. Baseball, Mickey Mantle. We liked Elvis, too. Ice cream, and the Lone Ranger. Stuff like that. Normal stuff.'

'His dad said he always wanted to be a soldier.'

'We all did. First it was cowboys and Indians, then it was soldiers.'

'So did you go to 'Nam?'

Steven shook his head. 'No, I kind of moved on from the soldier thing. Not because I disapproved. You got to understand, this was way, way before all that long-hair stuff arrived up here. Nobody objected to the military. I wasn't afraid of it, either. Back then there was nothing to be afraid of. We were the US, right? We were going to whip the ass off those slanty-eyed gooks, six months maximum. Nobody was worried about going. It just seemed old-fashioned. We all respected it, we all loved the stories, but it seemed like yesterday's thing, you know what I mean? I wanted to go into business. I wanted to build my dad's yard up into a big corporation. That seemed like the thing to do. To me, that seemed like more of an American thing than going into the military. Back then, it seemed just as patriotic.'

'So you beat the draft?' Reacher asked.

Steven nodded. 'Draft board called me, but I had college applications pending and they skipped right over me. My dad was close to the board chairman, which didn't hurt any, I guess.'

'How did Victor react to that?'

'He was fine with it. There was no issue about it. I wasn't anti-war or anything. I supported Vietnam, same as anybody else. It was just a personal choice, yesterday's thing or tomorrow's thing. I wanted tomorrow's thing, Victor wanted the Army. He kind of knew it was kind of, well, staid. Truth is, he was pretty much influenced by his old man. He was Four-F in World War Two. Mine was a foot soldier, went to the Pacific. Victor kind of felt his family hadn't done its bit. So he wanted to do it, like a duty. Sounds stuffy now, right? Duty? But we all thought like that, back then. No comparison at all with the kids of today. We were all pretty serious and old-fashioned around here, Victor maybe slightly more than the rest of us. Very serious, very earnest. But not really a whole lot out of the ordinary.'

Reacher was three-quarters through with the bags. He stopped and rested against the pick-up door. 'Was he smart?'

'Smart enough, I guess,' Steven said. 'He did well in school, without exactly setting the world on fire. We had a few kids here, over the years, gone to be lawyers or doctors or whatever. One of them went to NASA, a bit younger than Victor and me. Victor was smart enough, but he had to work to get his grades, as I recall.'

Reacher started with the bags again. He had filled the farthest shelves first, which he was glad about, because his forearms were starting to burn.

'Was he ever in any kind of trouble?'

Steven look impatient. 'Trouble? You haven't been listening to me, mister. Victor was straight as an arrow, back when the worst kid would look like a complete angel today.'

Six bags to go. Reacher wiped his palms on his pants.

'What was he like when you last saw him? Between the two tours?'

Steven paused to think about it. 'A little older, I guess. I'd grown up a year, it seemed like he'd grown up five. But he was no different. Same guy. Still serious, still earnest. They gave him a parade when he came home, because he had a medal. He was real embarrassed about it, said the medal was nothing. Then he went away again, and he never came back.'

'How did you feel about that?'

Steven paused again. 'Pretty bad, I guess. This was a guy I'd known all my life. I'd have preferred him to come back, of course, but I was real glad he didn't come back in a wheelchair or something, like a lot of them did.'

Reacher finished the work. He butted the last bag into position on the shelf with the heel of his hand and leaned on the post opposite Steven.

'What about the mystery? About what happened to him?'

Steven shook his head and smiled, sadly. 'There's no mystery. He was killed. This is about two old folks refusing to accept three unpleasant truths, is all.'

'Which are?'

'Simple,' Steven said. 'Truth one is their boy died. Truth two is he died out there in some godforsaken impenetrable jungle where nobody will ever find him. Truth three is the government got dishonest around that time, and they stopped listing the MIAs as casualties, so they could keep the numbers reasonable. There were . . . what? Maybe ten boys on Vic's chopper when it went down? That's ten names they kept off the nightly news. It was a policy, and it's too late for them to admit to anything now.'

234

'That's your take?'

'Sure is,' Steven said. 'The war went bad, and the government went bad with it. Hard enough for my generation to accept, let me tell you. You younger guys are probably more at home with it, but you better believe the old folk like the Hobies are never going to square up to it.'

He lapsed into silence, and glanced absently back and forth between the empty pick-up and the full shelves. 'That's a ton of cement you shifted. You want to come in and wash up and let me buy you a soda?'

'I need to eat,' Reacher said. 'I missed lunch.'

Steven nodded, and then he smiled, ruefully. 'Head south. There's a diner right after the train station. That's where we used to drink milk shakes, half past nine Saturday night, thinking we were practically Frank Sinatra.'

The diner had obviously changed many times since daring boys with baseball cards in the wheels of their bicycles had sipped milk shakes there on Saturday nights. Now it was a seventies-style eaterie, low and square, a brick facade, green roof, with a nineties-style gloss in the form of elaborate neon signs in every window, hot pinks and blues. Reacher took the leather-bound folder with him and pulled the door and stepped into chilly air smelling of Freon and burgers and the strong stuff they squirt on the tables before wiping them down. He sat at the counter and a cheerful heavy girl of twenty-something boxed him in with flatware and a napkin and handed him a menu card the size of a billboard with photographs of the food positioned next to the written descriptions. He ordered a half-pounder, Swiss, rare, slaw and onion

235

rings, and made a substantial wager with himself that it wouldn't resemble the photograph in any way at all. Then he drank his iced water and got a refill before opening the folder.

He concentrated on Victor's letters to his folks. There were twenty-seven of them in total, thirteen from his training postings and fourteen from Vietnam. They bore out everything he'd heard from Ed Steven. Accurate grammar, accurate spelling, plain terse phrasing. The same handwriting used by everybody educated in America between the twenties and the sixties, but with a backward slant. A left-handed person. None of the twenty-seven letters ran more than a few lines over the page. A dutiful person. A person who knew it was considered impolite to end a personal letter on the first page. A polite, dutiful, left-handed, dull, conventional, normal person, solidly educated, but no kind of a rocket scientist.

The girl brought him the burger. It was adequate in itself, but very different from the gigantic feast depicted in the photograph on the menu. The slaw was floating in whitened vinegar in a crimped paper cup, and the onion rings were bloated and uniform, like small brown automobile tyres. The Swiss was sliced so thin it was transparent, but it tasted like cheese.

The photograph taken after the passing-out parade down at Rucker was harder to interpret. The focus was off, and the peak of his cap put Victor's eyes into deep shadow. His shoulders were back, and his body was tense. Bursting with pride, or embarrassed by his mother? It was hard to tell. In the end, Reacher voted for pride, because of the mouth. It was a tight line, slightly down at the edges, the sort of mouth that needs firm control from the facial muscles to stop a

236

huge joyful grin. This was a photograph of a guy at the absolute peak of his life so far. Every goal attained, every dream realized. Two weeks later, he was overseas. Reacher shuffled through the letters for the note from Mobile. It was written from a bunk, before sailing. Mailed by a company clerk in Alabama. Sober phrases, a page and a quarter. Emotions tightly checked. It communicated nothing at all.

He paid the check and left the girl a two-dollar tip for being so cheerful. Would she have written home a page and a quarter of tight-assed nothingness the day she was sailing off to war? No, but she would never sail off to war. Victor's helicopter went down maybe seven years before she was born, and Vietnam was just something she had suffered through in eleventh-grade history class.

It was way too early to head straight back to Wall Street. Jodie had said seven o'clock. At least two hours to kill, minimum. He slid into the Taurus and put the air on high to blow the heat away. Then he flattened the Hertz map on the stiff leather of the folder and traced a route away from Brighton. He could take Route 9 south to the Bear Mountain Parkway, the Bear east to the Taconic, the Taconic south to the Sprain, and the Sprain would dump him out on the Bronx River Parkway. That road would take him straight down to the Botanical Gardens, which was a place he had never been, and a place he was pretty keen to visit.

Marilyn got to her lunch a little after three o'clock. She had checked the cleaning crew's work before she let them leave, and they had done a perfect job. They had used a steam-cleaner on the hall rug, not because it was dirty, but because it was the best way of raising up the dents in the pile left by the credenza's feet. The steam swelled the wool fibres, and after a thorough vacuuming nobody was ever going to know a heavy piece of furniture had once rested there.

She took a long shower and wiped out the stall with a kitchen towel to leave the tiling dry and shiny. She combed her hair and left it to air-dry. She knew the June humidity would put a slight curl in it. Then she got dressed, which involved one garment only. She put on Chester's favourite thing, a dark pink silk sheath which worked best with nothing on underneath. It came just above the knee, and although it wasn't exactly tight, it clung in all the right places, as if it had been made for her, which in fact it had been, although Chester wasn't aware of that. He thought it was just a lucky off-the-peg accident. She was happy to let him think that, not because of the money, but because it felt a little, well, *brazen* to admit to having such a sexy thing custom-made. And the effect on him was, frankly, brazen. It was like a trigger. She used it when she thought he needed rewarding. Or deflecting. And he was going to need deflecting tonight. He was going to arrive home and find his house up for sale and his wife in charge. Any old way she looked at it, it was going to be a difficult evening, and she was prepared to use any advantage she could to get through it, brazen or not.

She chose the Gucci heels that matched the sheath's colour and made her legs look long. Then she went down to the kitchen and ate her lunch, which was an apple and a square of reduced-fat cheese, and then she went back upstairs and brushed her teeth again and thought about make-up. Being naked under the dress

238

and with her hair down in a natural style, the way to go was really no make-up at all, but she was prepared to admit she was just a little beyond being able to get away with that, so she set out on the long haul of making herself up so she would look like she hadn't troubled to.

It took her twenty minutes, and then she did her nails, toes too, because she felt that counted when it was likely her shoes would be coming off early. Then she dabbed her favourite perfume on, enough to be noticed without being overwhelming. Then the phone rang. It was Sheryl.

'Marilyn?' she said. 'Six hours on the market, and you've got a nibble!'

'I have? But who? And how?'

'I know, the very first day, before you're even listed anywhere, isn't it wonderful? It's a gentleman who's relocating with his family, and he was cruising the area, getting a feel for it, and he saw your sign. He came straight over here for the particulars. Are you ready? Can I bring him right over?'

'Wow, right now? Already? This is quick, isn't it? But yes, I guess I'm ready. Who is it, Sheryl? You think he's a serious buyer?'

'Definitely I do, and he's only here today. He has to go back west tonight.'

'OK, well, bring him on over, I guess. I'll be ready.'

She realized she must have been rehearsing the whole routine, unconsciously, without really being aware of it. She moved fast, but she wasn't flustered. She hung up the phone and ran straight down to the kitchen and switched the oven on low. Spooned a heap of coffee beans on to a saucer and placed them on the middle shelf. Shut the oven door and turned to the sink. Dropped the apple core into the waste disposal and stacked the plate in the dishwasher. Wiped the sink down with a paper towel and stood back, hands on hips, scanning the room. She walked to the window and angled the blind until the light caught the shine on the floor.

'Perfect,' she said to herself.

She ran back up the stairs and started at the top of the house. She ducked into every room, scanning, checking, adjusting flowers, angling blinds, plumping pillows. She turned lamps on everywhere. She had read that to turn them on after the buyer was already in the room was a clear message the house was gloomy. Better to have them on from the outset, which was a clear message of cheerful welcome.

She ran back down the stairs. In the family room, she opened the blind all the way to show off the pool. In the den, she turned on the reading lamps and tilted the blind almost closed, to give a dark, comfortable look. Then she ducked into the living room. Shit, Chester's side-table was still there, right next to where his armchair had been. How could she have missed that? She grabbed it two-handed and ran with it to the basement stairs. She heard Sheryl's car on the gravel. She opened the basement door and ran down and dumped the table and ran back up. Closed the door on it and ducked into the powder room. Straightened the guest towel and dabbed at her hair and checked herself in the mirror. God! She was wearing her silk sheath. With nothing underneath. The silk was clinging to her skin. What the hell was this poor guy going to think?

The doorbell rang. She was frozen. Did she have time to change? Of course not. They were at the door, right now, ringing the bell. A jacket or something? The doorbell rang again. She took a breath and shook her hips to loosen the fabric and walked down the hall. Took another breath and opened the door.

Sheryl beamed in at her, but Marilyn was already looking at the buyer. He was a tallish man, maybe fifty or fifty-five, grey, in a dark suit, standing side-on, looking out and back at the plantings along the driveway. She glanced down at his shoes, because Chester always said wealth and breeding shows up on the feet. These looked pretty good. Heavy Oxfords, polished to a shine. She started a smile. Was this going to be it? Sold within six hours? That would be a hell of a thing. She smiled a quick conspirator's smile with Sheryl and turned to the man.

'Come in,' she said brightly, and held out her hand.

He turned back from the garden to face her. He stared straight at her, frankly and blatantly. She felt naked under his gaze. She practically *was* naked. But she found herself staring right back at him, because he was terribly burned. One side of his head was just a mass of shiny pink scars. She kept her polite smile frozen in place and kept her hand extended towards him. He paused. Brought his hand up to meet it. But it wasn't a hand. It was a shining metal hook. Not an artificial hand, not a clever prosthetic device, just a wicked metal curve made of gleaming steel.

Reacher was at the kerb outside the sixty-storey building on Wall Street ten minutes before seven o'clock. He kept the motor running and scanned a triangle that had its point on the building's exit door and spread sideways across the plaza past the distance where somebody could get to her before he could.

241

There was nobody inside the triangle who worried him. Nobody static, nobody watching, just a thin stream of office workers jostling out to the street, jackets over their arms, bulky briefcases in their hands. Most of them were making a left on the sidewalk, heading for the subway. Some of them were threading through the cars at the kerb, looking for cabs out in the traffic stream.

The other parked cars were harmless. There was a UPS truck two places ahead, and a couple of chauffeur driven with drivers standing next to them, scanning for their passengers. Innocent bustle, at the weary end of a busy day. Reacher settled back in his seat to wait, his eyes flicking left and right, ahead and behind, always returning to the revolving door.

She came out before seven, which was sooner than he expected. He saw her through the glass, in the lobby. He saw her hair, and her dress, and the flash of her legs as she skipped sideways to the exit. He wondered for a second if she had just been waiting up on her high floor. The timing was plausible. She could have seen the car from her window, gone straight to the elevator. She pushed the door and spilled out on to the plaza. He got out of the car and moved around the bonnet to the sidewalk and stood waiting. She was carrying the pilot's case. She skipped through a shaft of sun and her hair lit up like a halo. Ten yards from him, she smiled.

'Hello, Reacher,' she called.

'Hello, Jodie,' he said.

She knew something. He could see it in her face. She had big news for him, but she was smiling like she was going to tease him with it.

'What?' he asked.

She smiled again and shook her head. 'You first, OK?'

They sat in the car and he ran through everything the old couple had told him. Her smile faded and she turned sombre. Then he gave her the leather-bound folder and left her to scan it through while he fought the traffic in a narrow counterclockwise square that left them facing south on Broadway, two blocks from her place. He pulled in at the kerb outside an espresso bar. She was reading the reconnaissance report from Rutter and studying the photograph of the emaciated grey man and the Asian soldier.

'Incredible,' she said, quietly.

'Give me your keys,' he said back. 'Get a coffee and I'll walk up for you when I know your building's OK.'

She made no objection. The photograph had shaken her up. She just went into her bag for her keys and got out of the car and skipped straight across the sidewalk and into the coffee shop. He watched her inside and then eased south down the street. He turned directly into her garage. It was a different car, and he figured if anybody was waiting down there they would hesitate long enough to give him all the advantage he would need. But the garage was quiet. Just the same group of parked vehicles, looking like they hadn't moved all day. He put the Taurus in her slot and went up the metal stairs to the lobby. Nobody there. Nobody in the elevator, nobody in the fourth-floor hallway. Her door was undamaged. He opened it up and stepped inside. Quiet, still air. Nobody there.

He used the fire stairs to get back to the lobby and went out the glass doors to the street. Walked the two blocks north and ducked into the coffee shop and found her alone at a chrome table, reading Victor

243

Hobie's letters, an espresso untouched at her elbow.

'You going to drink that?' he asked.

She stacked the jungle photograph on top of the letters.

'This has big implications,' she said.

He took that for a no, and pulled the cup over and swallowed the coffee in one mouthful. It had cooled slightly and was wonderfully strong.

'Let's go,' she said. She let him carry her case and took his arm for the two-block walk. He gave back her keys at the street door and they went in through the lobby together and up in the elevator in silence. She unlocked the apartment door and went inside ahead of him.

'So it's government people after us,' she said.

He made no reply. Just shrugged off his new jacket and dropped it on the sofa under the Mondrian copy.

'Has to be,' she said.

He walked to the windows and cracked the blinds. Shafts of daylight poured in and the white room glowed.

'We're close to the secret of these camps,' she said. 'So the government is trying to silence us. CIA or somebody.'

He walked through to the kitchen. Pulled the refrigerator door and took out a bottle of water.

'We're in serious danger,' she said. 'You don't seem very worried about it.'

He shrugged and took a swallow of water. It was too cold. He preferred it room temperature.

'Life's too short for worrying,' he said.

'Dad was worrying. It was making his heart worse.'

He nodded. 'I know. I'm sorry.'

'So why aren't you taking it seriously? Don't you believe it?'

'I believe it,' he said. 'I believe everything they told me.'

'And the photograph proves it, right? The place obviously exists.'

'I know it exists,' he said. 'I've been there.'

She stared at him. 'You've been there? When? How?'

'Not long ago,' he said. 'I got just about as close as this Rutter guy got.'

'Christ, Reacher,' she said. 'So what are you going to do about it?'

'I'm going to buy a gun.'

'No, we should go to the cops. Or the newspapers, maybe. The government can't do this.'

'You wait for me here, OK?'

'Where are you going?'

'I'm going to buy a gun. Then I'll buy us some pizza. I'll bring it back.'

'You can't buy a gun, not in New York City, for God's sake. There are laws. You need ID and permits and things and you've got to wait five days anyway.'

'I can buy a gun anywhere,' he said. 'Especially New York City. What do you want on the pizza?'

'Have you got enough money?'

'For the pizza?'

'For the gun,' she said.

'The gun will cost me less than the pizza,' he said. 'Lock the door behind me, OK? And don't open it unless you see it's me in the spy hole.'

He left her standing in the centre of the kitchen. He used the fire stairs to the lobby and stood in the bustle on the sidewalk long enough to get himself lined up with the geography. There was a pizza parlour on the block to the south. He ducked inside and ordered a large pie, half anchovies and capers, half hot pepperoni, to go in thirty minutes. Then he dodged traffic on Broadway and struck out east. He'd been in New York enough times to know what people say is true. Everything happens fast in New York. Things change fast. Fast in terms of chronology, and fast in terms of geography. One neighbourhood shades into another within a couple of blocks. Sometimes, the front of a building is a middle-class paradise, and around the back bums are sleeping in the alley. He knew a fast ten-minute walk was going to take him worlds away from Jodie's expensive apartment block.

He found what he was looking for in the shadows under the approach to the Brooklyn Bridge. There was a messy tangle of streets crouching there, and a giant housing project sprawling to the north and east. Some ragged cluttered stores, and a basketball court with chains under the hoops instead of nets. The air was hot and damp and filled with fumes and noise. He turned a corner and stood leaning on the chain-link with the basketball noises behind him, watching two worlds collide. There was a rapid traffic flow of vehicles driving and people walking fast, and an equal quantity of cars stopped and idling and people standing around in bunches. The moving cars tacked around the stopped ones, honking and swerving, and the walking people pushed and complained and dodged into the gutter to pass the knots of loiterers. Sometimes a car would stop short and a boy would dart forward to the driver's window. There would be a short conversation and money would change hands like a conjuring trick and the boy would dart back to a doorway and disappear. He would reappear a moment later and hustle back to the car. The driver

246

would glance left and right and accept a small package and force back into the traffic in a burble of exhaust and a blast of horns. Then the boy would return to the sidewalk and wait.

Sometimes the trade was on foot, but the system was always the same. The boys were the cut-outs. They carried the money in and the packages out, and they were too young to go to trial. Reacher was watching them use three doorways in particular, spaced out along the block frontage. The centre of the three was doing the busiest trade. About two-to-one, in terms of commercial volume. It was the eleventh building, counting up from the south corner. He pushed off the fence and turned east. There was a vacant lot ahead which gave him a glimpse of the river. The bridge soared over his head. He turned north and came up behind the buildings in a narrow alley. Scanned ahead as he walked and counted eleven fire escapes. Dropped his glance to ground level and saw a black sedan jammed into the narrow space outside the eleventh rear entrance. There was a boy of maybe nineteen sitting on the trunk lid, with a mobile phone in his hand. The back-door guard, one step up the promotion ladder from his baby brothers shuttling back and forward across the sidewalk.

There was nobody else around. The boy was on his own. Reacher stepped into the alley. The way to do it is to walk fast and focus on something way beyond your target. Make the guy feel like he's got nothing to do with anything. Reacher made a show of checking his watch and glancing far ahead into the distance. He hustled along, almost running. At the last minute, he dropped his gaze to the car, like he was suddenly dragged back into the present by the obstacle. The boy was watching him. Reacher dodged left, where he knew the angle of the car wouldn't let him through. He pulled up in exasperation and dodged right, turning with the pent-up fury of a hurrying man baulked by a nuisance. He swung his left arm with the turn and hit the kid square in the side of the head. The kid toppled and he hit him again, right-handed, just a short-arm jab, relatively gentle. No reason to put him in the hospital.

He let him fall off the trunk lid unaided, to see how far away he'd put him. A conscious person will always break his fall. This kid didn't. He hit the alley floor with a dusty thump. Reacher rolled him over and checked his pockets. There was a gun in there, but it wasn't the sort of thing he was going to bear home in triumph. It was a Chinese .22, some imitation of a Soviet imitation of something that was probably useless to start with. He pitched it out of reach under the car.

He knew the back door of the tenement would be unlocked, because that's the point of a back door when you're doing a roaring trade about 150 yards south of Police Plaza. They come in the front, you need to be able to get out the back without fumbling for the key. He inched it open with his toe and stood gazing into the gloom. There was an inner door off the back hallway, leading to the right, into a room with a light on inside. It was about ten paces away.

No point in waiting. They weren't about to take a dinner break. He walked ahead ten paces and stopped at the door. The building stank of decay and sweat and urine. It was quiet. An abandoned building. He listened. There was a low voice inside the room. Then an answer to it. Two people, minimum.

Swinging the door open and standing and taking stock of the scene inside is not the way to do it. The guy who pauses even for a millisecond is the guy who dies earlier than his classmates. Reacher's guess was the tenement was maybe fifteen feet wide, of which three were represented by the hallway he was standing in. So he aimed to be the other twelve feet into the room before they even knew he was there. They would still be looking at the door, wondering who else was coming in after him.

He took a breath and burst through the door like it wasn't there at all. It crashed back against the hinge and he was across the room in two huge strides. Dim light. A single electric bulb. Two men. Packages on the table. Money on the table. A handgun on the table. He hit the first guy a wide swinging roundhouse blow square on the temple. The guy fell sideways and Reacher drove through him with a knee in the gut on his way back to the second man, who was coming up out of his chair with his eyes wide and his mouth open in shock. Reacher aimed high and smacked him with a forearm smash exactly horizontal between his eyebrows and his hairline. Do it hard enough, and the guy goes down for an hour, but his skull stays in one piece. This was supposed to be a shopping trip, not an execution.

He stood still and listened through the door. Nothing. The guy in the alley was sleeping and the noise on the street was occupying the kids on the sidewalk. He glanced at the table and glanced away again, because the handgun lying there was a Colt Detective Special. A six-shot .38-calibre revolver in blued steel with black plastic grips. Stubby little two-inch barrel. No good at all. Nowhere near the sort of thing he was

249

looking for. The short barrel was a drawback, and the calibre was a disappointment. He remembered a Louisiana cop he'd met, a police captain from some small jurisdiction out in the bayou. The guy had come to the military police for firearms advice and Reacher had been detailed to deal with him. The guy had all kinds of tales of woe about the .38-calibre revolvers his men were using. He said *you just can't rely on them to put a guy down, not if he's coming at you all pumped up on angel dust*. He told a story about a suicide. The guy needed five shots to the head with a .38 to put himself away. Reacher had been impressed by the guy's unhappy face and he had decided then and there to stay away from .38s, which was a policy he was not about to change now. So he turned his back on the table and stood still and listened again. Nothing. He squatted next to the guy he'd hit in the head and started through his jacket.

The busiest dealers make the most money, and the most money buys the best toys, which was why he was in this building, and not in one of the slower rivals up or down the street. He found exactly what he wanted in the guy's left-hand inner pocket. Something a whole lot better than a puny .38 Detective Special. It was a big black automatic, a Steyr GB, a handsome nine-millimetre which had been a big favourite of his Special Forces friends through most of his career. He pulled it out and checked it over. The magazine had all eighteen shells in it and the chamber smelled like it had never been fired. He pulled the trigger and watched the mechanism move. Then he re-assembled the gun and jammed it under his belt in the small of his back and smiled. Stayed down next to the unconscious guy and whispered, 'I'll buy your

Steyr for a buck. Just shake your head if you've got a problem with that, OK?'

Then he smiled again and stood up. Peeled a dollar bill off his roll and left it weighted down on the tabletop under the Detective Special. Stepped back to the hallway. All quiet. He made the ten paces to the back and came out into the light. Checked left and right up and down the alley and stepped over to the parked sedan. Opened the driver's door and found the lever and popped the trunk. There was a black nylon sports bag in there, empty. A small cardboard box of nine-millimetre reloads under a tangle of red and black jump leads. He put the ammunition in the bag and walked away with it. The pizza was waiting for him when he arrived back on Broadway.

It was sudden. It happened without warning. As soon as they were inside and the door was closed, the man hit Sheryl, a vicious backhand blow to the face with whatever was inside his empty sleeve. Marilyn was frozen with shock. She saw the man twisting violently and the hook swinging through its glittering arc and she heard the wet crunch as his arm hit Sheryl's face and she clamped both hands over her mouth as if it were somehow vitally important she didn't scream. She saw the man spinning back towards her and reaching up under his right armpit and coming out with a gun in his left hand. She saw Sheryl going over backward and sprawling on the rug, right where it was still damp from the steam cleaning. She saw the gun arcing at her along the exact same radius he had used before, but in the reverse direction, coming straight at her. The gun was made of dark metal, grey, dewed with oil. It was dull, but it shone. It stopped level with

251

her chest, and she stared down at its colour, and all she could think was *that's what they mean when they say gunmetal*.

'Step closer,' the man said.

She was paralysed. Her hands were clamped to her face and her eyes were open so wide she thought the skin on her face would tear.

'Closer,' the man said again.

She stared down at Sheryl. She was struggling up on her elbows. Her eyes were crossed and blood was running from her nose. Her top lip was swelling and the blood was dripping off her chin. Her knees were up and her skirt was rucked. She could see her panty hose change from thin to thick at the top. Her breathing was ragged. Then her elbows gave way again and slid forward and her knees splayed out. Her head hit the floor with a soft thump and rolled sideways.

'Step closer,' the man said.

She stared at his face. It was rigid. The scars looked like hard plastic. One eye was hooded under an eyelid as thick and coarse as a thumb. The other was cold and unblinking. She stared at the gun. It was a foot away from her chest. Not moving. The hand that held it was smooth. The nails were manicured. She stepped forward a quarter of a step.

'Closer.'

She slid her feet forward until the gun was touching the fabric of her dress. She felt the hardness and the coldness of the grey metal through the thin silk.

'Closer.'

She stared at him. His face was a foot away from hers. On the left the skin was grey and lined. The good eye was webbed with lines. The right eye blinked. The eyelid was slow and heavy. It went down, then up, deliberately, like a machine. She leaned forward an inch. The gun pressed into her breast.

'Closer.'

She moved her feet. He answered with matching pressure on the gun. The metal was pressing hard into the softness of her flesh. It was crushing her breast. The silk was yielding into a deep crater. It was pulling her nipple sideways. It was hurting her. The man raised his right arm. The hook. He held it up in front of her eyes. It was a plain steel curve, rubbed and polished until it shone. He rotated it slowly, with an awkward movement of his forearm. She heard leather inside his sleeve. The tip of the hook was machined to a point. He rotated the tip away and laid the flat of the curve against her forehead. She flinched. It was cold. He scraped it down her forehead and traced the curve of her nose. In under her nose. He pressed it against her top lip. Brought it down and in and pressed until her mouth opened. He tapped it gently against her teeth. It caught on her bottom lip, because her lip was dry. He dragged her lip down with the steel until the soft rubbery flesh pulled free. He traced over the curve of her chin. Down under her chin to her throat. Up again an inch, and back, under the shelf of her jaw, until he was forcing her head up with the strength in his shoulder. He stared into her eyes.

'My name is Hobie,' he said.

She was up on tiptoes, trying to take the weight off her throat. She was starting to gag. She couldn't remember taking a breath since she had opened the door.

'Did Chester mention me?'

Her head was tilting upwards. She was staring at the

253

ceiling. The gun was digging into her breast. It was no longer cold. The heat of her body had warmed it. She shook her head, a small urgent motion, balanced on the pressure of the hook.

'He didn't mention me?'

'No,' she gasped. 'Why? Should he have?'

'Is he a secretive man?'

She shook her head again. The same small urgent motion, side to side, the skin of her throat snagging left and right against the metal.

'Did he tell you about his business problems?'

She blinked. Shook her head again.

'So he *is* a secretive man.'

'I guess,' she gasped. 'But I knew anyway.'

'Does he have a girlfriend?'

She blinked again. Shook her head.

'How can you be sure?' Hobie asked. 'If he's a secretive man?'

'What do you want?' she gasped.

'But I guess he doesn't need a girlfriend. You're a very beautiful woman.'

She blinked again. She was up on her toes. The Gucci heels were off the ground.

'I just paid you a compliment,' Hobie said. 'Oughtn't you say something in response? Politely?'

He increased the pressure. The steel dug into the flesh of her throat. One foot came free of the ground.

'Thank you,' she gasped.

The hook eased down. Her eye line came back to the horizontal and her heels touched the rug. She realized she was breathing. She was panting, in and out, in and out.

'A very beautiful woman.'

He dropped the hook away from her throat. It

254

touched her waist. Traced down over the curve of her hip. Down over her thigh. He was staring at her face. The gun was jammed hard in her flesh. The hook turned, and the flat face of the curve lifted off her thigh, leaving just the point behind. It traced downward. She felt it slide off the silk onto her bare leg. It was sharp. Not like a needle. Like a pencil point. It stopped moving. It started back up. He was pressing with it, gently. It wasn't cutting her. She knew that. But it was furrowing against the firmness of her skin. It moved up. It slid under the silk. She felt the metal on the skin of her thigh. It moved up. She could feel the silk of her dress bunching and gathering in the radius of the hook. The hook moved up. The back of the hem was sliding up the backs of her legs. Sheryl stirred on the floor. The hook stopped moving and Hobie's awful right eye swivelled slowly across and down.

'Put your hand in my pocket,' he said.

She stared at him.

'Your left hand,' he said. 'My right pocket.'

She had to move closer and reach over and down between his arms. Her face was close to his. He smelled of soap. She felt around to his pocket. Darted her fingers inside and closed them over a small cylinder. Slid it out. It was a used roll of duct tape, an inch in diameter. Silver. Maybe five yards remaining. Hobie stepped away from her.

'Tape Sheryl's wrists together,' he said.

She wriggled her hips to make the hem of her dress fall down into place. He watched her do it and smiled. She glanced between the roll of silver tape and Sheryl, down on the floor.

'Turn her over,' he said.

The light from the window was catching the gun. She knelt next to Sheryl. Pulled on one shoulder and pushed on the other until she flopped over on her front.

'Put her elbows together,' he said.

She hesitated. He raised the gun a fraction, and then the hook, arms wide, a display of superior weaponry. She grimaced. Sheryl stirred again. Her blood had pooled on the rug. It was brown and sticky. Marilyn used both hands and forced her elbows together, behind her back. Hobie looked down.

'Get them real close,' he said.

She picked at the tape with her nail and got a length free. Wrapped it around and around Sheryl's fore-arms, just below her elbows.

'Tight,' he said. 'All the way up.'

She wound the tape around and around, up above her elbows and down to her wrists. Sheryl was stirring and struggling.

'OK, sit her up,' Hobie said.

She dragged her into a sitting position with her taped arms behind her. Her face was masked in blood. Her nose was swollen, going blue. Her lips were puffy.

'Put the tape on her mouth,' Hobie said.

She used her teeth and bit off a six-inch length. Sheryl was blinking and focusing. Marilyn shrugged unhappily at her, like a helpless apology, and stuck the tape over her mouth. It was thick tape, with tough reinforcing threads baked into the silver plastic coating. It was shiny, but not slippery, because of the raised criss-cross threads. She rubbed her fingers side to side across them to make it stick. Sheryl's nose started bubbling and her eyes opened wide in panic.

'God, she can't breathe,' Marilyn gasped.

256

She went to rip the tape off again, but Hobie kicked her hand away.

'You broke her nose,' Marilyn said. 'She can't breathe.'

The gun was pointing down at her head. Held steady. Eighteen inches away.

'She's going to die,' Marilyn said.

'That's for damn sure,' Hobie said back.

She stared up at him in horror. Blood was rasping and bubbling in Sheryl's fractured airways. Her eyes were staring in panic. Her chest was heaving. Hobie's eyes were on Marilyn's face.

'You want me to be nice?' he asked.

She nodded wildly.

'Are you going to be nice back?'

She stared at her friend. Her chest was convulsing, heaving for air that wasn't there. Her head was shaking from side to side. Hobie leaned down and turned the hook so the point was rasping across the tape on Sheryl's mouth as her head jerked back and forth. Then he jabbed hard and forced the point through the silver. Sheryl froze. Hobie moved his arm, left and right, up and down. Pulled the hook back out. There was a ragged hole left in the tape, with air whistling in and out. The tape sucked and blew against her lips as Sheryl gasped and panted.

'I was nice,' Hobie said. 'So now you owe me, OK?'

Sheryl's breathing was sucking hard through the hole in the tape. She was concentrating on it. Her eyes were squinting down, like she was confirming there was air in front of her to use. Marilyn was watching her, sitting back on her heels, cold with terror.

'Help her to the car,' Hobie said.

TEN

Chester Stone was alone in the bathroom on the eighty-eighth floor. Tony had forced him to go in there. Not physically. He had just stood there and pointed silently, and Stone had scuttled across the carpet in his undershirt and shorts, with his dark socks and polished shoes on his feet. Then Tony had lowered his arm and stopped pointing and told him to stay in there and closed the door on him. There had been muffled sounds out in the office, and after a few minutes the two men must have left, because Stone heard doors shutting and the nearby whine of the elevator. Then it had gone dark and silent.

He sat on the bathroom floor with his back against the grey granite tiling, staring into the silence. The bathroom door was not locked. He knew that. There had been no fiddling or clicking when the door closed. He was cold. The floor was hard tile, and the chill was striking up through the thin cotton of his boxers. He started shivering. He was hungry, and thirsty.

He listened carefully. Nothing. He eased himself up off the floor and stepped to the sink. Turned the tap and listened again over the trickle of water. Nothing. He bent his head and drank. His teeth touched the metal of the tap and he tasted the chlorine taste of city water. He held a mouthful unswallowed and let it soak into his dry tongue. Then he gulped it down and turned the tap off.

He waited an hour. A whole hour, sitting on the floor, staring at the unlocked door, listening to the silence. It was hurting where the guy had hit him. A hard ache, where the fist had glanced off his ribs. Bone against bone, solid, jarring. Then a soft, nauseated feeling in his gut where the blow had landed. He kept his eyes on the door, trying to tune out the pain. The building boomed and rumbled gently, like there were other people in the world, but they were far away. The elevators and the air-conditioning and the rush of water in the pipes and the play of the breeze on the windows added and cancelled to a low, comfortable whisper, just below the point of easy audibility. He thought he could hear elevator doors opening and closing, maybe eighty-eight floors down, faint bass thumps shivering upward through the shafts.

He was cold, and cramped, and hungry, and hurting, and scared. He stood up, bent with cramp and pain, and listened. Nothing. He slid his leather soles across the tile. Stood with his hand on the doorknob. Listened hard. Still nothing. He opened the door. The huge office was dim and silent. Empty. He padded straight across the carpet and stopped near the door out to the reception area. Now he was nearer the elevator banks. He could hear the cars whining up and down inside the shafts. He listened at the door. Nothing. He opened the door. The reception area was dim and deserted. The oak gleamed pale and there were random gleams coming off the brass accents. He could hear the motor running inside a refrigerator in

259

the kitchen to his right. He could smell cold stale coffee.

The door out to the lobby was locked. It was a big, thick door, probably fire-resistant in line with severe city codes. It was faced in pale oak, and he could see the dull gleam of steel in the gap where it met the frame. He shook the handle, and it didn't move at all. He stood there for a long time, facing the door, peering out through the tiny wired glass window, thirty feet away from the elevator buttons and freedom. Then he turned back to the counter.

It was chest high, viewed from the front. In back, there was a desktop level, and the chest-high barrier was made up of cubbyholes with office stationery and folders stacked neatly inside. There was a telephone on the desktop part, in front of Tony's chair. The telephone was a complicated console, with a handset on the left and buttons on the right under a small oblong window. The window was a grey LCD readout that said OFF. He picked up the handset and heard nothing except the blood hissing in his ear. He pressed random buttons. Nothing. He quartered the console, tracing his finger left-to-right across every button, searching. He found a button marked OPERATE. He pressed it and the little screen changed to ENTER CODE. He pressed random numbers and the screen changed back to OFF.

There were cupboards under the desktop. Little oak doors. They were all locked. He shook each of them in turn and heard little metal tongues striking metal plates. He walked back into Hobie's office. Walked through the furniture to the desk. There was nothing on the sofas. His clothes were gone. Nothing on the desktop. The desk drawers were locked. It was a solid desk, expensive, ruined by the gouges from the hook, and the drawer locks felt tight. He squatted down, ridiculous in his underwear, and pulled at the handles. They moved a fraction, then stopped. He saw the trash can, under the desk. It was a brass cylinder, not tall. He tilted it over. His wallet was in there, empty and forlorn. The picture of Marilyn was next to it, face down. The paper was printed over and over on the back: KODAK. He reached into the can and picked it up. Turned it over. She smiled out at him. It was a casual head-and-shoulders shot. She was wearing the silk dress. The sexy one, the one she'd had custom-made. She didn't know he knew she'd had it made. He had been home alone when the store called. He'd told them to call back, and let her believe he thought it was off-the-peg. In the photo, she was wearing it for the first time. She was smiling shyly, her eyes animated with daring, telling him not to go too low with the lens, not down to where the thin silk clung to her breasts. He cradled the picture in his palm and stared at it, and then he placed it back in the can, because he had no pockets.

He stood up urgently and stepped around the leather chair to the wall of windows. Pushed the slats of the blind apart with both hands and looked out. *He had to do something*. But he was eighty-eight floors up. Nothing to see except the river and New Jersey. No neighbours opposite to gesture urgently at. Nothing at all opposite, until the Appalachians reached Pennsylvania. He let the blinds fall back and paced every inch of the office, every inch of the reception area, and back into the office to do it all over again. *Hopeless*. He was in a prison. He stood in the centre of the floor, shivering, focusing on nothing.

He was hungry. He had no idea what time it was. The office had no clock and he had no watch. The sun was getting low in the west. Late afternoon or early evening, and he hadn't eaten lunch. He crept to the office door. Listened again. Nothing except the comfortable hum of the building and the rattle of the refrigerator motor. He stepped out and crossed to the kitchen. He paused with his finger on the light switch, and then he dared to turn it on. A fluorescent tube kicked in. It flickered for a second and threw a flat glare across the room and added an angry buzz from its circuitry. The kitchen was small, with a token stainless-steel sink and an equal length of counter. Rinsed mugs upside down, and a filter machine tarred with old coffee. A tiny refrigerator under the counter. There was milk in there and a six-pack of beer, and a Zabar's bag, neatly folded shut. He pulled it out. There was something wrapped in newspaper. It was heavy, and solid. He stood up and unrolled the paper on the counter. There was a plastic bag inside. He gripped the bottom, and the severed hand thumped out on the counter. The fingers were white and curled, and there was spongy purple flesh and splintered white bone and empty blue tubes trailing at the wrist. Then the glare of the fluorescent light spun around and tilted past his gaze as he fainted to the floor.

Reacher put the pizza box on the elevator floor and took the gun out of his belt and zipped it into the sports bag with the spare shells. Then he crouched and picked up the pizza again in time for the elevator door to slide back on the fourth floor. The apartment opened up as soon as he stepped within range of the fish-eye in the door. Jodie was standing just inside the hallway, waiting for him. She was still in the linen dress. It was slightly creased across the hips, from sitting all day. Her long brown legs were scissored, one foot in front of the other.

'I brought dinner,' he said.

She looked at the sports bag instead.

'Last chance, Reacher. We should talk with somebody about all of this.'

'No,' he said.

He put the bag on the floor and she stepped behind him to lock the door.

'OK,' she said. 'If this is the government doing something, maybe you're right. Maybe we should stay away from the cops.'

'Right,' he said.

'So I'm with you on this.'

'Let's eat,' he said.

He walked through to the kitchen with the pizza. She had set the table. There were two place settings, opposite each other. Plates, knives and forks, paper napkins, glasses of iced water. Like two people were resident in the apartment. He put the box on the counter and opened it up.

'You choose,' he said.

She was standing close behind him. He could feel her there. He could smell her perfume. He felt the flat of her hand touch his back. It burned. She left it there for a second, then she used it to move him out of the way.

'Let's split it,' she said.

She balanced the box on her arm and carried it back to the table. Pulled the slices off each other while the box canted and wobbled. Shared them between the plates. He sat and sipped the water and watched her. She was slender and energetic and could make any mundane activity look like a graceful ballet. She turned away and dumped the greasy box and turned back. The dress twisted and flowed with her. She sat down. He heard the whisper of linen on skin and her foot hit his knee under the table.

'Sorry,' she said.

She wiped her fingers on the napkin and tossed her hair behind her shoulders and held her head at an angle for the first bite. She ate left-handed, rolling the wedge into a point, attacking it hungrily.

'No lunch,' she said. 'You told me not to leave the building.'

She darted her tongue out and caught a thread of cheese. Smiled self-consciously as she hooked it back between her lips. They shone with the oil. She took a long drink of water. 'Anchovies, my favourite. How did you know? But they make you thirsty later, don't they? So salty.'

Her dress was sleeveless and he could see her arms, all the way down from the little knob of bone at the top of the shoulder. They were slim and brown and narrow. Almost no muscle there at all, just tiny biceps like tendons. She was gorgeous and she took his breath away, but she was a puzzle, physically. She was tall, but she was so tiny he didn't see how there was room for all the essential organs inside her. She was as thin as a stick, but looked vibrant and firm and strong. A puzzle. He remembered the feel of her arm around his waist, fifteen years before. Like somebody was tightening a thick rope around his middle.

'I can't stay here tonight,' he said.

She looked across at him. 'Why not? You got something to do, I'll come do it too. Like I said, I'm with you on this.'

'No, I just can't stay,' he said.

'Why not?' she asked again.

He took a deep breath and held it. Her hair was shimmering in the light.

'It's not appropriate that I should stay here,' he said.

'But why not?'

He shrugged, embarrassed. 'Just because, Jodie. Because you're thinking of me like a brother or an uncle or something, because of Leon, but I'm not that, am I?'

She was staring at him.

'I'm sorry,' he said.

Her eyes were wide. 'What?'

'This is not right,' he said gently. 'You're not my sister or my niece. That's just an illusion because I was close to your dad. To me, you're a beautiful woman, and I can't be here alone with you.'

'Why not?' she asked again, breathless.

'Christ, Jodie, why not? Because it's not appropriate, that's why not. You don't need to hear all the details. You're not my sister or my niece, and I can't keep on pretending you are. It's driving me crazy, pretending.'

She was very still. Staring at him. Still breathless.

'How long have you felt this way?' she asked.

He shrugged, embarrassed again. 'Always, I guess. Since I first met you. Give me a break, Jodie, you weren't a kid. I was nearer your age than Leon's.'

She was silent. He held his breath, waiting for the tears. The outrage. The trauma. She was just staring at him. He was already regretting having spoken. He should have just kept his damn mouth shut. Bitten his damn lip and gotten through it. He had been through worse, although he couldn't exactly remember where or when.

'I'm sorry,' he said again.

Her face was blank. Wide blue eyes staring at him. Her elbows were on the table. The dress fabric was bunching at the front and cupping forward. He could see the strap of her bra, thin and white against the skin of her shoulder. He stared at her anguished face and closed his eyes and sighed in despair. Honesty was the best policy? Forget about it.

Then she did a curious thing. She stood up slowly, and turned and hauled her chair out of the way. Stepped forward and gripped the table edge, both hands, slim muscles standing out like cords. She dragged the table off to one side. Then she changed position and turned and butted it with her thighs until it was hard back against the counter. Reacher was left sitting on his chair, suddenly isolated in the middle of the room. She stepped back and stood in front of him. His breath froze in his chest.

'You're thinking of me like just a woman?' she asked, slowly.

He nodded.

'Not like a kid sister? Not like your niece?'

He shook his head. She paused.

'Sexually?' she asked quietly.

He nodded, still embarrassed, resigned. 'Of course sexually. What do you think? Look at yourself. I could hardly sleep last night.'

She just stood there.

'I had to tell you,' he said. 'I'm really sorry, Jodie.'

She closed her eyes. Screwed them tight shut. Then

266

he saw a smile. It spread across her whole face. Her hands clenched at her side. She exploded forward and hurled herself at him. She landed on his lap and her arms clamped tight behind his head and she kissed him like she would die if she stopped.

It was Sheryl's car, but he made Marilyn drive it. He sat in the back, behind Marilyn, with Sheryl next to him with her arms crushed behind her. The tape was still on her mouth, and she was breathing hard. He kept the hook resting on her lap, with the point dug in against the skin of her thigh. His left hand held the gun. He touched it to the back of Marilyn's neck often enough that she never forgot it was there.

Tony met them in the underground garage. Office hours were over and the place was quiet. Tony handled Sheryl and Hobie took Marilyn and the four of them rode up in the freight elevator. Hobie unlocked the door from the corridor and stepped into the reception area. The kitchen light was on. Stone was sprawled on the floor, in his underwear. Marilyn gasped and ran to him. Hobie watched the sway of her body under the thin dress and smiled. Turned back and locked the door. Pocketed the keys and the gun. Marilyn had stopped short and was staring into the kitchen, hands up at her mouth again, eyes wide, horror in her face. Hobie followed her gaze. The hand was lying on the counter, palm up, fingers curled like a beggar's. Then Marilyn was looking downward in terror.

'Don't worry,' Hobie said. 'It's not one of his. But it's a thought, isn't it? I could cut his hand off if he doesn't do what I want.'

Marilyn stared at him.

'Or I could cut yours off,' he said to her. 'I could make him watch. Maybe I could make him do it for me.'

'You're insane,' Marilyn said.

'He would, you know,' Hobie said. 'He'd do anything. He's pathetic. Look at him, in his underwear. You think he looks good in his underwear?'

She said nothing.

'What about you?' Hobie asked. 'Do you look good in your underwear? You want to take that dress off and show me?'

She stared at him in panic.

'No?' he said. 'OK, maybe later. But what about your real-estate agent? You think she'd look good in her underwear?'

He turned to Sheryl. She was backing away against the door, leaning hard on her taped arms. She stiffened.

'What about it?' he said to her. 'You look good in your underwear?'

She stared and shook her head wildly. Her breathing whistled through the hole in the tape. Hobie stepped nearer and pinned her against the door and forced the tip of his hook under the waistband of her skirt.

'Let's check it out.'

He wrenched with the hook and Sheryl staggered off-balance and the fabric tore open. Buttons scattered and she fell to her knees. He raised his foot and used the flat of his sole to push her all the way over. He nodded to Tony. Tony ducked down and pulled the torn skirt down off her thrashing legs.

'Panty hose,' Hobie said. 'God, I hate panty hose. So unromantic.'

He stooped and used the tip of the hook to tear the nylon to shreds. Her shoes came off. Tony balled the skirt and the shoes and the torn nylon and carried it to the kitchen. Dropped it into the trash. Sheryl scrabbled her bare legs under her and sat there gasping through the tape. She was wearing tiny white panties and was trying to make the tails of her blouse fall down over them. Marilyn was watching her, open mouthed in horror.

'OK, *now* we're having fun,' Hobie said. 'Aren't we?'

'You bet,' Tony said. 'But not as much fun as we're going to have.'

Hobie laughed and Stone stirred. Marilyn ducked down and helped him to a sitting position on the kitchen floor. Hobie stepped over and picked up the severed hand from the countertop.

'This came off the last guy who annoyed me,' he said.

Stone was opening and closing his eyes like he could make the scene change by wiping it away. Then he stared out at Sheryl. Marilyn realized he had never met her before. He didn't know who she was.

'Into the bathroom,' Hobie said.

Tony pulled Sheryl to her feet and Marilyn helped Chester. Hobie walked behind them. They filed into the big office and crossed to the bathroom door.

'Inside,' Hobie said.

Stone led the way. The women followed him. Hobie watched them go and stood at the door. Nodded in at Stone. 'Tony's going to sleep the night out here, on the sofa. So don't come out again. And spend your time fruitfully. Talk things over with your wife. We're going to do the stock transfer tomorrow. Much better

269

for her if we do it in an atmosphere of mutual agreement. Much better. Any other way, there could be bad consequences. You get my meaning?'

Stone just stared at him. Hobie let his glance linger on the women and then he waved the severed hand in farewell and pulled the door closed.

Jodie's white bedroom was flooded with light. For five minutes every evening in June, the sun dropped away to the west and found a slim straight path through Manhattan's tall buildings and hit her window with its full force. The blind burned like it was incandescent and the walls picked it up and bounced it around until the whole place was glowing like a soft white explosion. Reacher thought it was entirely appropriate. He was lying on his back, happier than he could ever remember getting.

If he'd thought about it, he might have worried. He could remember mean little proverbs that said things like *pity the man who gets what he wants*. And *it's better to travel hopefully than to arrive*. To get something you want after fifteen years of wanting it could have felt strange. But it didn't. It had felt like a blissful rocket trip to somewhere he had no idea existed. It had been everything he had dreamed it would be, multiplied by a million. She wasn't a myth. She was a living breathing creature, hard and strong and sinewy and perfumed, warm and shy and giving.

She lay nestled in the crook of his arm, with her hair over his face. It was in his mouth as he breathed. His hand was resting on her back. He was rocking it back and forth over her ribs. Her backbone was in a cleft formed by long shallow muscle. He traced his finger down the groove. Her eyes were closed and she was

270

smiling. He knew that. He had felt the scrape of her lashes on his neck, and his shoulder could feel the shape of her mouth. It could decode the feel of the muscles in her face. She was smiling. He moved his hand. Her skin was cool and soft.

'I should be crying now,' she said, quietly. 'I always thought I would be. I used to think, if this ever, ever happens, I'll cry afterwards.'

He squeezed her tighter. 'Why should we cry?'

'Because of all those wasted years,' she said.

'Better late than never,' he said.

She came up on her elbows. Climbed half on top of him, her breasts crushed into his chest. 'That stuff you said to me, I could have said to you, exactly word for word. I wish I had, a long time ago. But I couldn't.'

'I couldn't, either,' he said. 'It felt like a guilty secret.'

'Yes,' she said. 'My guilty secret.'

She climbed up all the way and sat astride him, back straight, smiling.

'But now it's not a secret,' she said.

'No,' he said.

She stretched her arms up high and started a yawn that ended in a contented smile. He put his hands on her tiny waist. Traced them upward to her breasts. Her smile broadened to a grin. 'Again?'

He nudged her sideways with his hips and rolled her over and laid her down gently on the bed. 'We're playing catch-up, right? All those wasted years.'

She nodded. Just a tiny motion, smiling, rubbing her hair against the pillow.

Marilyn took charge. She felt she was the strong one. Chester and Sheryl were dazed, which she felt was

271

understandable, because they were the two who had suffered the abuse. She could guess how vulnerable they must be feeling, half-dressed. She felt half-dressed herself, but she wasn't going to worry about that now. She pulled the tape off Sheryl's mouth and held her while she cried. Then she ducked behind her and worked the binding free from her wrists and unwound it up to her elbows. She balled up the sticky mass and dropped it in the trash and went back to help massage some feeling into her shoulders. Then she found a washcloth and ran hot water into the sink and sponged the crusted blood off Sheryl's face. Her nose was swollen and going black. She started worrying about getting her to a doctor. She started rehearsing things in her head. She had seen movies where hostages get taken. Somebody always elects herself spokesman and says *no police* and gets the sick released to the hospital. But how exactly do they do it?

She took the towels from the bar and gave Sheryl a bath sheet to use as a skirt. Then she divided up the remainder into three piles and laid them on the floor. She could see the tiles were going to be cold. Thermal insulation was going to be important. She slid the three piles into a row against the wall. She sat with her back against the door, and put Chester on her left and Sheryl on her right. She took their hands and squeezed them hard. Chester squeezed back.

'I'm so sorry,' he said.

'How much do you owe?' she asked.

'More than seventeen million.'

She didn't bother to ask if he could pay it back. He wouldn't be half-naked on a bathroom floor if he could pay it back.

'What does he want?' she asked.

He shrugged at her side, miserably.

'Everything,' he said. 'He wants the whole company.'

She nodded, and focused on the plumbing under the sink.

'What would that leave us with?'

He paused and then shrugged again. 'Whatever crumb he would feel like throwing us. Probably nothing at all.'

'What about the house?' she asked. 'We'd still have that, right? I put it on the market. This lady is the broker. She says it'll sell for nearly two million.'

Stone glanced across at Sheryl. Then he shook his head. 'The house belongs to the company. It was a technical thing, easier to finance that way. So Hobie will get it, along with everything else.'

She nodded and stared into space. On her right, Sheryl was sleeping, sitting up. The terror had exhausted her.

'You go to sleep, too,' she said. 'I'll figure something out.'

He squeezed her hand again and leaned his head back. Closed his eyes.

'I'm so sorry,' he said again.

She made no reply. Just smoothed the thin silk down over her thighs and stared straight ahead, thinking hard.

The sun was gone before they finished for the second time. It became a bright bar sliding sideways off the window. Then it became a narrow horizontal beam, playing across the white wall, travelling slowly, dust dancing through it. Then it was gone, shut off like a light, leaving the room with the cool dull glow of

273

evening. They lay spent and nuzzling in a tangle of sheets, bodies slack, breathing low. Then he felt her smile again. She came up on one elbow and looked at him with the same teasing grin he'd seen outside her office building.

'What?' he asked.

'I've got something to tell you,' she said.

He waited.

'In my official capacity.'

He focused on her face. She was still smiling. Her teeth were white and her eyes were bright blue, even in the new cool dimness. He thought *what official capacity?* She was a lawyer who cleaned up the mess when somebody owed somebody else a hundred million dollars.

'I don't owe money,' he said. 'And I don't think anybody owes me.'

She shook her head. Still smiling. 'As executor of Dad's will.'

He nodded. It made sense that Leon should appoint her. A lawyer in the family, the obvious choice.

'I opened it up and read it,' she said. 'Today, at work.'

'So what's in it? He was a secret miser? A closet billionaire?'

She shook her head again. Said nothing.

'He knows what happened to Victor Hobie and wrote it all down in his will?'

She was still smiling. 'He left you something. A bequest.'

He nodded again, slowly. That made sense, too. That was Leon. He'd remember, and he'd pick out some little thing, for the sake of sentiment. But what? He scanned back. Probably a souvenir. Maybe his medals? Maybe the sniper rifle he brought home from Korea. It was an old Mauser, originally German, presumably captured by the Soviets on the Eastern Front and sold on ten years later to their Korean customers. It was a hell of a piece of machinery. Leon and he had speculated on the action it must have seen, many times. It would be a nice thing to have. A nice memory. But where the hell would he keep it?

'He left you his house,' she said.

'His what?'

'His house,' she said again. 'Where we were, up in Garrison.'

He stared at her blankly. 'His house?'

She nodded. Still smiling.

'I don't believe it,' he said. 'And I can't accept it. What would I do with it?'

'What would you do with it? You'd live in it, Reacher. That's what houses are for, right?'

'But I don't live in houses,' he said. 'I've never lived in a house.'

'Well, you can live in one now.'

He was silent. Then he shook his head. 'Jodie, I just can't accept it. It should be yours. He should have left it to you. It's your inheritance.'

'I don't want it,' she said simply. 'He knew that. I like the city better.'

'OK, so sell it. But it's yours, right? Sell it and keep the money.'

'I don't need money. He knew that, too. It's worth less than I make in a year.'

He looked at her. 'I thought that was an expensive area, right by the river?'

She nodded. 'It is.'

He paused, confused.

'His house?' he said again.

She nodded.

'Did you know he was doing this?'

'Not specifically,' she said. 'But I knew he wasn't leaving it to me. I thought he might want me to sell it, give the money to charity. Old soldiers, or something.'

'OK, so you should do that instead.'

She smiled again. 'Reacher, I can't. It's not up to me. It's a binding instruction in his will. I've got to obey it.'

'His house,' he said vaguely. 'He left me his house?'

'He was worried about you. For two years, he was worrying. Since they cut you loose. He knew how it could be, you spend the whole of your life in the service, and suddenly you find you've got nothing at the end of it. He was concerned about how you were living.'

'But he didn't know how I was living,' he said.

She nodded again. 'But he could guess, right? He was a smart old guy. He knew you'd be drifting around somewhere. He used to say, drifting around is great, maybe three or four years. But what about when he's fifty? Sixty? Seventy? He was thinking about it.'

Reacher shrugged, flat on his back, naked, staring at the ceiling.

'I was never thinking about it. One day at a time was my motto.'

She made no reply. Just ducked her head and kissed his chest.

'I feel like I'm stealing from you,' he said. 'It's your inheritance, Jodie. You should have it.'

She kissed him again. 'It was his house. Even if I wanted it, we'd have to respect his wishes. But the fact is I don't want it. I never did. He knew that. He was

276

totally free to do whatever he wanted with it. And he did. He left it to you because he wanted you to have it.'

He was staring at the ceiling, but he was wandering through the house in his mind. Down the driveway, through the trees, the garage on his right, the breezeway, the low bulk of the place on his left. The den, the living room, the wide slow Hudson rolling by. The furniture. It had looked pretty comfortable. Maybe he could get a stereo. Some books. A house. His house. He tried the words in his head: *my* house. My *house*. He barely knew how to say them. *My house*. He shivered.

'He wanted you to have it,' she said again. 'It's a bequest. You can't argue against it. It's happened. And it's not any kind of a problem to me, I promise, OK?'

He nodded, slowly.

'OK,' he said. 'OK, but weird. Really, truly weird.'

'You want coffee?' she asked.

He turned and focused on her face. He could get his own coffee machine. In his kitchen. In his house. Connected to the electricity. *His* electricity.

'Coffee?' she asked again.

'I guess,' he said.

She slid off the bed and found her shoes.

'Black, no sugar, right?'

She was standing there, naked except for her shoes. Patent, with heels. She saw him looking at her.

'Kitchen floor feels cold. I always wear shoes in there.'

'Forget the coffee, OK?'

They slept in her bed, all night, way past dawn. Reacher woke first and eased his arm out from under

277

her and checked his watch. Almost seven. He had slept nine hours. The finest sleep of his life. The best bed. He had slept in a lot of beds. Hundreds, maybe even thousands. This was the best of all of them. Jodie was asleep beside him. She was on her front and had thrown the sheet off during the night. Her back was bare, all the way down to her waist. He could see the swell of her breast under her. Her hair spilled over her shoulders. One knee was pulled up, resting on his thigh. Her head was bent forward on the pillow, curving in, following the direction of her knee. It gave her a compact, athletic look. He kissed her neck. She stirred.

'Morning, Jodie,' he said.

She opened her eyes. Then she closed them, and opened them again. She smiled. A warm, morning smile.

'I was afraid I'd dreamed it,' she said. 'I used to, once.'

He kissed her again. Tenderly, on the cheek. Then less tenderly, on the mouth. Her arms came around behind him and he rolled over with her. They made love again, the fourth time in fifteen years. Then they showered together, the first time ever. Then breakfast. They ate like they were starving.

'I need to go to the Bronx,' he said.

She nodded. 'This Rutter guy? I'll drive. I know roughly where it is.'

'What about work? I thought you had to go in.'

She looked at him, mystified.

'You told me you had hours to bill,' he said. 'You sounded real busy.'

She smiled, shyly. 'I made that up. I'm well ahead, really. They said I should take the whole week off. I

278

just didn't want to be hanging around with you, feeling what I was feeling. That's why I just ran off to bed, the first night. I should have shown you the guest room, you know, like a proper little hostess. But I didn't want to be alone in a bedroom with you. It would have driven me crazy. So near, but so far, you know what I mean?'

He nodded. 'So what did you do in the office all day?'

She giggled. 'Nothing. Just sat there all day, doing nothing.'

'You're nuts,' he said. 'Why didn't you just tell me?'

'Why didn't you just tell me?'

'I did tell you.'

'Eventually,' she said. 'After fifteen years.'

He nodded. 'I know, but I was worried about it. I thought you'd be hurt or something. I thought it would be the last thing you wanted to hear.'

'Same here,' she said. 'I thought you'd hate me for ever.'

They looked at each other and they smiled. Then they grinned. Then they laughed, and kept on laughing for five solid minutes.

'I'm going to get dressed,' she said, still laughing. He followed her through to the bedroom and found his clothes on the floor. She was halfway into her closet, selecting something clean. He watched her, and started wondering if Leon's house had closets. No, if *his* house had them. Of course it did. All houses had closets, right? So did that mean he'd have to start assembling stuff to fill them all with?

She chose jeans and a shirt, dressed up with a leather belt and expensive shoes. He took his new jacket out to the hallway and loaded it with the Steyr from the sports bag. He poured twenty loose refills into the opposite pocket. All the metal made the jacket feel heavy. She came out to join him with the leather-bound folder. She was checking Rutter's address.

'Ready?' she asked.

'As I'll ever be,' he said.

He made her wait at every stage while he checked ahead. The exact same procedures he had used the day before. Her safety had felt important then. Now it felt vital. But everything was clean and quiet. Empty hallway, empty elevator, empty lobby, empty garage. They got in the Taurus together and she drove it around the block and headed back north and east.

'East River Drive to I-95 OK with you?' she asked. 'Going east, it's the Cross Bronx Expressway.'

He shrugged and tried to recall the Hertz map. 'Then take the Bronx River Parkway north. We need to go to the zoo.'

'The zoo? Rutter doesn't live near the zoo.'

'Not the zoo, exactly. The Botanical Gardens. Something you need to see.'

She glanced sideways at him and then concentrated on driving. Traffic was heavy, just past the peak of rush hour, but it was moving. They followed the river north and then north-west to the George Washington Bridge and turned their backs on it and headed east into the Bronx. The expressway was slow, but the parkway north was faster, because it was leading out of town and New York was sucking people inward at that hour. Across the barrier, the southbound traffic was snarled.

'OK, where to?' she asked.

'Go past Fordham University. Past the conservatory, and park at the top.'

She nodded and made the lane changes. Fordham slid by on the left, and then the conservatory on the right. She used the museum entrance and found the lot just beyond it. It was mostly empty.

'Now what?'

He took the leather-bound folder with him.

'Just keep an open mind,' he said.

The conservatory was a hundred yards ahead of them. He had read all about it in a free leaflet, the day before. It was named for somebody called Enid Haupt and had cost a fortune to build in 1902, and ten times as much to renovate ninety-five years later, which was money well spent because the result was magnificent. It was huge and ornate, the absolute definition of urban philanthropy expressed in iron and milky white glass.

It was hot and damp inside. Reacher led Jodie around to the place he was looking for. The exotic plants were massed in huge beds bounded by little walls and railings. There were benches set on the edges of the walkways. The milky glass filtered the sunlight to a bright overcast. There was a strong smell of heavy damp earth and pungent blooms.

'What?' she asked. She was partly amused, partly impatient. He found the bench he was looking for and stepped away from it, close to the low wall. He stepped half a pace left, then another, until he was sure.

'Stand here,' he said.

He took her shoulders from behind and moved her into the same position he had just occupied. Ducked his head to her level and checked.

'Stand on tiptoes,' he told her. 'Look straight ahead.'

She made herself taller and stared ahead. Her back

was straight and her hair was spilled on her shoulders.

'OK,' he said. 'Tell me what you see.'

'Nothing,' she said. 'Well, plants and things.'

He nodded and opened the leather folder. Took out the glossy photograph of the grey emaciated Westerner, flinching away from his guard's rifle. He held it out, arm's length in front of her, just on the edge of her vision. She looked at it.

'What?' she asked again, half amused, half frustrated.

'Compare,' he said.

She kept her head still and flicked her eyes left and right between the photograph and the scene in front of her. Then she snatched the picture from him and held it herself, arm's length in front of her. Her eyes widened and her face went pale.

'Christ,' she said. 'Shit, this picture was taken here? Right here? It was, wasn't it? All these plants are exactly the same.'

He ducked down again and checked once more. She was holding the picture so the shapes of the plants corresponded exactly. A mass of some kind of palm on the left, fifteen feet high, fronds of fern to the right and behind in a tangled spray. The two figures would have been twenty feet into the dense flower bed, picked out by a telephoto lens that compressed the perspective and threw the nearer vegetation out of focus. Well to the rear was a jungle hardwood, which the camera had blurred with distance. It was actually growing in a different bed.

'Shit,' she said again. 'Shit, I don't believe it.'

The light was right, too. The milky glass way above them gave a pretty good impersonation of jungle overcast. Vietnam is a mostly cloudy place. The jagged mountains suck the clouds down, and most people remember the fogs and the mists, like the ground itself is always steaming. Jodie stared between the photo and the reality in front of her, dodging fractionally left and right to get a perfect fit.

'But what about the wire? The bamboo poles? It looks so real.'

'Stage props,' he said. 'Three poles, ten yards of barbed wire. How difficult is that to get? They carried it in here, probably all rolled up.'

'But when? How?'

He shrugged. 'Maybe early one morning? When the place was still closed? Maybe they know somebody who works here. Maybe they did it while the place was closed for the renovations.'

She was staring at the picture, close up to her eyes. 'Wait a damn minute. You can see that bench. You can see the corner of that bench over there.'

She showed him what she meant, with her fingernail placed precisely on the glossy surface of the photograph. There was a tiny square blur, white. It was the corner of an iron bench, off to the right, behind the main scene. The telephoto lens had been framed tight, but not quite tight enough.

'I didn't spot that,' he said. 'You're getting good at this.'

She turned around to face him. 'No, I'm getting good and mad, Reacher. This guy Rutter took eighteen thousand dollars for a faked photograph.'

'Worse than that. He gave them false hope.'

'So what are we going to do?'

'We're going to pay him a visit,' he said.

They were back at the Taurus sixteen minutes after leaving it. Jodie threaded back towards the parkway, drumming her fingers on the wheel and talking fast.

'But you told me you believed it. I said the photo proved the place existed, and you agreed it did. You said you'd been there, not long ago, got about as close as Rutter had.'

'All true,' Reacher said. 'I believed the Botanical Gardens existed. I'd just come back from there. And I got as close as Rutter did. I was standing right next to the little wall where he must have taken the picture from.'

'Jesus, Reacher, what is this? A game?'

He shrugged. 'Yesterday I didn't know what it was. I mean in terms of how much I needed to share with you.'

She nodded and smiled through her exasperation. She was remembering the difference between yesterday and today. 'But how the hell did he expect to get away with it? The greenhouse in the New York Botanical Gardens, for God's sake?'

He stretched in his seat. Eased his arms all the way forward to the windshield.

'Psychology,' he said. 'It's the basis of any scam, right? You tell people what they want to hear. Those old folks, they wanted to hear their boy was still alive. So he tells them their boy probably is. So they invest a lot of hope and money, they're waiting on pins three whole months, he gives them a photo, and basically they're going to see whatever they want to see. And he was smart. He asked them for the exact name and unit, he wanted existing pictures of the boy, so he could pick out a middle-aged guy roughly the right size and shape for the photo, and he fed them back the right name and the right unit. Psychology. They see what they want to see. He could have had a guy in a gorilla suit in the picture and they'd have believed

284

it was representative of the local wildlife.'

'So how did you spot it?'

'Same way,' he said. 'Same psychology, but in reverse. I wanted to disbelieve it, because I knew it couldn't be true. So I was looking for something that seemed wrong. It was the fatigues the guy was wearing that did it for me. You notice that? Old worn-out US Army fatigues? This guy went down thirty years ago. There is absolutely no way a set of fatigues would last thirty years in the jungle. They'd have rotted off in six weeks.'

'But why there? What made you look in the Botanical Gardens?'

He spread his fingers against the windshield glass, pushing to ease the tension in his shoulders. 'Where else would he find vegetation like that? Hawaii, maybe, but why spend the airfare for three people when it's available free right on his doorstep?'

'And the Vietnamese boy?'

'Probably a college kid,' he said. 'Probably right here at Fordham. Maybe Columbia. Maybe he wasn't Vietnamese at all. Could have been a waiter from a Chinese restaurant. Rutter probably paid him twenty bucks for the photo. He's probably got four friends taking turns playing the American captive. A big white guy, a small white guy, a big black guy, a small black guy, all the bases covered. All of them bums, so they look thin and haggard. Probably paid them in bourbon. Probably took all the pictures at the same time, uses them as appropriate. He could have sold that exact same picture a dozen times over. Anyone whose missing boy was tall and white, they get a copy. Then he swears them all to secrecy with this government-conspiracy shit, so nobody will ever compare notes afterward.'

'He's disgusting,' she said.

He nodded. 'That's for damn sure. BNR families are still a big, vulnerable market, I guess, and he's feeding off it like a maggot.'

'BNR?' she asked.

'Body not recovered,' he said. 'That's what they are. KIA/BNR. Killed in action, body not recovered.'

'Killed? You don't believe there are still any prisoners?'

He shook his head.

'There are no prisoners, Jodie,' he said. 'Not any more. That's all bullshit.'

'You sure?'

'Totally certain.'

'How can you be certain?'

'I just know,' he said. 'Like I know the sky is blue and the grass is green and you've got a great ass.'

She smiled as she drove. 'I'm a lawyer, Reacher. That kind of proof just doesn't do it for me.'

'Historical facts,' he said. 'The story about holding hostages to get American aid is all baloney, for a start. They were planning to come running south down the Ho Chi Minh Trail as soon as we were out of there, which was right against the Paris Accords, so they knew they were never going to get any aid no matter what they did. So they let all the prisoners go in '73, a bit slowly, I know, but they let them go. When we left in '75, they scooped up about a hundred stragglers, and then they handed them all straight back to us, which doesn't jibe with any kind of a hostage strategy. Plus they were desperate for us to de-mine their harbours, so they didn't play silly games.'

'They were slow about returning remains,' she said. 'You know, our boys killed in plane crashes or

286

battles. They played silly games about that.'

He nodded. 'They didn't really understand. It was important to us. We wanted two thousand bodies back. They couldn't understand why. They'd been at war more than forty years: Japanese, French, the US, China. They probably lost a million people missing in action. Our two thousand was a drop in the bucket. Plus they were Communists. They didn't share the value we put on individuals. It's a psychological thing again. But it doesn't mean they kept secret prisoners in secret camps.'

'Not a very conclusive argument,' she said drily.

He nodded again. 'Leon's the conclusive argument. Your old man, and people just like him. I know those people. Brave, honourable people, Jodie. They fought there, and then they rose to power and prominence later. The Pentagon is stuffed full of assholes, I know that as well as anybody, but there were always enough people like Leon around to keep them honest. You answer me a question: if Leon had known there were still prisoners kept back in 'Nam, what would he have done?'

She shrugged. 'I don't know. Something, obviously.'

'You bet your ass something,' he said. 'Leon would have torn the White House apart brick by brick, until all those boys were safely back home. But he didn't. And that's not because he didn't know. Leon knew everything there was to know. There's no way they could have kept a thing like that a secret from all the Leons, not all the time. A big conspiracy lasting six administrations? A conspiracy people like Leon couldn't sniff out? Forget about it. The Leons of this world never reacted, so it was never happening. That's conclusive proof, as far as I'm concerned, Jodie.'

'No, that's faith,' she said.

'Whatever, it's good enough for me.'

She watched the traffic ahead, and thought about it. Then she nodded, because in the end, faith in her father was good enough for her, too.

'So Victor Hobie's dead?'

Reacher nodded. 'Has to be. Killed in action, body not recovered.'

She drove on, slowly. They were heading south, and the traffic was bad.

'OK, no prisoners, no camps,' she said. 'No government conspiracy. So they weren't government people who were shooting at us and crashing their cars into us.'

'I never thought it was,' he said. 'Most government people I met were a lot more efficient than that. I was a government person, in a manner of speaking. You think I'd miss two days in a row?'

She slewed the car right and jammed to a stop on the shoulder. Turned in her seat to face him, blue eyes wide.

'So it must be Rutter,' she said. 'Who else can it be? He's running a lucrative scam, right? And he's prepared to protect it. He thinks we're going to expose it. So he's been looking for us. And now we're planning to walk right into his arms.'

Reacher smiled.

'Hey, life's full of dangers,' he said.

Marilyn realized she must have fallen asleep, because she woke up stiff and cold with noises coming through the door at her. The bathroom had no window, and she had no idea what time it was. Morning, she guessed, because she felt like she had been asleep some

288

time. On her left, Chester was staring into space, his gaze fixed a thousand miles beyond the fixtures under the sink. He was inert. She turned and looked straight at him, and got no response at all. On her right, Sheryl was curled on the floor. She was breathing heavily through her mouth. Her nose had turned black and shiny and swollen. Marilyn stared at her and swallowed. Turned again and pressed her ear to the door. Listened hard.

There were two men out there. The sound of two deep voices, talking low. She could hear elevators in the distance. A very faint traffic rumble, with occasional sirens, vanishing into stillness. Aircraft noise, like a big jet from JFK was wheeling away west across the harbour. She eased herself off the floor.

Her shoes had come off during the night. She found them scuffed under her pile of towels. She slipped them on and walked quietly to the sink. Chester was staring straight through her. She checked herself in the mirror. *Not too bad*, she thought. The last time she had spent the night on a bathroom floor was after a sorority party more than twenty years before, and she looked no worse now than she had then. She combed her hair with her fingers and patted water on her eyes. Then she crept back to the door and listened again.

Two men, but she was pretty sure Hobie wasn't one of them. There was some equality in the tenor of the voices. It was back-and-forth conversation, not orders and obedience. She slid the pile of towels backward with her foot and took a deep breath and opened the door.

Two men stopped talking and turned to stare at her. The one called Tony was sitting sideways on the sofa in front of the desk. Another she had not seen before

289

was squatted next to him on the coffee table. He was a thickset man in a dark suit, not tall, but heavy. The desk was not occupied. No sign of Hobie. The window blinds were closed to a crack, but she could see bright sun outside. It was later than she thought. She glanced back to the sofa and saw Tony smiling at her.

'Sleep well?' he asked.

She made no reply. Just kept a neutral look fixed on her face until Tony's smile died away. *Score one*, she thought.

'I talked things over with my husband,' she lied.

Tony looked at her, expectantly, waiting for her to speak again. She let him wait. *Score two*, she thought.

'We agree to the transfer,' she said. 'But it's going to be complicated. It's going to take some time. There are factors I don't think you appreciate. We'll do it, but we're going to expect some minimum co-operation from you along the way.'

Tony nodded. 'Like what?'

'I'll discuss that with Hobie,' she said. 'Not with you.'

There was silence in the office. Just faint noises from the world outside. She concentrated on her breathing. In and out, in and out.

'OK,' Tony said.

Score three, she thought.

'We want coffee,' she said. 'Three cups, cream and sugar.'

More silence. Then Tony nodded and the thickset man stood up. He looked away and walked out of the office towards the kitchen. *Score four*, she thought.

The return address on Rutter's letter corresponded to a dingy storefront some blocks south of any hope of urban renewal. It was a clapboard building sandwiched between crumbling four-storey brick structures that may have been factories or warehouses before they were abandoned decades ago. Rutter's place had a filthy window on the left and an entrance in the centre and a roll-up door standing open on the right revealing a narrow garage area. There was a brand-new Lincoln Navigator squeezed in the space. Reacher recognized the model from advertisements he'd seen. It was a giant four-wheel-drive Ford, with a thick gloss of luxury added in order to justify its elevation to the Lincoln division. This one was metallic black, and it was probably worth more than the real estate wrapped around it.

Jodie drove right past the building, not fast, not slow, just plausible city-street speed over the potholed road. Reacher craned his head around, getting a feel for the place. Jodie made a left and came back around the block. Reacher glimpsed a service alley running behind the row, with rusted fire escapes hanging above piles of garbage.

'So how do we do this?' Jodie asked him.

'We walk right in,' he said. 'First thing we do is we watch his reaction. If he knows who we are, we'll play it one way. If he doesn't, we'll play it another.'

She parked two spaces south of the storefront, in the shadow of a blackened brick warehouse. She locked the car and they walked north together. From the sidewalk they could make out what was behind the dirty window. There was a lame display of Army-surplus equipment, dusty old camouflage jackets and water canteens and boots. There were field radios and MRE rations and infantry helmets. Some of the stuff was already obsolete before Reacher graduated from West Point.

The door was stiff and it worked a bell when it opened. It was a crude mechanical system whereby the moving door flicked a spring that flicked the bell and made the sound. The store was deserted. There was a counter on the right with a door behind it to the garage. There was a display of clothing on a circular chrome rack and more random junk piled high on a single shelf. There was a rear door out to the alley, locked shut and alarmed. In a line next to the rear door were five padded vinyl chairs. Scattered all around the chairs were cigarette butts and empty beer bottles. The lighting was dim, but the dust of years was visible everywhere.

Reacher walked ahead of Jodie. The floor creaked under him. Two paces inside, he could see a trapdoor open beyond the counter. It was a sturdy door, made from old pine boards, hinged with brass and rubbed to a greasy shine where generations of hands had folded it back. Floor joists were visible inside the hole, and a narrow staircase built from the same old wood was leading down towards hot electric light. He could hear feet scraping on a cement cellar floor below him.

'I'll be right there, whoever the hell you are,' a voice called up from the hole.

It was a man's voice, middle-aged, suspended somewhere between surprise and bad temper. The voice of a man not expecting callers. Jodie looked at Reacher and Reacher closed his hand around the butt of the Steyr in his pocket.

A man's head appeared at floor level, then his shoulders, then his torso, as he came on up the ladder. He was a bulky figure and had difficulty climbing out of the hole. He was dressed in faded olive fatigues. He had greasy grey hair, a ragged grey beard, a fleshy face, small eyes. He came out on hands and knees and stood up.

'Help you?' he said.

Then another head and shoulders appeared behind him. And another. And another. And another. Four men stamped up the ladder from the cellar. Each one straightened and paused and looked hard at Reacher and Jodie and then stepped away to the line of chairs. They were big men, fleshy, tattooed, dressed in similar old fatigues. They sat with big arms crossed against big stomachs.

'Help you?' the first guy said again.

'Are you Rutter?' Reacher asked.

The guy nodded. There was no recognition in his eyes. Reacher glanced at the line of men on their chairs. They represented a complication he had not anticipated.

'What do you want?' Rutter asked.

Reacher changed his plan. Took a guess about the true nature of the store's transactions and what was stacked up down in the cellar.

'I want a silencer,' he said. 'For a Steyr GB.'

Rutter smiled, real amusement in the set of his jaw and the light in his eyes.

'Against the law for me to sell you one, against the law for you to own one.'

The singsong way he said it was an outright confession that he had them and sold them. There was a patronizing undercurrent in the tone that said *I've got something you want and that makes me better than you.* There was no caution in his voice. No suspicion that Reacher was a cop trying to set him up. Nobody ever thought Reacher was a cop. He was too big and too rough. He didn't have the precinct pallor or the urban furtiveness people subconsciously associate with cops. Rutter was not worried about him. He was worried about Jodie. He didn't know what she was. He had spoken to Reacher but looked at her. She was looking back at him, steadily.

'Against whose law?' she asked dismissively.

Rutter scratched at his beard. 'Makes them expensive.'

'Compared to what?' she asked.

Reacher smiled to himself. Rutter wasn't sure about her, and with two answers, just six words, she had him adrift, thinking she could be anything from a Manhattan socialite worried about a kidnap threat against her kids, to a billionaire's wife intending to inherit early, to a Rotary wife aiming to survive a messy love triangle. She was looking at him like she was a woman used to getting her own way without opposition from anybody. Certainly not from the law, and certainly not from some squalid little Bronx trader.

'Steyr GB?' Rutter asked. 'You want the proper Austrian piece?'

Reacher nodded, like he was the guy who dealt with the trivial details. Rutter clicked his fingers and one of the heavy men peeled off from the line of chairs and dropped down the hole. He came back up a long moment later with a black cylinder wrapped in paper that gun oil had turned transparent.

'Two thousand bucks,' Rutter said.

Reacher nodded. The price was almost fair. The pistol was no longer manufactured, but he figured it probably last retailed around eight or nine hundred bucks. Final factory price for the suppressor was probably more than two hundred. Two grand for

294

illegal supply ten years later and four thousand miles from the factory gate was almost reasonable.

'Let me see it,' he said.

Rutter wiped the tube on his pants. Handed it over. Reacher came out with the gun and clicked the tube in place. Not like in the movies. You don't hold it up to your eyes and screw it on, slowly and thoughtfully and lovingly. You use light fast pressure and a half-turn and it clicks on like a lens fits a camera.

It improved the weapon. Improved its balance. Ninety-nine times in a hundred, a handgun gets fired high because the recoil flips the muzzle upward. The weight of the silencer was going to counteract that likelihood. And a silencer works by dispersing the blast of gas relatively slowly, which weakens the recoil in the first place.

'Does it work real good?' Reacher asked.

'Sure it does,' Rutter said. 'It's the genuine factory piece.'

The guy who had brought it upstairs was back on his chair. Four guys, five chairs. The way to take out a gang is to hit the leader first. It's a universal truth. Reacher had learned it at the age of four. Figure out who the leader is, and put him down first, and put him down hard. This situation was going to be different. Rutter was the leader, but he had to stay in one piece for the time being, because Reacher had other plans for him.

'Two thousand bucks,' Rutter said again.

'Field test,' Reacher said.

There is no safety catch on a Steyr GB. The first pull needs a pressure of fourteen pounds on the trigger, which is judged to be enough to avoid an accidental discharge if the gun is dropped, because fourteen pounds is a very deliberate pull. So there is no separate safety mechanism. Reacher flicked his hand left and pulled the fourteen pounds. The gun fired and the empty chair blew apart. The sound was loud. Not like in the movies. It's not a little cough. Not a polite little spit. It's like taking the Manhattan phone book and raising it way over your head and smashing it down on a desk with all your strength. Not a quiet sound. But quieter than it could be.

The four guys were frozen with shock. Shredded vinyl and dirty horsehair stuffing were floating in the air. Rutter was staring, motionless. Reacher hit him hard, left-handed in the stomach, and kicked his feet away and dumped him on the floor. Then he lined up the Steyr on the guy next to the shattered chair.

'Downstairs,' he said. 'All of you. Right now, OK?'

Nobody moved. So Reacher counted out loud *one, two,* and on *three* he fired again. The same loud blast. The floorboards splintered at the first guy's feet. *One, two,* and Reacher fired again. And again, *one, two,* and *fire.* Dust and wood splinters were bursting upward. The noise of the repeated shots was crushing. There was the strong stink of burned powder and hot steel wool inside the suppressor. The men moved all at once after the third bullet. They fought and crowded to the hatch. Crashed and tumbled through. Reacher dropped the door closed on them and dragged the counter over the top of it. Rutter was up on his hands and knees. Reacher kicked him over on his back and kept on kicking him until he had scrambled all the way backward and his head was jammed up hard against the displaced counter.

Jodie had the faked photograph in her hand. She crouched and held it out to him. He blinked and focused on it. His mouth was working, just a ragged hole in his beard. Reacher ducked down and caught his left wrist. Dragged his hand up and took hold of the little finger.

'Questions,' he said. 'And I'll break a finger every time you lie to me.'

Rutter started struggling, using all his strength to twist up and away. Reacher hit him again, a solid blow to the gut, and he went back down.

'You know who we are?'

'No,' Rutter gasped.

'Where was this picture taken?'

'Secret camps,' Rutter gasped. 'Vietnam.'

Reacher broke his little finger. He just wrenched it sideways and snapped the knuckle. Sideways is easier than bending it all the way back. Rutter shrieked in pain. Reacher took hold of the next finger. There was a gold ring on it.

'Where?'

'Bronx Zoo,' Rutter gasped.

'Who's the boy?'

'Just some kid.'

'Who's the man?'

'Friend,' Rutter gasped.

'How many times have you done it?'

'Fifteen, maybe,' Rutter said.

Reacher bent the ring finger sideways.

'That's the truth,' Rutter screamed. 'No more than fifteen, I promise. And I never did anything to you. I don't even know you.'

'You know the Hobies?' Reacher asked. 'Up in Brighton?'

He saw Rutter searching through a mental list, dazed. Then he saw him remember. Then he saw him struggling to comprehend how those pathetic old suckers could possibly have brought all this down on his head.

'You're a disgusting piece of shit, right?'

Rutter was rolling his head from side to side in panic.

'Say it, Rutter,' Reacher yelled.

'I'm a piece of shit,' Rutter whimpered.

'Where's your bank?'

'My bank?' Rutter repeated blankly.

'Your bank,' Reacher said.

Rutter hesitated. Reacher put some weight back on the ring finger.

'Ten blocks,' Rutter shrieked.

'Title deed for your truck?'

'In the drawer.'

Reacher nodded to Jodie. She stood up and went around behind the counter. Rattled open the drawers and came out with a sheaf of paperwork. She flicked through and nodded. 'Registered in his name. Cost forty thousand bucks.'

Reacher switched his grip and caught Rutter by the neck. Bunched his shoulder and pushed hard until the web of his hand was forcing up under Rutter's jaw.

'I'll buy your truck for a dollar,' he said. 'Just shake your head if you've got a problem with that, OK?'

Rutter was totally still. His eyes were popping under the force of Reacher's grip on his throat.

'And then I'll drive you to your bank,' he said. 'In my new truck. You'll take out eighteen thousand dollars in cash and I'll give it back to the Hobies.'

'No,' Jodie called. 'Nineteen-six-fifty. It was in a safe mutual. Call it six per cent, for a year and a half compounded.'

298

'OK,' Reacher said. He increased the pressure. 'Nineteen-six-fifty for the Hobies, and nineteen-six-fifty for us.'

Rutter's eyes were searching Reacher's face. Pleading. Not understanding.

'You cheated them,' Reacher said. 'You told them you'd find out what happened to their boy. You didn't do that. So now we'll have to do it for them. So we need expense money.'

Rutter was turning blue in the face. His hands were clamped hard on Reacher's wrist, desperately trying to ease the pressure.

'OK?' Reacher asked. 'So that's what we're going to do. Just shake your head if you've got any kind of a problem with any part of it.'

Rutter was dragging hard on Reacher's wrist, but his head stayed still.

'Think of it like a tax,' Reacher said. 'A tax on cheating little pieces of shit.'

He jerked his hand away and stood up. Fifteen minutes later, he was in Rutter's bank. Rutter was nursing his left hand in his pocket and signing a cheque with his right. Five minutes after that, Reacher had 39,300 cash dollars zipped into the sports bag. Fifteen minutes after that, he left Rutter in the alley behind his store, with two dollar bills stuffed in his mouth, one for the silencer, and one for the truck. Five minutes after that, he was following Jodie's Taurus up to the Hertz return at LaGuardia. Fifteen minutes after that, they were in the new Lincoln together, heading back to Manhattan.

ELEVEN

Evening falls in Hanoi a full twelve hours earlier than in New York, so the sun which was still high as Reacher and Jodie left the Bronx had already slipped behind the highlands of northern Laos, two hundred miles away to the west of Noi Bai Airport. The sky was glowing orange and the long shadows of late afternoon were replaced by the sudden dull gloom of tropical dusk. The smells of the city and the jungle were masked under the reek of kerosene, and the noises of car horns and night-time insects were blown away by the steady whine of jet engines idling.

A giant US Air Force C-141 Starlifter transport was standing on the forecourt, a mile from the crowded passenger terminals, next to an unmarked hangar. The plane's rear ramp was down, and its engines were running fast enough to power the interior lighting. Inside the unmarked hanger, too, lights were on. There were a hundred arc lights, slung high up under the corrugated metal roof, washing the cavernous space with their bright yellow glow.

The hangar was as large as a stadium, but it held nothing except seven caskets. Each one of them was six and a half feet long, made from ribbed aluminium polished to a high shine and shaped roughly like a coffin, which is exactly what each one of them was. They were standing in a neat row, on trestles, each one draped with an American flag. The flags were newly laundered and crisply pressed, and the centre stripe of each flag was precisely aligned with the centre rib of each casket.

There were nine men and two women in the hangar, standing next to the seven aluminium caskets. Six of the men were there as the honour guard. They were regular soldiers of the United States Army, newly shaved, dressed in immaculate ceremonial uniforms, holding themselves at rigid attention, away from the other five people. Three of those were Vietnamese, two men and a woman, short, dark, impassive. They were dressed in uniform, too, but theirs were everyday uniforms, not ceremonial. Dark olive cloth, worn and creased, badged here and there with the unfamiliar insignia of their rank.

The last two people were Americans, dressed in civilian clothes, but the sort of civilian clothes that indicate military status as clearly as any uniform. The woman was young, with a mid-length canvas skirt and a long-sleeved khaki blouse, with heavy brown shoes on her feet. The man was tall, silver-haired, maybe fifty-five years old, dressed in tropical khakis under a lightweight belted raincoat. He was carrying a battered brown leather briefcase in his hand, and there was a garment bag of similar vintage on the ground at his feet.

The tall silver-haired man nodded to the honour guard, a tiny signal, almost imperceptible. The senior soldier spoke a muted command and the six men formed up in two lines of three. They slow-marched forward, and right-turned, and slow-marched again until they were lined up precisely, three each side of the first casket. They paused a beat and stooped and lifted the casket to their shoulders in a single fluid movement. The senior man spoke again, and they slow-marched forward towards the hangar door, the casket supported exactly level on their linked arms, the only sounds the crunch of their boots on the concrete and the whine of the waiting engines.

On the forecourt, they turned right and wheeled a wide slow semicircle through the hot jet wash until they were lined up with the Starlifter's ramp. They slow-marched forward, up the exact centre of the ramp, feeling carefully with their feet for the metal ribs bolted there to help them, and on into the belly of the plane. The pilot was waiting for them. She was a US Air Force captain, trim in a tropical-issue flight suit. Her crew was standing at attention with her, a co-pilot, a flight engineer, a navigator, a radio operator. Opposite them were the loadmaster and his crew, silent in green fatigues. They stood face-to-face in two still lines, and the honour guard filed slowly between them, all the way up to the forward loading bay. There they bent their knees and gently lowered the casket on to a shelf built along the fuselage wall. Four of the men stood back, heads bowed. The forward man and the rear man worked together to slide the casket into place. The loadmaster stepped forward and secured it with rubber straps. Then he stepped back and joined the honour guard and held a long silent salute.

It took an hour to load all seven caskets. The people inside the hangar stood silent throughout, and then they followed the seventh casket on to the forecourt. They matched their walk to the honour guard's slow pace, and waited at the bottom of the Starlifter's ramp in the hot noisy damp of the evening. The honour guard came out, duty done. The tall silver-haired American saluted them and shook hands with the three Vietnamese officers and nodded to the American woman. No words were exchanged. He shouldered his garment bag and ran lightly up the ramp into the plane. A slow powerful motor whirred and the ramp closed shut behind him. The engines ran up to speed and the giant plane came off its brakes and started to taxi. It wheeled a wide cumbersome left and disappeared behind the hangar. Its noise grew faint. Then it grew loud again in the distance and the watchers saw it come back along the runway, engines screaming, accelerating hard, lifting off. It yawed right, climbing fast, turning, dipping a wing, and then it was gone, just a triangle of winking lights tiny in the distance and a vague smudge of black kerosene smoke tracing its curved path into the night air.

The honour guard dispersed in the sudden silence and the American woman shook hands with the three Vietnamese officers and walked back to her car. The three Vietnamese officers walked in a different direction, back to theirs. It was a Japanese sedan, repainted a dull military green. The woman drove, and the two men sat in the back. It was a short trip to the centre of Hanoi. The woman parked in a chain-link compound behind a low concrete building painted the colour of sand. The men got out without a word and went inside through an unmarked door. The woman locked the car and walked around the building to a different entrance. She went inside and up a short flight of stairs to her office. There was a bound ledger open on her desk. She recorded the safe despatch of the cargo in neat handwriting and closed the ledger. She carried it to a filing cabinet near her office door. She locked it inside, and glanced through the door, up and down the corridor. Then she returned to her desk and picked up her telephone and dialled a number eleven thousand miles away in New York.

Marilyn got Sheryl woken up and Chester brought round into some sort of consciousness before the thickset man came into the bathroom with the coffee. It was in mugs, and he was holding them two in one hand and one in the other, unsure of where to leave them. He paused and stepped to the sink and lined them up on the narrow granite ledge under the mirror. Then he turned without speaking and walked back out. Pulled the door closed after him, firmly, but without slamming it.

Marilyn handed out the mugs one at a time, because she was trembling and pretty sure she was going to spill them if she tried them two at a time. She squatted down and gave the first one to Sheryl, and helped her take the first sip. Then she went back for Chester's. He took it from her blankly and looked at it like he didn't know what it was. She took the third for herself and stood against the sink and drank it down, thirstily. It was good. The cream and the sugar tasted like energy.

'Where are the stock certificates?' she whispered.

Chester looked up at her, listlessly. 'At my bank, in my box.'

Marilyn nodded. Came face-to-face with the fact she didn't know which Chester's bank was. Or where it was. Or what stock certificates were for.

'How many are there?'

He shrugged. 'A thousand, originally. I used three

304

hundred for security against the loans. I had to give them up to the lender, temporarily.'

'And now Hobie's got those?'

He nodded. 'He bought the debt. They'll messenger the security to him, today, maybe. They don't need it any more. And I pledged him another ninety. They're still in the box. I guess I was due to deliver them soon.'

'So how does the transfer actually happen?'

He shrugged again, wearily, vaguely. 'I sign the stock over to him, he takes the certificates and registers them with the Exchange, and when he's got five hundred and one registered in his name, then he's the majority owner.'

'So where's your bank?'

Chester took his first sip of coffee. 'About three blocks from here. About five minutes' walk. Then another five minutes to the Exchange. Call it ten minutes beginning to end, and we're penniless and homeless on the street.'

He set the mug on the floor and lapsed back into staring. Sheryl was listless. Not drinking her coffee. Her skin looked clammy. Maybe concussed, or something. Maybe still in shock. Marilyn didn't know. She had no experience. Her nose was awful. Black and swollen. The bruising was spreading under her eyes. Her lips were cracked and dry, from breathing through her mouth all night.

'Try some more coffee,' she said. 'It'll be good for you.'

She squatted beside her and guided her hand up to her mouth. Tilted the mug. Sheryl took a sip. Some of the hot liquid ran down her chin. She took another sip. She glanced up at Marilyn, with something in her eyes. Marilyn didn't know what it was, but she smiled back anyway, bright with encouragement.

'We'll get you to the hospital,' she whispered.

Sheryl closed her eyes and nodded, like she was suddenly filled with relief. Marilyn knelt beside her, holding her hand, staring at the door, wondering how she was going to deliver on that promise.

'Are you going to keep this thing?' Jodie asked.

She was talking about the Lincoln Navigator. Reacher thought about it as he waited. They were jammed up on the approach to the Triborough.

'Maybe,' he said.

It was more or less brand new. Very quiet and smooth. Black metallic outside, tan leather inside, four hundred miles on the clock, still reeking of new hide and new carpet and the strong plastic smell of a box-fresh vehicle. Huge seats, each one identical with the driver's chair, lots of fat consoles with drinks holders and little lids suggestive of secret storage spaces.

'I think it's gross,' she said.

He smiled. 'Compared to what? That tiny little thing you were driving?'

'That was much smaller than this.'

'You're much smaller than me.'

She was quiet for a beat.

'It was Rutter's,' she said. 'It's tainted.'

The traffic moved, and then stopped again halfway over the Harlem River. The buildings of Midtown were far away to his left, and hazy, like a vague promise.

'It's just a tool,' he said. 'Tools have no memory.'

'I hate him,' she said. 'I think more than I've ever hated anybody.'

306

He nodded.

'I know,' he said. 'The whole time we were in there I was thinking about the Hobies, up there in Brighton, alone in their little house, the look in their eyes. Sending your only boy off to war is a hell of a thing, and to be lied to and cheated afterward, Jodie, there's no excuse for that. Swap the chronology, it could have been my folks. And he did it fifteen times. I should have hurt him worse.'

'As long as he doesn't do it again,' she said.

He shook his head. 'The list of targets is shrinking. Not too many BNR families left now to fall for it.'

They made it off the bridge and headed south on Second Avenue. It was fast and clear ahead for sixty blocks.

'And it wasn't him coming after us,' she said quietly. 'He didn't know who we were.'

Reacher shook his head again. 'No. How many fake photographs do you have to sell to make it worth trashing a Chevy Suburban? We need to analyse it right from the beginning, Jodie. Two full-time employees get sent to the Keys and up to Garrison, right? Two full-time salaries, plus weapons and airfare and all, and they're riding around in the Tahoe, then a third employee shows up with a Suburban he can afford to just dump on the street? That's a lot of money, and it's probably just the visible tip of some kind of an iceberg. It implies something worth maybe millions of dollars. Rutter was never making that kind of money, ripping off old folks for eighteen thousand bucks a pop.'

'So what the hell *is* this about?'

Reacher just shrugged and drove, and watched the mirror all the way.

Hobie took the call from Hanoi at home. He listened to the Vietnamese woman's short report and hung up without speaking. Then he stood in the centre of his living room and tilted his head to one side and narrowed his good eye like he was watching something physical happening in front of him. Like he was watching a baseball soaring out of the diamond, looping upward into the glare of the lights, an outfielder tracking back under it, the fence getting closer, the glove coming up, the ball soaring, the fence looming, the outfielder leaping. Will the ball clear the fence? Or not? Hobie couldn't tell.

He stepped across the living room and out to the terrace. The terrace faced west across the park, from thirty floors up. It was a view he hated, because all the trees reminded him of his childhood. But it enhanced the value of his property, which was the name of the game. He wasn't responsible for the way other people's tastes drove the market. He was just there to benefit from them. He turned and looked left, to where he could see his office building, all the way downtown. The Twin Towers looked shorter than they should, because of the curvature of the earth. He turned back inside and slid the door closed. Walked through the apartment and out to the elevator. Rode down all the way to the parking garage.

His car was not modified in any way to help him with his handicap. It was a late-model Cadillac sedan with the ignition and the selector on the right of the steering column. Using the key was awkward, because he had to lean across with his left hand and jab it in backward and twist. But after that, he never had much of a problem. He put it in drive by using the hook on the selector and drove out of the garage one-handed, using his left, the hook resting down in his lap.

He felt better once he was south of Fifty-ninth Street. The park disappeared and he was deep in the noisy canyons of Midtown. The traffic comforted him. The Cadillac's air-conditioning relieved the itching under his scars. June was the worst time for that. Some particular combination of heat and humidity acted together to drive him crazy. But the Cadillac made it better. He wondered idly whether Stone's Mercedes would be as good. He thought not. He had never trusted the air on foreign cars. So he would turn it into cash. He knew a guy in Queens who would spring for it. But it was another chore on the list. A lot to do, and not much time to do it in. The outfielder was right there, under the ball, leaping, with the fence at his back.

He parked in the underground garage, in the slot previously occupied by the Suburban. He reached across and pulled the key and locked the Cadillac. Rode upstairs in the express elevator. Tony was at the reception counter.

'Hanoi called again,' Hobie told him. 'It's in the air.'

Tony looked away.

'What?' Hobie asked him.

'So we should just abandon this Stone thing.'

'It'll take them a few days, right?'

'A few days might not be enough,' Tony said. 'There are complications. The woman says she's talked it over with him, and they'll do the deal, but there are complications we don't know about.'

'What complications?'

Tony shook his head. 'She wouldn't tell me. She wants to tell you, direct.'

Hobie stared at the office door. 'She's kidding,

309

right? She damn well better be kidding. I can't afford any kind of complications now. I just pre-sold the sites, three separate deals. I gave my word. The machinery is in motion. What complications?'

'She wouldn't tell me,' Tony said again.

Hobie's face was itching. There was no air-conditioning in the garage. The short walk to the elevator had upset his skin. He pressed the hook to his forehead, looking for some relief from the metal. But the hook was warm, too.

'What about Mrs Jacob?' he asked.

'She was home all night,' Tony said. 'With this Reacher guy. I checked. They were laughing about something this morning. I heard them from the corridor. Then they drove somewhere, north on the FDR Drive. Maybe going back to Garrison.'

'I don't need her in Garrison. I need her right here. And him.'

Tony was silent.

'Bring Mrs Stone to me,' Hobie said.

He walked into his office and across to his desk. Tony went the opposite way, towards the bathroom. He came out a moment later, pushing Marilyn in front of him. She looked tired. The silk sheath looked ludicrously out of context, like she was a partygoer caught out by a blizzard and stranded in town the morning after.

Hobie pointed to the sofa.

'Sit down, Marilyn,' he said.

She remained standing. The sofa was too low. Too low to sit on in a short dress, and too low to achieve the psychological advantage she was going to need. But to stand in front of his desk was wrong, too. Too supplicant. She walked around to the wall of windows.

Eased the slats apart and gazed out at the morning. Then she turned and propped herself against the ledge. Made him rotate his chair to face her.

'What are these complications?' he asked.

She looked at him and took a deep breath.

'We'll get to that,' she said. 'First we get Sheryl to the hospital.'

There was silence. No sound at all, except the rumbling and booming of the populated building. Far away to the west, a siren sounded faintly. Maybe all the way over in Jersey City.

'What are these complications?' he asked again. He used the same exact voice, the same exact intonation. Like he was prepared to overlook her mistake.

'The hospital first.'

The silence continued. Hobie turned back to Tony.

'Get Stone out of the bathroom,' he said.

Stone stumbled out, in his underwear, with Tony's knuckles in his back, all the way to the desk. He hit his shins on the coffee table and gasped in pain.

'What are these complications?' Hobie asked him.

He just glanced wildly left and right, like he was too scared and disorientated to speak. Hobie waited. Then he nodded.

'Break his leg,' he said.

He turned to look at Marilyn. There was silence. No sound, except Stone's ragged breathing and the faint boom of the building. Hobie stared on at Marilyn. She stared back at him.

'Go ahead,' she said quietly. 'Break his damn leg. Why should I care? He's made me penniless. He's ruined my life. Break both his damn legs if you feel like it. But it won't get you what you want any quicker. Because there are complications, and the sooner we

311

get to them, the better it is for you. And we won't get to them until Sheryl is in the hospital.'

She leaned back on the window ledge, palms down, arms locked from the shoulder. She hoped it made her look relaxed and casual, but she was doing it to keep herself from falling on the floor.

'The hospital first,' she said again. She was concentrating so hard on her voice, it sounded like somebody else's. She was pleased with it. It sounded OK. A low, firm voice, steady and quiet in the silent office.

'Then we deal,' she said. 'Your choice.'

The outfielder was leaping, glove high, and the ball was dropping. The glove was higher than the fence. The trajectory of the ball was too close to call. Hobie tapped his hook on the desk. The sound was loud. Stone was staring at him. Hobie ignored him and glanced up at Tony.

'Take the bitch to the hospital,' he said sourly.

'Chester goes with them,' Marilyn said. 'For verification. He needs to see her go inside to the ER, alone. I stay here, as surety.'

Hobie stopped tapping. Looked at her and smiled. 'Don't you trust me?'

'No, I don't trust you. We don't do it this way, you'll just take Sheryl out of here and lock her up someplace else.'

Hobie was still smiling. 'Farthest thing from my thoughts. I was going to have Tony shoot her and dump her in the sea.'

There was silence again. Marilyn was shaking inside.

'You sure you want to do this?' Hobie asked her. 'She says one word to the hospital people, she gets you killed, you know that, right?'

Marilyn nodded. 'She won't say anything to

312

anybody. Not knowing you've still got me here.'

'You better pray she doesn't.'

'She won't. This isn't about us. It's about her. She needs to get help.'

She stared at him, leaning back, feeling faint. She was searching his face for a sign of compassion. Some acceptance of his responsibility. He stared back at her. There was no compassion in his face. Nothing there at all, except annoyance. She swallowed and took a deep breath.

'And she needs a skirt. She can't go out without one. It'll look suspicious. The hospital will get the police involved. Neither of us wants that. So Tony needs to go out and buy her a new skirt.'

'Lend her your dress,' Hobie said. 'Take it off and give it to her.'

There was a long silence.

'It wouldn't fit her,' Marilyn said.

'That's not the reason, is it?'

She made no reply. Silence. Hobie shrugged.

'OK,' he said.

She swallowed again. 'And shoes.'

'What?'

'She needs shoes,' Marilyn said. 'She can't go without shoes.'

'Jesus,' Hobie said. 'What the hell next?'

'Next, we deal. Soon as Chester is back here and tells me he saw her walk in alone and unharmed, then we deal.'

Hobie traced the curve of his hook with the fingers of his left hand.

'You're a smart woman,' he said.

I know I am, Marilyn thought. *That's the first of your complications.*

*   *   *

Reacher placed the sports bag on the white sofa underneath the Mondrian copy. He unzipped it and turned it over and spilled out the bricks of fifties. Thirty-nine thousand three hundred dollars in cash. He split it in half by tossing the bricks alternately left and right to opposite ends of the sofa. He finished up with two very impressive stacks.

'Four trips to the bank,' Jodie said. 'Under ten thousand dollars, the reporting rules don't apply, and we don't want to be answering any questions about where we got this from, right? We'll put it in my account and cut the Hobies a cashier's cheque for nineteen-six-fifty. Our half, we'll access through my gold card, OK?'

Reacher nodded. 'We need airfare to St Louis, Missouri, plus a hotel. Nineteen grand in the bank, we can stay in decent places and go business class.'

'It's the only way to fly,' she said. She put her arms around his waist and stretched up on tiptoes and kissed him on the mouth. He kissed her back, hard.

'This is fun, isn't it?' she said.

'For us, maybe,' he said. 'Not for the Hobies.'

They made three trips together to three separate banks and wound up at a fourth, where she made the final deposit and bought a cashier's cheque made out to Mr T. and Mrs M. Hobie in the sum of $19,650. The bank guy put it in a creamy envelope and she zipped it into her pocketbook. Then they walked back to Broadway together, holding hands, so she could pack for the trip. She put the bank envelope in her bureau and he got on the phone and established that United from JFK was the best bet for St Louis, that time of day.

'Cab?' she asked.

He shook his head. 'We'll drive.'

The big V-8 made a hell of a sound in the basement garage. He blipped the throttle a couple of times and grinned. The torque rocked the heavy vehicle, side to side on its springs.

'The price of their toys,' Jodie said.

He looked at her.

'You never heard that?' she said. 'Difference between the men and the boys is the price of their toys?'

He blipped the motor and grinned again. 'Price on this was a dollar.'

'And you just blipped away two dollars in gas,' she said.

He shoved it in drive and took off up the ramp. Worked around east to the Midtown Tunnel and took 495 to the Van Wyck and down into the sprawl of JFK.

'Park in short-term,' she said. 'We can afford it now, right?'

He had to leave the Steyr and the silencer behind. No easy way to get through the airport security hoops with big metal weapons in your pocket. He hid them under the driver's seat. They left the Lincoln in the lot right opposite the United building and five minutes later were at the counter buying two business-class one-ways to St Louis. The expensive tickets entitled them to wait in a special lounge, where a uniformed steward served them good coffee in china cups with saucers, and where they could read the *Wall Street Journal* without paying for it. Then Reacher carried Jodie's bag down the jet way into the plane. The business-class seats were two-on-a-side, the first half-dozen rows. Wide, comfortable seats. Reacher smiled.

'I never did this before,' he said.

He slid into the window seat. He had room to stretch out a little. Jodie was lost in her seat. There was room enough for three of her, side by side. The attendant brought them juice before the plane even taxied. Minutes later they were in the air, wheeling west across the southern tip of Manhattan.

Tony came back into the office with a shiny red Talbot's bag and a brown Bally carrier hanging by their rope handles from his clenched fist. Marilyn carried them into the bathroom and five minutes later Sheryl came out. The new skirt was the right size, but the wrong colour. She was smoothing it down over her hips with vague movements of her hands. The new shoes didn't match the skirt and they were too big. Her face looked awful. Her eyes were blank and acquiescent, like Marilyn had told her they should be.

'What are you going to tell the doctors?' Hobie called to her.

Sheryl looked away and concentrated on Marilyn's script.

'I walked into a door,' she said.

Her voice was low and nasal. Dull, like she was still in shock.

'Are you going to call the cops?'

She shook her head. 'No, I'm not going to do that.'

Hobie nodded. 'What would happen if you did?'

'I don't know,' she replied. Blank and dull.

'Your friend Marilyn would die, in terrible pain. You understand that?'

He raised the hook and let her focus on it from

across the room. Then he came out from behind the desk. Walked around and stood directly behind Marilyn. Used his left hand to lift her hair aside. His hand brushed her skin. She stiffened. He touched her cheek with the curve of the hook. Sheryl nodded, vaguely.

'Yes, I understand that,' she said.

It had to be done quickly, because although Sheryl was now in her new skirt and shoes, Chester was still in his boxers and undershirt. Tony made them both wait in reception until the freight elevator arrived, and then he hustled them along the corridor and inside. He stepped out in the garage and scanned ahead. Hustled them over to the Tahoe and pushed Chester into the back seat and Sheryl into the front. He fired it up and locked the doors. Took off up the ramp and out to the street.

He could recall offhand maybe two dozen hospitals in Manhattan, and as far as he knew most of them had emergency rooms. His instinct was to drive all the way north, maybe up to Mount Sinai on 100th Street, because he felt it would be safer to put some distance between themselves and wherever Sheryl was going to be. But they were tight for time. To drive all the way Uptown and back was going to take an hour, maybe more. An hour they couldn't spare. So he decided on St Vincent's on Eleventh Street and Seventh Avenue. Bellevue, over on Twenty-seventh and First, was better geographically, but Bellevue was usually swarming with cops, for one reason or another. That was his experience. They practically lived there. So St Vincent's it would be. And he knew St Vincent's had a big wide area facing the ER entrance, where

Greenwich Avenue sliced across Seventh. He remembered the layout from when they had gone out to capture Costello's secretary. A big wide area, almost like a plaza. They could watch her all the way inside, without having to stop too close.

The drive took eight minutes. He eased into the kerb on the west side of Seventh and clicked the button to unlock the doors.

'Out,' he said.

She opened the door and slid down to the sidewalk. Stood there, uncertain. Then she moved away to the pedestrian crossing, without looking back. Tony leaned over and slammed the door behind her. Turned in his seat towards Stone.

'So watch her,' he said.

Stone was already watching her. He saw the traffic stop and the walk light change. He saw her step forward with the crowd, dazed. She walked slower than the others, shuffling in her big shoes. Her hand was up at her face, masking it. She reached the opposite sidewalk well after the walk light changed back to DON'T. An impatient truck pulled right and eased around her. She walked on towards the hospital entrance. Across the wide sidewalk. Then she was in the ambulance circle. A pair of double doors ahead of her. Scarred, floppy plastic doors. A trio of nurses standing next to them, on their cigarette break, smoking. She walked past the nurses, straight to the doors, slowly. She pushed at them, tentatively, both hands. They opened. She stepped inside. The doors fell shut behind her.

'OK, you see that?'

Stone nodded. 'Yes, I saw it. She's inside.'

Tony checked his mirror and fought his way out

into the traffic stream. By the time he was a hundred yards south, Sheryl was waiting in the triage line, going over and over in her head what Marilyn had told her to do.

It was a short and cheap cab ride from the St Louis airport to the National Personnel Records Center building, and familiar territory for Reacher. Most of his Stateside tours of duty had involved at least one trip through the archives, searching backward in time for one thing or another. But this time, it was going to be different. He would be going in as a civilian. Not the same thing as going in dressed in a major's uniform. Not the same thing at all. He was clear on that.

Public access is controlled by the counter staff in the lobby. The whole archive is technically part of the public record, but the staff take a lot of trouble to keep that fact well obscured. In the past Reacher had agreed with that tactic, no hesitation. Military records can be very frank, and they need to be read and interpreted in strict context. He'd always been very happy they were kept away from the public. But now he *was* the public, and he was wondering how it was going to play. There were millions of files piled up in dozens of huge storerooms, and it would be very easy to wait days or weeks before anything got found, even with the staff running around like crazy and looking exactly like they were doing their absolute best. He had seen it happen before, from the inside, many times. It was a very plausible act. He had watched it, with a wry smile on his face.

So they paused in the hot Missouri sunshine after they paid off the cab and agreed on how to do it. They walked inside and saw the big sign: One File at a Time. They lined up in front of the clerk and waited. She was a heavy woman, middle-aged, dressed in a master sergeant's uniform, busy with the sort of work designed to achieve nothing at all except make people wait until it was done. After a long moment she pushed two blank forms across the counter and pointed to where a pencil was tied down to a desk with a piece of string.

The forms were access requests. Jodie filled in her last name as Jacob and requested all and any information on *Major Jack-none-Reacher, US Army Criminal Investigation Division*. Reacher took the pencil from her and asked for all and any information on *Lieutenant General Leon Jerome Garber*. He slid both forms back to the master sergeant, who glanced at them and dropped them in her out-tray. She rang a bell at her elbow and went back to work. The idea was some private would hear the bell, come pick up the forms, and start the patient search for the files.

'Who's working supervisor today?' Reacher asked.

It was a direct question. The sergeant looked for a way to avoid answering it, but she couldn't find one.

'Major Theodore Conrad,' she said reluctantly.

Reacher nodded. Conrad? Not a name he recalled.

'Would you tell him we'd like to meet with him, just briefly? And would you have those files delivered to his office?'

The way he said it was exactly halfway between a pleasant, polite request and an unspoken command. It was a tone of voice he had always found very useful with master sergeants. The woman picked up the phone and made the call.

'He'll have you shown upstairs,' she said, like in her

opinion she was amazed Conrad was doing them such a massive favour.

'No need,' Reacher said. 'I know where it is. I've been there before.'

He showed Jodie the way, up the stairs from the lobby to a spacious office on the second floor. Major Theodore Conrad was waiting at the door. Hot-weather uniform, his name on an acetate plate above his breast pocket. He looked like a friendly guy, but maybe slightly soured by his posting. He was about forty-five, and to still be a major on the second floor of the NPRC at forty-five meant he was going nowhere in a hurry. He paused, because a private was racing along the hallway towards him with two thick files in his hand. Reacher smiled to himself. They were getting the A-grade service. When this place wanted to be quick, it could be real quick. Conrad took the files and dismissed the runner.

'So what can I do for you folks?' he asked. His accent was slow and muddy, like the Mississippi where it originated, but it was hospitable enough.

'Well, we need your best help, Major,' Reacher said. 'And we're hoping if you read those files, maybe you'll feel willing to give it up.'

Conrad glanced at the files in his hand and stood aside and ushered them into his office. It was a quiet, panelled space. He showed them to a matched pair of leather armchairs and stepped around his desk. Sat down and squared the files on his blotter, one on top of the other. Opened the first, which was Leon's, and started skimming.

It took him ten minutes to see what he needed. Reacher and Jodie sat and gazed out of the window. The city baked under a white sun. Conrad finished with the files and studied the names on the request forms. Then he glanced up.

'Two very fine records,' he said. 'Very, very impressive. And I get the point. You're obviously Jack-none-Reacher himself, and I'm guessing Mrs Jodie Jacob here is the Jodie Garber referred to in the file as the general's daughter. Am I right?'

Jodie nodded and smiled.

'I thought so,' Conrad said. 'And you think being family, so to speak, will buy you better and faster access to the archive?'

Reacher shook his head solemnly.

'It never crossed our minds,' he said. 'We know all access requests are treated with absolute equality.'

Conrad smiled, and then he laughed out loud.

'You kept a straight face,' he said. 'Very, very good. You play much poker? You damn well should, you know. So how can I help you folks?'

'We need what you've got on a Victor Truman Hobie,' Reacher said.

'Vietnam?'

'You familiar with him?' Reacher asked, surprised.

Conrad looked blank. 'Never heard of him. But with Truman for a middle name, he was born somewhere between 1945 and 1952, wasn't he? Which made him too young for Korea and too old for the Gulf.'

Reacher nodded. He was starting to like Theodore Conrad. He was a sharp guy. He would have liked to pull his file to see what was keeping him a major, behind a desk out in Missouri at the age of forty-five.

'We'll work in here,' Conrad said. 'My pleasure.'

He picked up the phone and called directly to the storerooms, by-passing the master sergeant at the front desk. He winked at Reacher and ordered up the Hobie file. Then they sat in comfortable silence until the runner came in with the folder five minutes later.

'That was quick,' Jodie said.

'Actually it was a little slow,' Conrad said back. 'Think about it from the private's point of view. He hears me say H for Hobie, he runs to the H section, he locates the file by first and middle initials, he grabs it, he runs up here with it. My people are subject to the Army's normal standards for physical fitness, which means he could probably run most of a mile in five minutes. And although this is a very big place, there was a lot less than a mile to cover in the triangle between his desk and the H section and this office, believe me. So he was actually a little slow. I suspect the master sergeant interrupted him, just to frustrate me.'

Victor Hobie's file jacket was old and furred, with a printed grid on the cover where access requests were noted in neat handwriting. There were only two. Conrad traced the names with a finger.

'Requests by telephone,' he said. 'General Garber himself, in March of this year. And somebody called Costello, calling from New York, beginning of last week. Why all the sudden interest?'

'That's what we hope to find out,' Reacher said.

A combat soldier has a thick file, especially a combat soldier who did his fighting thirty years ago. Three decades is long enough for every report and every note to end up in exactly the right place. Victor Hobie's paperwork was a compressed mass about two inches deep. The old furred jacket was moulded tight around it. It reminded Reacher of Costello's black leather wallet, which he'd seen in the Keys bar. He hitched his chair closer to Jodie's and closer to the front edge of

Conrad's desk. Conrad laid the file down and reversed it on the shiny wood and opened it up, like he was displaying a rare treasure to interested connoisseurs.

Marilyn's instructions had been precise, and Sheryl followed them to the letter. The first step was *get treatment*. She went to the desk and then waited on a hard plastic chair in the triage bay. The St Vincent's ER was less busy than it sometimes is and she was seen within ten minutes by a woman doctor young enough to be her daughter.

'How did this happen?' the doctor asked.

'I walked into a door,' Sheryl said.

The doctor led her to a curtain area and sat her down on the examination table. Started checking the reflex responses in her limbs.

'A door? You absolutely sure about that?'

Sheryl nodded. Stuck to her story. Marilyn was counting on her to do that.

'It was half-open. I turned around, just didn't see it.'

The doctor said nothing and shone a light into Sheryl's left eye, then her right.

'Any blurring of your vision?'

Sheryl nodded. 'A little.'

'Headache?'

'Like you wouldn't believe.'

The doctor paused and studied the admission form.

'OK, we need X-rays of the facial bones, obviously, but I also want a full skull film and a CAT scan. We need to see what exactly happened in there. Your insurance is good, so I'm going to get a surgeon to take a look at you right away, because if you're going to need reconstructive work it's a lot better to start on that sooner rather than later, OK? So you need to get

324

into a gown and lie down. Then I'll put you on a painkiller to help with the headache.'

Sheryl heard Marilyn insist *make the call before the painkiller, or you'll fuzz out and forget.*

'I need to get to a phone,' she said, worried.

'We can call your husband, if you want,' the doctor said, neutrally.

'No, I'm not married. It's a lawyer. I need to call somebody's lawyer.'

The doctor looked at her and shrugged.

'OK, down the hall. But be quick.'

Sheryl walked to the bank of phones opposite the triage bay. She called the operator and asked for collect, like Marilyn had told her to. Repeated the number she'd memorized. The phone was answered on the second ring.

'Forster and Abelstein,' a bright voice said. 'How may we help you?'

'I'm calling on behalf of Mr Chester Stone,' Sheryl said. 'I need to speak with his attorney.'

'That would be Mr Forster himself,' the bright voice said. 'Please hold.'

While Sheryl was listening to the hold music, the doctor was twenty feet away, at the main desk, also making a call. Her call featured no music. Her call was to the NYPD's Domestic Violence Unit.

'This is St Vincent's,' she was saying. 'I've got another one for you. This one says she walked into a damn door. Won't even admit she's married, much less he's beating on her. You can come on down and talk to her any time you want.'

The first item in the file was Victor Hobie's original application to join the Army. It was brown at the edges and crisp with age, handwritten in the same neat left-handed schoolboy script they had seen in the letters home to Brighton. It listed a summary of his education, his desire to fly helicopters, and not very much else. On the face of it, not an obvious rising star. But around that time for every one boy stepping up to volunteer, there were two dozen others buying one-way tickets on the Greyhound to Canada, so the Army recruiters had grabbed Hobie with both hands and sent him straight to the doctor.

He had been given a flight medical, which was a tougher examination than standard, especially concerning eyesight and balance. He had passed A-1. Six feet one inch, 170 pounds, 20/20 vision, good lung capacity, free of infectious diseases. The medical was dated early in the spring, and Reacher could picture the boy, pale from the New York winter, standing in his boxers on a bare wooden floor with a tape measure tight around his chest.

Next item in the file showed he was given travel vouchers and ordered to report to Fort Dix in two weeks' time. The following batch of paperwork originated from down there. It started with the form he signed on his arrival, irrevocably committing himself to loyal service in the United States Army. Fort Dix was twelve weeks of basic training. There were six proficiency assessments. He scored well above average in all of them. No comments were recorded.

Then there was a requisition for travel vouchers to Fort Polk, and a copy of his orders to report there for a month of advanced infantry training. There were notes about his progress with weapons. He was rated good, which meant something at Polk. At Dix, you were rated good if you could recognize a rifle at ten paces. At Polk, such a rating spoke of excellent hand-to-eye co-ordination, steady muscle control, calm temperament. Reacher was no expert on flying, but he guessed the instructors would have been fairly sanguine about eventually letting this guy loose with a helicopter.

There were more travel vouchers, this time to Fort Wolters in Texas, where the US Army Primary Helicopter School was located. There was a note attached from the Polk CO indicating Hobie had turned down a week's leave in favour of heading straight there. It was just a bald statement, but it carried an approving resonance, even after all those years. Here was a guy who was just about itching to get going.

The paperwork thickened up at Wolters. It was a five-month stay, and it was serious stuff, like college. First came a month of pre-flight training, with heavy academic concentration on physics and aeronautics and navigation, taught in classrooms. It was necessary to pass to progress. Hobie had creamed it. The maths talent his father had hoped to turn to accountancy ran riot through those textbook subjects. He passed out of pre-flight top of his class. The only negative was a short note about his attitude. Some officer was criticizing him for trading favours for coaching. Hobie was helping some strugglers through the complex equations and in return they were shining his boots and cleaning his kit. Reacher shrugged to himself. The officer was clearly an asshole. Hobie was training to be a helicopter pilot, not a damn saint.

The next four months at Wolters were airborne for primary flight training, initially on H-23 Hillers. Hobie's first instructor was a guy called Lanark. His

training notes were written in a wild scrawl, very anec-
dotal, very un-military. Sometimes very funny. He
claimed learning to fly a helicopter was like learning
to ride a bike as a kid. You screwed it up, and you
screwed it up, and you screwed it up, and then all of a
sudden it came right and you never again forgot how
to do it. In Lanark's opinion, Hobie had maybe taken
longer than he ought to master it, but thereafter his
progress moved from excellent to outstanding. He
signed him off the Hiller and on to the H-19 Sikorsky,
which was like moving up to a ten-speed English racer.
He performed better on the Sikorsky than he had on
the Hiller. He was a natural, and he got better the more
complicated the machines became.

He finished Wolters overall second in his class,
rated outstanding, just behind an ace called A. A.
DeWitt. More travel vouchers had them heading out
together, over to Fort Rucker in Alabama, for another
four months in advanced flight training.

'Have I heard of this guy DeWitt?' Reacher asked.
'The name rings a bell.'

Conrad was following progress upside down.

'Could be General DeWitt,' he said. 'He runs the
Helicopter School back at Wolters now. That would
be logical, right? I'll check it out.'

He called direct to the storeroom and ordered up
Major General A. A. DeWitt. Checked his watch as the
phone went back down. 'Should be faster, because the
D section is nearer his desk than the H section. Unless
the damn master sergeant interferes with him again.'

Reacher smiled briefly and rejoined Jodie thirty
years in the past. Fort Rucker was the real thing, with
brand-new frontline assault helicopters replacing the
trainers. Bell UH-1 Iroquois, nicknamed Hueys. Big,

fierce machines, gas turbine engines, the unforgettable *wop-wop-wop* sound of a rotor blade forty-eight feet long and twenty-one inches wide. Young Victor Hobie had hurled one around the Alabama skies for seventeen long weeks, and then he passed out with credits and distinctions at the parade his father had photographed.

'Three minutes forty seconds,' Conrad whispered.

The runner was on his way in with the DeWitt jacket. Conrad leaned forward and took it from him. The guy saluted and went back out.

'I can't let you see this,' Conrad said. 'The general's still a serving officer, right? But I'll tell you if it's the same DeWitt.'

He opened the file at the beginning and Reacher saw flashes of the same paper as in Hobie's. Conrad skimmed and nodded. 'Same DeWitt. He survived the jungle and stayed onboard afterward. Total helicopter nut. My guess is he'll serve out his time down at Wolters.'

Reacher nodded. Glanced out of the window. The sun was falling away into afternoon.

'You guys want some coffee?' Conrad asked.

'Great,' Jodie said. Reacher nodded again.

Conrad picked up the phone and called the storeroom.

'Coffee,' he said. 'That's not a file. It's a request for refreshment. Three cups, best china, OK?'

The runner brought it in on a silver tray, by which time Reacher was up at Fort Belvoir in Virginia, with Victor Hobie and his new pal A. A. DeWitt reporting to the 3rd Transportation Company of the First Cavalry Division. The two boys were there two weeks, long enough for the Army to add *air-mobile* to their unit designation, and then to change it completely to Company B, 229th Assault Helicopter Battalion. At the end of the two weeks, the renamed company sailed away from the Alabama coast, part of a seventeen-ship convoy on a thirty-one-day sea voyage to Long Mai Bay, twenty miles south of Qui Nhon and eleven thousand miles away in Vietnam.

Thirty-one days at sea is a whole month, and the company brass invented make-work to keep boredom at bay. Hobie's file indicated he signed up for maintenance, which meant endlessly rinsing and greasing the disassembled Hueys to beat the salt air down in the ship's hold. The note was approving, and Hobie stepped on to the Indochina beach a first lieutenant, after leaving the States a second, and thirteen months after joining the Army as an officer candidate. Merited promotions for a worthy recruit. One of the good kids. Reacher recalled Ed Steven's words, in the hot sunshine outside the hardware store: *very serious, very earnest, but not really a whole lot out of the ordinary.*

'Cream?' Conrad asked.

Reacher shook his head, in time with Jodie.

'Just black,' they said, together.

Conrad poured and Reacher kept on reading. There were two variants of Huey in use at that time: one was a gunship, and the other was a transport chopper nicknamed a *slick*. Company B was assigned to fly slicks, servicing the First Cavalry's battlefield transport needs. The slick was a transport hack, but it was not unarmed. It was a standard Huey, with the side doors stripped off and a heavy machine-gun hung on a bungee cord in each open doorway. There were a pilot and a co-pilot, two gunners, and a crew chief acting as an all-purpose engineer and mechanic. The slick could lift as many grunts as could pack themselves into the boxy space between the two gunners' backs, or a ton of ammunition, or any combination.

There was on-the-job training to reflect the fact that Vietnam was very different from Alabama. There was no formal grading attached to it, but Hobie and DeWitt were the first new pilots assigned to the jungle. Then the requirement was to fly five combat missions as a co-pilot, and if you handled that, you took the pilot's seat and got your own co-pilot. Then the serious business started, and it was reflected in the file. The whole second half of the jacket was stuffed with mission reports on flimsy onion-skin paper. The language was dry and matter of fact. They were not written by Hobie himself. They were the work of the company despatch clerk.

It was very episodic fighting. The war was boiling all around him unabated, but Hobie spent a long time on the ground, because of the weather. For days at a time, the fogs and mists of Vietnam made it suicidal to fly a helicopter low-level into the jungle valleys. Then the weather would suddenly clear and the reports would clump together all under the same date: three, five, sometimes seven missions a day, against furious enemy opposition, inserting, recovering, supplying and resupplying the ground troops. Then the mists would roll back in, and the Hueys would wait inert once more in their laagers. Reacher pictured Hobie, lying in his hooch for days on end, frustrated or relieved, bored or tense, then bursting back into ter-rifying action for frantic exhausting hours of combat.

The reports were separated into two halves by paperwork documenting the end of the first tour, the routine award of the medal, the long furlough back in

New York, the start of the second tour. Then more combat reports. Same exact work, same exact pattern. There were fewer reports from the second tour. The very last sheet in the file recorded Lieutenant Victor Hobie's 991st career combat mission. Not routine First Cavalry business. It was a special assignment. He took off from Pleiku, heading east for an improvised landing zone near the An Khe Pass. His orders were to fly in as one of two slicks and exfiltrate the personnel waiting on the landing zone. DeWitt was flying back-up. Hobie got there first. He landed in the centre of the tiny landing zone, under heavy machine-gun fire from the jungle. He was seen to take onboard just three men. He took off again almost immediately. His Huey was taking hits to the airframe from the machine-guns. His own gunners were returning fire blind through the jungle canopy. DeWitt was circling as Hobie was heading out. He saw Hobie's Huey take a sustained burst of heavy machine-gun fire through the engines. His formal report as recorded by the despatch clerk said he saw the Huey's rotor stop and flames appear in the fuel tank area. The helicopter crashed through the jungle canopy four miles west of the landing zone, at a low angle and at a speed estimated by DeWitt to be in excess of eighty miles an hour. DeWitt reported a green flash visible through the foliage, which was normally indicative of a fuel-tank explosion on the forest floor. A search-and-rescue operation was mounted and aborted because of weather. No fragments of wreckage were observed. Because the area four miles west of the pass was considered inaccessible virgin jungle, it was procedure to assume there were no NVA troops on foot in the immediate vicinity. Therefore there had been no risk of immediate capture by the enemy. Therefore the eight men in the Huey were listed as missing in action.

'But why?' Jodie asked. 'DeWitt saw the thing blow up. Why list them as missing? They were obviously all killed, right?'

Major Conrad shrugged.

'I guess so,' he said. 'But nobody knew it for sure. DeWitt saw a flash through the leaves, is all. Could theoretically have been an NVA ammo dump, hit by a lucky shot from the machine as it went down. Could have been anything. They only ever said killed in action when they knew for damn sure. When somebody literally eyeballed it happening. Fighter planes went down alone two hundred miles out in the ocean, the pilot was listed as missing, not killed, because perhaps he could have swum away somewhere. To list them as killed, someone had to see it happen. I could show you a file ten times thicker than this one, packed with orders defining and redefining exactly how to describe casualties.'

'Why?' Jodie asked again. 'Because they were afraid of the press?'

Conrad shook his head. 'No, I'm talking about internal stuff here. Any time they were afraid of the press, they just told lies. This all was for two reasons. First, they didn't want to get it wrong for the next of kin. Believe me, weird things happened. It was a totally alien environment. People survived things you wouldn't expect them to survive. People turned up later. They found people. There was a massive search-and-recover deal running, all the time. People got taken prisoner, and Charlie never issued prisoner lists, not until years later. And you couldn't tell folks their boy was killed, only to have him turn up alive later on.

So they were anxious to keep on saying missing, just as long as they could.'

Then he paused for a long moment.

'Second reason is yes, they were afraid. But not of the press. They were afraid of themselves. They were afraid of telling themselves they were getting beat, and beat bad.'

Reacher was scanning the final mission report, picking out the co-pilot's name. He was a second lieutenant named F. G. Kaplan. He had been Hobie's regular partner throughout most of the second tour.

'Can I see this guy's jacket?' he asked.

'K section?' Conrad said. 'Be about four minutes.'

They sat in silence with the cold coffee until the runner brought F.G. Kaplan's life story to the office. It was a thick old file, similar size and vintage as Hobie's. There was the same printed grid on the front cover, recording access requests. The only note less than twenty years old showed a telephone enquiry had been made last April by Leon Garber. Reacher turned the file facedown and opened it up from the back. Started with the second-to-last sheet of paper. It was identical to the last sheet in Hobie's jacket. The same mission report, with the same eyewitness account from DeWitt, written up by the same clerk in the same handwriting.

But the final sheet in Kaplan's file was dated exactly two years later than the final mission report. It was a formal determination made after due consideration of the circumstances by the Department of the Army that F. G. Kaplan had been killed in action four miles west of the An Khe Pass when the helicopter he was co-piloting was brought down by enemy ground-to-air fire. No body had been recovered, but the death was

to be considered as actual for purposes of memorial-
izing and payment of pensions. Reacher squared the
sheet of paper on the desk.

'So why doesn't Victor Hobie have one of these?'

Conrad shook his head. 'I don't know.'

'I want to go to Texas,' Reacher said.

Noi Bai Airport outside Hanoi and Hickam Field
outside Honolulu share exactly the same latitude, so
the US Air Force Starlifter flew neither north nor
south. It just followed a pure west-east flight path
across the Pacific, holding comfortably between the
Tropic of Cancer and the Twentieth Parallel. Six
thousand miles, six hundred miles an hour, ten hours'
flight time, but it was on approach seven hours before
it took off, at three o'clock in the afternoon of the
day before. The Air Force captain made the usual
announcement as they crossed the date line and the tall
silver-haired American in the rear of the cockpit
wound his watch back and added another bonus day
to his life.

Hickam Field is Hawaii's main military air facility,
but it shares runway space and air-traffic control with
Honolulu International, so the Starlifter had to turn a
wide weary circle above the sea, waiting for a JAL 747
from Tokyo to get down. Then it turned in and flattened and came down behind it, tyres shrieking,
engines screaming with reverse thrust. The pilot was
not concerned with the niceties of civilian flying, so she
jammed the brakes on hard and stopped short enough
to get off the runway on the first taxiway. There was a
standing request from the airport to keep the military
planes away from the tourists. Especially the Japanese
tourists. This pilot was from Connecticut and had no

335

real interest in Hawaii's staple industry or Oriental sensitivities, but the first taxiway gave her a shorter run to the military compound, which is why she always aimed to take it.

The Starlifter taxied slowly, as was appropriate, and stopped fifty yards from a long low cement building near the wire. The pilot shut down her engines and sat in silence. Ground crew in full uniform marched slowly towards the belly of the plane, dragging a fat cable behind them. They latched it into a port under the nose and the plane's systems kicked in again under the airfield's own power. That way, the ceremony could be conducted in silence.

The honour guard at Hickam that day was the usual eight men in the usual mosaic of four different full-dress uniforms, two from the United States Army, two from the United States Navy, two from the United States Marine Corps, and two from the United States Air Force. The eight slow-marched forward and waited in silent formation. The pilot hit the switch and the rear ramp came whining down. It settled against the hot tarmac of American territory and the guard slow-marched up its exact centre into the belly of the plane. They passed between the twin lines of silent aircrew and moved forward. The loadmaster removed the rubber straps and the guard lifted the first casket off the shelves and on to their shoulders. They slow-marched back with it through the darkened fuselage and down the ramp and out into the blazing afternoon, the shined aluminium winking and the flag glowing bright in the sun against the blue Pacific and the green highlands of Oahu. They right-wheeled on the forecourt and slow-marched the fifty yards to the long, low cement building. They went inside and

336

bent their knees and laid the casket down. They stood in silence, hands folded behind them, heads bowed, and then they about-turned and slow-marched back towards the plane.

It took an hour to unload all seven of the caskets. Only when the task was complete did the tall silver-haired American leave his seat. He used the pilot's stairway, and paused at the top to stretch his weary limbs in the sun.

TWELVE

Stone had to wait five minutes behind the black glass in the rear of the Tahoe, because the loading dock under the World Trade Center was busy. Tony loitered near by, leaning on a pillar in the noisy dark, waiting until a delivery truck moved out in a blast of diesel and there was a moment before the next one could move in. He used that moment to hustle Stone across the garage to the freight elevator. He hit the button and they rode up in silence, heads down, breathing hard, smelling the strong smell of the tough rubber floor. They came out in the back of the eighty-eighth-floor lobby and Tony scanned ahead. The way was clear to the door of Hobie's suite.

The thickset man was at the reception counter. They walked straight past him into the office. It was dark, as usual. The blinds were pulled tight and it was quiet. Hobie was at the desk, sitting still and silent, gazing at Marilyn, who was on the sofa with her legs tucked underneath her.

'Well?' he asked. 'Mission accomplished?'

Stone nodded. 'She got inside OK.'

'Where?' Marilyn asked. 'Which hospital?'

'St Vincent's,' Tony said. 'Straight into the ER.'

338

Stone nodded to confirm it and he saw Marilyn smile a slight smile of relief.

'OK,' Hobie said into the silence. 'That's the good deed for the day. Now we do business. What are these complications I need to know about?'

Tony shoved Stone around the coffee table to the sofa. He sat down heavily next to Marilyn and stared straight ahead, focusing on nothing.

'Well?' Hobie said again.

'The stock,' Marilyn said. 'He doesn't own it outright.'

Hobie stared at her. 'Yes he damn well does. I checked it at the Exchange.'

She nodded. 'Well, yes, he owns it. What I mean is, he doesn't control it. He doesn't have free access to it.'

'Why the hell not?'

'There's a trust. Access is regulated by the trustees.'

'What trust? Why?'

'His father set it up, before he died. He didn't trust Chester to handle it all outright. He felt he needed supervision.'

Hobie stared at her.

'Any major stock disposals need to be co-signed,' she said. 'By the trustees.'

There was silence.

'Both of them,' she said.

Hobie switched his gaze to Chester Stone. It was like a searchlight beam flicking sideways. Marilyn watched his good eye. Watched him thinking. Watched him buying into the lie, like she knew he would, because it jibed with what he thought he already knew. Chester's business was failing, because he was a bad businessman. A bad businessman would have been spotted early by a close relative like a father.

339

And a responsible father would have protected the family heritage with a trust.

'It's unbreakable,' she said. 'God knows we've tried often enough.'

Hobie nodded. Just a slight movement of his head. Almost imperceptible. Marilyn smiled inside. Smiled with triumph. Her final comment had done it to him. A trust was a thing to be broken. It had to be fought. Therefore the attempts to fight it proved it existed.

'Who are the trustees?' he asked quietly.

'I'm one of them,' she said. 'The other is the senior partner at his law firm.'

'Just two trustees?'

She nodded.

'And you're one of them?'

She nodded again. 'And you've already got my vote. I just want to get rid of the whole damn thing and get you off our backs.'

Hobie nodded back to her. 'You're a smart woman.'

'Which law firm?' Tony asked.

'Forster and Abelstein,' she said. 'Right here in town.'

'Who's the senior partner?' Tony asked.

'A guy called David Forster,' Marilyn said.

'How do we set up the meeting?' Hobie asked.

'I call him,' Marilyn said. 'Or Chester does, but I think right now it would be better if I did.'

'So call him, set it up for this afternoon.'

She shook her head. 'Won't be that quick. Could be a couple of days.'

There was silence. Just the boom and shudder of the giant building breathing. Hobie tapped his hook on the desk. He closed his eyes. The damaged eyelid

340

stayed open a fraction. The eyeball rolled up and showed white, like a crescent moon.

'Tomorrow morning,' he said quietly. 'At the very latest. Tell him it's a matter of considerable urgency to you.'

Then his eyes snapped open.

'And tell him to fax the trust deeds to me,' he whispered. 'Immediately. I need to know what the hell I'm dealing with.'

Marilyn was shaking inside. She pushed down on the soft upholstery, trying to ground herself. 'There won't be a problem. It's really just a formality.'

'So let's go make the call,' Hobie said.

Marilyn was unsteady on her feet. She stood swaying, smoothing the dress down over her thighs. Chester touched her elbow, just for a second. A tiny gesture of support. She straightened and followed Hobie out to the reception counter.

'Dial nine for a line,' he said.

She moved behind the counter and the three men watched her. The phone was a small console. She scanned across the buttons and saw no speakerphone facility. She relaxed a fraction and picked up the handset. Pressed nine and heard a dial tone.

'Behave yourself,' Hobie said. 'You're a smart woman, remember, and right now you need to stay smart.'

She nodded. He raised the hook. It glittered in the artificial light. It looked heavy. It was beautifully made and lovingly polished, mechanically simple and terribly brutal. She saw him inviting her to imagine the things that could be done with it.

'Forster and Abelstein,' a bright voice said in her ear. 'How may we help you?'

'Marilyn Stone,' she said. 'For Mr Forster.'

Her throat was suddenly dry. It made her voice low and husky. There was a snatch of electronic music and then the boomy acoustic of a large office.

'Forster,' a deep voice said.

'David, it's Marilyn Stone.'

There was dead silence for a second. In that second, she knew Sheryl had done it right.

'Are we being overheard?' Forster asked quietly.

'No, I'm fine,' Marilyn said, brightness in her voice. Hobie rested the hook on the counter, the steel glittering chest high, eighteen inches in front of her eyes.

'You need the police for this,' Forster said.

'No, it's just about a trustees meeting. What's the soonest we can do?'

'Your friend Sheryl told me what you want,' Forster said. 'But there are problems. Our staff people can't handle this sort of stuff. We're not equipped for it. We're not that sort of law firm. I'll have to find you a private detective.'

'Tomorrow morning would be good for us,' she said back. 'There's an element of urgency, I'm afraid.'

'Let me call the police for you,' Forster said.

'No, David, next week is really too late. We need to move fast, if we can.'

'But I don't know where to look. We've never used private detectives.'

'Hold on a moment, David.' She covered the mouthpiece with the heel of her hand and glanced up at Hobie. 'If you want it tomorrow, it's got to be at their offices.'

Hobie shook his head. 'It has to be here, on my turf.'

She took her hand away. 'David, what about the

342

day after tomorrow? It really needs to be here, I'm afraid. It's a delicate negotiation.'

'You really don't want the police? You absolutely sure about that?'

'Well, there are complications. You know how things can be sometimes, sort of delicate?'

'OK, but I'm going to have to find somebody suitable. It could take me some time. I'll have to ask around for recommendations.'

'That's great, David,' she said.

'OK,' Forster said again. 'If you're sure, I'll get on it right away. But I'm really not clear exactly what you're hoping to achieve.'

'Yes, I agree,' she said. 'You know we've always hated the way Dad set it up. Outside interference can change things, can't it?'

'Two in the afternoon,' Forster said. 'Day after tomorrow. I don't know who it'll be, but I'll get you someone good. Will that be OK?'

'Day after tomorrow, two in the afternoon,' she repeated. She recited the address. 'That's great. Thanks, David.'

Her hand was shaking and the phone rattled in the cradle as she hung it up.

'You didn't ask for the trust deeds,' Hobie said.

She shrugged nervously.

'There was no need. It's a formality. It would have made him suspicious.'

There was silence. Then Hobie nodded.

'OK,' he said. 'Day after tomorrow. Two in the afternoon.'

'We need clothes,' she said. 'It's supposed to be a business meeting. We can't be dressed like this.'

Hobie smiled. 'I like you dressed like that. Both of

343

you. But I guess old Chester here can borrow my suit back for the meeting. You'll stay as you are.'

She nodded, vaguely. She was too drained to push it.

'Back in the bathroom,' Hobie said. 'You can come out again day after tomorrow, two o'clock. Behave yourselves and you'll eat twice a day.'

They walked silently ahead of Tony. He closed the bathroom door on them and walked back through the dark office and rejoined Hobie in the reception area.

'Day after tomorrow is way too late,' he said. 'For God's sake, Hawaii is going to know *today*. Tomorrow, at the very latest, right?'

Hobie nodded. The ball was dropping through the glare of the lights. The outfielder was leaping. The fence was looming.

'Yes, it's going to be tight, isn't it?' he said.

'It's going to be crazy tight. You should just get the hell out.'

'I can't, Tony. I've given my word on the deal, so I need that stock. But it'll be OK. Don't you worry about it. Day after tomorrow at two-thirty, the stock will be mine, it'll be registered by three, it'll be sold on by five, we'll be out of here by suppertime. Day after tomorrow, it'll all be over.'

'But it's crazy. Involving a lawyer? We can't let a lawyer in here.'

Hobie stared at him.

'A lawyer,' he repeated slowly. 'You know what the basis of justice is?'

'What?'

'Fairness,' Hobie said. 'Fairness, and equality. They bring a lawyer, we should bring a lawyer, too, shouldn't we? Keep things fair?'

344

'Christ, Hobie, we can't have *two* lawyers in here.'

'We can,' Hobie said. 'In fact, I think we should.'

He walked around the reception counter and sat down where Marilyn had sat. The leather was still warm from her body. He took the Yellow Pages from a cubbyhole and opened it up. Picked up the phone and hit nine for a line. Then he used the top of the hook in seven precise little motions to dial the number.

'Spencer Gutman,' a bright voice said in his ear. 'How may we help you?'

Sheryl was on her back on a bed, with an IV needle taped into a vein in her left hand. The IV was a square polythene bag hanging off a curled steel stand behind her. The bag contained liquid, and she could feel the pressure as it seeped down into her hand. She could feel it pushing her blood pressure higher than usual. There was hissing in her temples, and she could feel the pulses behind her ears. The liquid in the bag was clear, like thick water, but it was doing the job. Her face had stopped hurting. The pain had just faded away, leaving her feeling calm and sleepy. She had almost called out to the nurse that she could manage without the painkiller now, because the pain had gone away anyhow, but then she caught herself and realized it was the drug that was taking it away, and it would come right back if the IV stopped. She tried to giggle at her confusion, but her breathing was too slow to get much of a sound out. So she just smiled to herself and closed her eyes and swam down into the warm depths of the bed.

Then there was a sound somewhere in front of her. She opened her eyes and saw the ceiling. It was white and illuminated from above. She swivelled her gaze towards her feet. It was a big effort. There were two people standing at the end of the bed. A man, and a woman. They were looking at her. They were dressed in uniforms. Short-sleeved blue shirts, long dark pants, big comfortable shoes for walking. Their shirts were all covered in badges. Bright embroidered badges and metal signs and plates. They had belts, all loaded down with equipment. There were nightsticks and radios and handcuffs. Revolvers with big wooden handles were strapped into holsters. They were police officers. Both of them were old. Quite short. Quite broad. The heavy loaded belts made them ungainly.

They were looking at her, patiently. She tried to giggle again. They were looking at the patient, patiently. The man was balding. The illuminated ceiling was reflected in his shiny forehead. The woman had a tight perm, dyed orange, like a carrot. She was older than he was. She must have been fifty. She was a mother. Sheryl could tell that. She was gazing down with a kind expression, like a mother would.

'Can we sit down?' the woman asked.

Sheryl nodded. The thick liquid was buzzing in her temples, and it was confusing her. The woman scraped a chair across the floor and sat down on Sheryl's right, away from the IV stand. The man sat directly behind her. The woman leaned towards the bed, and the man leaned the other way, so his head was visible in a line behind hers. They were close, and it was a struggle to focus on their faces.

'I'm Officer O'Hallinan,' the woman said.

Sheryl nodded again. The name suited her. The gingery hair, the heavy face, the heavy body, she needed an Irish name. And a lot of New York cops were Irish. Sheryl knew that. Sometimes it was like a family trade. One generation would follow the other.

'I'm Officer Sark,' the man said, from behind her.

He was pale. He had the sort of pale white skin that looks papery. He had shaved, but there was grey shadow showing. His eyes were deep set, but kindly. They were in a web of lines. He was an uncle. Sheryl was sure of that. He had nephews and nieces who liked him.

'We want you to tell us what happened,' the woman called O'Hallinan said.

Sheryl closed her eyes. She couldn't really remember what happened. She knew she had stepped in through Marilyn's door. She remembered the smell of rug shampoo. She remembered thinking that was a mistake. Maybe the client would wonder what needed covering up. Then she was suddenly on her back on the hallway floor with agony exploding from her nose.

'Can you tell us what happened?' the man called Sark asked.

'I walked into a door,' she whispered. Then she nodded, like she was confirming it to them. It was important. Marilyn had told her *no police*. Not yet.

'Which door?'

She didn't know which door. Marilyn hadn't told her. It was something they hadn't talked about. Which door? She panicked.

'Office door,' she said.

'Is your office here in the city?' O'Hallinan asked.

Sheryl made no reply. She just stared blankly into the woman's kindly face.

'Your insurance carrier says you work up in Westchester,' Sark said. 'At a real estate broker in Pound Ridge.'

Sheryl nodded, cautiously.

'So you walked into your office door in Westchester,' O'Hallinan said. 'And now you're in the hospital fifty miles away in New York City.'

'How did that happen, Sheryl?' Sark asked.

She made no reply. There was silence inside the curtained area. Hissing and buzzing in her temples.

'We can help, you know,' O'Hallinan said. 'That's why we're here. We're here to help you. We can make sure this doesn't happen again.'

Sheryl nodded again, cautiously.

'But you have to tell us how it came about. Does he do this often?'

Sheryl stared at her, confused.

'Is that why you're down here?' Sark asked. 'You know, new hospital, no records from the other times? If we were to ask up in Mount Kisco or White Plains, what would we find? Would we find they know you up there? From before, maybe? From the other times he's done this to you?'

'I walked into a door,' Sheryl whispered.

O'Hallinan shook her head. 'Sheryl, we know you didn't.'

She stood up and peeled the X-ray films off the light box on the wall. Held them up to the light from the ceiling, like a doctor would.

'Here's your nose,' she said pointing. 'Here's your cheekbones, and here's your brow, and here's your chin. See here? Your nose is broken, and your cheekbones, Sheryl. There's a depressed fracture. That's what the doctor is calling it. A depressed fracture. The bones are pushed down below the level of your chin and your brow. But your chin and your brow are OK. So this was done by something horizontal, wasn't it? Something like a bat? Swinging sideways?'

Sheryl stared at the films. They were grey and milky. Her bones looked like vague blurred shapes. Her eye sockets were enormous. The painkiller buzzed in her head, and she felt weak and sleepy.

'I walked into a door,' she whispered.

'The edge of a door is vertical,' Sark said, patiently. 'There would be damage to your chin and your brow as well, wouldn't there? It stands to reason, doesn't it? If a vertical thing had depressed your cheek-bones, it would have hit your brow and your chin pretty hard as well, wouldn't it?'

He gazed at the X-rays, sadly.

'We can help you,' O'Hallinan said. 'You tell us all about it, and we can keep it from happening again. We can keep him from doing this to you again.'

'I want to sleep now,' Sheryl whispered.

O'Hallinan leaned forward and spoke softly. 'Would it help if my partner left? You know, just you and me talking?'

'I walked into a door,' Sheryl whispered. 'Now I want to go to sleep.'

O'Hallinan nodded, wisely and patiently. 'I'll leave you my card. So if you want to talk to me when you wake up, you can just call me, OK?'

Sheryl nodded vaguely and O'Hallinan slipped a card from her pocket and bent down and placed it on the cabinet next to the bed.

'Don't forget, we can help you,' she whispered.

Sheryl made no reply. She was either asleep, or pretending to be. O'Hallinan and Sark pulled the curtain and walked away to the desk. The doctor looked up at them. O'Hallinan shook her head.

'Complete denial,' she said.

'Walked into a door,' Sark said. 'A door who was

probably juiced up, weighs about two hundred pounds and swings a baseball bat.'

The doctor shook her head. 'Why on earth do they protect the bastards?'

A nurse looked up. 'I saw her come in. It was really weird. I was on my cigarette break. She got out of a car, way on the far side of the street. Walked herself all the way in. Her shoes were too big, you notice that? There were two guys in the car, watched her every step of the way, and then they took off in a big hurry.'

'What was the car?' Sark asked.

'Big black thing,' the nurse said.

'You recall the plate?'

'What am I, Mr Memory?'

O'Hallinan shrugged and started to move away.

'But it'll be on the video,' the nurse said suddenly.

'What video?' Sark asked.

'Security camera, above the doors. We stand right underneath it, so the management can't clock how long we take out there. So what we see, it sees too.'

The exact time of Sheryl's arrival was recorded in the paperwork at the desk. It took just a minute to wind the tape back to that point. Then another minute to run her slow walk in reverse, backward across the ambulance circle, across the plaza, across the sidewalk, through the traffic, into the front of a big black car. O'Hallinan bent her head close to the screen.

'Got it,' she said.

Jodie chose the hotel for the night. She did it by finding the travel section in the nearest bookstore to the NPRC building. She stood there and leafed through the local guides until she found a place recommended in three of them.

350

'It's funny, isn't it?' she said. 'We're in St Louis here, and the travel section has more guides to St Louis than anyplace else. So how is that a travel section? Should be called the stay-at-home section.'

Reacher was a little nervous. This method was new to him. The sort of places he normally patronized never advertised in books. They relied on neon signs on tall poles, boasting attractions that had stopped being attractions and had become basic human rights about twenty years ago, like air and cable and a pool.

'Hold this,' she said.

He took the book from her and kept his thumb on the page while she squatted down and opened her carry-on. She rooted around and found her mobile phone. Took the book back from him and stood right there in the aisle and called the hotel. He watched her. He had never called a hotel. The places he stayed always had a room, no matter when. They were delirious if their occupancy rates ever made it above 50 per cent. He listened to Jodie's end of the conversation and heard her mentioning sums of money that would have bought him a bed for a month, given a little haggling.

'OK,' she said. 'We're in. It's their honeymoon suite. Four-poster bed. Is that neat, or what?'

He smiled. The honeymoon suite.

'We need to eat,' he said. 'They serve dinner there?'

She shook her head and thumbed through the book to the restaurant section.

'More fun to go someplace else for dinner,' she said. 'You like French?'

He nodded. 'My mother was French.'

She checked the book and used the mobile again and reserved a table for two at a fancy place in the

351

historic section, near the hotel.

'Eight o'clock,' she said. 'Gives us time to look around a little. Then we can check in at the hotel and get freshened up.'

'Call the airport,' he said. 'We need early flights out. Dallas–Fort Worth should do it.'

'I'll do that outside,' she said. 'Can't call the airport from a bookstore.'

He carried her bag and she bought a gaudy tourist map of St Louis and they stepped out into the heat of the late-afternoon sun. He looked at the map and she called the airline from the sidewalk and reserved two business-class seats to Texas, eight thirty in the morning. Then they set out to walk the banks of the Mississippi where it ran through the city.

They strolled arm in arm for ninety minutes, which took them about four miles, all the way around to the historic part of town. The hotel was a medium-sized old mansion set on a wide quiet street lined with chestnut trees. It had a big door painted shiny black and oak floors the colour of honey. Reception was an antique mahogany desk standing alone in the corner of the hallway. Reacher stared at it. The places he normally stayed, reception was behind a wire grille or boxed in with bulletproof plexiglas. An elegant lady with white hair ran Jodie's card through the swipe machine and the charge slip came chattering out. Jodie bent to sign it and the lady handed Reacher a brass key.

'Enjoy your stay, Mr Jacob,' she said.

The honeymoon suite was the whole of the attic. It had the same honey oak floor, thickly varnished to a high shine, with antique rugs scattered across it. The ceiling was a complicated geometric arrangement of slopes and dormer windows. There was a sitting room at one end with two sofas in pale floral patterns. The bathroom was next, and then the bedroom area. The bed was a gigantic four-poster, swathed in the same floral fabric and high off the ground. Jodie jumped up and sat there, her hands under her knees, her legs swinging in space. She was smiling and the sun was in the window behind her. Reacher put her bag down on the floor and stood absolutely still, just looking at her. Her shirt was blue, somewhere between the blue of a cornflower and the blue of her eyes. It was made from soft material, maybe silk. The buttons looked like small pearls. The first two were undone. The weight of the collar was pulling the shirt open. Her skin showed through at the neck, paler honey than the oak floor. The shirt was small, but it was still loose around her body. It was tucked deep into her belt. The belt was black leather, cinched tight around her tiny waist. The free end was long, hanging down outside the loops on her jeans. The jeans were old, washed many times and immaculately pressed. She wore her shoes on bare feet. They were small blue penny loafers, fine leather, low heels, probably Italian. He could see the soles as she swung her legs. The shoes were new. Barely worn at all.

'What are you looking at?' she asked.

She held her head at an angle, shy and mischievous. 'You,' he said.

The buttons *were* pearls, exactly like the pearls from a necklace, taken off the string and sewn individually on to the shirt. They were small and slippery under his clumsy fingers. There were five of them. He fiddled four of them out through their buttonholes and gently tugged the shirt out of the waistband of her jeans and undid the fifth. She held up her hands, left and right in turn, so he could undo the cuffs. He eased the shirt backward off her shoulders. She was wearing nothing underneath it.

She leaned forward and started on his buttons. She started from the bottom. She was dextrous. Her hands were small and neat and quick. Quicker than his had been. His cuffs were already open. His wrists were too wide for any store-bought cuff to close over them. She smoothed her hands up over the slab of his chest and pushed the shirt away with her forearms. It fell off his shoulders and she tugged it down over his arms. It fell to the floor with the sigh of cotton and the lazy click of buttons on wood. She traced her finger across the teardrop-shaped burn on his chest.

'You bring the salve?'

'No,' he said.

She locked her arms around his waist and bent her head down and kissed the wound. He felt her mouth on it, firm and cool against the tender skin. Then they made love for the fifth time in fifteen years, in the four-poster bed at the top of the old mansion while the sun in the window fell away west towards Kansas.

The NYPD's Domestic Violence Unit borrowed squad-room space wherever it could find it, which was currently in a large upstairs room above the administrative offices at One Police Plaza. O'Hallinan and Sark got back there an hour before the end of their shift. That was the paperwork hour, and they went straight to their desks and opened their notebooks to the start of the day and began typing.

They reached their visit to the St Vincent's ER with fifteen minutes to go. They wrote it up as a probable

354

incident with a non-co-operative victim. O'Hallinan spooled the form out of her typewriter and noticed the Tahoe's plate number scrawled at the bottom of her notebook page. She picked up the phone and called it in to the Department of Motor Vehicles.

'Black Chevrolet Tahoe,' the clerk told her. 'Registered to Cayman Corporate Trust with an address in the World Trade Center.'

O'Hallinan shrugged to herself and wrote it all down in her notebook. She was debating whether to put the form back in the typewriter and add the information to it when the DMV clerk came back on the line.

'I've got another tag here,' he said. 'Same registered owner abandoned a black Chevrolet Suburban on lower Broadway yesterday. Three-vehicle moving traffic incident. Fifteenth Precinct towed the wreck.'

'Who's dealing with it? You got a name at Fifteenth?'

'Sorry, no.'

O'Hallinan hung up and called traffic in the Fifteenth Precinct, but it was shift change at the end of the day and she got no farther with it. She scrawled a reminder to herself and dropped it in her in-tray. Then the clock ticked around to the top of the hour and Sark stood up opposite her.

'And we're out of here,' he said. 'All work and no play makes us dull people, right?'

'Right,' she said. 'You want to get a beer?'

'At least a beer,' Sark said. 'Maybe two beers.'

'Steady,' she said.

They took a long shower together in the honeymoon suite's spacious bathroom. Then Reacher sprawled in his towel on a sofa and watched her get ready. She went into her bag and came out with a dress. It was the same line as the yellow linen shift she'd worn to the office, but it was midnight blue and silk. She slipped it over her head and wriggled it down into place. It had a simple scoop neck and came just above the knee. She wore it with the same blue loafers. She patted her hair dry with the towel and combed it back. Then she went into the bag again and came out with the necklace he'd bought her in Manila.

'Help me with this?'

She lifted her hair away from her neck and he bent to fasten the clasp. The necklace was a heavy gold rope. Probably not real gold, not at the price he'd paid, although anything was possible in the Philippines. His fingers were wide and his nails were scuffed and broken from the physical labour with the shovel. He held his breath and needed two attempts to close the catch. Then he kissed her neck and she let her hair fall back into place. It was heavy and damp and smelled like summer.

'Well, I'm ready at least,' she said.

She grinned and tossed him his clothes from the floor and he put them on, with the cotton dragging against his damp skin. He borrowed her comb and ran it through his hair. In the mirror he caught a glimpse of her behind him. She looked like a princess about to go out to dinner with her gardener.

'They might not let me in,' he said.

She stretched up and smoothed the back of his collar down over the now exaggerated bulk of his deltoid muscle.

'How would they keep you out? Call the National Guard?'

It was a four-block walk to the restaurant. A June evening in Missouri, near the river. The air was soft and damp. The stars were out above them, in an inky sky the colour of her dress. The chestnut trees rustled in a slight warm breeze. The streets got busier. There were the same trees, but cars were moving and parking under them. Some of the buildings were still hotels, but some of them were smaller and lower, with painted signs showing restaurant names in French. The signs were lit with aimed spotlights. No neon anywhere. The place she'd picked was called La Préfecture. He smiled and wondered if lovers in a minor city in France were eating in a place called the Municipal Offices, which was the literal translation, as far as he recalled.

But it was a pleasant enough place. A boy from somewhere in the Midwest trying a French accent greeted them warmly and showed them to a table in a candlelit porch overlooking the rear garden. There was a fountain with underwater lighting playing softly and the trees were lit with spotlamps fastened to their trunks. The tablecloth was linen and the silverware was silver. Reacher ordered American beer and Jodie ordered Pernod and water.

'This is nice, isn't it?' she said.

He nodded. The night was warm and still, and calm.

'Tell me how you feel,' he said.

She looked at him, surprised. 'I feel good.'

'Good how?'

She smiled, shyly. 'Reacher, you're fishing.'

He smiled back. 'No, I'm just thinking about some-thing. You feel relaxed?'

She nodded.

'Safe?'

She nodded again.

'Me too,' he said. 'Safe and relaxed. So what does that mean?'

The boy arrived with the drinks on a silver tray. The Pernod was in a tall glass and he served it with an authentic French water jug. The beer was in a frosted mug. No long-neck bottles in a place like this.

'So what does it mean?' Jodie asked.

She splashed water into the amber liquid and it turned milky. She swirled the glass to mix it. He caught the strong aniseed smell.

'It means whatever is happening is small,' he said. 'A small operation, based in New York. We felt nervous there, but we feel safe here.'

He took a long sip of the beer.

'That's just a feeling,' she said. 'Doesn't prove anything.'

He nodded. 'No, but feelings are persuasive. And there's some hard evidence. We were chased and attacked there, but nobody out here is paying any attention to us.'

'You been checking?' she asked, alarmed.

'I'm always checking,' he said. 'We've been walking around, slow and obvious. Nobody's been after us.'

'No manpower?'

He nodded again. 'They had the two guys who went to the Keys and up to Garrison, and the guy driving the Suburban. My guess is that's all they've got, or they'd be out here looking for us. So it's a small unit, based in New York.'

She nodded.

'I think it's Victor Hobie,' she said.

The waiter was back, with a pad and a pencil. Jodie ordered pâté and lamb, and Reacher ordered soup and *porc aux pruneaux,* which had always been his Sunday lunch as a kid, any time his mother could find pork and prunes in the distant places they were stationed. It was a regional dish from the Loire, and although his mother was from Paris she liked to make it for her sons because she felt it was a kind of shorthand introduction to her native culture.

'I don't think it's Victor Hobie,' he said.

'I think it is,' she said. 'I think he survived the war somehow, and I think he's been hiding out somewhere ever since, and I think he doesn't want to be found.'

He shook his head. 'I thought about that, too, right from the start. But the psychology is all wrong. You read his record. His letters. I told you what his old buddy Ed Steven said. This was a straight-arrow kid, Jodie. Totally dull, totally normal. I can't believe he'd leave his folks hanging like that. For thirty years? Why would he? It just doesn't jibe with what we know about him.'

'Maybe he changed,' Jodie said. 'Dad always used to say Vietnam changed people. Usually for the worse.'

Reacher shook his head.

'He died,' he said. 'Four miles west of An Khe, thirty years ago.'

'He's in New York,' Jodie said. 'Right now, trying to stay hidden.'

He was on his terrace, thirty floors up, leaning on the railing with his back to the park. He had a cordless phone pressed to his ear, and he was selling Chester Stone's Mercedes to the guy out in Queens.

'There's a BMW too,' he was saying. 'Eight-series coupé. It's up in Pound Ridge right now. I'll take fifty cents on the dollar for cash in a bag, tomorrow.'

He stopped and listened to the guy sucking in air through his teeth, like car guys always do when you talk to them about money.

'Call it thirty grand for the both of them, cash in a bag, tomorrow.'

The guy grunted a yes, and Hobie moved on down his mental list.

'There's a Tahoe and a Cadillac. Call it forty grand, you can add either one of them to the deal. Your choice.'

The guy paused and picked the Tahoe. More resale in a four-wheel drive, especially some way south, which is where Hobie knew he was going to move it. He clicked the phone off and went inside through the sliders to the living room. He used his left hand to open his little leather diary and kept it open by flattening it down with the hook. He clicked the button again and dialled a real-estate broker who owed him serious money.

'I'm calling the loan,' he said.

He listened to the swallowing sounds as the guy started panicking. There was desperate silence for a long time. Then he heard the guy sit down, heavily.

'Can you pay me?'

There was no reply.

'You know what happens to people who can't pay me?'

More silence. More swallowing.

'Don't worry,' he said. 'We can work something out. I got two properties to sell. A mansion up in Pound Ridge, and my apartment on Fifth. I want two million for the house, and three-point-five for the apartment. You get me that and I'll write off the loan against your commission, OK?'

The guy had no choice but to agree. Hobie had him copy down the bank details in the Caymans and told him to wire the proceeds within a month.

'A month is pretty optimistic,' the guy said.

'How are your kids?' Hobie asked.

More swallowing.

'OK, a month,' the guy said.

Hobie clicked the phone off and wrote *$5,540,000* on the page where he had scored out three automobiles and two residences. Then he called the airline and enquired about flights to the coast, evening of the day after tomorrow. There was plenty of availability. He smiled. The ball was soaring right over the fence, heading for the fifth row of the bleachers. The outfielder was leaping like crazy, but he was absolutely nowhere near it.

With Hobie gone, Marilyn felt safe enough to take a shower. She wouldn't have done it with him out there in the office. There was too much in his leer. She would have felt he could see right through the bathroom door. But the one called Tony was not such a problem. He was anxious and obedient. Hobie had told him to make sure they didn't come out of the bathroom. He would do that, for sure, but nothing more. He wouldn't come in and hassle them. He would leave them alone. She was confident of that. And the other guy, the thickset one who had brought the coffee, he was doing what Tony told him. So she felt safe enough, but she still had Chester stand by the door with his hand on the handle.

She leaned in and set the shower running hot and stripped off her dress and her shoes. She folded the dress neatly over the curtain rail, out of the water

361

stream, but near enough for the steam to take the creases out. Then she stepped into the stall and washed her hair and soaped herself from head to foot. It felt good. It was relaxing. It took away the tension. She stood face up and soaked for a long time. Then she left the water running and stepped out and took a towel and changed places with Chester.

'Go ahead,' she said. 'It'll do you good.'

He was numb. He just nodded and let the door handle go. Stood for a second and stripped off his undershirt and his boxers. Sat naked on the floor and took off his shoes and socks. She saw the yellow bruise on his side.

'They hit you?' she whispered.

He nodded again. Stood up and stepped into the stall. He stood under the torrent with his eyes closed and his mouth open. Then the water seemed to revive him. He found the soap and the shampoo and washed himself all over.

'Leave the water running,' she said. 'It's warming the place up.'

It was true. The hot water was making the room comfortable. He stepped out and took a towel. Dabbed his face with it and wrapped it around his waist.

'And the noise means they can't hear us talking,' she said. 'And we need to talk, right?'

He shrugged, like there wasn't much to talk about. 'I don't understand what you're doing. There are no trustees. He's going to find that out, and then he'll just get mad.'

She was towelling her hair. She stopped and looked at him through the gathering cloud of steam. 'We need a witness. Don't you see that?'

362

'A witness to what?'

'To what happens,' she said. 'David Forster will send some private detective over here, and what can Hobie do? We'll just admit there is no trust, and then we'll all of us go down to your bank, and we'll hand Hobie the stock. In a public place, with a witness. A witness, and a sort of bodyguard. Then we can just walk away.'

'Will that work?'

'I think so,' she said. 'He's in some kind of a hurry. Can't you see that? He's got some kind of a deadline. He's panicking. Our best bet is to delay as long as we can, and then just slip away, with a witness watching the whole thing and guarding us. Hobie will be too uptight about time to react.'

'I don't understand,' he said again. 'You mean this private dick will testify we were acting under duress? You mean so we can sue Hobie to get the stock back?'

She was quiet for a beat. Amazed. 'No, Chester, we're not going to sue anybody. Hobie gets the stock, and we forget all about it.'

He stared at her through the steam. 'But that's no good. That won't save the company. Not if it means Hobie gets the stock and we've got no comeback.'

She stared back at him. 'God's sake, Chester, don't you understand anything? The company is gone. The company is history, and you better face it. This is not about saving the damn company. This is about saving our lives.'

The soup was wonderful and the pork was even better. His mother would have been proud of it. They shared a half-bottle of Californian wine and ate in contented silence. The restaurant was the sort of place that gave you a long pause between the main course and the dessert. No rush to get you out and reclaim the table. Reacher was enjoying the luxury. Not something he was used to. He sprawled back in his chair and stretched his legs out. His ankles were rubbing against Jodie's, under the table.

'Think about his parents,' he said. 'Think about him, as a kid. Open up the encyclopedia to N for 'normal American family' and you're going to see a picture of the Hobies, all three of them, staring right out at you. I accept that 'Nam changed people. I can see it kind of expanding his horizons a little. They knew that, too. They knew he wasn't going to come back and work for some dumb little print shop in Brighton. They saw him going down to the rigs, flying around the Gulf for the oil companies. But he would have kept in touch, right? To some extent? He wouldn't have just abandoned them. That's real cruelty, cold and consistent for thirty straight years. You see anything in his record that makes him that kind of a guy?'

'Maybe he did something,' she said. 'Something shameful. Maybe something like My Lai, you know, a massacre or something? Maybe he was ashamed to go home. Maybe he's hiding a guilty secret.'

He shook his head impatiently. 'It would be in his record. And he didn't have the opportunity, anyway. He was a helicopter pilot, not an infantryman. He never saw the enemy close up.'

The waiter came back with his pad and pencil.

'Dessert?' he asked. 'Coffee?'

They ordered raspberry sorbet and black coffee. Jodie drained the last of her wine. It shone dull red in the glass in the candlelight.

'So what do we do?'

'He died,' Reacher said. 'We'll get the definitive evidence, sooner or later. Then we'll go back and tell the old folks they've wasted thirty years fretting about it.'

'And what do we tell ourselves? We were attacked by a ghost?'

He shrugged and made no reply to that. The sorbet arrived and they ate it in silence. Then the coffee came, and the bill in a padded leather folder bearing the restaurant logo printed in gold. Jodie laid her credit card on it without looking at the total. Then she smiled.

'Great dinner,' she said.

He smiled back. 'Great company.'

'Let's forget all about Victor Hobie for a while,' she said.

'Who?' he asked, and she laughed.

'So what shall we think about instead?' she said.

He smiled. 'I was thinking about your dress.'

'You like it?'

'I think it's great,' he said.

'What?'

'But it could look better. You know, maybe thrown in a heap on the floor.'

'You think so?'

'I'm pretty sure,' he said. 'But that's just a guess, right now. I'd need some experimental data. You know, a before-and-after comparison.'

She sighed in mock exhaustion. 'Reacher, we need to be up at seven. Early flights, right?'

'You're young,' he said. 'If I can take it, you sure as hell can.'

She smiled. Scraped her chair back and stood up.

365

Stepped away from the table and turned a slow turn in the aisle. The dress moved with her. It was like a sheath, but not tight. It looked wonderful from the back. Her hair was gold against it in the candlelight. She stepped close and bent down and whispered in his ear.

'OK, that's the before part. Let's go before you forget the comparison.'

Seven o'clock in the morning in New York happened an hour before seven o'clock in the morning in St Louis, and O'Hallinan and Sark spent that hour in the squad room planning their shift. The overnight messages were stacked deep in the in-trays. There were calls from the hospitals, and reports from nightshift beat cops who had gone out to domestic disturbances. They all needed sifting and evaluating, and an itinerary had to be worked out, based on geography and urgency. It had been an average night in New York City, which meant O'Hallinan and Sark compiled a list of twenty-eight brand new cases which required their attention, which meant the call to the fifteenth precinct traffic squad got delayed until ten minutes to eight in the morning.

O'Hallinan dialled the number and reached the desk sergeant on the tenth ring. 'You towed a black Suburban,' she said. 'It got wrecked on lower Broadway couple of days ago. You doing anything about it?'

There was the sound of the guy scraping through a pile of paperwork.

'It's in the pound. You got an interest in it?'

'We got a woman with a busted nose in the hospital, got delivered there in a Tahoe owned by the same people.'

'Maybe she was the driver. We had three vehicles involved, and we only got one driver. There was the Suburban that caused the accident, driver disappeared. Then there was an Olds Bravada which drove away into an alley, driver and passenger disappeared. The Suburban was corporate, some financial trust in the district.'

'Cayman Corporate Trust?' O'Hallinan asked. 'That's who owns our Tahoe.'

'Right,' the guy said. 'The Bravada is down to a Mrs Jodie Jacob, but it was reported stolen prior. That's not your woman with the busted nose, is it?'

'Jodie Jacob? No, our woman is Sheryl somebody.'

'OK, probably the Suburban driver. Is she small?'

'Small enough, I guess,' O'Hallinan said. 'Why?'

'The airbag deployed,' the guy said. 'Possible a small woman could be injured that way, by the airbag. It happens.'

'You want to check it out?'

'No, our way of thinking, we got their vehicle, they want it, they'll come to us.'

O'Hallinan hung up and Sark looked at her enquiringly.

'So what's that about?' he asked. 'Why would she say she walked into a door if it was really a car wreck?'

O'Hallinan shrugged. 'Don't know. And why would a real-estate woman from Westchester be driving for a firm out of the World Trade Center?'

'Could explain the injuries,' Sark said. 'The airbag, maybe the rim of the steering wheel, that could have done it to her.'

'Maybe,' O'Hallinan said.

'So should we check it out?'

'We should try, I guess, because if it was a car

wreck it makes it a closed instead of a probable.'

'OK, but don't write it down anywhere, because if it wasn't a car wreck it'll make it open and pending again, which will be a total pain in the ass later.'

They stood up together and put their notebooks in their uniform pockets. Used the stairs and enjoyed the morning sun on the way across the yard to their cruiser.

The same sun rolled west and made it seven o'clock in St Louis. It came in through an attic dormer and played its low beam across the four-poster from a new direction. Jodie had gotten up first, and she was in the shower. Reacher was alone in the warm bed, stretching out, aware of a muffled chirping sound somewhere in the room.

He checked the nightstand to see if the phone was ringing, or if Jodie had set an alarm clock he hadn't noticed the night before. Nothing there. The chirping kept on going, muffled but insistent. He rolled over and sat up. The new angle located the sound inside Jodie's carry-on bag. He slid out of bed and padded naked across the room. Unzipped the bag. The chirping sounded louder. It was her mobile telephone. He glanced at the bathroom door and pulled out the phone. It was chirping loudly in his hand. He studied the buttons on it and pressed SEND. The chirping stopped.

'Hello?' he said.

There was a pause. 'Who's that? I'm trying to reach Mrs Jacob.'

It was a man's voice, young, busy, harassed. A voice he knew. Jodie's secretary at the law firm, the guy who had dictated Leon's address.

'She's in the shower.'

'Ah,' the voice said.

There was another pause.

'I'm a friend,' Reacher said.

'I see,' the voice said. 'Are you still up in Garrison?'

'No, we're in St Louis, Missouri.'

'Goodness, that complicates things, doesn't it? May I speak with Mrs Jacob?'

'She's in the shower,' Reacher said again. 'She could call you back. Or I could take a message, I guess.'

'Would you mind?' the guy said. 'It's urgent, I'm afraid.'

'Hold on,' Reacher said. He walked back to the bed and picked up the little pad and the pencil the hotel had placed on the nightstand next to the telephone. Sat down and juggled the mobile into his left hand.

'OK, shoot,' he said. The guy ran through his message. It was very non-specific. The guy was choosing his words carefully to keep the whole thing vague. Clearly a friend couldn't be trusted with any secret legal details. He put the pad and pencil down again. He wasn't going to need them.

'I'll have her call you back if that's not clear,' he said ambiguously.

'Thank you, and I'm sorry to interrupt, well, whatever it is I'm interrupting.'

'You're not interrupting anything,' Reacher said. 'Like I told you, she's in the shower right now. But ten minutes ago might have been a problem.'

'Goodness,' the guy said again, and the phone went dead.

Reacher smiled and studied the buttons again and pressed END. He dropped the phone on the bed and heard the water cut off in the bathroom. The door opened and she came out, wrapped in a towel and a cloud of steam.

'Your secretary just called on your mobile,' he said. 'I think he was a little shocked when I answered.'

She giggled. 'Well, there goes my reputation. It'll be all over the office by lunchtime. What did he want?'

'You've got to go back to New York.'

'Why? He give you the details?'

He shook his head.

'No, he was very confidential, very proper, like a secretary should be, I guess. But you're an ace lawyer, apparently. Big demand for your services.'

She grinned. 'I'm the best there is. Didn't I tell you that? So who needs me?'

'Somebody called your firm. Some financial corporation with something to handle. Asked for you personally. Presumably because you're the best there is.'

She nodded and smiled. 'He say what the problem is?'

He shrugged. 'Your usual, I guess. Somebody owes somebody else some money, sounds like they're all squabbling over it. You have to go to a meeting tomorrow afternoon and try to talk some sense into one side or the other.'

Another of the thousands of phone calls taking place during the same minute in the Wall Street area was a call from the law offices of Forster and Abelstein to the premises of a private detective called William Curry. Curry was a twenty-year veteran of the NYPD's detective squads, and he had taken his pension at the age of forty-seven and was looking to pay his alimony by working private until his ex-wife got married again or died or forgot about him. He had been in business for two lean years, and a personal call from the senior partner of a white-shoe Wall Street law firm was a breakthrough event, so he was pleased, but not too surprised. He had done two years of good work at reasonable rates with the exact aim of creating some kind of reputation, so if the reputation was finally spreading and the big hitters were finally calling, he was pleased about it without being astonished by it.

But he was astonished by the nature of the job.

'I have to impersonate you?' he repeated.

'It's important,' Forster told him. 'They're expecting a lawyer called David Forster, so that's what we have to give them. There won't be any law involved. There probably won't be anything involved at all. Just being there will keep the lid on things. It'll be straightforward enough. OK?'

'OK, I guess,' Curry said. He wrote down the names of the parties involved and the address where the performance was due to take place. He quoted double his normal fee. He didn't want to look cheap, not in front of these Wall Street guys. They were always impressed by expensive services. He knew that. And, given the nature of the job, he figured he would be earning it. Forster agreed the price without hesitation and promised a cheque in the mail. Curry hung up the phone and started through his closets in his head, wondering what the hell he could wear to make himself look like the head of a big Wall Street firm.

THIRTEEN

St Louis to Dallas–Fort Worth is 568 miles by air, and it took a comfortable ninety minutes, thirty of them climbing hard, thirty of them cruising fast, and thirty of them descending on approach. Reacher and Jodie were together in business class, this time on the port side of the plane, among a very different clientele than had flown with them out of New York. Most of the cabin was occupied by Texan businessmen in shark-skin suits in various shades of blue and grey, with alligator boots and big hats. They were larger and ruddier and louder than their East Coast counter-parts, and they were working the stewardesses harder. Jodie was in a simple rust-coloured dress like some-thing Audrey Hepburn might have worn, and the businessmen were stealing glances at her and avoiding Reacher's eye. He was on the aisle, in his crumpled khakis and his ten-year-old English shoes, and they were trying to place him. He saw them going around in circles, looking at his tan and his hands and his companion, figuring him for a roughneck who got lucky with a claim, then figuring that doesn't really happen any more, then starting over with new specu-lations. He ignored them and drank the airline's best coffee from a china cup and started thinking about how to get inside Wolters and get some sense out of DeWitt.

A military policeman trying to get some sense out of a two-star general is like a guy tossing a coin. Heads brings you a guy who knows the value of co-operation. Maybe he's had difficulties in the past inside some unit or another, and maybe he's had them solved for him by the MPs in an effective and perceptive manner. Then he's a believer, and his instinct goes with you. You're his friend. But tails brings you a guy who has maybe caused his own difficulties. Maybe he's botched and blundered his way through some command and maybe the MPs haven't been shy about telling him so. Then you get nothing from him except aggravation. Heads or tails, but it's a bent coin, because on top of everything any institution despises its own policemen, so it comes down tails a lot more than it comes up heads. That had been Reacher's experience. And, worse, he was a military policeman who was now a civilian. He had two strikes against him before he even stepped up to the plate.

The plane taxied to the gate and the businessmen waited and ushered Jodie down the aisle ahead of them. Either plain Texan courtesy or they wanted to watch her legs and her ass as she walked, but Reacher couldn't mount any serious criticism on that issue because he wanted to do exactly the same thing. He carried her bag and followed her down the jet way and into the terminal. He stepped alongside her and put his arm around her shoulders and felt a dozen pairs of eyes drilling into his back.

'Claiming what's yours?' she asked.

'You noticed them?' he asked back.

She threaded her arm around his waist and pulled him closer as they walked.

'They were kind of hard to miss. I guess it would have been easy enough to get a date for tonight.'

'You'd have been beating them off with a stick.'

'It's the dress. Probably I should have worn trousers, but I figured it's kind of traditional down here.'

'You could wear a Soviet tank driver's suit, all grey-green and padded with cotton, and they'd still have their tongues hanging out.'

She giggled. 'I've seen Soviet tank drivers. Dad showed me pictures. Two hundred pounds, big moustaches, smoking pipes, tattoos, and that was just the women.'

The terminal was chilled with air conditioning and they were hit with a forty-degree jump in temperature when they stepped out to the taxi line. June in Texas, just after ten in the morning, and it was over a hundred and humid.

'Wow,' she said. 'Maybe the dress makes sense.'

They were in the shade of an overhead roadway, but beyond it the sun was white and brassy. The concrete baked and shimmered. Jodie bent and found some dark glasses in her bag and slipped them on and looked more like a blonde Audrey Hepburn than ever. The first taxi was a new Caprice with the air going full blast and religious artefacts hanging from the rearview mirror. The driver was silent and the trip lasted forty minutes, mostly over concrete highways that shone white in the sun and started out busy and got emptier.

Fort Wolters was a big permanent facility in the middle of nowhere with low elegant buildings and landscaping kept clean and tidy in the sterile way only the Army can achieve. There was a high fence stretching miles around the whole perimeter, taut and level all the way, no weeds at its base. The inner kerb of the road was whitewashed. Beyond the fence internal roads faced with grey concrete snaked here and there between the buildings. Windows winked in the sun. The taxi rounded a curve and revealed a field the size of a stadium with helicopters lined up in neat rows. Squads of flight trainees moved about between them.

The main gate was set back from the road, with tall white flagpoles funnelling down towards it. Their flags hung limp in the heat. There was a low square gate-house with a red-and-white barrier controlling access. The gatehouse was all windows above waist level and Reacher could see MPs inside watching the approach of the taxi. They were in full service gear, including the white helmets. Regular Army MPs. He smiled. This part was going to be no problem. They were going to see him as more their friend than the people they were guarding.

The taxi dropped them in the turning circle and drove back out. They walked through the blinding heat to the shade of the guardhouse eaves. An MP sergeant slid the window back and looked at them enquiringly. Reacher felt the chilled air spilling out over him.

'We need to get together with General DeWitt,' he said. 'Is there any chance of that happening, Sergeant?'

The guy looked him over. 'Depends who you are, I guess.'

Reacher told him who he was and who he had been, and who Jodie was and who her father had been, and a minute later they were both inside the cool of the guardhouse. The MP sergeant was on the phone to his opposite number in the command office.

'OK, you're booked in,' he said. 'General's free in half an hour.'

Reacher smiled. The guy was probably free right now, and the half-hour was going to be spent checking that they were who they said they were.

'What's the general like, Sergeant?' he asked.

'We'd rate him SAS, sir,' the MP said, and smiled.

Reacher smiled back. The guardhouse felt surprisingly good to him. He felt at home in it. SAS was MP code for 'stupid asshole sometimes', and it was a reasonably benevolent rating for a sergeant to give a general. It was the kind of rating that meant if he approached it right, the guy might co-operate. On the other hand, it meant he might not. It gave him something to ponder during the waiting time.

After thirty-two minutes a plain green Chevy with neat white stencils pulled up inside the barrier and the sergeant nodded them towards it. The driver was a private soldier who wasn't about to speak a word. He just waited until they were seated and turned the car around and headed slowly back through the buildings. Reacher watched the familiar sights slide by. He had never been to Wolters, but he knew it well enough because it was identical to dozens of other places he had been. The same layout, the same people, the same details, like it was built to the same master plan. The main building was a long two-storey brick structure facing a parade ground. Its architecture was exactly the same as the main building on the Berlin base where he was born. Only the weather was different.

The Chevy eased to a stop opposite the steps up into

the building. The driver moved the selector into park and stared silently ahead through the windshield. Reacher opened the door and stepped out into the heat with Jodie.

'Thanks for the ride, soldier,' he said.

The boy just sat in park with the motor running and stared straight ahead. Reacher walked with Jodie to the steps and in through the door. There was an MP private stationed in the cool of the lobby, white helmet, white gaiters, a gleaming M-16 held easy across his chest. His gaze was fixed on Jodie's bare legs as they danced in towards him.

'Reacher and Garber to see General DeWitt,' Reacher said.

The guy snapped the rifle upright, which was symbolic of removing a barrier. Reacher nodded and walked ahead to the staircase. The place was like every other place, built to a specification poised uneasily somewhere between lavish and functional, like a private school occupying an old mansion. It was immaculately clean, and the materials were the finest available, but the decor was institutional and brutal. At the top of the stairs was a desk in the corridor. Behind it was a portly MP sergeant, swamped with paperwork. Behind him was an oak door with an acetate plate bearing DeWitt's name, his rank and his decorations. It was a large plate.

'Reacher and Garber to see the general,' Reacher said.

The sergeant nodded and picked up his telephone. He pressed a button.

'Your visitors, sir,' he said into the phone.

He listened to the reply and stood up and opened the door. Stepped aside to allow them to walk past.

Closed the door behind them. The office was the size of a tennis court. It was panelled in oak and had a huge dark rug on the floor, threadbare with vacuuming. The desk was large and oak, and DeWitt was in the chair behind it. He was somewhere between fifty and fifty-five, dried out and stringy, with thinning grey hair shaved down close to his scalp. He had half-closed grey eyes and he was using them to watch their approach with an expression Reacher read as halfway between curiosity and irritation.

'Sit down,' he said. 'Please.'

There were leather visitor chairs drawn up near the desk. The office walls were crowded with mementoes, but they were all battalion and division mementoes, war-game trophies, battle honours, old platoon photographs in faded monochrome. There were pictures and cutaway diagrams of a dozen different helicopters. But there was nothing personal to DeWitt on display. Not even family snaps on the desk.

'How can I help you folks?' he asked.

His accent was the bland Army accent that comes from serving all over the world with people from all over the country. He was maybe a midwesterner, originally. Maybe from somewhere near Chicago, Reacher thought.

'I was an MP major,' he said, and waited.

'I know you were. We checked.'

A neutral reply. Nothing there at all. No hostility. But no approval, either.

'My father was General Garber,' Jodie said.

DeWitt nodded without speaking.

'We're here in a private capacity,' Reacher said.

There was a short silence.

'A civilian capacity, in fact,' DeWitt said slowly.

378

Reacher nodded. *Strike one.*

'It's about a pilot called Victor Hobie. You served with him in Vietnam.'

DeWitt looked deliberately blank. He raised his eyebrows.

'Did I?' he said. 'I don't remember him.'

Strike two. Unco-operative.

'We're trying to find out what happened to him.'

Another short silence. Then DeWitt nodded, slowly, amused.

'Why? Was he your long-lost uncle? Or maybe he was secretly your father? Maybe he had a brief sad affair with your mother when he was her pool boy. Or did you buy his old childhood home and find his long-lost teenage diaries hidden behind the wainscoting with a 1968 issue of *Playboy* magazine?'

Strike three. Aggressively unco-operative. The office went silent again. There was the thumping of rotor blades somewhere in the far distance. Jodie hitched forward on her chair. Her voice was soft and low in the quiet room.

'We're here for his parents, sir. They lost their boy thirty years ago, and they've never known what happened to him. They're still grieving, General.'

DeWitt looked at her with the grey eyes and shook his head.

'I don't remember him. I'm very sorry.'

'He trained with you right here at Wolters,' Reacher said. 'You went to Rucker together and you sailed to Qui Nhon together. You served the best part of two tours together, flying slicks out of Pleiku.'

'Your old man in the service?' DeWitt asked.

Reacher nodded. 'The Corps. Thirty years, *Semper Fi.*'

379

'Mine was Eighth Air Force,' DeWitt said. 'World War Two, flying bombers out of East Anglia in England all the way to Berlin and back. You know what he told me when I signed up for helicopters?'

Reacher waited.

'He gave me some good advice,' DeWitt said. 'He told me, don't make friends with pilots. Because they all get killed, and it just makes you miserable.'

Reacher nodded again. 'You really can't recall him?'

DeWitt just shrugged.

'Not even for his folks?' Jodie asked. 'Doesn't seem right they'll never know what happened to their boy, does it?'

There was silence. The distant rotor blades faded to nothing. DeWitt gazed at Jodie. Then he spread his small hands on the desk and sighed heavily.

'Well, I guess I can recall him a little,' he said. 'Mostly from the early days. Later on, when they all started dying, I took the old man's advice to heart. Kind of closed in on myself, you know?'

'So what was he like?' Jodie asked.

'What was he like?' DeWitt repeated. 'Not like me, that's for sure. Not like anybody else I ever knew, either. He was a walking contradiction. He was a volunteer, you know that? I was too, and so were a lot of the guys. But Vic wasn't like the others. There was a big divide back then between the volunteers and the drafted guys. The volunteers were all rah-rah boys, you know, going for it because they believed in it. But Vic wasn't like that. He volunteered, but he was about as mousy quiet as the sulkiest draftee you ever saw. But he could fly like he was born with a rotor blade up his ass.'

380

'So he was good?' Jodie prompted.

'Better than good,' DeWitt replied. 'Second only to me in the early days, which is saying something, because I was definitely born with a rotor blade up my ass. And Vic was smart with the book stuff. I remember that. He had it all over everybody else in the classroom.'

'Did he have an attitude problem with that?' Reacher asked. 'Trading favours for help?'

DeWitt swung the grey eyes across from Jodie.

'You've done your research. You've been in the files.'

'We just came from the NPRC,' Reacher said.

DeWitt nodded, neutrally. 'I hope you didn't read my jacket.'

'Supervisor wouldn't let us,' Reacher said.

'We were anxious not to poke around where we're not wanted,' Jodie said.

DeWitt nodded again.

'Vic traded favours,' he said. 'But they claimed he did it in the wrong way. There was a little controversy about it, as I recall. You were supposed to do it because you were glad to help your fellow candidates, you know? For the good of the unit, right? You remember how that shit went?'

He stopped and glanced at Reacher, amused. Reacher nodded. Jodie's being there was helping him. Her charm was inching him back towards approval.

'But Vic was cold about it,' DeWitt said. 'Like it was all just another math equation. Like x amount of lift moves the chopper off the ground, like this much help with that complicated formula gets his boots bulled up. They saw it as cold.'

'Was he cold?' Jodie asked.

DeWitt nodded. 'Emotionless, the coldest guy I ever saw. It always amazed me. At first I figured it was because he came from some little place where he'd never done anything or seen anything. But later I realized he just felt nothing. Nothing at all. It was weird. But it made him a hell of a tremendous flyer.'

'Because he wasn't afraid?' Reacher asked.

'Exactly,' DeWitt said. 'Not courageous, because a courageous guy is somebody who feels the fear but conquers it. Vic never felt it in the first place. It made him a better war flyer than me. I was the one passed out of Rucker head of the class, and I've got the plaque to prove it, but when we got in-country, he was better than me, no doubt about it.'

'In what kind of way?'

DeWitt shrugged, like he couldn't explain it. 'We learned everything as we went along, just made it all up. Fact is, our training was shit. It was like being shown a little round thing and being told *this is a baseball* and then getting sent straight out to play in the major leagues. That's something I'm trying to put right, now I'm here running this place. I never want to send boys out as unprepared as we were.'

'Hobie was good at learning on the job?' Reacher asked.

'The best,' DeWitt said. 'You know anything about helicopters in the jungle?'

Reacher shook his head. 'Not a lot.'

'First main problem is the LZ,' DeWitt said. 'LZ, landing zone, right? You got a desperate bunch of tired infantry under fire somewhere, they need exfiltrating, they get on the radio and our despatcher tells them, *sure, make us an LZ and we'll be right over to pull you out.* So they use explosives and saws and whatever the hell else they got and they blast a temporary LZ in the jungle. Now a Huey with the rotor turning needs a space exactly forty-eight feet wide and fifty-seven feet nine-point-seven inches long to land in. But the infantry is tired and in a big hurry and Charlie is raining mortars down on them and generally they don't make the LZ big enough. So we can't get them out. This happened to us two or three times, and we're sick about it, and one night I see Vic studying the leading edge of the rotor blade on his Huey. So I say to him, *what are you looking at?* And he says, *these are metal.* I'm thinking, like what else would they be? Bamboo? But he's looking at them. Next day, we're called to a temporary LZ again, and sure enough the damn thing is too small, by a couple of feet all around. So I can't get in. But Vic goes down anyway. He spins the chopper around and around and cuts his way in with the rotor. Like a gigantic flying lawn mower? It was awesome. Bits of tree flying everywhere. He pulls out seven or eight guys and the rest of us go down after him and get all the rest. That became SOP afterward, and he invented it, because he was cold and logical and he wasn't afraid to try. That manoeuvre saved hundreds of guys over the years. Literally hundreds, maybe even thousands.'

'Impressive,' Reacher said.

'You bet your ass impressive,' DeWitt said back. 'Second big problem we had was weight. Suppose you were out in the open somewhere, like a field. The infantry would come swarming in on you until the damn chopper was too heavy to take off. So your own gunners would be beating them off and leaving them there in the field, maybe to die. Not a nice feeling. So one day Vic lets them all onboard, and sure enough he can't get off the ground. So he shoves the stick forward and sort of skitters horizontally along the field until the airspeed kicks in under the rotor and unsticks him. Then he's up and away. The running jump. It became another SOP, and he invented it too. Sometimes he would do it downhill, even down the mountainsides, like he was heading for a certain crash, and then up he went. Like I told you, we were just making it up as we went along, and the truth is a lot of the good stuff got made up by Victor Hobie.'

'You admired him,' Jodie said.

DeWitt nodded. 'Yes, I did. And I'm not afraid to admit it.'

'But you weren't close.'

He shook his head. 'Like my daddy told me, don't make friends with the other pilots. And I'm glad I didn't. Too many of them died.'

'How did he spend his time?' Reacher asked. 'The files show a lot of days you couldn't fly.'

'Weather was a bitch. A real bitch. You got no idea. I want this facility moved someplace else, maybe Washington State, where they get some mists and fogs. No point training down in Texas and Alabama if you want to go fighting someplace you get weather.'

'So how did you spend the down-time?'

'Me? I did all kinds of things. Sometimes I partied, sometimes I slept. Sometimes I took a truck out and went scavenging for things we needed.'

'What about Vic?' Jodie asked. 'What did he do?'

DeWitt just shrugged again. 'I have no idea. He was always busy, always up to something, but I don't know what it was. Like I told you, I didn't want to mix with the other flyers.'

'Was he different on the second tour?' Reacher asked.

384

DeWitt smiled briefly. 'Everybody was different second time around.'

'In what way?' Jodie asked.

'Angrier,' DeWitt said. 'Even if you signed up again right away it was nine months minimum before you got back, sometimes a whole year. Then you got back and you figured the place had gone to shit while you were away. You figured it had gotten sloppy and half-assed. Facilities you'd built would be all falling down, trenches you'd dug against the mortars would be half full of water, trees you'd cleared away from the heli-copter parking would be all sprouting up again. You'd feel your little domain had been ruined by a bunch of know-nothing idiots while you were gone. It made you angry and depressed. And generally speaking it was true. The whole 'Nam thing went steadily downhill, right out of control. The quality of the personnel just got worse and worse.'

'So you'd say Hobie got disillusioned?' Reacher asked.

DeWitt shrugged. 'I really don't remember much about his attitude. Maybe he coped OK. He had a strong sense of duty, as I recall.'

'What was his final mission about?'

The grey eyes suddenly went blank, like the shutters had just come down.

'I can't remember.'

'He was shot down,' Reacher said. 'Shot out of the air, right alongside you. You can't recall what the mission was?'

'We lost eight thousand helicopters in 'Nam,' DeWitt said. 'Eight thousand, Mr Reacher, beginning to end. Seems to me I personally saw most of them go down. So how should I recall any particular one of them?'

'What was it about?' Reacher asked again.

'Why do you want to know?' DeWitt asked back.

'It would help me.'

'With what?'

Reacher shrugged. 'With his folks, I guess. I want to be able to tell them he died doing something useful.'

DeWitt smiled. A bitter, sardonic smile, worn and softened at the edges by thirty years of regular use. 'Well, my friend, you sure as hell can't do that.'

'Why not?'

'Because none of our missions were useful. They were all a waste of time. A waste of lives. We lost the war, didn't we?'

'Was it a secret mission?'

There was a pause. Silence in the big office.

'Why should it be secret?' DeWitt asked back, neutrally.

'He only took onboard three passengers. Seems like a special sort of a deal to me. No running jump required there.'

'I don't remember,' DeWitt said again.

Reacher just looked at him, quietly. DeWitt stared back.

'How should I remember? I hear about something for the first time in thirty years and I'm supposed to remember every damn detail about it?'

'This isn't the first time in thirty years. You were asked all about it a couple of months ago. In April of this year.'

DeWitt was silent.

'General Garber called the NPRC about Hobie,' Reacher said. 'It's inconceivable he didn't call you afterward. Won't you tell us what you told him?'

DeWitt smiled. 'I told him I didn't remember.'

There was silence again. Distant rotor blades, coming closer.

'On behalf of his folks, won't you tell us?' Jodie asked softly. 'They're still grieving for him. They need to know about it.'

DeWitt shook his head. 'I can't.'

'Can't or won't?' Reacher asked.

DeWitt stood up slowly and walked to the window. He was a short man. He stood in the light of the sun and squinted left, across to where he could see the helicopter he could hear, coming in to land on the field.

'It's classified information,' he said. 'I'm not allowed to make any comment, and I'm not going to. Garber asked me, and I told him the same thing. No comment. But I hinted he should maybe look closer to home, and I'll advise you to do the exact same thing, Mr Reacher. Look closer to home.'

'Closer to home?'

DeWitt put his back to the window. 'Did you see Kaplan's jacket?'

'His co-pilot?'

DeWitt nodded. 'Did you read his last but one mission?'

Reacher shook his head.

'You should have,' DeWitt said. 'Sloppy work from somebody who was once an MP major. But don't tell anybody I suggested it, because I'll deny it, and they'll believe me, not you.'

Reacher looked away. DeWitt walked back to his desk and sat down.

'Is it possible Victor Hobie is still alive?' Jodie asked him.

The distant helicopter shut off its engines. There was total silence.

387

'I have no comment on that,' DeWitt said.

'Have you been asked that question before?' Jodie said.

'I have no comment on that,' DeWitt said again.

'You saw the crash. Is it possible anybody survived it?'

'I saw an explosion under the jungle canopy, is all. He was way more than half-full with fuel. Draw your own conclusion, Ms Garber.'

'Did he survive?'

'I have no comment on that.'

'Why is Kaplan officially dead and Hobie isn't?'

'I have no comment on that.'

She nodded. Thought for a moment and regrouped exactly like the lawyer she was, boxed in by some recalcitrant witness. 'Just theoretically, then. Suppose a young man with Victor Hobie's personality and character and background survived such an incident, OK? Is it possible a man like that would never even have made contact with his own parents again afterward?'

DeWitt stood up again. He was clearly uncomfortable.

'I don't know, Ms Garber. I'm not a damn psychiatrist. And like I told you, I was careful not to get to know him too well. He seemed like a real dutiful guy, but he was cold. Overall, I guess I would rate it as very unlikely. But don't forget, Vietnam changed people. It sure as hell changed me, for instance. I used to be a nice guy.'

Officer Sark was forty-four years old, but he looked older. His physique was damaged by a poor childhood and ignorant neglect through most of his adult years. His skin was dull and pale, and he had lost his hair early. It left him looking sallow and sunken and old before his time. But the truth was he had woken up to it and was fighting it. He had read stuff the NYPD's medical people were putting about, concerning diet and exercise. He had eliminated most of the fats from his daily intake, and he had started sunbathing a little, just enough to take the pallor off his skin without provoking the risk of melanomas. He walked whenever he could. Going home, he would get off the subway a stop short and hike the rest of the way, fast enough to get his breath going and his heart-beat raised, like the stuff he'd read said he should. And during the workday, he would persuade O'Hallinan to park the prowl car somewhere that would give them a short walk to wherever it was they were headed.

O'Hallinan had no interest in aerobic exercise, but she was an amiable woman and happy enough to co-operate with him, especially during the summer months, when the sun was shining. So she put the car against the kerb in the shadow of Trinity Church and they approached the World Trade Center on foot from the south. It gave them a brisk six-hundred-yard walk in the sun, which made Sark happy, but it left the car exactly equidistant from a quarter of a million separate postal addresses, and with nothing on paper in the squad room it left nobody with any clue about which one of them they were heading for.

'You want a ride back to the airport?' DeWitt asked.

Reacher interpreted the offer as a dismissal mixed in with a gesture designed to soften the stonewall performance the guy had been putting up. He nodded. The Army Chevrolet would get them there faster than

389

a taxi, because it was already waiting right outside with the motor running.

'Thanks,' he said.

'Hey, my pleasure,' DeWitt said back.

He dialled a number from his desk and spoke like he was issuing an order.

'Wait right here,' he said. 'Three minutes.'

Jodie stood up and smoothed her dress down. Walked to the windows and gazed out. Reacher stepped the other way and looked at the mementoes on the wall. One of the photographs was a glossy reprint of a famous newspaper picture. A helicopter was lifting off from inside the embassy compound in Saigon, with a crowd of people underneath it, arms raised like they were trying to force it to come back down for them.

'You were that pilot?' Reacher asked, on a hunch.

DeWitt glanced over and nodded.

'You were still there in '75?'

DeWitt nodded again. 'Five combat tours, then a spell on HQ duty. Overall, I guess I preferred the combat.'

There was noise in the distance. The bass thumping of a powerful helicopter, coming closer. Reacher joined Jodie at the window. A Huey was in the air, drifting over the distant buildings from the direction of the field.

'Your ride,' DeWitt said.

'A helicopter?' Jodie said.

DeWitt was smiling. 'What did you expect? This is the helicopter school, after all. That's why these boys are down here. It ain't driver's ed.'

The rotor noise was building to a loud *wop-wop-wop*. Then it slowly blended to a higher-pitched *whip-whip-whip* as it came closer and the jet whine mixed in.

'Bigger blade now,' DeWitt shouted. 'Composite materials. Not metal any more. I don't know what old Vic would have made of it.'

The Huey was sliding sideways and hovering over the parade ground in front of the building. The noise was shaking the windows. Then the helicopter was straightening and settling to the ground.

'Nice meeting you,' DeWitt shouted.

They shook his hand and headed out. The MP sergeant at the desk nodded to them through the noise and went back to his paperwork. They went down the stairs and outside into the blast of heat and dust and sound. The co-pilot was sliding the door for them. They ran bent-over across the short distance. Jodie was grinning and her hair was blowing everywhere. The co-pilot offered his hand and pulled her up inside. Reacher followed. They strapped themselves into the bench seat in the back and the co-pilot slid the door closed and climbed through to the cabin. The familiar shudder of vibration started up as the craft hauled itself into the air. The floor tilted and swung and the buildings rotated in the windows, and then their roofs were visible, and then the outlying grassland, with the highways laid through it like grey pencil lines. The nose went down and the engine noise built to a roar as they swung on course and settled to a hundred-mile-an-hour cruise.

The stuff Sark had read called it 'power walking', and the idea was to push yourself towards a speed of four miles an hour. That way your heartbeat was raised, which was the key to the aerobic benefit, but you avoided the impact damage to your shins and knees that you risked with proper jogging. It was a convincing proposition, and he believed in it. Doing it properly, six hundred yards at four miles an hour should have taken a fraction over five minutes, but it actually took nearer eight, because he was walking with O'Hallinan at his side. She was happy to walk, but she wanted to do it slowly. She was not an unfit woman, but she always said *I'm built for comfort, not for speed.* It was a compromise. He needed her co-operation to get to walk at all, so he never complained about her pace. He figured it was better than nothing. It had to be doing him some kind of good.

'Which building?' he asked.

'The south, I think,' she said.

They walked around to the main entrance of the south tower and inside to the lobby. There were guys in security uniforms behind a counter, but they were tied up with a knot of foreign men in grey suits, so Sark and O'Hallinan stepped over to the building directory and consulted it direct. Cayman Corporate Trust was listed on the eighty-eighth floor. They walked to the express elevator and stepped inside without the security force being aware they had ever entered the building.

The elevator floor pressed against their feet and sped them upward. It slowed and stopped at eighty-eight. The door slid back and a muted bell sounded and they stepped out into a plain corridor. The ceilings were low and the space was narrow. Cayman Corporate Trust had a modern oak door with a small window and a brass handle. Sark pulled the door and allowed O'Hallinan to go inside ahead of him. She was old enough to appreciate the courtesy.

There was an oak-and-brass reception area with a thickset man in a dark suit behind a chest-high counter. Sark stood back in the centre of the floor, his loaded belt emphasizing the width of his hips, making him seem large and commanding. O'Hallinan stepped up to the counter, planning her approach. She wanted to shake something loose, so she tried the sort of frontal attack she had seen detectives use.

'We've come about Sheryl,' she said.

'I have to go home, I guess,' Jodie said.

'No, you're coming to Hawaii, with me.'

They were back inside the freezing terminal at Dallas–Fort Worth. The Huey had put down on a remote forecourt and the co-pilot had driven them over in a golf cart painted dull green. He had shown them an unmarked door that led them up a flight of stairs into the bustle of the public areas.

'Hawaii? Reacher, I can't go to Hawaii. I need to be back in New York.'

'You can't go back there alone. New York is where the danger is, remember? And I need to go to Hawaii. So you'll have to come with me, simple as that.'

'Reacher, I can't,' she said again. 'I have to be in a meeting tomorrow. You know that. You took the call, right?'

'Tough, Jodie. You're not going back there alone.'

Checking out of the St Louis honeymoon suite that morning had done something to him. The lizard part of his brain buried deep behind the frontal lobes had shrieked *the honeymoon is over, pal. Your life is changing and the problems start now.* He had ignored it. But now he was paying attention to it. For the first time in his life, he had a hostage to fortune. He had somebody to worry about. It was mostly a pleasure, but it was also a burden.

'I have to go back, Reacher,' she said. 'I can't let them down.'

'Call them, tell them you can't make it. Tell them you're sick or something.'

'I can't do that. My secretary knows I'm not sick, right? And I've got a career to think about. It's important to me.'

'You're not going back there alone,' he said again.

'Why do you need to go to Hawaii anyway?'

'Because that's where the answer is,' he said.

He stepped away to a ticket counter and took a thick timetable from a small chrome rack. Stood in the cold fluorescence and opened it up to D for the Dallas–Fort Worth departures and ran his finger down the list of destinations as far as H for Honolulu. Then he flipped ahead to the Honolulu departures and checked the flights going back to New York. He double-checked, and then he smiled with relief.

'We can make it anyway, do both things. Look at this. There's a twelve-fifteen out of here. Flight time minus the time change going west gets us to Honolulu at three o'clock. Then we get the seven o'clock back to New York, flight time plus the time change coming back east gets us into JFK at twelve noon tomorrow. Your guy said it was an afternoon meeting, right? So you can still make it.'

'I need to get briefed in,' she said. 'I have no idea what it's about.'

'You'll have a couple of hours. You're a quick study.'

'It's crazy. Only gives us four hours in Hawaii.'

'All we need. I'll call ahead, set it up.'

'We'll be on a plane all night. I'll be going to my meeting after a sleepless night on a damn plane.'

'So we'll go first class,' he said. 'Rutter's paying, right? We can sleep in first class. The chairs look comfortable enough.'

She shrugged and sighed. 'Crazy.'

'Let me use your phone,' he said.

She handed him the mobile from her bag and he called long-distance information and asked for the number. Dialled it and heard it ring six thousand miles away. It rang eight times and the voice he wanted to hear answered it.

'This is Jack Reacher,' he said. 'You going to be in the office all day?'

The answer was slow and sleepy, because it was very early in the morning in Hawaii, but it was the answer he wanted to hear. He clicked the phone off and turned back to Jodie. She sighed at him again, but this time there was a smile mixed in with it. She stepped to the counter and used the gold card to buy two first-class tickets, Dallas–Fort Worth to Honolulu to New York. The guy at the counter made the seat assignment on the spot, slightly bewildered in front of people paying the price of a used sportscar to buy twenty hours on a plane and four on the ground on Oahu. He handed the wallets over and twenty minutes later Reacher was settling into an enormous leather-and-sheepskin chair with Jodie safely a yard away at his side.

There was a routine to be followed in this situation. It had never before been employed, but it had been rehearsed often and thoroughly. The thickset man at the chest-high counter moved his hand casually sideways and used his index finger on one button and his middle finger on another. The first button locked the oak door out to the elevator lobby. There was an electromagnetic mechanism that snicked the steel tongue into place, silently and unobtrusively. Once it was activated, the door stayed locked until the mechanism was released again, no matter what anybody did with the latch or the key. The second button set a red light flashing in the intercom unit on Hobie's desk. The red light was bright and the office was always dark, and it was impossible to miss it.

'Who?' the thickset guy said.

'Sheryl,' O'Hallinan repeated.

'I'm sorry,' the guy said. 'There's nobody called Sheryl working here. Currently we have a staff of three, and they're all men.'

He moved his hand to the left and rested it on a button marked TALK, which activated the intercom.

'You operate a black Tahoe?' O'Hallinan asked him.

He nodded. 'We have a black Tahoe on the corporate fleet.'

'What about a Suburban?'

'Yes, I think we have one of those too. Is this about a traffic violation?'

'It's about Sheryl being in the hospital,' O'Hallinan said.

'Who?' the guy asked again.

Sark came up behind O'Hallinan. 'We need to speak with your boss.'

'OK,' the guy said. 'I'll see if that can be arranged. May I have your names?'

'Officers Sark and O'Hallinan, City of New York Police Department.'

Tony opened the inner office door, and stood there, enquiringly.

'May I help you, Officers?' he called.

In the rehearsals, the cops would turn away from the counter and look at Tony. Maybe take a couple of steps towards him. And that is exactly what happened. Sark and O'Hallinan turned their backs and walked towards the middle of the reception area. The thickset man at the counter leaned down and opened a cupboard. Unclipped the shotgun from its rack and held it low, out of sight.

'It's about Sheryl,' O'Hallinan said again.

'Sheryl who?' Tony asked.

'The Sheryl in the hospital with the busted nose,' Sark said. 'And the fractured cheekbones and the concussion. The Sheryl who got out of your Tahoe outside St Vincent's ER.'

'Oh, I see,' Tony said. 'We didn't get her name. She couldn't speak a word, because of the injuries to her face.'

'So why was she in your car?' O'Hallinan asked.

'We were up at Grand Central, dropping a client there. We found her on the sidewalk, kind of lost. She was off the train from Mount Kisco, and just kind of wandering about. We offered her a ride to the hospital, which seemed to be what she needed. So we dropped her at St Vincent's, because it's on the way back here.'

'Bellevue is nearer Grand Central,' O'Hallinan said.

'I don't like the traffic over there,' Tony said neutrally. 'St Vincent's was more convenient.'

'And you didn't wonder about what had happened to her?' Sark asked. 'How she came by the injuries?'

'Well, naturally we wondered,' Tony said. 'We asked her about it, but she couldn't speak, because of the injuries. That's why we didn't recognize the name.'

397

O'Hallinan stood there, unsure. Sark took a step forward.

'You found her on the sidewalk?'

Tony nodded. 'Outside Grand Central.'

'She couldn't speak?'

'Not a word.'

'So how do you know she was off the Kisco train?'

The only grey area in the rehearsals had been picking the exact moment to drop the defence and start the offence. It was a subjective issue. They had trusted that when it came, they would recognize it. And they did. The thickset man stood up and crunched a round into the shotgun's chamber and levelled it across the counter.

'Freeze!' he screamed.

A nine-millimetre pistol appeared in Tony's hand. Sark and O'Hallinan stared at it and glanced back at the shotgun and jerked their arms upward. Not a rueful little gesture like in the movies. They stretched them violently upward like their lives depended on touching the acoustic tile directly above their heads. The guy with the shotgun came up from the rear and jammed the muzzle hard into Sark's back and Tony stepped around behind O'Hallinan and did the same thing with his pistol. Then a third man came out from the darkness and paused in the office doorway.

'I'm Hook Hobie,' he said.

They stared at him. Said nothing. Their gazes started on his disfigured face and travelled slowly down to the empty sleeve.

'Which of you is which?' Hobie asked.

No reply. They were staring at the hook. He raised it and let it catch the light.

'Which of you is O'Hallinan?'

O'Hallinan ducked her head in acknowledgement. Hobie turned.

'So you're Sark.'

Sark nodded. Just a fractional inclination of his head.

'Undo your belts,' Hobie said. 'One at a time. And be quick.'

Sark went first. He was quick. He dropped his hands and wrestled with his buckle. The heavy belt thumped to the floor at his feet. He stretched up again for the ceiling.

'Now you,' Hobie said to O'Hallinan.

She did the same thing. The heavy belt with the revolver and the radio and the handcuffs and the nightstick thumped on the carpet. She stretched her hands back up, as far as they would go. Hobie used the hook. He leaned down and swept the point through both buckles and swung the belts up in the air, posing like a fisherman at the end of a successful day on the riverbank. He reached around and used his good hand to pull the two sets of handcuffs out of their worn leather cups.

'Turn around.'

They turned and faced the guns head-on.

'Hands behind you.'

It is possible for a one-armed man to put handcuffs on a victim, if the victim stands still, wrists together. Sark and O'Hallinan stood very still indeed. Hobie clicked one wrist at a time, and then tightened all four cuffs against their ratchets until he heard gasps of pain from both of them. Then he swung the belts high enough not to drag on the floor and walked back inside the office.

'Come in,' he called.

He walked around behind the desk and laid the belts on it like items for close examination. He sat heavily in his chair and waited while Tony lined up the prisoners in front of him. He left them in silence while he emptied their belts. He unstrapped their revolvers and dropped them in a drawer. Took out their radios and fiddled with the volume controls until they were hissing and crackling loudly. He squared them together at the end of the desktop with their antennas pointed towards the wall of windows. He inclined his head for a moment and listened to the squelch of radio atmospherics. Then he turned back and pulled both nightsticks out of the loops on the belts. He placed one on the desk and hefted the other in his left hand and examined it closely. It was the modern kind, with a handle, and a telescopic section below. He peered at it, interested.

'How does this work, exactly?'

Neither Sark nor O'Hallinan replied. Hobie played with the stick for a second, and then he glanced at the thickset guy, who jabbed the shotgun forward and hit Sark in the kidney.

'I asked you a question,' Hobie said to him.

'You swing it,' he muttered. 'Swing it, and sort of flick it.'

He needed space, so he stood up. Swung the stick and flicked it like he was cracking a whip. The telescopic section snapped out and locked into place. He grinned with the unburned half of his face. Collapsed the mechanism and tried again. Grinned again. He took to pacing big circles around the desk, swinging the stick and cracking it open. He did it vertically, and then horizontally. He used more and more force. He spun tight circles, flashing the stick. He whipped it

400

backhanded and the mechanism sprang open and he whirled and smashed it into O'Hallinan's face.

'I like this thing,' he said.

She was swaying backward, but Tony jabbed her upright with his pistol. Her knees gave way and she fell forward in a heap, pressed up against the front of the desk, arms cuffed tight behind her, bleeding from the mouth and nose.

'What did Sheryl tell you?' Hobie asked.

Sark was staring down at O'Hallinan.

'She said she walked into a door,' he muttered.

'So why the hell are you bothering me? Why are you here?'

Sark moved his gaze upward. Looked Hobie full in the face.

'Because we didn't believe her. It was clear somebody beat on her. We followed up on the Tahoe plate, and it looks like it led us to the right place.'

The office went silent. Nothing except the hiss and the squelch from the police radios on the end of the desk. Hobie nodded.

'Exactly the right place,' he said. 'There was no door involved.'

Sark nodded back. He was a reasonably courageous man. The Domestic Violence Unit was no kind of safe refuge for cowards. By definition it involved dealing with men who had the capacity for brutal violence. And Sark was as good at dealing with them as anybody.

'This is a big mistake,' he said quietly.

'In what way?' Hobie asked interested.

'This is about what you did to Sheryl, is all. It doesn't have to be about anything else. You really shouldn't mix anything else in with it. It's a big step up to violence against police officers. It might be possible to work something out about the Sheryl issue. Maybe there was provocation there, you know, some mitigating circumstance. But you keep on messing with us, then we can't work anything out. Because you're just digging yourself into bigger trouble.'

He paused and watched carefully for the response. The approach often worked. Self-interest on the part of the perpetrator often made it work. But there was no response from Hobie. He said nothing. The office was silent. Sark was shaping the next gambit on his lips when the radios crackled and some distant despatcher came over the air and sentenced him to death.

'Five one and five two, please confirm your current location.'

Sark was so conditioned to respond that his hand jerked towards where his belt had been. It was stopped short by the handcuff. The radio call died into silence. Hobie was staring into space.

'Five one, five two, I need your current location, please.'

Sark was staring at the radios in horror. Hobie followed his gaze and smiled.

'They don't know where you are,' he said.

Sark shook his head. Thinking fast. A courageous man.

'They know where we are. They know we're here. They want confirmation, is all. They check we're where we're supposed to be, all the time.'

The radios crackled again. *'Five one, five two, respond, please.'*

Hobie stared at Sark. O'Hallinan was struggling to her knees and staring towards the radios. Tony moved his pistol to cover her.

'*Five one, five two, do you copy?*'

The voice slid under the sea of static and then came back stronger.

'*Five one, five two, we have a violent domestic emergency at Houston and Avenue D. Are you anywhere near that vicinity?*'

Hobie smiled.

'That's two miles from here,' he said. 'They have absolutely no idea where you are, do they?'

Then he grinned. The left side of his face folded into unaccustomed lines, but on the right the scar tissue stayed tight, like a rigid mask.

FOURTEEN

For the first time in his life, Reacher was truly comfortable in a plane. He had been flying since birth, first as a soldier's kid and then as a soldier himself, millions of miles in total, but all of them hunched in roaring spartan military transports or folded into hard civilian seats narrower than his shoulders. Travelling first class on a scheduled airline was a completely new luxury.

The cabin was dramatic. It was a calculated insult to the passengers who filed down the jet way and glanced into it before shuffling along the aisle to their own mean accommodations. It was cool and pastel in first class, with four seats to a row where there were ten in coach. Arithmetically, Reacher figured that made each seat two and a half times as wide, but they felt better than that. They felt enormous. They felt like sofas, wide enough for him to squirm left and right without bruising his hips against the arms. And the leg room was amazing. He could slide right down and stretch right out without touching the seat in front. He could hit the button and recline almost horizontal without bothering the guy behind. He operated the mechanism a couple of times like a kid with a toy, and then he settled on a sensible halfway position and opened the in-flight magazine, which was crisp and new and not creased and sticky like the ones they were reading forty rows back.

Jodie was lost in her own seat, with her shoes off and her feet tucked up under her, the same magazine open on her lap and a glass of chilled champagne at her elbow. The cabin was quiet. They were a long way forward of the engines, and their noise was muted to a hiss no louder than the hiss of the air coming through the vents in the overhead. There was no vibration. Reacher was watching the sparkling gold wine in Jodie's glass, and he saw no tremor on its surface.

'I could get accustomed to this,' he said.

She looked up and smiled.

'Not on your wages,' she said.

He nodded and went back to his arithmetic. He figured a day's earnings from digging swimming pools would buy him fifty miles of first-class air travel. Cruising speed, that was about five minutes' worth of progress. Ten hours of work, all gone in five minutes. He was spending money 120 times faster than he had been earning it.

'What are you going to do?' she asked. 'When this is all over?'

'I don't know,' he said.

The question had been in the back of his mind ever since she told him about the house. The house itself sat there in his imagination, sometimes benign, sometimes threatening, like a trick picture that changed depending on how you tilted it against the light. Sometimes it sat there in the glow of the sun, comfortable, low and spreading, surrounded by its amiable jungle of a yard, and it looked like home. Other times, it looked like a gigantic millstone, requiring him to run and run and run just to stay level with the starting line. He knew people with houses. He had talked to them, with the same kind of detached interest he would talk to a person who kept snakes as pets or entered ballroom dancing competitions. Houses forced you into a certain lifestyle. Even if somebody gave you one for nothing, like Leon had, it committed you to a whole lot of different things. There were property taxes. He knew that. There was insurance, in case the place burned down or was blown away in a high wind. There was maintenance. People he knew with houses were always doing something to them. They would be replacing the heating system at the start of the winter, because it had failed. Or the basement would be leaking water, and complicated things with excavations would be required. Roofs were a problem. He knew that. People had told him. Roofs had a finite life span, which surprised him. The shingles needed stripping off and replacing with new. Siding, also. Windows, too. He had known people who had put new windows in their houses. They had deliberated long and hard about what type to buy.

'Are you going to get a job?' Jodie asked.

He stared out through the oval window at southern California, dry and brown seven miles below him. What sort of a job? The house was going to cost him maybe ten thousand dollars a year in taxes and premiums and maintenance. And it was an isolated house, so he would have to keep Rutter's car, too. It was a free car, like the house, but it would cost him money just to own. Insurance, oil changes, inspections, title, gasoline. Maybe another three grand a year. Food and clothes and utilities were on top of all

406

that. And if he had a house, he would want other things. He would want a stereo. He would want Wynonna Judd's record, and a whole lot of others, too. He thought back to old Mrs Hobie's handwritten calculations. She had settled on a certain sum of money she needed every year, and he couldn't see getting it any lower than she had got it. The whole deal added up to maybe thirty thousand dollars a year, which meant earning maybe fifty, to take account of income taxes and the cost of five days a week travelling back and forth to wherever the hell he was going to earn it.

'I don't know,' he said again.

'Plenty of things you could do.'

'Like what?'

'You've got talents. You're a hell of an investigator, for instance. Dad always used to say you're the best he ever saw.'

'That was in the Army,' he said. 'That's all over now.'

'Skills are portable, Reacher. There's always demand for the best.'

Then she looked up, a big idea in her face. 'You could take over Costello's business. He's going to leave a void. We used him all the time.'

'That's great. First I get the guy killed, then I steal his business.'

'It wasn't your fault,' she said. 'You should think about it.'

So he looked back down at California and thought about it. Thought about Costello's well-worn leather chair and his ageing, comfortable body. Thought about sitting in his pastel room with its pebble-glass windows, spending his whole life on the telephone.

Thought about the cost of running the Greenwich Avenue office and hiring a secretary and providing her with new computers and telephone consoles and health insurance and paid vacations. All on top of running the Garrison place. He would be working ten months of the year before he got ahead by a single dollar.

'I don't know,' he said again. 'I'm not sure I want to think about it.'

'You're going to have to.'

'Maybe,' he said. 'But not necessarily right now.'

She smiled like she understood and they lapsed back into silence. The plane hissed onward and the stewardess came back with the drinks cart. Jodie got a refill of champagne and Reacher took a can of beer. He flipped through the airline magazine. It was full of bland articles about nothing much in particular. There were advertisements for financial services and small complicated gadgets, all of which were black and ran on batteries. He arrived at the section where the airline's operational fleet was pictured in little coloured drawings. He found the plane they were on and read about its passenger capacity and its range and the power of its engines. Then he arrived at the crossword in the back. It filled a page and looked pretty hard. Jodie was already there in her own copy, ahead of him.

'Look at eleven down,' she said.

He looked.

'They can weigh heavy,' he read. 'Sixteen letters.'

'Responsibilities,' she said.

Marilyn and Chester Stone were huddled together on the left-hand sofa in front of the desk, because Hobie was in the bathroom, alone with the two cops. The thickset man in the dark suit sat on the opposite sofa with the shotgun resting in his lap. Tony was sprawled out next to him with his feet on the coffee table. Chester was inert, just staring into the gloom. Marilyn was cold and hungry, and terrified. Her eyes were darting all around the room. There was total silence from the bathroom.

'What's he doing in there with them?' she whispered.

Tony shrugged. 'Probably just talking to them right now.'

'About what?'

'Well, asking them questions about what they like and what they don't. In terms of physical pain, you understand. He likes to do that.'

'God, why?'

Tony smiled. 'He feels it's more democratic, you know, letting the victims decide their own fate.'

Marilyn shuddered. 'Oh God, can't he just let them go? They thought Sheryl was a battered wife, that's all. They didn't know anything about him.'

'Well, they'll know something about him soon,' Tony said. 'He makes them pick a number. They never know whether to pick high or low, because they don't know what it's for. They think it might please him, you know, if they pick right. They spend for ever trying to figure it out.'

'Can't he just let them go? Maybe later?'

Tony shook his head.

'No,' he said. 'He's very tense right now. This will relax him. Like therapy.'

Marilyn was silent for a long moment. But then she had to ask.

'What is the number for?' she whispered.

'How many hours it takes them to die,' Tony said. 'The ones who pick high get real pissed when they find out.'

'You bastards.'

'Some guy once picked a hundred, but we let him off with ten.'

'You bastards.'

'But he won't make you pick a number. He's got other plans for you.'

Total silence from the bathroom.

'He's insane,' Marilyn whispered.

Tony shrugged. 'A little, maybe. But I like him. He's had a lot of pain in his life. I think that's why he's so interested in it.'

Marilyn stared at him in horror. Then the buzzer sounded at the oak door out to the elevator lobby. Very loud in the awful silence. Tony and the thickset man with the shotgun spun around and stared in that direction.

'Check it out,' Tony said.

He went into his jacket and came out with his gun. He held it steady on Chester and Marilyn. His partner with the shotgun jacked himself up out of the low sofa and stepped around the table to the door. He closed it behind him and the office went quiet again. Tony stood up and walked to the bathroom door. Knocked on it with the butt of his gun and opened it a fraction and ducked his head inside.

'Visitors,' he whispered.

Marilyn glanced left and right. Tony was twenty feet from her, and he was the nearest. She jumped to her feet and snatched a deep breath. Hurdled the coffee table and scrambled around the opposite sofa and made it all the way to the office door. She

410

wrenched it open. The thickset man in the dark suit was on the far side of the reception area, talking to a short man framed in the doorway out to the elevator lobby.

'Help us!' she screamed to him.

The man stared over at her. He was dressed in dark blue pants and a blue shirt, with a short jacket open over it, the same blue as the pants. Some kind of uniform. There was a small design on the jacket, left side of the chest. He was carrying a brown grocery sack cradled in his arms.

'Help us!' she screamed again.

Two things happened. The thickset man in the dark suit darted forward and bundled the visitor all the way inside and slammed the door after him. And Tony grabbed Marilyn from behind with a strong arm around her waist. He dragged her backward into the office. She arched forward against the pressure of his arms. She was bending herself double and fighting.

'God's sake, help us!'

Tony lifted her off her feet. His arm was bunching under her breasts. The short dress was riding up over her thighs. She was kicking and struggling. The short man in the blue uniform was staring. Her shoes came off. Then the short man was smiling. He walked forward into the office after her, stepping carefully over her abandoned shoes, carrying his grocery sack.

'Hey, I'd like to get me a piece of that,' he said.

'Forget it,' Tony gasped from behind her. 'This one's off limits, time being.'

'Pity,' the new guy said. 'Not every day you see a thing like that.'

Tony struggled with her all the way back to the sofa. Dumped her down next to Chester. The new guy

411

shrugged wistfully and emptied the grocery sack on the desk. Bricks of cash money thumped out on the wood. The bathroom door opened and Hobie stepped into the room. His jacket was off and his shirt sleeves were rolled up to the elbow. On the left was a forearm. It was knotted with muscle and thick with dark hair. On the right was a heavy leather cup, dark brown, worn and shiny, with straps riveted to it running away up into the shirt sleeve. The bottom of the cup was narrowed to a neck, with the bright steel hook coming down out of it, running straight for six or eight inches and then curving around to the point.

'Count the money, Tony,' Hobie said.

Marilyn jerked upright. Turned to face the new guy.

'He's got two cops in there,' she said urgently. 'He's going to kill them.'

The guy shrugged at her.

'Suits me,' he said. 'Kill them all, is what I say.'

She stared at him blankly. Tony moved behind the desk and sorted through the bricks of money. He stacked them neatly and counted out loud, moving them from one end of the desk to the other.

'Forty thousand dollars.'

'So where are the keys?' the new guy asked.

Tony rolled open the desk drawer. 'These are for the Benz.'

He tossed them to the guy and went into his pocket for another bunch.

'And these are for the Tahoe. It's in the garage downstairs.'

'What about the BMW?' the guy asked.

'Still up in Pound Ridge,' Hobie called across the room.

'Keys?' the guy asked.

'In the house, I guess,' Hobie said. 'She didn't bring a pocketbook, and it doesn't look like she's concealing them about her person, does it?'

The guy stared at Marilyn's dress and smiled an ugly smile, all lips and tongue.

'There's something in there, that's for damn sure. But it don't look like keys.'

She looked at him in disgust. The design on his jacket said *Mo's Motors*. It was embroidered in red silk. Hobie walked across the room and stood directly behind her. He leaned forward and brought the hook around into her line of vision. She stared at it, close up. She shuddered.

'Where are the keys?' he asked.

'The BMW is mine,' she said.

'Not any more it isn't.'

He moved the hook closer. She could smell the metal and the leather.

'I could search her,' the new guy called. 'Maybe she is concealing them after all. I can think of a couple of interesting places to look.'

She shuddered.

'Keys,' Hobie said to her softly.

'Kitchen counter,' she whispered back.

Hobie took the hook away and walked around in front of her, smiling. The new guy looked disappointed. He nodded to confirm he'd heard the whisper and walked slowly to the door, jingling the Benz keys and the Tahoe keys in his hands.

'Pleasure doing business,' he said as he walked.

Then he paused at the door and looked back, straight at Marilyn.

'You completely sure that's off limits, Hobie?

413

Seeing as how we're old friends and all? Done a lot of business together?'

Hobie shook his head like he meant it. 'Forget about it. This one's mine.'

The guy shrugged and walked out of the office, swinging the keys. The door closed behind him and they heard the second thump of the lobby door a moment later. Then there was elevator whine and the office fell silent again. Hobie glanced at the stacks of dollar bills on the desk and headed back to the bathroom. Marilyn and Chester were kept side by side on the sofa, cold, sick and hungry. The light coming in through the chinks in the blinds faded away to the yellow dullness of evening, and the silence from the bathroom continued until a point Marilyn guessed was around eight o'clock in the evening. Then it was shattered by screaming.

The plane chased the sun west but lost time all the way and arrived on Oahu three hours in arrears, in the middle of the afternoon. The first-class cabin was emptied ahead of business class and coach, which meant Reacher and Jodie were the first people outside the terminal and into the taxi line. The temperature and the humidity out there were similar to Texas, but the damp had a saline quality to it because of the Pacific close by. And the light was calmer. The jagged green mountains and the blue of the sea bathed the island with the jewelled glow of the Tropics. Jodie put her dark glasses on again and gazed beyond the airport fences with the mild curiosity of somebody who had passed through Hawaii a dozen times in her father's service days without ever really stopping there. Reacher did the same. He had used it as a Pacific

414

stepping-stone more times than he could count, but he had never served in Hawaii.

The taxi waiting at the head of the line was a replica of the one they'd used at Dallas–Fort Worth, a clean Caprice with the air roaring full blast and the driver's compartment decorated halfway between a religious shrine and a living room. They disappointed the guy by asking him for the shortest ride available on Oahu, which was the half-mile hop around the perimeter road to the Hickam Air Force Base entrance. The guy glanced backward at the line of cars behind him, and Reacher saw him thinking about the better fares the other drivers would get.

'Ten-dollar tip in it for you,' he said.

The guy gave him the same look the ticket clerk at Dallas–Fort Worth had used. A fare that was going to leave the meter stuck on the basic minimum, but a ten-dollar tip? Reacher saw a photograph of what he guessed was the guy's family, taped to the vinyl of the dash. A big family, dark smiling children and a dark smiling woman in a cheerful print dress, all standing in front of a clean simple home with something vigorous growing in a dirt patch to the right. He thought about the Hobies, alone in the dark silence up in Brighton with the hiss of the oxygen bottle and the squeak of the worn wooden floors. And Rutter, in the dusty squalor of his Bronx storefront.

'Twenty dollars,' he said. 'If we get going right now, OK?'

'Twenty dollars?' the guy repeated, amazed.

'Thirty. For your kids. They look nice.'

The guy grinned in the mirror and touched his fingers to his lips and laid them gently on the shiny surface of the photograph. He swung the cab through

415

the lane changes on to the perimeter track and came off again more or less immediately, eight hundred yards into the journey, outside a military gate which looked identical to the one fronting Fort Wolters. Jodie opened the door and stepped out into the heat and Reacher went into his pocket and came out with his roll of cash. Top bill was a fifty, and he peeled it off and pushed it through the little hinged door in the Plexiglas.

'Keep it.'

Then he pointed at the photograph. 'That your house?'

The driver nodded.

'Is it holding up OK? Anything need fixing on it?'

The guy shook his head. 'Tip-top condition.'

'The roof OK?'

'No problems at all.'

Reacher nodded. 'Just checking.'

He slid across the vinyl and joined Jodie on the blacktop. The taxi moved off through the haze, back towards the civilian terminal. There was a faint breeze coming off the ocean. Salt in the air. Jodie pushed the hair off her face and looked around.

'Where are we going?'

'CIL-HI,' Reacher said. 'It's right inside here.'

He pronounced it phonetically, and it made her smile.

'Silly?' she repeated. 'So what's that?'

'C, I, L, H, I,' he said. 'Central Identification Laboratory, Hawaii. It's the Department of the Army's main facility.'

'For what?'

'I'll show you for what,' he said.

Then he paused. 'At least I hope I will.'

They walked up to the gatehouse and waited at the window. There was a sergeant inside, same uniform, same haircut, same suspicious expression on his face as the guy at Wolters. He made them wait in the heat for a second, and then he slid the window back. Reacher stepped forward and gave their names.

'We're here to see Nash Newman,' he said.

The sergeant looked surprised and picked up a clipboard and peeled thin sheets of paper back. He slid a thick finger along a line and nodded. Picked up a phone and dialled a number. Four digits. An internal call. He announced the visitors and listened to the reply, and then he looked puzzled. He covered the phone with his palm and turned back to Jodie.

'How old are you, miss?' he asked.

'Thirty,' Jodie said, puzzled in turn.

'Thirty,' the MP repeated into the phone. Then he listened again and hung it up and wrote something on the clipboard. Turned back to the window.

'He'll be right out, so come on through.'

They squeezed through the narrow gap between the gatehouse wall and the heavy counterweight on the end of the vehicle barrier and waited on the hot pavement six feet away from where they had started, but now it was military pavement, not Hawaii Department of Transportation pavement, and that made a lot of difference to the look on the sergeant's face. The suspicion was all gone, replaced by frank curiosity about why the legendary Nash Newman was in such a big hurry to get these two civilians inside the base.

There was a low concrete building maybe sixty yards away with a plain personnel door set in the blank end wall. The door opened up and a silver-haired man stepped out. He turned back to close it and lock it and then set out at a fast walk towards the gate-house. He was in the pants and the shirt of an Army tropical-issue uniform, with a white lab coat flapping open over them. There was enough metal punched through the collar of the shirt to indicate he was a high-ranking officer, and nothing in his distinguished bearing to contradict that impression. Reacher moved to meet him and Jodie followed. The silver-haired guy was maybe fifty-five, and up close he was tall, with a handsome patrician face and a natural athletic grace in his body that was just beginning to yield to the stiffness of age.

'General Newman,' Reacher said. 'This is Jodie Garber.'

Newman glanced at Reacher and took Jodie's hand, smiling.

'Pleased to meet you, General,' she said.

'We already met,' Newman said.

'We did?' she said, surprised.

'You wouldn't recall it,' he said. 'At least I'd be terribly surprised if you did. You were three years old at the time, I guess. In the Philippines. It was in your father's backyard. I remember you brought me a glass of planter's punch. It was a big glass, and a big yard, and you were a very little girl. You carried it in both hands, with your tongue sticking out, concentrating. I watched you all the way, with my heart in my mouth in case you dropped it.'

She smiled. 'Well, you're right, I'm afraid I don't recall it. I was three? That's an awful long time ago now.'

Newman nodded. 'That's why I checked how old you looked. I didn't mean for the sergeant to come right out and ask you straight. I wanted his subjective impression, is all. It's not the sort of thing one should ask a lady, is it? But I was wondering if you could really be Leon's daughter, come to visit me.'

He squeezed her hand and let it go. Turned to Reacher and punched him lightly on the shoulder.

'Jack Reacher,' he said. 'Damn, it's good to see you again.'

Reacher caught Newman's hand and shook it hard, sharing the pleasure.

'General Newman was my teacher,' he said to Jodie. 'He did a spell at staff college about a million years ago. Advanced forensics, taught me everything I know.'

'He was a pretty good student,' Newman said to her. 'Paid attention at least, which is more than most of them did.'

'So what is it you do, General?' she asked.

'Well, I do a little forensic anthropology,' Newman said.

'He's the best in the world,' Reacher said.

Newman waved away the compliment. 'Well, I don't know about that.'

'Anthropology?' Jodie said. 'But isn't that studying remote tribes and things? How they live? Their rituals and beliefs and so on?'

'No, that's cultural anthropology,' Newman said. 'There are many different disciplines. Mine is forensic anthropology, which is a part of physical anthropology.'

'Studying human remains for clues,' Reacher said.

'A bone doctor,' Newman said. 'That's about what it amounts to.'

They were drifting down the sidewalk as they talked, getting nearer the plain door in the blank wall.

419

It opened up and a younger man was standing there waiting for them in the entrance corridor. A nondescript guy, maybe thirty years old, in a lieutenant's uniform under a white lab coat. Newman nodded towards him. 'This is Lieutenant Simon. He runs the lab for me. Couldn't manage without him.'

He introduced Reacher and Jodie and they shook hands all around. Simon was quiet and reserved. Reacher figured him for a typical lab guy, annoyed at the disruption to the measured routine of his work. Newman led them inside and down the corridor to his office, and Simon nodded silently to him and disappeared.

'Sit down,' Newman said. 'Let's talk.'

'So you're a sort of pathologist?' Jodie asked him.

Newman took his place behind his desk and rocked his hand from side to side, indicating a disparity. 'Well, a pathologist has a medical degree, and we anthropologists don't. We studied anthropology, pure and simple. The physical structure of the human body, that's our field. We both work post-mortem, of course, but generally speaking if a corpse is relatively fresh, it's a pathologist's job, and if there's only a skeleton left, then it's our job. So I'm a bone doctor.'

Jodie nodded.

'Of course, that's a slight simplification,' Newman said. 'A fresh corpse can raise questions concerning its bones. Suppose there's a dismemberment involved? The pathologist would refer to us for help. We can look at the saw marks on the bones and help out. We can say how weak or strong the perpetrator was, what kind of saw he used, was he left-handed or right-handed, things like that. But ninety-nine times out of a hundred, I'm working on skeletons. Dry old bones.'

Then he smiled again. A private, amused smile. 'And pathologists are useless with dry old bones. Really, really hopeless. They don't know the first thing about them. Sometimes I wonder what the hell they teach them in medical school.'

The office was quiet and cool. No windows, indirect lighting from concealed fixtures, carpet on the floor. A rosewood desk, comfortable leather chairs for the visitors. And an elegant clock on a low shelf, ticking quietly, already showing three thirty in the afternoon. Just three and a half hours until the return flight.

'We're here for a reason, General,' Reacher said. 'This isn't entirely a social call, I'm afraid.'

'Social enough to stop calling me General and start calling me Nash, OK? And tell me what's on your mind.'

Reacher nodded. 'We need your help, Nash.'

Newman looked up. 'With the MIA lists?'

Then he turned to Jodie, to explain.

'That's what I do here,' he said. 'Twenty years I've done nothing else.'

She nodded. 'It's about a particular case. We sort of got involved in it.'

Newman nodded back, slowly, but this time the light was gone from his eyes.

'Yes, I was afraid of that,' he said. 'There are eighty-nine thousand one hundred twenty MIA cases here, but I bet I know which one you're interested in.'

'Eighty-nine thousand?' Jodie repeated, surprised.

'And a hundred twenty. Two thousand, two hundred missing from Vietnam, eight thousand, one hundred seventy missing from Korea, and seventy-eight thousand, seven hundred fifty missing from World War Two. We haven't given up on any single

421

one of them, and I promise you we never will.'

'God, why so many?'

Newman shrugged, a bitter sadness suddenly there in his face.

'Wars,' he said. 'High explosive, tactical movement, airplanes. Wars are fought, some combatants live, some die. Some of the dead are recovered, some of them aren't. Sometimes there's nothing left to recover. A direct hit on a man by an artillery shell will reduce him to his constituent molecules. He's just not there any more. Maybe a fine red mist drifting through the air, maybe not even that, maybe he's completely boiled off to vapour. A near miss will blow him to pieces. And fighting is about territory, isn't it? So even if the pieces of him are relatively large, enemy tank movement or friendly tank movement back and forth across the disputed territory will plough the pieces of him into the earth, and then he's gone for ever.'

He sat in silence, and the clock ticked slowly around.

'And airplanes are worse. Many of our air campaigns have been fought over oceans. A plane goes down in the ocean and the crew is missing until the end of time, no matter how much effort we expend in a place like this.'

He waved his hand in a vague gesture that took in the office and all the unseen space beyond and ended up resting towards Jodie, palm up, like a mute appeal.

'Eighty-nine thousand,' she said. 'I thought the MIA stuff was just about Vietnam. Two thousand or so.'

'Eighty-nine thousand, one hundred twenty,' Newman said again. 'We still get a few from Korea, the occasional one from World War Two, the

422

Japanese islands. But you're right, this is mostly about Vietnam. Two thousand, two hundred missing. Not so very many, really. They lost more than that in a single morning during World War One, every morning for four long years. Men and boys blown apart and mashed into the mud. But Vietnam was different. Partly because of things like World War One. We won't take that wholesale slaughter any more, and quite rightly. We've moved on. The population just won't stand for those old attitudes now.'

Jodie nodded, quietly.

'And partly because we lost the war in Vietnam,' Newman said quietly. 'That makes it very different. The only war we ever lost. Makes it all feel a hell of a lot worse. So we try harder to resolve things.'

He made the gesture with his hand again, indicating the unseen complex beyond the office door, and his voice ended on a brighter note.

'So that's what you do here?' Jodie asked. 'Wait for skeletons to be discovered overseas and then bring them back here to identify? So you can finally tick the names off the missing lists?'

Newman rocked his hand again, equivocating. 'Well, we don't wait, exactly. Where we can, we go out searching for them. And we don't always identify them, although we sure as hell try hard.'

'It must be difficult,' she said.

He nodded. 'Technically, it can be very challenging. The recovery sites are usually a mess. The field workers send us animal bones, local bones, anything. We sort it all out here. Then we go to work with what we've got. Which sometimes isn't very much. Sometimes all that's left of an American soldier is just a handful of bone fragments you could fit in a cigar box.'

'Impossible,' she said.

'Often,' he said back. 'We've got a hundred part-skeletons here right now, unidentified. The Department of the Army can't afford mistakes. They demand a very high standard of certainty, and sometimes we just can't meet it.'

'Where do you start?' she asked.

He shrugged. 'Well, wherever we can. Medical records, usually. Suppose Reacher here was an MIA? If he'd broken his arm as a boy, we'd be able to match the old X-ray against a healed break in the bones we found. Maybe. Or if we found his jaw, we could match the work on his teeth with his dental charts.'

Reacher saw her looking at him, imagining him reduced to dry yellowing bones on a jungle floor, scraped out of the dirt and compared to brittle fading X-rays taken thirty years earlier. The office went silent again, and the clock ticked around.

'Leon came here in April,' Reacher said.

Newman nodded. 'Yes, he visited with me. Foolish of him, really, because he was a very sick man. But it was good to see him.'

Then he turned to Jodie, sympathy on his face.

'He was a fine, fine man. I owed him a lot.'

She nodded. It wasn't the first time she'd heard it, and it wouldn't be the last.

'He asked you about Victor Hobie,' Reacher said.

Newman nodded again. 'Victor Truman Hobie.'

'What did you tell him?'

'Nothing,' Newman said. 'And I'm going to tell you nothing, too.'

The clock ticked on. A quarter to four.

'Why not?' Reacher asked.

'Surely you know why not.'

424

'It's classified?'

'Twice over,' Newman said.

Reacher moved in the silence, restless with frustration. 'You're our last hope, Nash. We've already been all over everything else.'

Newman shook his head. 'You know how it is, Reacher. I'm an officer in the US Army, damn it. I'm not going to reveal classified information.'

'Please, Nash,' Reacher said. 'We came all this way.'

'I can't,' Newman said.

'No such word,' Reacher said.

Silence.

'Well, I guess you could ask me questions,' Newman said. 'If a former student of mine comes in here and asks me questions based on his own skills and observations, and I answer them in a purely academic fashion, I don't see that any harm can come to anybody.'

It was like the clouds lifting away from the sun. Jodie glanced at Reacher. He glanced at the clock. Seven minutes to four. Less than three hours to go.

'OK, Nash, thanks,' he said. 'You're familiar with this case?'

'I'm familiar with all of them. This one especially, since April.'

'And it's classified twice over?'

Newman just nodded.

'At a level that kept Leon out of the loop?'

'That's a pretty high level,' Newman hinted. 'Wouldn't you agree?'

Reacher nodded. Thought hard. 'What did Leon want you to do?'

'He was in the dark,' Newman said. 'You need to bear that in mind, right?'

425

'OK,' Reacher said. 'What did he want you to do?'

'He wanted us to find the crash site.'

'Four miles west of An Khe.'

Newman nodded. 'I felt badly for Leon. No real reason for him to be out of the loop on this, and there was nothing I could do to alter the classification code. But I owed that man a lot, way more than I can tell you about, so I agreed to find the site.'

Jodie leaned forward. 'But why wasn't it found before? People seem to know roughly where it is.'

Newman shrugged. 'It's all incredibly difficult. You have no idea. The terrain, the bureaucracy. We lost the war, remember. The Vietnamese dictate the terms over there. We run a joint recovery effort, but they control it. The whole thing is constant manipulation and humiliation. We're not allowed to wear our uniforms over there, because they say the sight of a US Army uniform will traumatize the village populations. They make us rent their own helicopters to get around, millions and millions of dollars a year for ratty old rust-buckets with half the capability of our own machines. Truth is, we're *buying* those old bones back, and they set the price and the availability. Bottom line right now is the United States is paying more than three million dollars for every single identification we make, and it burns me up.'

Four minutes to four. Newman sighed again, lost in thought.

'But you found the site?' Reacher prompted.

'It was scheduled for some time in the future,' Newman said. 'We knew roughly where it was, and we knew exactly what we'd find when we got there, so it wasn't much of a high priority. But as a favour to Leon, I went over there and bargained to move it up the schedule. I wanted it next item on the list. It was a real bitch to negotiate. They get wind you want something in particular, they go stubborn as all hell. You've got no idea. Inscrutable? Tell me about it.'

'But you found it?' Jodie asked.

'It was a bitch, geographically,' Newman said. 'We talked to DeWitt over at Wolters, and he helped us pin down the exact location, more or less. Remotest place you ever saw. Mountainous and inaccessible. I can guarantee you no human being has ever set foot there, no time in the history of the planet. It was a nightmare trip. But it was a great site. Completely inaccessible, so it wasn't mined.'

'Mined?' Jodie repeated. 'You mean they booby-trap the sites?'

Newman shook his head. 'No, mined, as in excavated. Anything accessible, the population was all over it thirty years ago. They took dog tags, ID cards, helmets, souvenirs, but mostly they were after the metals. Fixed-wing sites, mostly, because of the gold and platinum.'

'What gold?' she asked.

'In the electrical circuits,' Newman said. 'The F-4 Phantoms, for instance, they had about five thousand dollars' worth of precious metals in the connections. Population used to hack it all out and sell it. You buy cheap jewellery in Bangkok, probably it's made out of old US fighter-bomber electronics.'

'What did you find up there?' Reacher asked.

'A relatively good state of preservation,' Newman said. 'The Huey was smashed up and rusted, but it was recognizable. The bodies were completely skeletonized, of course. Clothing was rotted and gone, long ago. But nothing else was missing. They all had dog tags. We packed them up and helicoptered them to Hanoi. Then we flew them back here in the Starlifter, full honours. We only just got back. Three months, beginning to end, one of the best we've ever done in terms of time scale. And the IDs are going to be a total formality, because we've got the dog tags. No role for a bone doctor on this one. Open and shut. I'm just sorry Leon didn't live to see it. It would have put his mind at rest.'

'The bodies are here?' Reacher asked.

Newman nodded. 'Right next door.'

'Can we see them?' Reacher asked.

Newman nodded again. 'You shouldn't, but you need to.'

The office went quiet and Newman stood up and gestured towards the door with both hands. Lieutenant Simon walked past. He nodded a greeting.

'We're going into the lab,' Newman said to him.

'Yes, sir,' Simon said back. He moved away into his own office cubicle and Reacher and Jodie and Newman walked in the other direction and paused in front of a plain door set in a blank cinder-block wall. Newman took keys from his pocket and unlocked it. He pulled it open and repeated the same formal gesture with both his hands. Reacher and Jodie preceded him into the lab.

Simon watched them go inside from his cubicle. When the door closed and locked behind them, he picked up his phone and dialled nine for a line and then a ten-figure number starting with the New York City area code. The number rang for a long time because it was already the middle of the evening six thousand miles to the east. Then it was answered.

'Reacher's here,' Simon whispered. 'Right now, with a woman. They're in the lab, right now. Looking.'

Hobie's voice came back low and controlled. 'Who's the woman?'

'Jodie Garber,' Simon said. 'General Garber's daughter.'

'Alias Mrs Jacob.'

'What do you want me to do?'

There was silence on the line. Just the whistle of the long-distance satellite.

'You could give them a ride back to the airport, maybe. The woman's got an appointment in New York tomorrow afternoon, so I guess they'll be trying to make the seven o'clock flight. Just make sure they don't miss it.'

'OK,' Simon said, and Hobie broke the connection.

The lab was a wide low room, maybe forty feet by fifty. There were no windows. The lighting was the bland wash of fluorescent tubes. There was the faint hiss of efficient air circulation, but there was a smell in the room, somewhere between the sharp tang of strong disinfectant and the warm odour of earth. At the far end of the space was an alcove filled with racks. On the racks were rows of cardboard boxes, marked with reference numbers in black. Maybe a hundred boxes.

'The unidentified,' Reacher said.

Newman nodded at his side.

'As of now,' he said quietly. 'We won't give up on them.'

Between them and the distant alcove was the main body of the room. The floor was tile, swabbed to a shine. Standing on it were twenty neat wooden tables set in precise rows. The tables were waist high and

429

topped with heavy polished slabs. Each table was a little shorter and a little narrower than an Army cot. They looked like sturdy versions of the tables decorators use for wallpaper pasting. Six of them were completely empty. Seven of them had the lids of seven polished aluminium caskets laid across them. The final seven tables held the seven aluminium caskets themselves, in neat alternate rows, each one adjacent to the table bearing its lid. Reacher stood silent with his head bowed, and then he drew himself up to attention and held a long silent salute for the first time in more than two years.

'Awful,' Jodie whispered.

She was standing with her hands clasped behind her, head bowed, like she was at a graveside ceremony. Reacher released his salute and squeezed her hand.

'Thank you,' Newman said quietly. 'I like people to show respect in here.'

'How could we not?' Jodie whispered.

She was staring at the caskets, with tears starting in her eyes.

'So, Reacher, what do you see?' Newman asked in the silence.

Reacher's eyes were wandering around the bright room. He was too shocked to move.

'I see seven caskets,' he said quietly. 'Where I expected to see eight. There were eight people in that Huey. Crew of five, and they picked up three. It's in DeWitt's report. Five and three make eight.'

'And eight minus one makes seven,' Newman said.

'Did you search the site? Thoroughly?'

Newman shook his head. 'No.'

'Why not?'

'You'll have to figure that out.'

430

Reacher shook himself and took a step forward. 'May I?'

'Be my guest,' Newman replied. 'Tell me what you see. Concentrate hard, and we'll see what you've remembered, and what you've forgotten.'

Reacher walked to the nearest casket and turned so that he was looking down into it along its length. The casket held a rough wooden box, six inches smaller in every dimension than the casket itself.

'That's what the Vietnamese make us use,' Newman said. 'They sell those boxes to us and make us use them. We put them in our own caskets in the hangar at the airfield in Hanoi.'

The wooden box had no lid. It was just a shallow tray. There was a jumble of bones in it. Somebody had arranged them in roughly the correct anatomical sequence. There was a skull at the top, yellowed and old. It grinned up with a grotesque smile. There was a gold tooth in the mouth. The empty eye sockets stared. The vertebrae of the neck were lined up neatly. Below them the shoulder blades and the collarbones and the ribs were laid out in their correct places above the pelvis. The arm bones and the leg bones were stacked to the sides. There was the dull glint of a metal chain draped over the vertebrae of the neck, running away under the flatness of the left shoulder blade.

'May I?' Reacher asked again.

Newman nodded. 'Please.'

Reacher stood silent for a long moment and then leaned in and hooked his finger under the chain and eased it out. The bones stirred and clicked and moved as the dog tags caught. He pulled them out and brought them up and rubbed the ball of his thumb across their faces. Bent down to read the stamped name.

'Kaplan,' he said. 'The co-pilot.'

'How did he die?' Newman asked.

Reacher draped the tags back across the bony ribs and looked hard for the evidence. The skull was OK. No trace of damage to the arms or legs or chest. But the pelvis was smashed. The vertebrae towards the bottom of the spine were crushed. And the ribs at the back were fractured, eight of them on both sides, counting upward from the bottom.

'Impact, when the Huey hit the ground. He took a big hit in the lower back. Massive internal trauma and haemorrhage. Probably fatal within a minute.'

'But he was strapped in his seat,' Newman said. 'Head-on crash into the ground, how does that injure him from behind?'

Reacher looked again. He felt the way he had years before in the classroom, nervous about screwing up in front of the legendary Nash Newman. He looked hard, and he put his hands lightly on the dry bones, feeling them. But he had to be right. This was a crushing impact to the lower back. There was no other explanation.

'The Huey spun,' he said. 'It came in at a shallow angle and the trees spun it around. It separated between the cabin and the tail and the cabin hit the ground travelling backward.'

Newman nodded. 'Excellent. That's exactly how we found it. It hit backward. Instead of his harness saving him, his chair killed him.'

Reacher moved on to the next casket. There was the same shallow wooden tray, the same jumble of yellow bones. The same grotesque, accusing, grinning skull. Below it, the neck was broken. He eased the dog tags out from between the shards of cracked bone.

432

'Tardelli,' he read.

'The starboard-side gunner,' Newman said.

Tardelli's skeleton was a mess. The gunners on a slick stand in the open doorway, basically unsecured, juggling with the heavy machine-gun swinging on a bungee cord. When the Huey went down, Tardelli had been thrown all over the cabin.

'Broken neck,' Reacher said. 'Crushing to the upper chest.'

He turned the awful yellow skull over. It was fractured like an eggshell.

'Head trauma also. I'd say he died instantaneously. Wouldn't like to say which exact injury killed him.'

'Neither would I,' Newman said. 'He was nineteen years old.'

There was silence. Nothing in the air except the faint sweet aroma of loam.

'Look at the next one,' Newman said.

The next one was different. There was a single injury to the chest. The dog tags were tangled into splintered bones. Reacher couldn't free them. He had to bend his head to get the name.

'Bamford.'

'The crew chief,' Newman said. 'He would have been sitting on the cabin bench, facing the rear, opposite the three guys they picked up.'

Bamford's bony face grinned up at him. Below it, his skeleton was complete and undamaged, except for the narrow crushing injury sideways across the upper body. It was like a three-inch trench in his chest. The sternum had been punched down to the level of the spine and had gone on and knocked three vertebrae out of line. Three ribs had gone with it.

'So what do you think?' Newman asked.

Reacher put his hand into the box and felt the dimensions of the injury. It was narrow and horizontal. Three fingers wouldn't fit into it, but two would.

'Some kind of an impact,' he said. 'Something between a sharp instrument and a blunt instrument. Hit him sideways in the chest, obviously. It would have stopped his heart immediately. Was it the rotor blade?'

Newman nodded. 'Very good. The way it looked, the rotor folded up against the trees and came down into the cabin. It must have struck him across the upper body. As you say, a blow like that would have stopped his heart instantaneously.'

In the next casket, the bones were very different. Some of them were the same dull yellow, but most of them were white and brittle and eroded. The dog tags were bent and blackened. Reacher turned them to throw the embossing into relief against the ceiling lights and read: Soper.

'The port-side gunner,' Newman said.

'There was a fire,' Reacher said.

'How can you tell?' Newman asked, like the teacher he was.

'Dog tags are burned.'

'And?'

'The bones are calcinated,' Reacher said. 'At least, most of them are.'

'Calcinated?' Newman repeated.

Reacher nodded and went back fifteen years to his textbooks.

'The organic components burned off, leaving only the inorganic compounds behind. Burning leaves the bones smaller, whiter, veined, brittle and eroded.'

'Good,' Newman nodded.

'The explosion DeWitt saw,' Jodie said. 'It was the fuel tank.'

Newman nodded. 'Classic evidence. Not a slow fire. A fuel explosion. It spills randomly and burns quickly, which explains the random nature of the burned bones. Looks to me like Soper caught the fuel across his lower body, but his upper body was lying outside of the fire.'

His quiet words died to silence and the three of them were lost in imagining the terror. The bellowing engines, the hostile bullets smashing into the airframe, the sudden loss of power, the spurt of spilling fuel, the fire, the tearing smashing impact through the trees, the screaming, the rotor scything down, the shuddering crash, the screeching of metal, the smashing of frail human bodies into the indifferent jungle floor where no person had ever walked since the dawn of time. Soper's empty eye sockets stared up into the light, challenging them to imagine.

'Look at the next one,' Newman said.

The next casket held the remains of a man called Allen. No burning. Just a yellow skeleton with bright dog tags around the broken neck. A noble, grinning skull. Even white teeth. A high, round, undamaged cranium. The product of good nutrition and careful upbringing in the America of the Fifties. His whole back was smashed, like a dead crab.

'Allen was one of the three they picked up,' Newman said.

Reacher nodded, sadly. The sixth casket was a burn victim. His name was Zabrinski. His bones were calcinated and small.

'He was probably a big guy in life,' Newman said.

'Burning can shrink your bones by fifty per cent, sometimes. So don't write him off as a midget.'

Reacher nodded again. Stirred through the bones with his hand. They were light and brittle. Like husks. The veining left them sharp with microscopic ribbing.

'Injuries?' Newman asked.

Reacher looked again, but he found nothing.

'He burned to death,' he said.

Newman nodded.

'Yes, I'm afraid he did,' he said.

'Awful,' Jodie whispered.

The seventh and final casket held the remains of a man named Gunston. They were terrible remains. At first Reacher thought there was no skull. Then he saw it was lying in the bottom of the wooden box. It was smashed into a hundred pieces. Most of them were no bigger than his thumbnail.

'What do you think?' Newman asked.

Reacher shook his head.

'I don't want to think,' he whispered. 'I'm all done thinking.'

Newman nodded, sympathetic. 'Rotor blade hit him in the head. He was one of the three they picked up. He was sitting opposite Bamford.'

'Five and three,' Jodie said quietly. 'So the crew was Hobie and Kaplan, pilot and co-pilot, Bamford the crew chief, Soper and Tardelli the gunners, and they went down and picked up Allen and Zabrinski and Gunston.'

Newman nodded. 'That's what the files tell us.'

'So where's Hobie?' Reacher asked.

'You're missing something,' Newman said. 'Sloppy work, Reacher, for somebody who used to be good at this.'

Reacher glanced at him. DeWitt had said something similar. He had said *sloppy work for somebody who was once an MP major.* And he had said *look closer to home.*

'They were MPs, right?' he said suddenly.

Newman smiled. 'Who were?'

'Two of them,' Reacher said. 'Two out of Allen and Zabrinski and Gunston. Two of them were arresting the other one. It was a special mission. Kaplan had put two MPs in the field the day before. His last but one mission, flying solo, the one I didn't read. They were going back to pick them up, plus the guy they'd arrested.'

Newman nodded. 'Correct.'

'Which was which?'

'Pete Zabrinski and Joey Gunston were the cops. Carl Allen was the bad guy.'

Reacher nodded. 'What had he done?'

'The details are classified,' Newman said. 'Your guess?'

'In and out like that, a quick arrest? Fragging, I suppose.'

'What's fragging?' Jodie asked.

'Killing your officer,' Reacher said. 'It happened, time to time. Some gung-ho lieutenant, probably new in-country, gets all keen on advancing into dangerous positions. The grunts don't like it, figure he's after a medal, figure they'd rather keep their asses in one piece. So he says *charge* and somebody shoots him in the back, or throws a grenade at him, which was more efficient, because it didn't need aiming and it disguised the whole thing better. That's where the name comes from, fragging, fragmentation device, a grenade.'

'So was it fragging?' Jodie asked.

437

'The details are classified,' Newman said again. 'But certainly there was fragging involved, at the end of a long and vicious career. According to the files, Carl Allen was definitely not the flavour of the month.'

Jodie nodded. 'But why on earth is that classified? Whatever he did, he's been dead thirty years. Justice is done, right?'

Reacher had stepped back to Allen's casket. He was staring down into it.

'Caution,' he said. 'Whoever the gung-ho lieutenant was, his family was told he died a hero, fighting the enemy. If they ever find out any different, it's a scandal. And the Department of the Army doesn't like scandals.'

'Correct,' Newman said again.

'But where's Hobie?' Reacher asked again.

'You're still missing something. One step at a time, OK?'

'But what is it?' Reacher asked. 'Where is it?'

'In the bones,' Newman said.

The clock on the laboratory wall showed five-thirty. Not much more than an hour to go. Reacher took a breath and walked back around the caskets in reverse order. Gunston, Zabrinski, Allen, Soper, Bamford, Tardelli, Kaplan. Six grinning skulls and one headless bony set of shoulders stared back up at him. He did the round again. The clock ticked on. He stopped next to each casket and gripped the cold aluminium sides and leaned over and stared in, desperate to spot what he was missing. In the bones. He started each search at the top. The skull, the neck, the collarbones, the ribs, the arms, the pelvis, the legs, the feet. He took to rummaging through the boxes, lightly, delicately, sorting the dry bones, looking for it. A quarter to six.

Ten to six. Jodie was watching him, anxiously. He did the round for the third time, starting again with Gunston, the cop. He moved on to Zabrinski, the other cop. On to Allen, the criminal. On to Soper, the gunner. On to Bamford, the crew chief. He found it right there in Bamford's box. He closed his eyes. It was obvious. It was so obvious it was like it was painted in Day-Glo paint and lit up with a searchlight. He ran back around the other six boxes, counting, double checking. He was right. He had found it. Six o'clock in the evening in Hawaii.

'There are seven bodies,' he said. 'But there are fifteen hands.'

Six o'clock in the evening in Hawaii is eleven o'clock at night in New York City, and Hobie was alone in his apartment, thirty floors above Fifth Avenue, in the bedroom, getting ready to go to sleep. Eleven o'clock was earlier than his normal bedtime. Usually he would stay awake, reading a book or watching a film on cable until one or two in the morning. But tonight he was tired. It had been a fatiguing day. There had been a certain amount of physical activity, and some mental strain.

He was sitting on the edge of his bed. It was a king-size bed, although he slept alone, and always had. There was a thick comforter in white. The walls were white and the venetian blinds were white. Not because he had wanted any kind of artistic consistency in his decor, but because white things were always the cheapest. Whatever you were dealing with, bed linen or paint or window coverings, the white option was always priced lowest. There was no art on the walls. No photographs, no ornaments, no souvenirs, no hangings. The floor was plain oak strips. No rug.

His feet were planted squarely on the floor. His shoes were black Oxfords, polished to a high shine, planted exactly at right angles to the oak strips. He reached down with his good hand and undid the laces, one at a time. Eased the shoes off, one at a time. Pushed them together with his feet and picked them up both together and squared them away under the bed. He slid his thumb into the top of his socks, one at a time, and eased them off his feet. Shook them out and dropped them on the floor. He unknotted his tie. He always wore a tie. It was a source of great pride to him that he could knot a tie with one hand.

He picked up the tie and stood and walked barefoot to his closet. Slid the door open and worked the thin end of the tie down behind the little brass bar where it hung at night. Then he dropped his left shoulder and let his jacket slide off his arm. Used the left hand to pull it off on the right. He reached into the closet and came out with a hanger and slid the jacket on to it, one-handed. He hung it up on the rail. Then he unbuttoned his pants and dropped the zip. Stepped out of them and crouched and straightened them on the shiny oak floor. No other way for a one-armed man to fold trousers. He put the cuffs together one on top of the other and trapped them under his foot and pulled the legs straight. Then he stood up and took a second hanger from the closet and bent down and flipped the bar under the cuffs and slid it along the floor to the knees. Then he stood up again and shook the hanger and the pants fell into perfect shape. He hung them alongside the jacket.

He curled his left wrist around the starched button-holes and undid his shirt. He opened the right cuff. He shrugged the shirt off his shoulders and used his left hand to pull it down over his hook. Then he leaned sideways and let it fall down his left arm. Trapped the tail under his foot and pulled his arm up through the sleeve. The sleeve turned inside out as it always did and his good hand squeezed through the cuff. The only modification he had been forced to make in his entire wardrobe was to move the cuff buttons on his shirts to allow them to pass over his left hand while they were still done up.

He left the shirt on the floor and pulled at the waistband of his boxers and wriggled them down over his hips. Stepped out of them and grasped the hem of his undershirt. This was the hardest part. He stretched the hem and ducked and whipped it up over his head. Changed his grip to the neck and pulled it up over his face. He pulled it down on the right and eased his hook out through the armhole. Then he cracked his left arm like a whip until the undershirt came off it and landed on the floor. He bent and scooped it up with the shirt and the boxers and the socks and carried them into the bathroom and dumped them all in the basket.

He walked naked back to the bed and sat down again on the edge. Reached across his chest with his left hand and unbuckled the heavy leather straps around his right bicep. There were three straps, and three buckles. He eased the leather corset apart and squeezed it backward off his upper arm. It creaked in the silence as it moved. The leather was thick and heavy, much thicker and heavier than any shoe leather. It was built up in shaped layers. It was brown and shiny with wear. Over the years it had moulded itself like steel to his shape. It crushed the muscle as he eased it back. He fiddled the riveted straps clear of his

441

elbow. Then he took the cold curve of the hook in his left hand and pulled gently. The cup sucked off the stump and he pulled it away. Clamped it vertically between his knees, the hook pointing downward to the floor and the cup facing upward. He leaned over to his nightstand and took a wad of tissues from a box and a can of talc from a drawer. He crushed the tissues in his left palm and pushed them down into the cup, twisting the wad like a screw to wipe away the sweat of the day. Then he shook the can of talc and powdered all around the inside. He took more tissues and polished the leather and the steel. Then he laid the whole assembly on the floor, parallel with the bed.

He wore a thin sock on the stump of his right forearm. It was there to stop the leather chafing the skin. It was not a specialist medical device. It was a child's sock. Just tubular, no heel, the sort of thing mothers choose before their babies can walk. He bought them a dozen pairs at a time from department stores. He always bought white ones. They were cheaper. He eased the sock off the stump and shook it out and laid it next to the box of tissues on the nightstand.

The stump itself was shrivelled. There was some muscle left, but with no work to do it had wasted to nothing. The bones were filed smooth on the cut ends, and the skin had been sewn tight down over them. The skin was white, and the stitches were red. They looked like Chinese writing. There was black hair growing on the bottom of the stump, because the skin there had been stretched down from the outside of his forearm.

He stood up again and walked to the bathroom. A previous owner had installed a wall of mirror above the sink. He looked at himself in it, and hated what he saw. His arm didn't bother him. It was just missing. It was his face he hated. The burns. The arm was a wound, but the face was a disfigurement. He turned half sideways so he didn't have to look at it. He cleaned his teeth and carried a bottle of lotion back to the bed. Squeezed a drop on to the skin of the stump and worked it in with his fingers. Then he placed the lotion next to the baby's sock on the nightstand and rolled under the covers and clicked the light off.

'Left or right?' Jodie asked. 'Which did he lose?'

Reacher was standing over Bamford's bright casket, sorting through bones.

'His right,' he said. 'The extra hand is a right hand.'

Newman moved across to Reacher's shoulder and leaned in and separated two splintered shards of bone, each one about five inches in length.

'He lost more than his hand,' he said. 'These are the radius and the ulna from his right arm. It was severed below the elbow, probably by a fragment of the rotor blade. There would have been enough left to make a decent stump.'

Reacher picked up the bones and ran his fingers across the splintered ends.

'I don't understand, Nash,' he said. 'Why didn't you search the area?'

'Why should we?' Newman said back, neutrally.

'Because why just assume he survived? He was grievously injured. The impact, the severed arm? Maybe other injuries, maybe internal? Massive blood loss at least? Maybe he was burned, too. There was burning fuel everywhere. Think about it, Nash. Probability is he crawled out from the wreck, bleeding from his arteries, maybe on fire, he dragged himself

443

twenty yards away and collapsed in the undergrowth and died. Why the hell didn't you look for him?'

'Ask yourself the question,' Newman said. 'Why didn't we look for him?'

Reacher stared at him. Nash Newman, one of the smartest guys he had ever known. A man so picky and precise he could take a fragment of skull an inch wide and tell you who it had belonged to, how he had lived, how he had died. A man so professional and meticulous he had run the longest-lasting and most complicated forensic investigation ever known in history and had received nothing but praise and plaudits all the way. How could Nash Newman have made such an elementary mistake? Reacher stared at him, and then he breathed out and closed his eyes.

'Christ, Nash,' he said slowly. 'You *know* he survived, don't you? You actually *know* it. You didn't look for him because you know it for sure.'

Newman nodded. 'Correct.'

'But how do you know?'

Newman glanced around the lab. Lowered his voice.

'Because he turned up afterward,' he said. 'He crawled into a field hospital fifty miles away and three weeks later. It's all in their medical files. He was racked with fever, serious malnutrition, terrible burns to one side of his face, no arm, maggots in the stump. He was incoherent most of the time, but they identified him by his dog tags. Then he came around after treatment and told the story, no other survivors but himself. That's why I said we knew exactly what we were going to find up there. That's why it was such a low priority, until Leon got all agitated about it.'

'So what happened?' Jodie asked. 'Why all the secrecy?'

'The hospital was way north,' Newman said. 'Charlie was pushing south and we were retreating. The hospital was getting ready for evacuation.'

'And?' Reacher asked.

'He disappeared the night before they were due to move him to Saigon.'

'He disappeared?'

Newman nodded. 'Just ran away. Got himself out of his cot and lit out. Never been seen since.'

'Shit,' Reacher said.

'I still don't understand the secrecy,' Jodie said.

Newman shrugged. 'Well, Reacher can explain it. More his area than mine.'

Reacher still had hold of Hobie's bones. The radius and the ulna from his right arm, neatly socketed on the lower end like nature intended, savagely smashed and splintered at the upper end by a fragment of his own rotor blade. Hobie had studied the leading edge of that blade and seen that it was capable of smashing through tree limbs as thick as a man's arm. He had used that inspiration to save other men's lives, over and over again. Then that same blade had come folding and whirling down into his own cockpit and taken his hand away.

'He was a deserter,' he said. 'Technically, that's what he was. He was a serving soldier and he ran away. But a decision was taken not to go after him. Had to be that way. Because what could the Army do? If they caught him, what next? They would be prosecuting a guy with an exemplary record, nine hundred ninety-one combat missions, a guy who deserted after the trauma of a horrendous injury and disfigurement. They couldn't do that. The war was unpopular. You can't send a disfigured hero to Leavenworth for

445

deserting under those circumstances. But equally you can't send out the message that you're letting deserters get away with it. That would have been a scandal of a different sort. They were still busting plenty of guys for deserting. The undeserving ones. They couldn't reveal they had different strokes for different folks. So Hobie's file was closed and sealed and classified secret. That's why the personnel record ends with the last mission. All the rest of it is in a vault, somewhere in the Pentagon.'

Jodie nodded.

'And that's why he's not on the Wall,' she said. 'They know he's still alive.'

Reacher was reluctant to put the arm bones down. He held them, and ran his fingers up and down their length. The good ends were smooth and perfect, ready to accept the subtle articulation of the human wrist.

'Have you logged his medical records?' he asked Newman. 'His old X-rays and dental charts and all that stuff?'

Newman shook his head. 'He's not MIA. He survived and deserted.'

Reacher turned back to Bamford's casket and laid the two yellow shards gently in one corner of the rough wooden box. He shook his head. 'I just can't believe it, Nash. Everything about this guy says he didn't have a deserter's mentality. His background, his record, everything. I know about deserters. I hunted plenty of them.'

'He deserted,' Newman said. 'It's a fact, it's in the files from the hospital.'

'He survived the crash,' Reacher said. 'I guess I can't dispute that any more. He was in the hospital. Can't dispute that, either. But suppose it wasn't really

446

desertion? Suppose he was just confused, or groggy from the drugs or something? Suppose he just wandered away and got lost?'

Newman shook his head. 'He wasn't confused.'

'But how do you know that? Loss of blood, malnutrition, fever, morphine?'

'He deserted,' Newman said.

'It doesn't add up,' Reacher said.

'War changes people,' Newman said.

'Not that much,' Reacher said back.

Newman stepped closer and lowered his voice again.

'He killed an orderly,' he whispered. 'The guy spotted him on the way out and tried to stop him. It's all in the file. Hobie said *I'm not going back* and hit the guy in the head with a bottle. Broke his skull. They put the guy in Hobie's bed and he didn't survive the trip back to Saigon. That's what the secrecy is all about, Reacher. They didn't just let him get away with deserting. They let him get away with murder.'

There was total silence in the lab. The air hissed and the loamy smell of the old bones drifted. Reacher laid his hand on the shiny lip of Bamford's casket, just to keep himself standing upright.

'I don't believe it,' he said.

'You should,' Newman said back. 'Because it's true.'

'I can't tell his folks that,' Reacher said. 'I just can't. It would kill them.'

'Hell of a secret,' Jodie said. 'They let him get away with murder?'

'Politics,' Newman said. 'The politics over there stunk to high heaven. Still do, as a matter of fact.'

'Maybe he died later,' Reacher said. 'Maybe he got

away into the jungle and died there later. He was still very sick, right?'

'How would that help you?' Newman asked.

'I could tell his folks he was dead, you know, gloss over the exact details.'

'You're clutching at straws,' Newman said.

'We have to go,' Jodie said. 'We need to make the plane.'

'Would you run his medical records?' Reacher asked. 'If I got hold of them from his family? Would you do that for me?'

There was a pause.

'I've already got them,' Newman said. 'Leon brought them with him. The family released them to him.'

'So will you run them?' Reacher asked.

'You're clutching at straws,' Newman said again.

Reacher turned around and pointed at the hundred cardboard boxes stacked in the alcove at the end of the room. 'He could already be here, Nash.'

'He's in New York,' Jodie said. 'Don't you see that?'

'No, I want him to be dead,' Reacher said. 'I can't go back to his folks and tell them their boy is a deserter and a murderer and has been running around all this time without contacting them. I need him to be dead.'

'But he isn't,' Newman said.

'But he could be, right?' Reacher said. 'He could have died later. Back in the jungle, someplace else, maybe far away, on the run? Disease, malnutrition? Maybe his skeleton was found already. Will you run his records? As a favour to me?'

'Reacher, we need to go now,' Jodie said.

'Will you run them?' Reacher asked again.

'I can't,' Newman said. 'Christ, this whole thing is

448

classified, don't you understand that? I shouldn't have told you anything at all. And I can't add another name to the MIA lists now. The Department of the Army wouldn't stand for it. We're supposed to be reducing the numbers here, not adding to them.'

'Can't you do it unofficially? Privately? You can do that, right? You run this place, Nash. Please? For me?'

Newman shook his head. 'You're clutching at straws, is all.'

'Please, Nash,' Reacher said.

There was a silence. Then Newman sighed.

'OK, damn it,' he said. 'For you, I'll do it, I guess.'

'When?' Reacher asked.

Newman shrugged. 'First thing tomorrow morning, OK?'

'Call me as soon as you've done it?'

'Sure, but you're wasting your time. Number?'

'Use the mobile,' Jodie said.

She recited the number. Newman wrote it on the cuff of his lab coat.

'Thanks, Nash,' Reacher said. 'I really appreciate this.'

'Waste of time,' Newman said again.

'We need to go,' Jodie called.

Reacher nodded vaguely and they all moved towards the plain door in the cinder-block wall. Lieutenant Simon was waiting on the other side of it with the offer of a ride around the perimeter road to the passenger terminals.

FIFTEEN

First class or not, the flight back was miserable. It was the same plane, going east to New York along the second leg of a giant triangle. It was cleaned and perfumed and checked and refuelled, and it had a new crew onboard. Reacher and Jodie were in the same seats they had left four hours earlier. Reacher took the window again, but it felt different. It was still two and a half times as wide as normal, still sumptuously upholstered in leather and sheepskin, but he took no pleasure in sitting in it again.

The lights were dimmed, to represent night. They had taken off into an outrageous tropical sunset boiling away beyond the islands and then they had turned away to fly towards darkness. The engines settled to a muted hiss. The flight attendants were quiet and unobtrusive. There was only one other passenger in the cabin. He was sitting two rows ahead, across the aisle. He was a tall spare man, dressed in a seersucker short-sleeve shirt printed with pale stripes. His right forearm was laid gently on the arm of the chair, and his hand hung down, limp and relaxed. His eyes were closed.

'How tall is he?' Jodie whispered.

Reacher leaned over and glanced ahead. 'Maybe six one.'

'Same as Victor Hobie,' she said. 'Remember the file?'

Reacher nodded. Glanced diagonally across at the pale forearm resting along the seat. The guy was thin, and he could see the prominent knob of bone at the wrist, standing out in the dimness. There was slim muscle and freckled skin and bleached hair. The radius bone was visible, running all the way back to the elbow. Hobie had left six inches of his radius bone behind at the crash site. Reacher counted with his eyes, up from the guy's wrist joint. Six inches took him halfway to the elbow.

'About half and half, right?' Jodie said.

'A little more than half,' Reacher said. 'The stump would have needed trimming. They'd have filed it down where it was splintered, I guess. If he survived.'

The guy two rows ahead turned sleepily and pulled his arm in close to his body and out of sight, like he knew they were talking about it.

'He survived,' Jodie said. 'He's in New York, trying to stay hidden.'

Reacher leaned the other way and rested his forehead on the cold plastic of the porthole.

'I would have bet my life he isn't,' he said.

He kept his eyes open, but there was nothing to see out of the window. Just black night sky all the way down to the black night ocean, seven miles below.

'Why does it bother you so much?' she asked, in the quiet.

He turned forward and stared at the empty seat six feet in front of him.

'Lots of reasons,' he said.

451

'Like what?'

He shrugged. 'Like everything, like a great big depressing spiral. It was a professional call. My gut told me something, and it looks like I was wrong.'

She laid her hand gently on his forearm, where the muscle narrowed a little above his wrist. 'Being wrong isn't the end of the world.'

He shook his head. 'Sometimes it isn't, sometimes it is. Depends on the issue, right? Somebody asks me who's going to win the series, and I say the Yankees, that doesn't matter, does it? Because how can I know stuff like that? But suppose I was a sportswriter who was supposed to know stuff like that? Or a professional gambler? Suppose baseball was my life? Then it's the end of the world if I start to screw up.'

'So what are you saying?'

'I'm saying judgements like that are my life. It's what I'm supposed to be good at. I used to be good at it. I could always depend on being right.'

'But you had nothing to go on.'

'Bullshit, Jodie. I had a whole lot to go on. A whole lot more than I sometimes used to have. I met with the guy's folks, I read his letters, I talked with his old friend, I saw his record, I talked with his old comrade-in-arms, and everything told me this was a guy who definitely could not behave the way he clearly did behave. So I was just plain wrong, and that burns me up, because where does it leave me now?'

'In what sense?'

'I've got to tell the Hobies,' he said. 'It'll kill them stone dead. You should have met them. They worshipped that boy. They worshipped the military, the patriotism of it all, serving your country, the whole damn thing. Now I've got to walk in there and tell

452

them their boy is a murderer and a deserter. And a cruel son who left them twisting in the wind for thirty long years. I'll be walking in there and killing them stone dead, Jodie. I should call ahead for an ambulance.'

He lapsed into silence and turned back to the black porthole.

'And?' she said.

He turned back to face her. 'And the future. What am I going to do? I've got a house, I need a job. What kind of a job? I can't put myself about as an investigator any more, not if I've started getting things completely ass-backward all of a sudden. The timing is wonderful, right? My professional capabilities have turned to mush right at the exact time I need to find work. I should go back to the Keys and dig pools the rest of my life.'

'You're being too hard on yourself. It was a feeling, was all. A gut feeling that turned out wrong.'

'Gut feelings should turn out right,' he said. 'Mine always did before. I could tell you about a dozen times when I stuck to gut feelings, no other reason than I felt them. They saved my life, time to time.'

She nodded, without speaking.

'And statistically I should have been right,' he said. 'You know how many men were officially unaccounted for after 'Nam? Only about five. Twenty-two hundred missing, but they're dead, we all know that. Eventually Nash will find them all, and tick them all off. But there were five guys left we can't categorize. Three of them changed sides and stayed on in the villages afterward, gone native. A couple disappeared in Thailand. One of them was living in a hut under a bridge in Bangkok. Five loose ends out of a million men, and Victor Hobie is one of them, and I was wrong about him.'

'But you weren't really wrong,' she said. 'You were judging the old Victor Hobie, is all. All that stuff was about Victor Hobie before the war and before the crash. War changes people. The only witness to the change was DeWitt, and he went out of his way not to notice it.'

He shook his head again. 'I took that into account, or at least I tried to. I didn't figure it could change him that much.'

'Maybe the crash did it,' she said. 'Think about it, Reacher. What was he, twenty-one years old? Twenty-two, something like that? Seven people died, and maybe he felt responsible. He was the captain of the ship, right? And he was disfigured. He lost his arm, and he was probably burned, too. That's a big trauma for a young guy, physical disfigurement, right? And then in the field hospital, he was probably woozy with drugs, terrified of going back.'

'They wouldn't have sent him back to combat,' Reacher said.

Jodie nodded. 'Yes, but maybe he wasn't thinking straight. The morphine, it's like being high, right? Maybe he thought they were going to send him straight back. Maybe he thought they were going to punish him for losing the helicopter. We just don't know his mental state at the time. So he tried to get away, and he hit the orderly on the head. Then later he woke up to what he'd done. Probably felt terrible about it. That was my gut feeling, all along. He's hiding out, because of a guilty secret. He should have turned himself in, because nobody was going to convict him of anything. The mitigating circumstances

454

were too obvious. But he hid out, and the longer it went on, the worse it got. It kind of snowballed.'

'Still makes me wrong,' he said. 'You've just described an irrational guy. Panicky, unrealistic, a little hysterical. I had him down as a plodder. Very sane, very rational, very normal. I'm losing my touch.'

The giant plane hissed on imperceptibly. Six hundred miles an hour through the thin air of altitude, and it felt like it was suspended immobile. A spacious pastel cocoon, hanging there seven miles up in the night sky, going nowhere at all.

'So what are you going to do?' she asked.

'About what?'

'The future?'

He shrugged again. 'I don't know.'

'What about the Hobies?'

'I don't know,' he said again.

'You could try to find him,' she said. 'You know, convince him no action would be taken now. Talk some sense into him. Maybe you could get him to meet with his folks again.'

'How could I find him? The way I feel right now, I couldn't find the nose on my face. And you're so keen on making me feel better, you're forgetting something.'

'What?'

'He doesn't *want* to be found. Like you figured, he wants to stay hidden. Even if he started out real confused about it, he evidently got the taste for it later. He had Costello killed, Jodie. He sent people after us. So he could stay hidden.'

Then the stewardess dimmed the cabin lights right down to darkness, and Reacher gave up and laid his seat back and tried to sleep, with his last thought uppermost in his mind: *Victor Hobie had Costello killed, so he could stay hidden.*

Thirty floors above Fifth Avenue, he woke up just after six o'clock in the morning, which for him was about normal, depending on how bad the fire dream had been. Thirty years is nearly eleven thousand days, and eleven thousand days have eleven thousand nights attached to them, and during every single one of those nights he had dreamed about fire. The cockpit broke away from the tail section, and the treetops flipped it backward. The fracture in the airframe split the fuel tank. The fuel hurled itself out. He saw it coming at him every night, in appalling slow motion. It gleamed and shimmered in the grey jungle air. It was liquid and globular and formed itself into solid shapes like giant distorted raindrops. They twisted and changed and grew, like living things floating slowly through the air. The light caught them and made them strange and beautiful. There were rainbows in them. They got to him before the rotor blade hit his arm. Every night he turned his head in the exact same convulsive jerk, but every night they still got to him. They splashed on his face. The liquid was warm. It puzzled him. It looked like water. Water should be cold. He should feel the thrill of cold. But it was warm. It was sticky. Thicker than water. It smelled. A chemical smell. It splashed across the left side of his head. It was in his hair. It plastered the hair to his forehead and ran slowly down into his eye.

Then he turned his head back, and he saw that the air was on fire. There were fingers of flame pointing down the floating rivulets of fuel like accusations. Then the fingers were mouths. They were eating the floating liquid shapes. They ate fast, and they left the shapes bigger and blazing with heat. Then the separate globules in the air were bursting into flames ahead of each other. There was no connection any more. No sequence. They were just exploding. He jerked his head down eleven thousand separate times, but the fire always hit him. It smelled hot, like burning, but it felt cold, like ice. A sudden ice-cold shock on the side of his face, in his hair. Then the black shape of the rotor blade, arcing down. It broke against the chest of the guy called Bamford and a fragment smacked him edge-on, precisely halfway along the length of his forearm.

He saw his hand come off. He saw it in detail. That part was never in the dream, because the dream was about fire, and he didn't need to dream about his hand coming off, because he could remember seeing it happen. The edge of the blade had a slim aerodynamic profile, and it was dull black. It punched through the bones of his arm and stopped dead against his thigh, its energy already expended. His forearm just fell in two. His watch was still strapped to the wrist. The hand and the wrist fell to the floor. He raised the severed forearm and touched his face with it, to try to find out why the skin up there felt so cold but smelled so hot.

He realized some time later that action had saved his life. When he could think straight again, he understood what he had done. The intense flames had cauterized his open forearm. The heat had seared the exposed flesh and sealed the arteries. If he hadn't touched his burning face with it, he would have bled to death. It was a triumph. Even in extreme danger and confusion, he had done the right thing. The smart

457

thing. He was a survivor. It gave him a deadly assurance he had never lost.

He stayed conscious for about twenty minutes. He did what he had to do inside the cockpit and crawled away from the wreck. He knew nobody was crawling with him. He made it into the undergrowth and kept on going. He was on his knees, using his remaining hand ahead of him, walking on the knuckles like an ape. He ducked his head to the ground and jammed his burned skin into the earth. Then the agony started. He survived twenty minutes of it and collapsed.

He remembered almost nothing of the next three weeks. He didn't know where he went, or what he ate, or what he drank. He had brief flashes of clarity, which were worse than not remembering. He was covered in leeches. His burned skin came off and the flesh underneath stank of rot and decay. There were things living and crawling in his raw stump. Then he was in the hospital. One morning he woke up floating on a cloud of morphine. It felt better than anything had felt in his whole life. But he pretended to be in agony throughout. That way, they would postpone sending him back.

They applied burn dressings to his face. They cleaned the maggots out of his wound. Years later, he realized the maggots had saved his life, too. He read a report about new medical research. Maggots were being used in a revolutionary new treatment for gangrene. Their tireless eating consumed the gangrenous flesh before the rot could spread. Experiments had proven successful. He had smiled. He knew.

The evacuation of the hospital caught him by surprise. They hadn't told him. He overheard the orderlies making plans for the morning. He got out, immediately. There were no guards. Just an orderly, by chance loitering on the perimeter. The orderly cost him a precious bottle of water broken across his head, but didn't delay him by more than a second.

His long journey home started right there, a yard into the undergrowth outside the hospital fence. First task was to retrieve his money. It was buried fifty miles away, in a secret spot outside his last base camp, inside a coffin. The coffin was just a lucky chance. It had been the only large receptacle he could lay his hands on at the time, but later it would prove to be a stroke of absolute genius. The money was all in hundreds and fifties and twenties and tens, and there was a hundred and seventy pounds of it. A plausible weight to find in a coffin. Just under two million dollars.

By then the base camp was abandoned and far behind enemy lines. But he got himself there, and faced the first of his many difficulties. How does a sick one-armed man dig up a coffin? At first, with blind perseverance. Then later, with help. He had already shifted most of the earth when he was discovered. The coffin lid was plainly visible, lying in the shallow grave. The VC patrol crashed in on him out of the trees, and he expected to die. But he didn't. Instead, he made a discovery. It ranked with the other great discoveries he made in his life. The VC stood back, fearful and muttering and uncertain. He realized they didn't know who he was. They didn't know *what* he was. The terrible burns robbed him of his identity. He was wearing a torn and filthy hospital nightshirt. He didn't look American. He didn't look like anything. He didn't look human. He learned that the combination of his terrible looks and his wild behaviour and the coffin had an effect on anybody who saw him. Distant atavistic fears of death and corpses and madness made them passive. He learned in an instant if he was prepared to act like a madman and cling to his coffin, these people would do anything for him. Their ancient superstitions worked in his favour. The VC patrol completed the excavation for him and loaded the coffin on to a buffalo cart. He sat up high on top of it and raved and gibbered and pointed west and they took him a hundred miles towards Cambodia.

Vietnam is a narrow country, side to side. He was passed from group to group and was in Cambodia within four days. They fed him rice and gave him water to drink and clothed him in black pyjamas, to tame him and assuage their primitive fears. Then Cambodians took him onward. He bounced and jabbered like a monkey and pointed west, west, west. Two months later, he was in Thailand. The Cambodians manhandled the coffin over the border and turned and ran.

Thailand was different. When he passed the border, it was like stepping out of the Stone Age. There were roads, and vehicles. The people were different. The babbling scarred man with the coffin was an object for wary pity and concern. He was not a threat. He got rides on old Chevrolet pick-ups and in old Peugeot trucks and within two weeks he found himself washed up with all the other Far Eastern flotsam in the sewer they called Bangkok.

He lived in Bangkok for a year. He reburied the coffin in the yard behind the shack he rented, working furiously all through his first night with a black-market entrenching tool stolen from the US Army. He could manage an entrenching tool. It was designed to be used one-handed, while the other hand held a rifle.

Once his money was safe again, he went looking for doctors. There was a large supply in Bangkok. Gin-soaked remnants of Empire, fired from every other job they ever had, but reasonably competent on the days they were sober. There wasn't much they could do with his face. A surgeon rebuilt his eyelid so that it would almost close, and that was it. But they were thorough with his arm. They opened the wound again and filed the bones round and smooth. They stitched the muscle down and folded the skin over tight and sealed it all back up. They told him to let it heal for a month, and then they sent him to a man who built false limbs.

The man offered him a choice of styles. They all involved the same corset to be worn around the bicep, the same straps, the same cup moulded to the exact contours of his stump. But there were different appendages. There was a wooden hand, carved with great skill and painted by his daughter. There was a three-pronged thing like some kind of a gardening tool. But he chose the simple hook. It appealed to him, though he couldn't explain why. The man forged it from stainless steel and polished it for a week. He welded it to a funnel-shaped steel sheet and built the sheet into the heavy leather cup. He carved a wooden replica of the stump and beat the leather into shape over it, and then he soaked it in resins to make it stiff. He sewed the corset and attached the straps and buckles. He fitted it carefully and charged five hundred American dollars for it.

He lived out the year in Bangkok. At first the hook chafed and was clumsy and uncontrollable. But he got better with it. With practice, he got along. By the time

461

he dug up the coffin again and booked passage to San Francisco on a tramp steamer, he had forgotten all about ever having two hands. It was his face that continued to bother him.

He landed in California and retrieved the coffin from the cargo sheds and used a small portion of its contents to buy a used station wagon. A trio of frightened longshoremen loaded the coffin inside and he drove it cross-country all the way to New York City, and he was still there twenty-nine years later, with the Bangkok craftsman's handiwork lying on the floor beside his bed, where it had lain every night for the last eleven thousand nights.

He rolled over on to his front and reached down with his left hand and picked it up. Sat up in bed and laid it across his knees and reached out to take the baby's sock from his nightstand. Ten past six in the morning. Another day of his life.

William Curry woke up at six-fifteen. It was an old habit from working the day shift on the detective squads. He had inherited the lease on his grandmother's apartment two floors above Beekman Street. It wasn't a great apartment, but it was cheap, and it was convenient for most of the precinct houses below Canal. So he had moved in after his divorce and stayed there after his retirement. His police pension covered the rent and the utilities and the lease on his one-room office on Fletcher. So the income from his fledgling private bureau had to cover his food and his alimony. And then, when he got established and built it up bigger, it was supposed to make him rich.

Six-fifteen in the morning, the apartment was cool. It was shaded from the early sun by taller buildings near by. He put his feet on the linoleum and stood up and stretched. Went to the kitchen corner and set the coffee going. Headed to the bathroom and washed up. It was a routine that had always gotten him to work by seven o'clock, and he stuck to it.

He came back to the closet with coffee in his hand and stood there with the door open, looking at what was on the rail. As a cop, he had always been a pants-and-jacket type of guy. Grey flannels, checked sportcoat. He had favoured tweed, although he wasn't strictly Irish. In the summer, he had tried linen jackets, but they wrinkled too easily and he had settled on thin polyester blends. But none of those outfits was going to do on a day when he had to show up somewhere looking like David Forster, high-priced attorney. He was going to have to use his wedding suit.

It was a plain black Brooks Brothers, bought for family weddings and christenings and funerals. It was fifteen years old, and being Brooks Brothers didn't look a whole lot different from contemporary items. It was a little loose on him, because losing his wife's cooking had brought his weight down in a hurry. The pants were a little wide by East Village standards, but that was OK because he planned on wearing two ankle holsters. William Curry was a guy who believed in being prepared. David Forster had said *probably won't be anything involved at all*, and if it worked out that way he would be happy enough, but a twenty-year man from the NYPD's worst years tends to get cautious when he hears a promise like that. So he planned on using both ankle holsters and putting his big .357 in the small of his back.

He put the suit in a plastic cover he had picked up somewhere and added a white shirt and his quietest tie. He threaded the .357 holster on to a black leather belt and put it in a bag with the two ankle holsters. He put three handguns in his briefcase, the .357 long-barrelled Magnum and two .38 snub-nosed Smith and Wessons for the ankles. He sorted twelve rounds for each gun into a box and packed it beside the guns. He stuffed a black sock into each of his black shoes and stowed them with the holsters. He figured he would get changed after an early lunch. No point in wearing the stuff all morning and showing up looking like a limp rag.

He locked up the apartment and walked south to his office on Fletcher, carrying his luggage, stopping only to get a muffin: banana and walnut, reduced fat.

Marilyn Stone woke up at seven o'clock. She was bleary-eyed and tired. They had been kept out of the bathroom until well after midnight. It had to be cleaned. The thickset guy in the dark suit did it. He came out in a bad temper and made them wait until the floor dried. They sat in the dark and the silence, numb and cold and hungry, too sickened to think about asking for something to eat. Tony made Marilyn plump up the sofa pillows. She guessed he planned to sleep there. Bending over in her short dress and preparing his bed was a humiliation. She patted the pillows into place while he smiled at her.

The bathroom was cold. It was damp everywhere and smelled of disinfectant. The towels had been folded and stacked next to the sink. She put them in two piles on the floor and she and Chester curled up on them without a word. Beyond the door, the office was silent. She didn't expect to sleep. But she must have, because she awoke with a clear sense of a new day beginning.

There were sounds in the office. She had rinsed her face and was standing upright when the thickset guy brought coffee. She took her mug without a word and he left Chester's on the ledge under the mirror. Chester was still on the floor, not asleep, just lying there inert. The guy stepped right over him on his way out.

'Nearly over,' she said.

'Just starting, you mean,' Chester said back. 'Where do we go next? Where do we go tonight?'

She was going to say *home, thank God*, but then she remembered he'd already realized that after about two-thirty they would have no home.

'A hotel, I guess,' she said.

'They took my credit cards.'

Then he went quiet. She looked at him. 'What?'

'It's never going to be over,' he said. 'Don't you see that? We're witnesses. To what they did to those cops. And Sheryl. How can they just let us walk away?'

She nodded, a small vague movement of her head, and looked down at him with disappointment. She was disappointed because he finally understood. Now he was going to be worried and frantic all day, and that would just make it harder.

It took five minutes to get the knot in the necktie neat, and then he slipped his jacket on. Dressing was the exact reverse of undressing, which meant the shoes came last. He could tie laces just about as fast as a two-handed person. The trick was to trap the loose end under the hook against the floor.

Then he started in the bathroom. He rammed all the

465

dirty laundry into a pillowcase and left it by the apartment door. He stripped the bed and balled the linen into another pillowcase. He put all the personal items he could find into a supermarket carrier. He emptied his closet into a garment bag. He propped the apartment door open and carried the pillowcases and the carrier to the refuse chute. Dropped them all down and clanged the slot closed after them. Dragged the garment bag out into the hallway and locked up the apartment and put the keys in an envelope from his pocket.

He detoured to the concierge's desk and left the envelope of keys for the real-estate guy. Used the stairway to the parking garage and carried the garment bag over to the Cadillac. He locked it into the trunk and walked around to the driver's door. Slid inside and leaned over with his left hand and fired it up. Squealed around the garage and up into the daylight. He drove south on Fifth, carefully averting his eyes until he was clear of the park and safe in the bustling canyons of Midtown.

He leased three bays under the World Trade Center, but the Suburban was gone, and the Tahoe was gone, so they were all empty when he arrived. He put the Cadillac in the middle slot and left the garment bag in the trunk. He figured he would drive the Cadillac to LaGuardia and abandon it in the long-term parking lot. Then he would take a cab to JFK, carrying the bag, looking like any other transfer passenger in a hurry. The car would sit there until the weeds grew up under it, and if anybody ever got suspicious they would comb through the LaGuardia manifests, not JFK's. It meant writing off the Cadillac along with the lease on the offices, but he was always comfortable about spending money when he got value for it, and saving his life was about the best value he could think of getting.

He used the express elevator from the garage and was in his brass-and-oak reception area ninety seconds later. Tony was behind the chest-high counter, drinking coffee, looking tired.

'Boat?' Hobie asked him.

Tony nodded. 'It's at the broker's. They'll wire the money. They want to replace the rail, where that asshole damaged it with the cleaver. I told them OK, just deduct it from the proceeds.'

Hobie nodded back. 'What else?'

Tony smiled, at an apparent irony. 'We got more money to move. The first interest payment just came in from the Stone account. Eleven thousand dollars, right on time. Conscientious little asshole, isn't he?'

Hobie smiled back. 'Robbing Peter to pay Paul, only now Peter and Paul are the same damn guy. Wire it down to the islands at start of business, OK?'

Tony nodded and read a note. 'Simon called from Hawaii again. They made the plane. Right now they're over the Grand Canyon somewhere.'

'Has Newman found it yet?' Hobie asked.

Tony shook his head. 'Not yet. He's going to start looking this morning. Reacher pushed him into doing it. Sounds like a smart guy.'

'Not smart enough,' Hobie said. 'Hawaii's five hours behind, right?'

'It'll be this afternoon. Call it he starts at nine, spends a couple of hours looking, that's four o'clock our time. We'll be out of here.'

Hobie smiled again. 'I told you it would work out. Didn't I tell you it would work out? Didn't I tell you to relax and let me do the thinking?'

467

Reacher woke up at seven o'clock on his watch, which was still set to St Louis time as far as he could remember, which made it three o'clock in the morning back in Hawaii, and six in Arizona or Colorado or wherever they were seven miles above, and already eight in New York. He stretched in his seat and stood up and stepped over Jodie's feet. She was curled in her chair, and a stewardess had covered her with a thin plaid blanket. She was fast asleep, breathing slow, her hair over her face. He stood in the aisle for a moment and watched her sleep. Then he went for a walk.

He walked through business class, and on into coach. The lights were dimmed and it got more crowded the farther back he walked. The tiny seats were packed with people huddled under blankets. There was a smell of dirty clothes. He walked right down to the rear of the plane and looped around through the galley past a quiet huddle of cabin staff leaning on the aluminium lockers. He walked back up the other aisle, through coach, into business class. He paused there a second and scanned the passengers. There were men and women in suits, jackets discarded, ties pulled down. There were laptop computers open. Briefcases stood on unoccupied seats, bulging with folders with plastic covers and comb bindings. Reading lights were focused on tray tables. Some of the people were still working, late in the night or early in the morning, depending on where you measured it from.

He guessed these were middle-ranking people. A long way from the bottom, but nowhere near the top. In Army terms, these were the majors and the colonels. They were the civilian equivalents of himself. He had finished a major, and might be a colonel now if he'd stayed in uniform. He leaned on a bulkhead and looked at the backs of the bent heads and thought *Leon made me, and now he's changed me*. Leon had boosted his career. He hadn't created it, but he had made it what it became. There was no doubt about that. Then the career ended and the drifting began, and now the drifting was ended, too, because of Leon. Not just because of Jodie. Because of Leon's last will and testament. The old guy had bequeathed him the house, and the bequest had sat there like a time bomb, waiting to anchor him. Because the vague promise was enough to do it. Before, settling down had seemed theoretical. It was a distant country he knew he would never visit. The journey there was too long to manage. The fare was too high. The sheer difficulty of insinuating himself into an alien lifestyle was impossibly great. But Leon's bequest had kidnapped him. Leon had kidnapped him and dumped him right on the border of the distant country. Now his nose was pressed right up against the fence. He could see life waiting for him on the other side. Suddenly it seemed insane to turn back and hike the impossible distance in the other direction. That would turn drifting into a conscious choice, and conscious choice would turn drifting into something else completely. The whole point of drifting was happy passive acceptance of no alternatives. Having alternatives ruined it. And Leon had handed him a massive alternative. It sat there, still and amiable above the rolling Hudson, waiting for him. Leon must have smiled as he sat and wrote out that provision. He must have grinned and thought *let's see how you get out of this one, Reacher*.

He stared at the laptops and the comb-bound

folders and winced inside. How was he going to cross the border of the distant country without getting issued with all this stuff? The suits and the ties and the black plastic battery-driven devices? The lizard-skin cases and the memorandums from the main office? He shuddered and found himself paralysed against the bulkhead, panicking, not breathing, completely unable to move. He recalled a day not more than a year ago, stepping out of a truck at a crossroads near a town he had never heard of in a state he had never been. He had waved the driver away and thrust his hands deep in his pockets and started walking, with a million miles behind him and a million miles ahead of him. The sun was shining and the dust was kicking up off his feet as he walked and he had smiled with the joy of being alone with absolutely no idea where he was headed.

But he also recalled a day nine months after that. Realizing he was running out of money, thinking hard. The cheapest motels still required some small amount of dollars. The cheapest diners, likewise. He had taken the job in the Keys, intending to work a couple of weeks. Then he had taken the evening job, too, and he was still working both of them when Costello came calling three whole months later. So the reality was that drifting was already over. *He was already a working man.* No point in denying it. Now it was just a question of where and how much and for who. He smiled. *Like prostitution*, he thought. *No going back.* He relaxed a little and pushed off the bulkhead and padded back through to first class. The guy with the striped shirt and the arms the same length as Victor Hobie's was awake and watching him. He nodded a greeting. Reacher nodded back and headed for the bathroom. Jodie was awake when he got back to his seat. She was sitting up straight, combing her hair with her fingers.

'Hi, Reacher,' she said.

'Hey, Jodie,' he said back.

He bent and kissed her on the lips. Stepped over her feet and sat down.

'Feel OK?' he asked.

She ducked her head in a figure eight to put her hair behind her shoulders.

'Not bad. Not bad at all. Better than I thought I would. Where did you go?'

'I took a walk,' he said. 'I went back to see how the other half lives.'

'No, you were thinking. I noticed that about you fifteen years ago. You always go walking when you have something to think about.'

'I do?' he said, surprised. 'I didn't know that.'

'Of course you do,' she said. 'I noticed it. I used to watch every detail about you. I was in love with you, remember?'

'What else do I do?'

'You clench your left hand when you're angry or tense. You keep your right hand loose, probably from weapons training. When you're bored, you play music in your head. I could see it in your fingers, like you're playing along on a piano or something. The tip of your nose moves a little bit when you talk.'

'It does?'

'Sure it does,' she said. 'What were you thinking about?'

He shrugged.

'This and that,' he said.

'The house, right?' she said. 'It's bothering you,

471

isn't it? And me. Me and the house, tying you down, like that guy in the book, Gulliver? You know that book?'

He smiled. 'He's a guy gets captured by tiny little people when he's asleep. They peg him down flat with hundreds of tiny little ropes.'

'You feel that way?'

He paused a beat. 'Not about you.'

But the pause had been a fraction of a second too long. She nodded.

'It's different than being alone, right?' she said. 'I know, I was married. Somebody else to take into account all the time? Somebody to worry about?'

He smiled. 'I'll get used to it.'

She smiled back. 'And there's the house, right?'

He shrugged. 'Feels weird.'

'Well, that's between you and Leon,' she said. 'I want you to know I'm not putting demands on you, either way. About anything. It's your life, and your house. You should do exactly what you want, no pressure.'

He nodded. Said nothing.

'So you going to look for Hobie?'

He shrugged again. 'Maybe. But it's a hell of a task.'

'Bound to be angles,' she said. 'Medical records and things? He must have a prosthesis. And if he's burned, too, there'll be records of that. And you wouldn't miss him in the street, would you? A one-armed man, all burned up?'

He nodded. 'Or I could just wait for him to find me. I could just hang out in Garrison until he sends his boys back.'

Then he turned to the window and stared out at his pale reflection against the darkness and realized *I'm*

472

just accepting he's alive. I'm just accepting I was wrong.
He turned back to Jodie.

'Will you give me the mobile? Can you manage without it today? In case Nash finds something and calls me? I want to hear right away, if he does.'

She held his gaze for a long moment, and then she nodded. Leaned down and unzipped her carry-on. Took out the phone and handed it to him.

'Good luck,' she said.

He nodded and put the phone in his pocket.

'I never used to need luck,' he said.

Nash Newman did not wait until nine o'clock in the morning to start the search. He was a meticulous man, attentive to tiny detail as much in his ethics as in his professional speciality. This was an unofficial search, undertaken out of compassion for a troubled friend, so it couldn't be done on company time. A private matter had to be settled privately.

So he got out of bed at six, watching the faint red glow of tropical dawn starting beyond the mountains. He made coffee and dressed. By six-thirty he was in his office. He figured he would give it two hours. Then he would have breakfast in the mess and start his proper work on time at nine.

He rolled open a desk drawer and lifted out Victor Hobie's medical records. Leon Garber had assembled them after patient enquiries in doctors' and dentists' offices in Putnam County. He had bundled them into an old military police folder and secured it shut with an old canvas strap. The strap had been red, but age had faded it to dusty pink. There was a fiddly metal buckle.

He undid the buckle. Opened the folder. The top

sheet was a release signed by both the Hobie parents in April. Underneath it was ancient history. He had scanned thousands of files similar to this one, and he could effortlessly place the boys they referred to in terms of their age, their geographic location, their parents' income, their ability at sports, all the numerous factors that affect a medical history. Age and location worked together. A new dental treatment might start out in California and sweep the country like a fashion, so the thirteen-year-old boy getting it in Des Moines had to have been born five years later than the thirteen-year-old boy getting it in Los Angeles. Their parents' income dictated whether they got it at all. The high school football stars had treatment for torn shoulders, the softball players had cracked wrists, the swimmers had chronic ear infections.

Victor Truman Hobie had very little at all. Newman read between the lines and pictured a healthy boy, properly fed, conscientiously cared for by dutiful parents. His health had been good. There had been colds and flu, and a bout of bronchitis at the age of eight. No accidents. No broken bones. Dental treatment had been very thorough. The boy had grown up through the era of aggressive dentistry. In Newman's experience, it was absolutely typical of any he had seen from the New York metropolitan area in the Fifties and early Sixties. Dentistry through that era consisted of a war on cavities. Cavities had to be hunted down. They were hunted with powerful X-rays, and when they were found they were enlarged with the drill and filled with amalgam. The result was a lot of trips to the dentist's office, which no doubt had been miserable for the young Victor Hobie, but from Newman's point of view the process had left him with a thick sheaf of

474

films of the boy's mouth. They were good enough and clear enough and numerous enough to be potentially definitive.

He stacked the films and carried them out into the corridor. Unlocked the plain door in the cinder-block wall and walked past the aluminium caskets to the alcove at the far end. There was a computer terminal on a wide shelf, out of sight around a corner. He booted it up and clicked on the search menu. The screen scrolled down and revealed a detailed questionnaire.

Filling out the questionnaire was a matter of simple logic. He clicked on ALL BONES and entered NO CHILDHOOD BREAKS, POTENTIAL ADULT BREAKS. The kid didn't break his leg playing football at high school, but he might have broken it later in a training accident. Service medical records were sometimes lost. He spent a lot of time on the dental section of the questionnaire. He entered a full description of each tooth as last recorded. He marked the filled cavities, and against each good tooth he entered POTENTIAL CAVITY. It was the only way to prevent mistakes. Simple logic. A good tooth can go bad later and need treatment, but a filled cavity can't ever disappear. He stared at the X-rays and against SPACING he entered EVEN, and against SIZE he entered EVEN again. The rest of the questionnaire he left blank. Some diseases showed up in the skeleton, but not colds and flu and bronchitis.

He reviewed his work and at seven o'clock exactly he hit SEARCH. The hard disk whirred and chattered in the morning silence and the software started its patient journey through the database.

They landed ten minutes ahead of schedule, just before the peak of noon, East Coast time. They came in low

475

over the glittering waters of Jamaica Bay and put down facing east before turning back and taxiing slowly to the terminal. Jodie reset her watch and was on her feet before the plane stopped moving, which was a transgression they don't chide you for in first class.

'Let's go,' she said. 'I'm real tight for time.'

They were lined up by the door before it opened. Reacher carried her bag out into the jet way and she hurried ahead of him all the way through the terminal and outside. The Lincoln Navigator was still there in the short-term lot, big and black and obvious, and it cost fifty-eight of Rutter's dollars to drive it out.

'Do I have time for a shower?' she asked herself.

Reacher put his comment into hustling faster than he should along the Van Wyck. The Long Island Expressway was moving freely west to the tunnel. They were in Manhattan within twenty minutes of touching down and heading south on Broadway near her place within thirty.

'I'm still going to check it out,' he told her. 'Shower or no shower.'

She nodded. Being back in the city had brought back the worry.

'OK, but be quick.'

He limited it to stopping on the street outside her door and making a visual check of the lobby. Nobody there. They dumped the car and went up to five and down the fire stairs to four. The building was quiet and deserted. The apartment was empty and undisturbed. The Mondrian copy glowed in the bright daylight. Twelve-thirty in the afternoon.

'Ten minutes,' she said. 'Then you can drive me to the office, OK?'

'How will you get to the meeting?'

'We have a driver,' she said. 'He'll take me.'

She ran through the living room to the bedroom, shedding clothes as she went.

'You need to eat?' Reacher called after her.

'No time,' she called back.

She spent five minutes in the shower and five minutes in the closet. She came out with a charcoal dress and a matching jacket.

'Find my briefcase, OK?' she yelled.

She combed her hair and used a hair dryer on it. Limited her make-up to a touch of eyeliner and lipstick. Checked herself in the mirror and ran back to the living room. He had her briefcase waiting for her. He carried it down to the car.

'Take my keys,' she said. 'Then you can get back in. I'll call you from the office and you can come pick me up.'

It took seven minutes to get opposite the little plaza outside her building. She slid out of the car at five minutes to one.

'Good luck,' Reacher called after her. 'Give them hell.'

She waved to him and skipped across to the revolving door. The security guys saw her coming and nodded her through to the elevator bank. She was upstairs in her office before one o'clock. Her secretary followed her inside with a thin file in his hand.

'There you go,' he said, ceremoniously.

She opened it up and flipped through eight sheets of paper.

'Hell is this?' she said.

'They were thrilled about it at the partners' meeting,' the guy said.

She went back through the pages in reverse order. 'I don't see why. I never heard of either of these corporations and the amount is trivial.'

'That's not the point, though, is it?' the guy said.

She looked at him. 'So what is the point?'

'It's the creditor who hired you,' he said. 'Not the guy who owes all the money. It's a pre-emptive move, isn't it? Because word is getting around. The creditor knows if you get alongside the guy who owes him money, you can cause him a big problem. So he hired you first, to keep that from happening. It means you're famous. That's what the partners are thrilled about. You're a big star now, Mrs Jacob.'

SIXTEEN

Reacher drove slowly back to lower Broadway. He bumped the big car down the ramp to the garage. Parked it in Jodie's slot and locked it. He didn't go upstairs to the apartment. He walked back up the ramp to the street and headed north in the sun to the espresso bar. He had the counter guy put four shots in a cardboard cup and sat at the chromium table Jodie had used when he was checking the apartment the night he had got back from Brighton. He had walked back up Broadway and found her sitting there, staring at Rutter's faked photograph. He sat down in the same chair she had used and blew on the espresso foam and smelled the aroma and took the first sip.

What to tell the old folks? The only humane thing to do would be to go up there and tell them nothing at all. Just tell them he had drawn a blank. Just leave it completely vague. It would be a kindness. Just go up there, hold their hands, break the news of Rutter's deception, refund their money, and then describe a long and fruitless search backward through history that ended up absolutely nowhere. Then plead with them to accept he must be long dead, and beg them to understand nobody would ever be able to tell them where or when or how. Then disappear and leave them to live out the short balance of their lives with whatever dignity they could find in being just two out of the tens of millions of parents who gave up their children to the night and the fog swirling through a ghastly century.

He sipped his way through the coffee, with his left hand clenched on the table in front of him. He would lie to them, but out of kindness. Reacher had no great experience of kindness. It was a virtue that had always run parallel to his life. He had never been in the sort of position where it counted for anything. He had never drawn duty breaking bad news to relatives. Some of his contemporaries had. After the Gulf, duty squads had been formed, a senior officer from the unit concerned teamed up with a military policeman, and they had visited the families of the casualties, walking up long lonely driveways, walking up stairs in apartment houses, breaking the news that their formal uniformed arrival had already announced in advance. He guessed kindness counted for a lot during that type of duty, but his own career had been locked tight inside the service itself, where things were always simple, either happening or not happening, good or bad, legal or not legal. Now two years after leaving the service, kindness was suddenly a factor in his life. And it would make him lie.

But he would find Victor Hobie. He unclenched his hand and touched the burn scar through his shirt. He had a score to settle. He tilted the cup until he felt the espresso mud on his teeth and tongue. Then he dropped the cup in the trash and stepped back out to the sidewalk. The sun was full on Broadway, coming slightly from the south and west of directly overhead.

He felt it on his face and turned towards it and walked down to Jodie's building. He was tired. He had slept only four hours on the plane. Four hours, out of more than twenty-four. He remembered reclining the enormous first-class seat and falling asleep in it. He had been thinking about Hobie then, like he was thinking about him now. *Victor Hobie had Costello killed, so he could stay hidden.* Crystal floated into his memory. The stripper, from the Keys. He shouldn't be thinking about her again. But he was saying something to her, in the darkened bar. She was wearing a T-shirt and nothing else. Then Jodie was talking to him, in the dim study at the back of Leon's house. *His house.* She was saying the same thing he was saying to Crystal. He was saying *he must have stepped on some toes up north, given somebody a problem.* She was saying *he must have tried some kind of a shortcut, got somebody alerted.*

He stopped dead on the street with his heart thumping. Leon. Costello. Leon and Costello, together, talking. Costello had gone up to Garrison and talked with Leon just before he died. Leon had run down the problem for him. *Find a guy called Jack Reacher because I want him to check on a guy called Victor Hobie,* Leon must have said. Costello, calm and businesslike, must have listened well. He had gone back to the city and scoped out the job. He had thought hard and tried a shortcut. *Costello had gone looking for the guy called Hobie before he had gone looking for the guy called Reacher.*

He ran the last block to Jodie's parking garage. Then lower Broadway to Greenwich Avenue was two and three-quarter miles, and he got there in eleven minutes by slipstreaming behind the taxis heading up to the west side of Midtown. He dumped the Lincoln on the sidewalk in front of the building and ran up the stone steps into the lobby. He glanced around and pressed three random buttons.

'UPS,' he called.

The inner screen buzzed open and he ran up the stairs to suite five. Costello's mahogany door was closed, just like he had left it four days ago. He glanced around the hallway and tried the knob. The door opened. The lock was still latched back, open for business. The pastel reception area was undisturbed. The impersonal city. Life swirled on, busy and oblivious and uncaring. The air inside felt stale. The secretary's perfume had faded to a trace. But her computer was still turned on. The watery screensaver was swirling away, waiting patiently for her return.

He stepped to her desk and nudged the mouse with his finger. The screen cleared and revealed the database entry for Spencer Gutman Ricker and Talbot, which was the last thing he had looked at before calling them, back when he had never heard of anybody called Mrs Jacob. He exited the entry and went back to the main listing without any real optimism. He had looked for JACOB on it and got nowhere. He didn't recall seeing HOBIE there, either, and *H* and *J* are pretty close together in the alphabet.

He spooled it up from bottom to top and back again, but there was nothing in the main listing. No real names in it at all, just acronyms for corporations. He stepped out from behind the desk and ran through to Costello's own office. No papers on the desk. He walked around behind it and saw a metal trash can in the kneehole space. There were crumpled papers in it. He squatted down and spilled them out on the floor. There were opened envelopes and discarded forms. A greasy sandwich wrapper. Some sheets of lined paper, torn out from a perforated book. He straightened them on the carpet with his palm. Nothing hit him in the eye, but they were clearly working notes. They were the kind of jottings a busy man makes to help him organize his thoughts. But they were all recent. Costello was clearly a guy who emptied his trash on a regular basis. There was nothing from more than a couple of days before he died in the Keys. Any short-cuts involving Hobie, he would have taken them twelve or thirteen days ago, right after talking with Leon, right at the outset of the investigation.

Reacher opened the desk drawers, each one in turn, and found the perforated book in the top on the left-hand side. It was a supermarket notebook, partly used up, with a thick backbone on the left and half the pages remaining on the right. He sat down in the crushed leather chair and leafed through the book. Ten pages in, he saw the name *Leon Garber*. It leapt out at him from a mess of pencilled notes. He saw *Mrs Jacob, SGR&T*. He saw *Victor Hobie*. That name was underlined twice, with the casual strokes a pensive man uses while he is thinking hard. It was circled lightly with overlapping oval shapes, like eggs. Next to it, Costello had scrawled *CCT??* There was a line running away across the page from *CCT??* to a note saying *9am. 9am* was circled, too, inside more oval scrawlings. Reacher stared at the page and saw an appointment with Victor Hobie, at a place called CCT, at nine o'clock in the morning. Presumably at nine o'clock in the morning of the day he was killed.

He bounced the chair backward and scrambled around the desk. Ran back to the computer. The data-base listing was still there. The screensaver had not cut in. He scrolled the list to the top and looked at everything between *B* and *D*. CCT was right there, jammed between CCR&W and CDAG&Y. He moved the mouse and clicked on it. The screen scrolled down and revealed an entry for CAYMAN CORPORATE TRUST. There was an address listed in the World Trade Center. There were telephone and fax numbers. There were notes listing enquiries from law firms. The proprietor was listed as Mr Victor Hobie. Reacher stared at the display and the phone started ringing.

He tore his eyes from the screen and glanced at the console on the desk. It was silent. The ringing was in his pocket. He fumbled Jodie's mobile out of his jacket and clicked the button.

'Hello?' he said.

'I've got some news,' Nash Newman replied.

'News about what?'

'About what? What the hell do you think?'

'I don't know,' Reacher said. 'So tell me.'

So Newman told him. Then there was silence. Just a soft hiss from the phone representing six thousand miles of distance and a soft whirring noise from the fan inside the computer. Reacher took the phone away from his ear and stared between it and the screen, left and right, left and right, dazed.

'You still there?' Newman asked. It came through faint and electronic, just a faraway squawk from the earpiece. Reacher put the phone back to his face.

'You sure about this?' he asked.

'I'm sure,' Newman said. 'One hundred per cent certain. It's totally definitive. Not one chance in a billion that I'm wrong. No doubt about it.'

'You sure?' Reacher asked again.

'Positive,' Newman said. 'Totally, utterly positive.'

Reacher was silent. He just stared around the quiet empty office. Light blue walls where the sun was coming through the pebbled glass of the window, light grey where it wasn't.

'You don't sound very happy about it,' Newman said.

'I can't believe it,' Reacher said. 'Tell me again.'

So Newman told him again.

'I can't believe it,' Reacher said. 'You're absolutely totally sure about this?'

Newman repeated it all. Reacher stared at the desk, blankly.

'Tell me again,' he said. 'One more time, Nash.'

So Newman went through it all for the fourth time.

'There's absolutely no doubt about it,' he added. 'Have you ever known me be wrong?'

'Shit,' Reacher said. 'Shit, you see what this means? You see what happened? You see what he did? I've got to go, Nash. I need to get back to St Louis, right now. I need to get into the archive again.'

'You do indeed, don't you?' Newman said. 'St Louis would certainly be my first port of call. As a matter of considerable urgency, too.'

'Thanks, Nash,' Reacher said, vaguely. He clicked the phone off and jammed it back in his pocket. Then he stood up and wandered slowly out of Costello's office suite to the stairs. He left the mahogany door standing wide open behind him.

Tony came into the bathroom carrying the Savile Row suit on a wire hanger inside a dry cleaner's bag. The shirt was starched and folded in a paper wrapper jammed under his arm. He glanced at Marilyn and hung the suit on the shower rail and tossed the shirt

485

into Chester's lap. He went into his pocket and came out with the tie. He pulled it out along its whole length, like a conjuror performing a trick with a concealed silk scarf. He tossed it after the shirt.

'Show time,' he said. 'Be ready in ten minutes.'

He went back out and closed the door. Chester sat on the floor, cradling the packaged shirt in his arms. The tie was draped across his legs, where it had fallen. Marilyn leaned down and took the shirt from him. Slipped her fingers flat under the edge of the paper and opened it up. She balled the paper and dropped it. Shook out the shirt and undid the top two buttons.

'Nearly over,' she said, like an incantation.

He looked at her neutrally and stood up. Took the shirt from her and pulled it on over his head. She stepped in front of him and snapped the collar up and fixed his tie.

'Thanks,' he said.

She helped him into the suit and came around in front of him and tweaked the lapels.

'Your hair,' she said.

He went to the mirror and saw the man he used to be in another life. He used his fingers and smoothed his hair into place. The bathroom door opened again and Tony stepped inside. He was holding the Mont Blanc fountain pen.

'We'll lend this back to you, so you can sign the transfer.'

Chester nodded and took the pen and slipped it into his jacket.

'And this. We need to keep up appearances, right? All these lawyers everywhere?' It was the platinum Rolex. Chester took it from him and latched it on his wrist. Tony left the room and closed the door. Marilyn was at the mirror, styling her hair with her fingers. She put it behind her ears and pursed her lips together like she'd just used lipstick, although she hadn't. She had none to use. It was just instinct. She stepped away to the middle of the floor and smoothed her dress down over her thighs.

'You ready?' she asked.

Chester shrugged. 'For what? Are you?'

'I'm ready,' she said.

Spencer Gutman Ricker and Talbot's driver was the husband of one of the firm's longest-serving secretaries. He had been a dead-wood clerk somewhere who hadn't survived his company's amalgamation with a lean and hungry competitor. Fifty-nine and unemployed with no skills and no prospects, he had sunk his payoff into a used Lincoln Town Car and his wife had written a proposal showing it would be cheaper for the firm to contract him exclusively rather than keep a car service account. The partners had turned a blind eye to the accounting mistakes in the proposal and hired him anyway, looking at it somewhere halfway between pro bono and convenience. Thus the guy was waiting in the garage with the motor running and the air on high when Jodie came out of the elevator and walked over to him. He buzzed his window down and she bent to speak.

'You know where we're going?' she asked.

He nodded and tapped the clipboard lying on the front passenger seat.

'I'm all set,' he said.

She got in the back. By nature she was a democratic person who would have preferred to ride in front with him, but he insisted passengers take the rear seat. It

487

made him feel more official. He was a sensitive old man, and he had caught the whiff of charity around his hiring. He felt that to act very properly would raise his perceived status. He wore a dark suit and a chauffeur's cap he had found in an outfitters in Brooklyn.

As soon as he saw in the mirror that Jodie was settled, he moved away around the garage and up the ramp and outside into the daylight. The exit was at the back of the building and it put him on Exchange Place. He made the left on to Broadway and worked across the lanes in time for the right into the Trinity Street dogleg. He followed it west and turned, coming up on the World Trade Center from the south. Traffic was slow past Trinity Church, because two lanes were blocked by a police tow truck stopped alongside an NYPD cruiser parked at the kerb. Cops were peering into the windows, as if they were unsure about something. He eased past and accelerated. Slowed and pulled in again alongside the plaza. His eyes were fixed at street level, and the giant towers loomed over him unseen. He sat with the motor running, silent and deferential.

'I'll be waiting here,' he said.

Jodie got out of the car and paused on the sidewalk. The plaza was wide and crowded. It was five minutes to two, and the lunch crowd was returning to work. She felt unsettled. She would be walking through a public space without Reacher watching over her, for the first time since things went crazy. She glanced around and joined a knot of hurrying people and walked with them all the way to the south tower.

The address in the file was the eighty-eighth floor. She joined the line for the express elevator behind a

488

medium-sized man in an ill-fitting black suit. He was carrying a cheap briefcase upholstered with brown plastic stamped to make it look like crocodile skin. She squeezed into the elevator behind him. The car was full and people were calling their floor numbers to the woman nearest the buttons. The guy in the bad suit asked for eighty-eight. Jodie said nothing.

The car stopped at most floors in its zone and people jostled out. Progress was slow. It was dead-on two o'clock when the car arrived on eighty-eight. Jodie stepped out. The guy in the bad suit stepped out behind her. They were in a deserted corridor. Undistinguished closed doors led into office suites. Jodie went one way and the guy in the suit went the other, both of them looking at the plates fixed next to the doors. They met up again in front of an oak slab marked *Cayman Corporate Trust*. There was a wired-glass porthole set off-centre in it. Jodie glanced through it and the guy in the suit leaned past her and pulled it open.

'We in the same meeting?' Jodie asked, surprised.

She followed him inside to a brass-and-oak reception area. There were office smells. Hot chemicals from copying machines, stewed coffee somewhere. The guy in the suit turned back to her and nodded.

'I guess we are,' he said.

She stuck out her hand as she walked.

'I'm Jodie Jacob,' she said. 'Spencer Gutman. For the creditor.'

The guy walked backward and juggled his plastic briefcase into his left hand and smiled and shook hands with her.

'I'm David Forster,' he said. 'Forster and Abelstein.'

489

They were at the reception counter. She stopped and stared at him.

'No, you're not,' she said blankly. 'I know David very well.'

The guy looked suddenly tense. The lobby went silent. She turned the other way and saw the guy she had last seen clinging to the door handle of her Bravada as Reacher hauled away from the collision on Broadway. He was sitting there calmly behind the counter, looking straight back at her. His left hand moved and touched a button. In the silence she heard a click from the entrance door. Then his right hand moved. It went down empty and came back up with a gun the colour of dull metal. It had a wide barrel like a tube and a metal handgrip. The barrel was more than a foot long. The guy in the bad suit dropped his plastic case and jerked his hands in the air. Jodie stared at the weapon and thought *but that's a shotgun*.

The guy holding it moved his left hand again and hit another button. The door to the inner office opened. The man who had crashed the Suburban into them was standing there framed in the doorway. He had another gun in his hand. Jodie recognized the type from movies she'd seen. It was an automatic pistol. On the cinema screen it fired loud bullets that smashed you six feet backward. The Suburban driver was holding it steady on a point to her left and the other guy's right, like he was ready to jerk his wrist either way.

The guy with the shotgun came out from behind the counter and pushed past Jodie. Went up behind the guy with the bad suit and rammed the shotgun barrel into the small of his back. There was a hard sound, metal on metal, muffled by cloth. The guy with the shotgun put his hand up under the jacket and came out with a big chromium revolver. He held it up, like an exhibit.

'Unusual accessory for a lawyer,' the man in the doorway said.

'He's not a lawyer,' his partner said. 'The woman says she knows David Forster very well and this ain't him.'

The man in the doorway nodded.

'My name is Tony,' he said. 'Come inside, both of you, please.'

He stepped to one side and covered Jodie with the automatic pistol while his partner pushed the guy claiming to be Forster in through the open door. Then he beckoned with the gun and Jodie found herself walking towards him. He stepped close and pushed her through the door with a hand flat on her back. She stumbled once and regained her balance. Inside was a big office, spacious and square. Dim light from shaded windows. There was living-room furniture arranged in front of a desk. Three identical sofas, with lamp tables. A huge brass-and-glass coffee table filled the space between the sofas. There were two people sitting on the left-hand sofa. A man and a woman. The man wore an immaculate suit and tie. The woman wore a wrinkled silk party dress. The man looked up, blankly. The woman looked up in terror.

There was a man at the desk. He was sitting in the gloom, in a leather chair. He was maybe fifty-five years old. Jodie stared at him. His face was divided roughly in two, like an arbitrary decision, like a map of the western states. On the right was lined skin and thinning grey hair. On the left was scar tissue, pink and thick and shiny like an unfinished plastic model

491

of a monster's head. The scars touched his eye, and the lid was a ball of pink tissue, like a mangled thumb.

He was wearing a neat suit, which fell over broad shoulders and a wide chest. His left arm was laid comfortably on the desk. There was the cuff of a white shirt, snowy in the gloom, and a manicured hand, palm down, the fingers tapping an imperceptible rhythm on the desktop. His right arm was laid exactly symmetrical with his left. There was the same fine summer-weight wool of the suit coat, and the same snowy white shirt cuff, but they were collapsed and empty. There was no hand. Just a simple steel hook protruding at a shallow angle, resting on the wood. It was curved and polished like a miniature version of a sculpture from a public garden.

'Hobie,' she said.

He nodded slowly, just once, and raised the hook like a greeting.

'Pleased to meet you, Mrs Jacob. I'm just sorry it took so long.'

Then he smiled.

'And I'm sorry our acquaintance will be so brief.'

He nodded again, this time to the man called Tony, who manoeuvred her alongside the guy claiming to be Forster. They stood side by side, waiting.

'Where's your friend Jack Reacher?' Hobie asked her.

She shook her head. 'I don't know.'

Hobie looked at her for a long moment.

'OK,' he said. 'We'll get to Jack Reacher later. Now sit down.'

He was pointing with the hook to the sofa opposite the staring couple. She stepped over and sat down, dazed.

'This is Mr and Mrs Stone,' Hobie said to her. 'Chester and Marilyn, to be informal. Chester ran a corporation called Stone Optical. He owes me more than seventeen million dollars. He's going to pay me in stock.'

Jodie glanced at the couple opposite. They both had panic in their eyes. Like something had just gone terribly wrong.

'Put your hands on the table,' Hobie called. 'All three of you. Lean forward and spread your fingers. Let me see six little starfish.'

Jodie leaned forward and laid her palms on the low table. The couple opposite did the same thing, automatically.

'Lean forward more,' Hobie called.

They all slid their palms towards the centre of the table until they were leaning at an angle. It put their weight on their hands and made them immobile. Hobie came out from behind the desk and stopped opposite the guy in the bad suit.

'Apparently you're not David Forster,' he said.

The guy made no reply.

'I would have guessed, you know,' Hobie said. 'In an instant. A suit like that? You've really got to be kidding. So who are you?'

Again the guy said nothing. Jodie watched him, with her head turned sideways. Tony raised his gun and pointed it at the guy's head. He used both hands and did something with the slide that made a menacing metallic sound in the silence. He tightened his finger on the trigger. Jodie saw his knuckle turn white.

'Curry,' the guy said quickly. 'William Curry. I'm a private detective, working for Forster.'

Hobie nodded, slowly. 'OK, Mr Curry.'

He walked back behind the Stones. Stopped directly behind the woman.

'I've been misled, Marilyn,' he said.

He balanced himself with his left hand on the back of the sofa and leaned all the way forward and snagged the tip of the hook into the neck of her dress. He pulled back against the strength of the fabric and hauled her slowly upright. Her palms slid off the glass and left damp shapes where they had rested. Her back touched the sofa and he slipped the hook around in front of her and nudged her lightly under the chin like a hairdresser adjusting the position of her head before starting work. He raised the hook and brought it back down gently and used the tip to comb through her hair, lightly, front to back. Her hair was thick and the hook ploughed through it, slowly, front to back, front to back. Her eyes were screwed shut in terror.

'You deceived me,' he said. 'I don't like being deceived. Especially not by you. I protected you, Marilyn. I could have sold you with the cars. Now maybe I will. I had other plans for you, but I think Mrs Jacob just usurped your position in my affections. Nobody told me how beautiful she was.'

The hook stopped moving and a thin thread of blood ran down out of Marilyn's hair on to her forehead. Hobie's gaze shifted across to Jodie. His good eye was steady and unblinking.

'Yes,' he said to her. 'I think maybe you're New York's parting gift to me.'

He pushed the hook hard against the back of Marilyn's head until she leaned forward again and put her hands back on the table. Then he turned around.

'You armed, Mr Curry?'

Curry shrugged. 'I was. You know that. You took it.'

The guy with the shotgun held up the shiny revolver. Hobie nodded.

'Tony?'

Tony started patting him down, across the tops of his shoulders, under his arms. Curry glanced left and right and the guy with the shotgun stepped close and jammed the barrel into his side.

'Stand still,' he said.

Tony leaned forward and smoothed his hands over the guy's belt area and between his legs. Then he slid them briskly downward and Curry twisted violently sideways and tried to knock the shotgun away with his arm, but the guy holding it was firmly grounded with his feet well apart and he stopped Curry short. He used the muzzle like a fist and hit him in the stomach. Curry's breath coughed out and he folded up and the guy hit him again, on the side of the head, hard with the stock of the shotgun. Curry went down on his knees and Tony rolled him over with his foot.

'Asshole,' he sneered.

The guy with the shotgun leaned down one-handed and rammed the muzzle into Curry's gut with enough weight on it to hurt. Tony squatted and fiddled under the legs of the pants and came back up with two identical revolvers. His left forefinger was threaded through the trigger guards and he was swinging them around. The metal clicked and scratched and rattled. The revolvers were small. They were made from stainless steel. Like shiny toys. They had short barrels. Almost no barrels at all.

'Stand up, Mr Curry,' Hobie said.

Curry rolled on to his hands and knees. He was

clearly dazed from the blow to the head. Jodie could see him blinking, trying to focus. Shaking his head. He reached out for the back of the sofa and hauled himself upright. Hobie stepped a yard closer and turned his back on him. He looked at Jodie and Chester and Marilyn like they were an audience. He held his left palm flat and started butting the curve of the hook into it. He was butting with the right and slapping with the left, and the impacts were building.

'A simple question of mechanics,' he said. 'The impact on the end of the hook transfers up to the stump. The shockwaves travel. They dissipate against what's left of the arm. Naturally the leatherwork was built by an expert, so the discomfort is minimized. But we can't beat the laws of physics, can we? So in the end the question is who does the pain get to first? Him or me?'

He spun on the ball of his foot and punched Curry full in the face with the blunt outside curve of the hook. It was a hard punch thrown all the way from the shoulder, and Curry staggered back and gasped.

'I asked you if you were armed,' Hobie said quietly. 'You should have told the truth. You should have said, *yes, Mr Hobie, I've got a revolver on each ankle.* But you didn't. You tried to deceive me. And like I told Marilyn, I don't like to be deceived.'

The next punch was a jab to the body. Sudden and hard.

'Stop it,' Jodie screamed. She pushed back and sat upright. 'Why are you doing this? What the hell happened to you?'

Curry was bent over and gasping. Hobie turned away from him to face her.

'What happened to me?' he repeated.

'You were a decent guy. We know all about you.'

He shook his head slowly.

'No, you don't,' he said.

Then the buzzer sounded at the door out to the elevator lobby. Tony glanced at Hobie, and slipped his automatic into his pocket. He took Curry's two small revolvers off his finger and stepped over and pressed one of them into Hobie's left hand. Then he leaned in close and slipped the other into the pocket of Hobie's jacket. It was a curiously intimate gesture. Then he walked out of the office. The guy with the shotgun stepped back and found an angle to cover all four prisoners. Hobie moved in the opposite direction and triangulated his aim.

'Be very quiet, everybody,' he whispered.

They heard the lobby door open. Then there was the low sound of conversation and then it closed again. A second later Tony walked back into the gloom with a package under his arm and a smile on his face.

'Messenger from Stone's old bank. Three hundred stock certificates.'

He held up the package.

'Open it,' Hobie said.

Tony found the plastic thread and tore open the envelope. Jodie saw the rich engraving of equity holdings. Tony flicked through them. He nodded. Hobie stepped back to his chair and laid the small revolver on the desktop.

'Sit down, Mr Curry,' he said. 'Next to your legal colleague.'

Curry dropped heavily into the space next to Jodie. He slid his hands across the glass and leaned forward, like the others. Hobie used the hook in a circular gesture.

497

'Take a good look around, Chester,' he said. 'Mr Curry, Mrs Jacob, and your dear wife Marilyn. Good people all, I'm sure. Three lives, full of their own petty concerns and triumphs. Three lives, Chester, and now they're entirely in your hands.'

Stone's head was up, moving in a circle as he looked at the other three at the table. He ended up looking straight across the desk at Hobie.

'Go get the rest of the stock,' Hobie said to him. 'Tony will accompany you. Straight there, straight back, no tricks, and these three people will live. Anything else, they'll die. You understand that?'

Stone nodded, silently.

'Pick a number, Chester,' Hobie said to him.

'One,' Stone said back.

'Pick two more numbers, Chester.'

'Two and three,' Stone said.

'OK, Marilyn gets the three,' Hobie said. 'If you decide to be a hero.'

'I'll get the stock,' Stone said.

Hobie nodded.

'I think you will,' he said. 'But you need to sign the transfer first.'

He rolled open a drawer and swept the small shiny revolver into it. Then he pulled out a single sheet of paper. Beckoned to Stone who slid himself upright and stood, shakily. He threaded around the desk and signed his name with the Mont Blanc pen from his pocket.

'Mrs Jacob can be the witness,' Hobie said. 'She's a member of the New York State Bar, after all.'

Jodie sat still for a long moment. She stared left at the guy with the shotgun, and straight ahead at Tony, and then right at Hobie behind the desk. She pulled herself upright. Stepped to the desk and reversed the form and took Stone's pen from him. Signed her name and wrote the date on the line next to it.

'Thank you,' Hobie said. 'Now sit down again and keep completely still.'

She went back to the sofa and leaned forward over the table. Her shoulders were starting to hurt. Tony took Stone's elbow and moved him towards the door.

'Five minutes there, five back,' Hobie called. 'Don't be a hero, Chester.'

Tony led Stone out of the office and the door closed gently behind them. There was the thump of the lobby door and the faraway whine of the elevator, and then there was silence. Jodie was in pain. The grip of the glass on her clammy palms was pulling the skin away from under her fingernails. Her shoulders were burning. Her neck was aching. She could see on their faces the others were suffering, too. There were sudden breaths and gasps. The beginnings of low moans.

Hobie gestured to the guy with the shotgun and they changed places. Hobie strolled nervously around the office and the shotgun guy sat at the desk with the weapon resting on its grips, swivelling randomly left and right like a prison searchlight. Hobie was checking his wristwatch, counting the minutes. Jodie saw the sun slipping south-west, lining up with the gaps in the window blinds and shooting steep angled beams into the room. She could hear the ragged breathing of the two others near her and she could feel the faint shudder of the building coming through the table under her hands.

Five minutes there and five minutes back add up to ten, but at least twenty minutes passed. Hobie paced and checked his watch a dozen times. Then he walked through into reception and the guy with the shotgun followed him to the office door. He kept the weapon pointed into the room, but his head was turned, watching his boss.

'Is he planning to let us go?' Curry whispered.

Jodie shrugged and lifted up on to her fingertips, hunching her shoulders and ducking her head to ease the pain.

'I don't know,' she whispered back.

Marilyn had her forearms pinched tight together, with her head resting on them. She looked up and shook her head.

'He killed two cops,' she whispered. 'We were witnesses.'

'Stop talking,' the guy called from the door.

They heard the whine of the elevator again and the faint bump through the floor as it stopped. There was a moment's quiet and then the lobby door opened and suddenly there was noise in reception, Tony's voice, and then Hobie's, loud and fuelled with relief. Hobie came back into the office carrying a white package and smiling with the mobile half of his face. He clamped the package under his right elbow and tore it open as he walked and Jodie saw more engraving on thick parchment. He took the long way around to the desk and dumped the certificates on top of the three hundred he already had. Stone followed Tony like he had been forgotten and stood gazing at the life's work of his ancestors piled casually on the scarred wood. Marilyn looked up and walked her fingers backward across the glass, jacking herself upright with her hands because she had no strength left in her shoulders.

'OK, you got them all,' she said quietly. 'Now you can let us go.'

Hobie smiled. 'Marilyn, what are you, a moron?'

Tony laughed. Jodie looked from him to Hobie. She saw they were very nearly at the end of some long process. Some goal had been in sight, and now it was very close. Tony's laughter was about release after days of strain and tension.

'Reacher is still out there,' she said quietly, like a move in a game of chess.

Hobie stopped smiling. He touched the hook to his forehead and rubbed it across his scars and nodded.

'Reacher,' he said. 'Yes, the last piece of the puzzle. We mustn't forget about Reacher, must we? He's still out there. But out where, exactly?'

She hesitated.

'I don't know, exactly,' she said.

Then her head came up, defiant.

'But he's in the city,' she said. 'And he'll find you.'

Hobie met her gaze. Stared at her, contempt in his face.

'You think that's some kind of threat?' he sneered. 'Truth is I *want* him to find me. Because he has something I require. Something vital. So help me out, Mrs Jacob. Call him and invite him right over.'

She was silent for a moment.

'I don't know where he is,' she said.

'Try your place,' Hobie said back. 'We know he's been staying there. He's probably there right now. You got off the plane at eleven-fifty, right?'

She stared at him. He nodded complacently.

'We check these things. We own a boy called Simon, who I believe you've met. He put you on the seven o'clock flight from Honolulu, and we called JFK and they told us it landed at eleven-fifty exactly. Old Jack Reacher was all upset in Hawaii, according to our boy

Simon, so he's probably still upset. And tired. Like you are. You look tired, Mrs Jacob, you know that? But your friend Jack Reacher is probably in bed at your place, sleeping it off, while you're here having fun with the rest of us. So call him, tell him to come over and join you.'

She stared down at the table. Said nothing.

'Call him. Then you can see him one more time before you die.'

She was silent. She stared down at the glass. It was smeared with her handprints. She wanted to call him. She wanted to see him. She felt like she had felt a million times over fifteen long years. *She wanted to see him again.* His lazy, lopsided grin. His tousled hair. His arms, so long they gave him a greyhound's grace even though he was built like the side of a house. His eyes, cold icy blue like the Arctic. His hands, giant battered mitts that bunched into fists the size of footballs. She wanted to see those hands again. She wanted to see them around Hobie's throat.

She glanced around the office. The sunbeams had crawled an inch across the desk. She saw Chester Stone, inert. Marilyn, trembling. Curry, white in the face and breathing hard next to her. The guy with the shotgun, relaxed. Reacher would break him in half without even thinking about it. She saw Tony, his eyes fixed on hers. And Hobie, caressing his hook with his manicured hand, smiling at her, waiting. She turned and looked at the closed door. She imagined it bursting open with a crash and Jack Reacher striding in through it. She wanted to see that happen. She wanted it more than she had ever wanted anything.

'OK,' she whispered. 'I'll call him.'

Hobie nodded. 'Tell him I'll be here a few more

hours. But tell him if he wants to see you again, he better come quick. Because you and I have a little date in the bathroom, about thirty minutes from now.'

She shuddered and pushed off the glass table and stood upright. Her legs were weak and her shoulders were on fire. Hobie came around and took her elbow and led her to the door. Led her over behind the reception counter.

'This is the only telephone in the place,' he said. 'I don't like telephones.'

He sat down in the chair and pressed nine with the tip of his hook. Handed the phone across to her. 'Come closer, so I can hear what he says to you. Marilyn deceived me with the phone, and I'm not going to let that happen to me again.'

He made her stoop down and put her face next to his. He smelled of soap. He put his hand in his pocket and came out with the tiny revolver Tony had slipped in there. He touched it to her side. She held the phone at an angle with the earpiece upward between them. She studied the console. There was a mass of buttons. A speed-dial facility for 911. She hesitated for a second and then dialled her own home number. It rang six times. Six long soft purrs. With each one, she willed him: *be there, be there*. But it was her own voice that came back to her, from her machine.

'He's not there,' she said blankly.

Hobie smiled.

'That's too bad,' he said.

She was stooped over next to him, numb with shock.

'He's got my mobile,' she said suddenly. 'I just remembered.'

'OK, press nine for a line.'

She dabbed the cradle and dialled nine and then her mobile number. It rang four times. Four loud urgent electronic squawks. Each one, she prayed: *answer, answer, answer, answer*. Then there was a click in the earpiece.

'Hello?' he said.

She breathed out.

'Hi, Jack,' she said.

'Hey, Jodie,' he said. 'What's new?'

'Where are you?'

She realized there was urgency in her voice. It made him pause.

'I'm in St Louis, Missouri,' he said. 'Just flew down. I had to go to the NPRC again, where we were before.'

She gasped. *St Louis?* Her mouth went dry.

'You OK?' he asked her.

Hobie leaned across and put his mouth next to her ear.

'Tell him to come right back to New York,' he whispered. 'Straight here, soon as he can.'

She nodded nervously and he pressed the gun harder against her side.

'Can you come back?' she asked. 'I sort of need you here, as soon as possible.'

'I'm booked on the six o'clock,' he said. 'Gets me in around eight-thirty, East Coast time. Will that do?'

She could sense Hobie grinning next to her.

'Can you make it any time sooner? Like maybe right away?'

She could hear talking in the background. Major Conrad, she guessed. She remembered his office, dark wood, worn leather, the hot Missouri sun in the window.

'Sooner?' he said. 'Well, I guess so. I could be there

504

in a couple of hours, depending on the flights. Where are you?'

'Come to the World Trade Center, south tower, eighty-eighth floor, OK?'

'Traffic will be bad. Call it two and a half hours, I'll be there.'

'Great,' she said.

'You OK?' he asked again.

Hobie brought the gun around into her view.

'I'm fine,' she said. 'I love you.'

Hobie leaned over and hit the cradle with the tip of his hook. The earpiece clicked and filled with dial tone. She put the phone down, slowly and carefully on to the console. She was shattered with shock and disappointment, numb, still stooped over the counter, one hand laid flat on the wood propping her weight, the other hand shaking in the air an inch above the phone.

'Two and a half *hours*,' Hobie said to her with exaggerated sympathy. 'Well, it looks like the cavalry ain't going to arrive in time for you, Mrs Jacob.'

He laughed to himself and put the gun back in his pocket. Got out of the chair and caught the arm that was supporting her weight. She stumbled and he dragged her towards the office door. She caught the edge of the counter and held on tight. He hit her, backhanded with the hook. The curve caught her high on the temple and she lost her grip on the counter. Her knees gave way and she fell and he dragged her to the door by the arm. Her heels scuffed and kicked. He swung her around in front of him and straight-armed her back into the office. She sprawled on the carpet and he slammed the door.

'Back on the sofa,' he snarled.

The sunbeams were off the desk. They were inching around the floor and creeping across the table. Marilyn Stone's splayed fingernails were vivid in their light. Jodie crawled on her hands and knees and pulled herself up on the furniture and staggered all the way back to her place alongside Curry. She put her hands back where they had been before. There was a narrow pain in her temple. It was an angry throb, hot and alien where the metal had thumped against bone. Her shoulder was twisted. The guy with the shotgun was watching her. Tony was watching her, the automatic pistol back in his hand. Reacher was far away from her, like he had been most of her life.

Hobie was back at the desk, squaring the stack of equity certificates into a pile. They made a brick four inches tall. He butted each side in turn with the hook. The heavy engraved papers slid neatly into place.

'UPS will be here soon,' he said happily. 'Then the developers get their stock, and I get my money, and I've won again. About half an hour, probably, and then it's all over, for me, and for you.'

Jodie realized he was talking to her alone. He had selected her as a conduit for information. Curry and the Stone couple were staring at her, not him. She looked away and gazed down through the glass at the rug on the floor. It had the same pattern as the faded old item in DeWitt's office in Texas, but it was much smaller and much newer. Hobie left the brick of paper where it was and walked around behind the square of furniture and took the shotgun away from the guy holding it.

'Go bring me some coffee,' he said to him.

The guy nodded and walked out to the lobby. Closed the door gently behind him. The office went

506

silent. There was just tense breathing and the faint rumble of the building underneath it. The shotgun was in Hobie's left hand. It was pointing at the floor. Swinging gently, back and forth through a tiny arc. A loose grip. Jodie could hear the rub of metal on the skin of his hand. She saw Curry glancing around. He was checking Tony's position. Tony had stepped back a yard. He had put himself outside the shotgun's field of fire and he was aiming directly across it at a right angle. His automatic was raised. Jodie felt Curry testing the strength in his shoulders. She felt him moving. She saw his arms bunching. She saw him glance ahead at Tony, maybe twelve feet in front of him. She saw him glance left at Hobie, maybe eight feet to the side. She saw the sunbeams, exactly parallel with the brass edges of the table. She saw Curry push up on to his fingertips.

'No,' she breathed.

Leon had always simplified his life with rules. He had a rule for every situation. As a kid, they had driven her crazy. His catch-all rule for everything from her term papers to his missions to legislation in Congress was *do it once and do it right*. Curry had no chance of doing it right. No chance at all. He was triangulated by two powerful weapons. His options were non-existent. If he jumped up and hurdled the table and headed for Tony, he would catch a bullet in the chest before he was even halfway there, and probably a shotgun blast in the side as well which would kill the Stone couple along with himself. And if he headed for Hobie first, then maybe Tony wouldn't fire for fear of hitting his boss, but Hobie would fire for sure, and the shotgun blast would shred Curry into a hundred small pieces, and she was in a direct line right behind him.

Another of Leon's rules was *hopeless is hopeless and don't ever pretend it ain't*.

'Wait,' she breathed.

She felt a fractional nod from Curry and she saw his shoulders go slack again. They waited. She stared down through the glass at the rug and fought the pain, minute by minute. Her torn shoulder was shrieking against her weight. She folded her fingers and rested on her knuckles. She could hear Marilyn Stone breathing hard opposite her. She looked defeated. Her head was resting sideways on her arms, and her eyes were closed. The sunbeams had moved away from parallel and were creeping towards her edge of the table.

'What the hell is that guy doing out there?' Hobie muttered. 'How long does it take to fetch me a damn cup of coffee?'

Tony glanced at him, but he made no reply. Just kept the automatic held forward, favouring Curry more than anybody. Jodie turned her hands and leaned on her thumbs. Her head throbbed and burned. Hobie kicked the shotgun up and rested the muzzle on the back of the sofa in front of him. He brought the hook up and rubbed the flat of the curve over his scars.

'Christ,' he said. 'What's taking so long? Go give him a hand, OK?'

Jodie realized he was looking straight at her. 'Me?'

'Why not? Make yourself useful. Coffee is woman's work, after all.'

She hesitated.

'I don't know where it is,' she said.

'Then I'll show you.'

He was staring at her, waiting. She nodded, suddenly glad to get a chance just to move a little. She

508

straightened her fingers and eased her hands backward and pushed herself upright. She felt weak and she stumbled once and caught her shin on the table's brass frame. She walked uneasily through Tony's field of fire. Up close, his automatic was huge and brutal. He tracked her with it all the way as she approached Hobie. Back there, she was beyond the reach of the sunbeams. Hobie led her through the gloom and juggled the shotgun up under his arm and grasped the handle and pulled the door open.

Check the outer door first, and then the telephone. That was what she had been rehearsing as she walked. If she could get out into the public corridor, she might have a chance. Failing that, there was the 911 speed-dial. Knock the handset out of the cradle, hit the button, and even if she got no opportunity to speak the automatic circuitry would give the cops a location. *The door, or the phone.* She rehearsed looking ahead at the door, looking left at the phone, the precise turn of her head in between. But when it came to it she looked at neither thing. Hobie stopped dead in front of her and she stepped alongside him and just looked at the guy who had gone to fetch the coffee.

He was a thickset man, shorter than Hobie or Tony, but broad. He was wearing a dark suit. He was lying on his back on the floor, precisely centred in front of the office door. His legs were straight. His feet were turned out. His head was propped at a steep angle on a stack of phone books. His eyes were wide open. They stared forward, sightlessly. His left arm was dragged up and back, and the hand was resting palm up on another stack of books in a grotesque parody of greeting. His right arm was pulled straight, at a shallow angle away from his body. His right hand was severed at the wrist. It was lying on the carpet six inches away from his shirt cuff, arranged in a precise straight line with the arm it had come from. She heard Hobie making a small sound in his throat and turned to see him dropping the shotgun and clutching at the door with his good hand. The burn scars were still vivid pink, but the rest of his face was turning a ghastly white.

SEVENTEEN

Reacher had been named Jack by his father, who was a plain New Hampshire Yankee with an implacable horror of anything fancy. He had walked into the maternity ward one late October Tuesday, the morning after the birth, and he had handed his wife a small bunch of flowers and told her *we'll call him Jack.* There was no middle name. Jack Reacher was the whole of it, and it was already on the birth certificate, because he had visited the company clerk on his way to the infirmary and the guy had written it down and reported it by telex to the Berlin Embassy. Another United States citizen, born overseas to a serving soldier, name of Jack-none-Reacher.

His mother made no objection. She loved her husband for his ascetic instincts, because she was French and they gave him a kind of European sensibility that made her feel more at home with him. She had found an enormous gulf between America and Europe in those postwar decades. The wealth and excess of America contrasted uneasily with the exhaustion and poverty of Europe. But her very own New Hampshire Yankee had no use for wealth and excess. No use at all. Plain simple things were what he liked, and that was absolutely fine with her, even if it did extend all the way to her babies' names.

He had called her firstborn Joe. Not Joseph, just Joe. No middle name. She loved the boy, of course, but the name was hard for her. It was very short and abrupt, and she struggled with the initial *J* because of her accent. It came out like *zh*. Like the boy was called *Zhoe*. Jack was much better. Her accent made it sound like Jacques, which was a very traditional old French name. Translated, it meant James. Privately, she always thought of her second boy as James.

But paradoxically nobody ever called him by his first name. Nobody knew how it came about, but Joe was always called Joe and Jack was always called Reacher. She did it herself, all the time. She had no idea why. She would stick her head out of some service bungalow window and yell *Zhoe! Come get your lunch! And bring Reacher with you!* And her two sweet little boys would come running inside for something to eat.

The exact same thing happened in school. It was Reacher's own earliest memory. He was an earnest, serious boy, and he was puzzled why his names were backward. His brother was called by his first name first and his last name last. Not him. There was a schoolyard softball game and the kid who owned the bat was choosing up sides. He turned to the brothers and called out *I'll have Joe and Reacher*. All the kids did the same thing. The teachers, too. They called him Reacher, even in kindergarten. And somehow it travelled with him. Like any Army kid, he changed elementary schools dozens of times. First day in some new place somewhere, maybe even on a new continent, some new teacher would be yelling *come here, Reacher!*

But he got used to it fast and had no problem living his whole life behind a one-word name. He was Reacher, always had been, always would be, to everybody. The first girl he ever dated was a tall brunette who sidled shyly up to him and asked *what's your name? Reacher*, he replied. The loves of his life had all called him that. *Mmm, Reacher, I love you*, they had whispered in his ear. All of them. Jodie herself had done the exact same thing. He had appeared at the top of the concrete steps in Leon's yard and she had looked up at him and said *hello, Reacher*. After fifteen long years, she still knew exactly what he was called.

But she hadn't called him Reacher on the mobile. He had clicked the button and said hello and she had said *hi, Jack*. It went off in his ear like a siren. Then she had asked *where are you?* and she had sounded so tense about it he panicked and his mind started racing and for a second he missed exactly what she meant. His given name, just a lucky chance. *Hi, Jack* meant *hijack*. It took him a second to catch on. She was in trouble. Big trouble, but she was still Leon's daughter, smart enough to think hard and warn him with two little syllables at the start of a desperate phone call.

Hijack. An alert. A combat warning. He blinked once and crushed down the fear and went to work. First thing he did was lie to her. Combat is about time and space and opposing forces. Like a huge four-dimensional diagram. First step is misinform the enemy. Let him think your diagram is a completely different shape. You assume all communications are penetrated, and then you use them to spread lies and deceit. You buy yourself an advantage.

He wasn't in St Louis. Why should he be? Why fly himself all the way down there when there were

513

telephones in the world and he had already built a working relationship with Conrad? He called him from the Greenwich Avenue sidewalk and told him what he needed and Conrad called back just three minutes later because the file in question was right there in the A section nearest the harassed runner's desk. He listened with the pedestrians swirling around him and Conrad read the file aloud and twelve minutes later he clicked the phone off with all the information he was ever going to need.

Then he hustled the Lincoln south on Seventh and dumped it in a garage a block north of the Twin Towers. He hurried down and crossed the plaza and he was already inside the south tower's lobby when Jodie called. Just eighty-eight floors below her. He was talking to the security guy at the desk, which was the voice she heard in the background. His face went blank with panic and he clicked the phone off and took the express elevator to eighty-nine. He stepped out and breathed hard and forced himself to calm down. *Stay calm and plan.* His guess was eighty-nine would be laid out the same as eighty-eight. It was quiet and empty. Corridors ran around the elevator cores, narrow, lit by bulbs in the ceiling. There were doors opening into the individual office suites. They had rectangular wired-glass portholes set off-centre at a short person's eye level. Each suite door had a metal plate listing the name of the occupant and a buzzer to press for entry.

He found the fire stairs and ran down one level. The stairwell was utilitarian. No finesse in the decor. Just plain dusty concrete with metal handrails. Behind every fire door was an extinguisher. Above the extinguisher was a bright red cabinet with a red-painted axe clipped into place behind glass. On the wall next

514

to the cabinet was a giant stencil in red, marking the floor number.

He came out into the eighty-eighth-floor corridor. It was equally quiet. Identical narrow width, identical lighting, same layout, same doors. He ran the wrong way and came around to CCT last. It had a light oak door, with a brass plate next to it, and a brass push-button for the buzzer. He pulled the door, gently. It was locked tight. He stooped and looked in through the wired-glass porthole. He saw a reception area. Bright lights. Brass-and-oak decor. A counter to his right. Another door, straight ahead. That door was shut, and the reception area was deserted. He stood and stared straight through at the closed inner door and felt panic rising in his throat.

She was in there. She was in the inner office. He could feel it. She was in there, alone, a prisoner, and she needed him. She was in there and he should be in there with her. *He should have gone with her*. He stooped down and put his forehead against the cold glass and stared through at the office door. Then he heard Leon in his head, starting up with another of his golden rules. *Don't worry about why it went wrong. Just damn well put it right*.

He stepped back and glanced left and right along the corridor. Put himself underneath the light nearest the door. Reached up and unscrewed the bulb until it went out. The hot glass burned his fingers. He winced and stepped back to the door and checked again, a yard from the porthole, well out in the corridor. The reception area was brightly lit and the corridor was now dark. He could see in, but nobody would see out. You can see from a dark place into a light place, but you can't see from a light place into

515

a dark place. A crucial difference. He stood and waited.

The inner door opened and a thickset guy stepped out of the office into reception. Closed the door gently behind him. A thickset guy in a dark suit. The guy he'd pushed down the stairs in the Key West bar. The guy who had fired the Beretta up in Garrison. The guy who had clung to the Bravada's door handle. He walked through reception and disappeared from view. Reacher stepped forward again and studied the inner door through the glass. It stayed closed. He knocked gently on the outer door. The guy came to the port-hole and peered through. Reacher stood up straight and turned his shoulder so his brown jacket filled the view.

'UPS,' he said softly.

It was an office building and it was dark and it was a brown jacket, and the guy opened the door. Reacher stepped around the arc of its swing and shot his hand in and caught the guy by the throat. Do it fast enough and hard enough and you numb the guy's voice box before he can get going with any sounds. Then you dig your fingers in and keep him from falling over. The guy went heavy against his grip and Reacher ran him all the way along the corridor to the fire door and threw him backward into the stairwell. The guy bounced off the far wall and went down on the concrete, with a cracked rasping sound coming from his throat.

'Time to choose,' Reacher whispered. 'You help me, or you die.'

A choice like that, there's only one sensible thing to do, but the guy didn't do it. He struggled up to his knees and made like he was going to fight it out. Reacher tapped him on the top of the head, just

516

enough to send some shock down through his neck bones, and then stepped back and asked him again.

'Help me out,' he said. 'Or I'll kill you.'

The guy shook his head to clear it and launched himself across the floor. Reacher heard Leon say *ask once, ask twice if you must, but for God's sake don't ask three times*. He kicked the guy in the chest and spun him around backward and wedged his forearm across the top of his shoulders and put a hand under his chin and wrenched it once and broke his neck.

One down, but he was down without releasing any information, and in combat information is king. His gut still told him this was a small operation, but two guys or three or five could equally be called small, and there was a hell of a big difference between going in blind against two or three or five opponents. He paused in the stairwell and glanced at the fire-axe in the red cabinet. Next best thing to solid information is some kind of an arresting diversion. Something to make them worried and unsettled. Something to make them pause.

He did it as quietly as he could and checked the corridor was truly empty before dragging the body back. He swung the door open soundlessly and got the guy arranged in the middle of the lobby floor. Then he closed the door again and dodged down behind the reception counter. It was chest high, and more than ten feet long. He lay on the floor behind it and eased the silenced Steyr out of his jacket and settled down to wait.

It felt like a long wait. He was pressed to the thin office carpet, and he could feel the unyielding concrete under it, alive with the tiny vibrations of a giant building at work. He could feel the faint bass shudder

517

of the elevators stopping and starting. He could feel the tingle of the tension in their cables. He could hear the hum of air-conditioning and the tremor of the wind. He hooked his toes back against the resistance of the nylon pile and bunched his legs against them, ready for action.

He felt the fall of footsteps a second before he heard the click of the latch. He knew the inner door had opened because he heard the change in the acoustic. The reception area was suddenly open to a larger space. He heard four feet on the carpet and he heard them stop, like he knew they would. He waited. Present somebody with an astonishing sight, and it takes about three seconds for the maximum effect to develop. That was Reacher's experience. They look at it, they see it, their brain rejects it, their eyes bounce it back again, and it sinks in. Three whole seconds, beginning to end. He counted silently *one, two, three*, and pushed out at the base of the counter, pressed to the floor, leading with the long black silencer on the end of the Steyr. He got his arms out, then his shoulders, then his eyes.

What he saw was a disaster. The guy with the hook and the burned face was dropping a weapon and gasping and clutching at the door frame, but he was on the wrong side of Jodie. The far side. He was on Jodie's right and the reception counter was on her left. She was a foot nearer than he was. She was much shorter but Reacher was down on the floor looking up at an angle that put her head directly in front of his head, her body directly in front of his body. There was no clear shot. No clear shot anywhere. Jodie was in the way.

The guy with the hook and the face was making

sounds in his throat and Jodie was staring down at the floor. Then there was a second guy behind them in the open doorway. The Suburban driver. He stopped behind Jodie's shoulder and stared. He was carrying a Beretta in his right hand. He stared forward and down at the floor and then he stepped alongside Jodie and pushed his way past her. He stepped a yard into the room. He stepped into clear air.

Reacher squeezed the trigger, fourteen whole pounds of pressure, and the silencer banged loud and the guy's face blew apart. It took the nine-millimetre bullet in the exact centre and exploded. Blood and bone hit the ceiling and sprayed the far wall behind him. Jodie froze in direct line with the guy with the hook. And the guy with the hook was very fast. Faster than he should have been for a crippled fifty-year-old. He went one way with his left arm and scooped the shotgun off the floor. He went the other way with his right arm and folded it around Jodie's waist. The steel hook was bright against her suit. He was moving her before the other guy had even hit the floor. He clamped his right arm hard around her and lifted her off her feet and dragged her backward. The crash of the shot from the Steyr was still rumbling.

'How many?' Reacher screamed.

She was as fast as Leon ever was.

'Two down, one up,' she screamed back.

So the guy with the hook was the only one, but he was already swinging the shotgun around. It arced up through the air and he used the momentum to crunch the pump. Reacher was caught half-exposed, low down, scrambling out from behind the counter. It was only a tiny fractional opportunity, but the guy went right ahead and took it. He fired low and the gun flashed and boomed and the reception counter splintered into ten thousand pieces. Reacher ducked his head but sharp needles of wood and metal and hot stray pellets smashed him in the side of the face like a blow from a sledgehammer, all the way from his cheek to his forehead. He felt the dull crump and the sharp agonizing sting of serious injury. It was like falling from a window and hitting the ground head first. He rolled up dazed and the guy was hauling Jodie backward through the doorway, crunching the pump once more against the shotgun's weight as it moved. Reacher was dull and motionless against the back wall and the muzzle was coming up on him. His forehead was numb and icy. There was terrible pain there. He raised the Steyr. The silencer pointed straight at Jodie. He jerked it a fraction left and right. It still pointed at Jodie. The guy was making himself small behind her. He was craning around with his left hand, levelling the shotgun. His finger was tightening on the trigger. Reacher was immobile against the wall. He stared at Jodie, fixing her face in his mind before he died. Then a fair-haired woman was suddenly behind her, shouldering desperately into the guy's back, pushing him off balance. He staggered and whirled and clubbed at her with the shotgun barrel. Reacher caught a glimpse of a pink dress as she went down.

Then the shotgun was swinging back towards him. But Jodie was bouncing and wrestling against the guy's arm. She was stamping and kicking. The guy was staggering around against her energy. He blundered with her all the way back out into the reception area and tripped against the Suburban driver's legs. He fell with Jodie and the shotgun fired against the corpse. There was deafening sound and smoke and the obscene bloom and spray of dead blood and tissue. The guy came up on his knees and Reacher tracked him all the way with the Steyr. The guy dropped the shotgun and went for his pocket and came back with a shiny short-barrel revolver. He thumbed the hammer. The click was loud. Jodie was heaving left and right against his arm tight around her waist. Left and right, left and right, furiously, randomly. Reacher had no clear shot. Blood was pouring into his left eye. His forehead was pounding and bleeding. He closed the useless eye against the wetness and squinted with the right. The shiny revolver came all the way up and jammed hard into Jodie's side. She gasped and stopped moving and the guy's face came out from behind her head, smiling savagely.

'Drop the gun, asshole,' he panted.

Reacher kept the Steyr exactly where it was. One eye open, one eye closed, jagged bolts of pain hammering in his head, the length of the silencer trained on the guy's distorted grin.

'I'll shoot her,' the guy snarled.

'Then I'll shoot you,' Reacher said. 'She dies, you die.'

The guy stared. Then he nodded.

'Impasse,' he said.

Reacher nodded back. It looked that way. He shook his head to clear it. It just made the pain worse. Stalemate. Even if he could fire first, the guy might still get a shot off. With his finger tense on the trigger like that and the gun hard in her side, the pulse of death would probably be enough to do it. It was too much to risk. He kept the Steyr where it was and stood up slowly and pulled his shirt tail out and wiped his face with it, all the time squinting one-eyed down the

521

barrel. The guy took a breath and stood up too, hauling Jodie with him. She tried to ease away from the pressure of the gun, but he kept her pulled in tight with his right arm. He turned his elbow outward and the hook pivoted and the point dug in against her waist.

'So we need to deal,' he said.

Reacher stood and mopped his eye and said nothing. His head was buzzing with pain. Buzzing and screaming. He was beginning to understand he was in serious trouble.

'We need to deal,' the guy said again.

'No deal,' Reacher replied.

The guy twisted the hook a little more and jammed the revolver in a little harder. Jodie gasped. It was a Smith and Wesson Model 60. Two-inch barrel, stainless steel, .38 calibre, five shots in the cylinder. The sort of thing a woman carries in her purse or a man conceals on his body. The barrel was so short and the guy was digging it in so hard his knuckles were hard up against Jodie's side. She was hanging forward against the pressure of his arm. Her hair was falling over her face. Her eyes were looking straight up at Reacher, and they were the loveliest eyes he had ever seen.

'Nobody says no deal to Victor Hobie,' the guy snarled.

Reacher fought the pain and kept the Steyr steady and level on the guy's forehead, right where the pink scars met the grey skin.

'You're not Victor Hobie,' he said. 'You're Carl Allen, and you're a piece of shit.'

There was silence. Pain was hammering in his head. Jodie was staring harder at him, questions in her eyes.

'You're not Victor Hobie,' he said again. 'You're Carl Allen.'

The name hung in the air and the guy seemed to recoil away from it. He dragged Jodie backward, stepping over the corpse of the thickset guy, turning her to keep her body between himself and Reacher, walking slowly backward into the dark office. Reacher followed unsteadily with the Steyr held high and level. There were people in the office. Reacher saw dimmed windows and living-room furniture and three people milling around, the fair-haired woman in the silk dress and two men in suits. They were all staring at him. Staring at his gun, and the silencer, and his forehead, and the blood pouring down on to his shirt. Then they were regrouping themselves like automatons and moving towards a tight square group of sofas. They threaded their separate ways inside and sat down and placed their hands on the glass coffee table which was filling the space. Six hands on the table, three faces turned towards him, expressions of hope and fear and astonishment visible on each of them.

'You're wrong,' the guy with the hook said.

He backed away with Jodie in a wide circle until he was behind the farthest sofa. Reacher moved with them all the way and stopped opposite. His Steyr was levelled right over the heads of the three cowering people leaning on the coffee table. His blood was dripping off his chin on to the back of the sofa below him.

'No, I'm right,' he said. 'You're Carl Allen. Born April eighteenth, 1949, south of Boston, some leafy suburb. Normal little family, going nowhere. You got drafted in the summer of 1968. Private soldier, capabilities rated below average in every category.

Sent to Vietnam as an infantryman. A grunt, a humble foot soldier. War changes people, and when you got there you turned into a real bad guy. You started scamming. Buying and selling, trading drugs and girls and whatever else you could get your filthy hands on. Then you started lending money. You turned really vicious. You bought and sold favours. You lived like a king for a long time. Then somebody got wise. Pulled you out of your cosy little situation and put you in-country. The jungle. The real war. A tough unit, with a tough officer riding you. It pissed you off. First chance you got, you fragged the officer. And then his sergeant. But the unit turned you in. Very unusual. They didn't like you, did they? Probably owed you money. They called it in and two cops called Gunston and Zabrinski came out to pick you up. You want to deny anything yet?'

The guy said nothing. Reacher swallowed. His head was hurting badly. There was real pain digging in deep behind the cuts. Real serious pain.

'They came in a Huey,' he said. 'A decent young kid called Kaplan was flying it. Next day he came back, flying co-pilot for an ace named Victor Hobie. Gunston and Zabrinski had you ready and waiting on the ground. But Hobie's Huey was hit on takeoff. It went down again, four miles away. He was killed, along with Kaplan and Gunston and Zabrinski and three other crew called Bamford and Tardelli and Soper. But you survived. You were burned and you lost your hand, but you were alive. And your evil little brain was still ticking over. You swapped dog tags with the first guy you got to. Happened to be Victor Hobie. You crawled away with his tags around your neck. Left yours on his body. Right then and there Carl Allen and his criminal past ceased to exist. You made it to a field hospital, and they thought they were treating Hobie. They wrote his name down in their records. Then you killed an orderly and got away. You said *I'm not going back*, because you knew as soon as you arrived anywhere somebody would realize you weren't Hobie. They'd find out who you were, and you'd be back in the shit. So you just disappeared. A new life, a new name. A clean slate. You want to deny anything yet?'

Allen tightened his grip on Jodie.

'It's all bullshit,' he said.

Reacher shook his head. Pain flashed in his eye like a camera.

'No, it's all true,' he said. 'Nash Newman just identified Victor Hobie's skeleton. It's lying in a casket in Hawaii with your dog tags around its neck.'

'Bullshit,' Allen said again.

'It was the teeth,' Reacher said. 'Mr and Mrs Hobie sent their boy to the dentist thirty-five times, to give him perfect teeth. Newman says they're definitive. He spent an hour with the X-rays, programming the computer. Then he recognized the exact same skull when he walked back past the casket. Definitive match.'

Allen said nothing.

'It worked for thirty years,' Reacher said. 'Until those two old people finally made enough noise and somebody poked around. And now it's not going to work any longer, because you've got me to answer to.'

Allen sneered. It made the unmarked side of his face as ugly as the burns.

'Why the hell should I answer to you?'

Reacher blinked the blood out of his eye over the unwavering Steyr.

525

'A lot of reasons,' he said quietly. 'I'm a representative. I'm here to represent a lot of people. Like Victor Truman Hobie. He was a hero, but because of you he was written off as a deserter and a murderer. His folks have been in agony, thirty long years. I represent them. And I represent Gunston and Zabrinski, too. They were both MP lieutenants, both twenty-four years old. I was an MP lieutenant when I was twenty-four. They were killed because of what you did wrong. That's why you're going to answer to me, Allen. Because I'm them. Scum like you gets people like me killed.'

Allen's eyes were blank. He shifted Jodie's weight to keep her directly in front of him. Twisted the hook and jammed the gun in harder. He nodded, just a fractional movement of his head.

'OK, I was Carl Allen,' he said. 'I admit it, smart guy. I was Carl Allen, and then that was over. Then I was Victor Hobie. I was Victor Hobie for a real long time, longer than I was ever Carl Allen, but I guess that's over now, too. So now I'm going to be Jack Reacher.'

'What?'

'That's what you've got,' Allen said. 'That's the deal. That's your trade. Your name, for this woman's life.'

'What?' Reacher said again.

'I want your identity,' Allen said. 'I want your name.'

Reacher just stared at him.

'You're a drifter, no family,' Allen said. 'Nobody will ever miss you.'

'Then what?'

'Then you die,' Allen said. 'We can't have two

526

people with the same name running around, can we? It's a fair trade. Your life, for the woman's life.'

Jodie was staring, straight at Reacher, waiting.

'No deal,' Reacher said.

'I'll shoot her,' Allen said.

Reacher shook his head again. The pain was fearsome. It was building stronger and spreading behind both his eyes.

'You won't shoot her,' he said. 'Think about it, Allen. Think about yourself. You're a selfish piece of shit. The way you are, you're always number one. You shoot her, I'll shoot you. You're twelve feet away from me. I'm aiming at your head. You pull your trigger, I pull mine. She dies, you die one-hundredth of a second later. You won't shoot me either, because you start to line up on me, you go down before you're even halfway there. Think about it. Impasse.'

He stared at him down through the pain and the gloom. A classic standoff. But there was a problem. A serious flaw in his analysis. He knew that. It came to him in a cold flash of panic. It came to Allen at the exact same moment. Reacher knew that, too, because he saw it settle in his eyes, complacently.

'You're miscalculating,' Allen said. 'You're missing something.'

Reacher made no response.

'Right now it's a stalemate,' Allen said. 'And it always will be, as long as I'm standing here and you're standing there. But how long are you going to be standing there?'

Reacher swallowed against the pain. It was hammering at him.

'I'll be standing here as long as it takes,' he said. 'I've got plenty of time. Like you figured, I'm a drifter. I don't have any pressing appointments to get to.'

Allen smiled.

'Brave words,' he said. 'But you're bleeding from the head. You know that? You've got a piece of metal sticking in your head. I can see it from here.'

Jodie nodded desperately, eyes full of terror.

'Check it out, Mr Curry,' Allen said. 'Tell him.'

The guy on the sofa underneath the Steyr crabbed around and knelt up. He kept well away from Reacher's gun arm and craned his head around to look. Then his face creased in horror.

'It's a nail,' he said. 'A woodworking nail. You've got a nail in your head.'

'From the reception desk,' Allen said.

The guy called Curry ducked down again and Reacher knew it was true. As soon as the words were spoken, the pain doubled and quadrupled and exploded. It was a piercing agony centred in his forehead, an inch above his eye. The adrenaline had masked it for a long time. But adrenaline doesn't last for ever. He forced his mind away from it with all the power of his will, but it was still there. Bad pain, razor-sharp and nausea-dull all at the same time, booming and throbbing through his head, sending brilliant lightning strikes into his eyes. The blood had soaked his shirt, all the way down to his waist. He blinked, and saw nothing at all with his left eye. It was full of blood. Blood was running down his neck and down his left arm and dripping off his fingertips.

'I'm fine,' he said. 'Don't anybody worry about me.'

'Brave words,' Allen said again. 'But you're in pain and you're losing a lot of blood. You won't outlast me, Reacher. You think you're tough, but you're nothing next to me. I crawled away from that helicopter with no hand. Severed arteries. I was on fire. I survived three weeks in the jungle like that. Then I got myself home free. Then I lived with danger for thirty years. So I'm the tough guy here. I'm the toughest guy in the world. Mentally and physically. You couldn't outlast me even if you didn't have a nail in your damn head. So don't kid yourself, OK?'

Jodie was staring at him. Her hair was golden in the faint diffused light from the window blinds. It was hanging forward over her face, parted by the sweep of her brow. He could see her eyes. Her mouth. The curve of her neck. Her slim strong body, tense against Allen's arm. The hook, shining against the colour of her suit. The pain was hammering in his head. His soaked shirt was cold against his skin. There was blood in his mouth. It tasted metallic, like aluminium. He was feeling the first faint tremors in his shoulder. The Steyr was starting to feel heavy in his hand.

'And I'm motivated,' Allen said. 'I've worked hard for what I've got. I'm going to keep it. I'm a genius and a survivor. You think I'm going to let you take me down? You think you're the first person who ever tried?'

Reacher swayed against the pain.

'Now let's up the stakes a little,' Allen called to him.

He forced Jodie upward with all the strength in his arm. Jammed the gun in so hard she bent away from it, folding forward against the arm and sideways against the gun. He hauled her up so he was invisible behind her. Then the hook moved. The arm came up from crushing her waist to crushing her chest. The hook ploughed over her breasts. She gasped in pain. The hook moved up until the arm was at a steep angle crushing her body and the hook was resting on the side of her face. Then the elbow turned out and the steel tip dug into the skin of her cheek.

'I could rip her open,' Allen said. 'I could tear her face off, and there's nothing you could do about it except feel worse. Stress makes it worse, right? The pain? You're starting to feel faint, right? You're on your way out, Reacher. You're going down. And when you're down, the stalemate is over, believe me.'

Reacher shuddered. Not from the pain, but because he knew Allen was right. He could feel his knees. They were there, and they were strong. But a fit man never feels his knees. They're just a part of him. Feeling them valiantly holding up 250 pounds of body weight means that pretty soon they won't be. It's an early warning.

'You're going down, Reacher,' Allen called again. 'You're shaking, you know that? You're slipping away from us. Couple of minutes I'll walk right over and shoot you in the head. All the time in the world.'

Reacher shuddered again and scoped it out. It was hard to think. He was dizzy. He had an open head wound. His skull was penetrated. Nash Newman flashed into his mind, holding up bones in a classroom. Maybe Nash would explain it, many years in the future. *A sharp object penetrated the frontal lobe – here – and pierced the meninges and caused a haemorrhage*. His gun hand was shaking. Then Leon was there, scowling and muttering *if plan A doesn't work, move on to plan B*.

Then the Louisiana cop was there, the guy from years ago in another life, talking about his .38-calibre revolvers, saying *you just can't rely on them to put a guy down, not if he's coming at you all pumped up on angel dust*. Reacher saw the guy's unhappy face. *You can't rely on a .38 to put a man down*. And a short-barrel .38, worse still. Hard to hit a target with a short barrel. And with a struggling woman in your arms, harder still. *Although her struggling might put the bullet dead centre by accident.* His head spun. It was being pounded by a giant with a jackhammer. His strength was draining out of him from the inside. His right eye was jacked open and it was dry and stinging, like needles were in it. *Five more minutes, maybe*, he was thinking. *Then I'm done for.* He was in a rented car, next to Jodie, driving back from the zoo. He was talking. It was warm in the car. There was sun and glass. He was saying *the basis of any scam is to show them what they want to see.* The Steyr wobbled in his hand and he thought *OK, Leon, here's plan B. See how you like it.*

His knees buckled and he swayed. He came back upright and brought the Steyr back to the only thin sliver of Allen's head he could make out. The muzzle wavered through a circle. A small circle at first, then a larger one as the weight of the gun overwhelmed the control in his shoulder. He coughed and pushed blood out of his mouth with his tongue. The Steyr was coming down. He watched the front sight dropping like a strong man was pulling on it. He tried to bring it up, but it wouldn't come. He forced his hand upward, but it just moved sideways like an invisible force was deflecting it. His knees went again and he jerked back upright like a spasm. The Steyr was miles away. It was hanging down to the right. It was pointing at the desk. His elbow was locked against its weight and his arm was bending. *Allen's hand was moving.* He watched it one-eyed and wondered *is what I feel for Jodie as good as being pumped up by angel dust?* The barrel snagged out from a fold of cloth and

531

came free of her jacket. *Am I going to make it?* His knees were going and he started shaking. *Wait. Just wait.* Allen's wrist snapped forward. He saw it move. It was very quick. He saw the black hole in the stainless barrel. *It was clear of her body.* She smashed her head down and he whipped the Steyr back and got it pretty close to the target before Allen fired. It was within a couple of inches. That was all. A couple of lousy inches. *Fast*, he thought, *but not fast enough*. He saw the revolver hammer click forward and then a flower of bright flame bloomed out from the barrel and a freight train hit him in the chest. The roar of the shot was completely lost behind the immense physical impact of the bullet hitting him. It was a blow from a giant hammer the size of a planet. It thumped and crashed and deafened him from the inside. There was no pain. No pain at all. Just a huge cold numbness in his chest and a silent vacuum of total calm in his mind. He thought hard for a split second and fought to stay firm on his feet and he kept his eye wide open long enough to concentrate on the puff of soot coming from the Steyr's silencer. Then he moved his eye the last little fraction and watched Allen's head burst open twelve feet away. There was an explosion of blood and bone in the air, a cloud three or four feet wide, and it was spreading like a mist. He asked himself *is he dead now?* and when he heard himself answer *surely he must be* he let himself go and rolled his eye up in his head and fell backward through perfect still silent blackness that continued for ever and ended nowhere.

EIGHTEEN

He knew he was dying because faces were coming towards him and all of them were faces he recognized. They came in a long stream, unending, ones and twos together, and there were no strangers among them. He had heard it would be like this. Your life was supposed to flash before your eyes. Everybody said so. And now it was happening. So he was dying.

He guessed when the faces stopped, that was it. He wondered who the last one would be. There were a number of candidates. He wondered who chose the order. Whose decision was it? He felt mildly irritated he wasn't allowed to specify. And what would happen next? When the last face had gone, what then?

But something was going seriously wrong. A face loomed up who he didn't know. It was then he realized the Army was in charge of the parade. It had to be. Only the Army could accidentally include someone he had never seen before. A complete stranger, in the wrong place at the wrong time. He supposed it was fitting. He had lived most of his life under the control of the Army. He supposed it was pretty natural they would take charge of organizing this final part. And one mistake was tolerable. Normal, even acceptable, for the Army.

But this guy was touching him. Hitting him. Hurting him. He suddenly realized the parade had finished *before* this guy. This guy wasn't *in* the parade at all. He came *after* it. Maybe this guy was here to finish him off. Yes, that was it. Had to be that way. This guy was here to make sure he died on schedule. The parade was over, and the Army couldn't let him survive it. Why should they go to all the trouble of putting it on and then have him survive it? That would be no good. No good at all. That would be a serious lapse in procedure. He tried to recall who had come before this guy. The second-to-last person, who was really the last person. He didn't remember. He hadn't paid attention. He slipped away and died without remembering who had been the last face in his parade.

He was dead, but he was still thinking. Was that OK? Was this the afterlife? That would be a hell of a thing. He had lived nearly thirty-nine years assuming there was no afterlife. Some people had agreed with him, others had argued with him. But he'd always been adamant about it. Now he was right there in it. Somebody was going to come sneering up to him and say *I told you so*. He would, if the boot was on the other foot. He wouldn't let somebody get away with being absolutely wrong about something, not without a little friendly ribbing at least.

He saw Jodie Garber. She was going to tell him. No, that wasn't possible. She wasn't dead. Only a dead person could yell at you in the afterlife, surely? A live person couldn't do it. That was pretty obvious. A live person wasn't *in* the afterlife. And Jodie Garber was a live person. He'd made certain of it. That had been the whole damn point. And anyway, he was pretty sure he had never discussed the afterlife with Jodie Garber. Or had he? Maybe many years ago, when she was still a kid? But it *was* Jodie Garber. And she *was* going to speak to him. She sat down in front of him and pushed her hair behind her ears. Long blond hair, small ears.

'Hi, Reacher,' she said.

It was her voice. No doubt about it. No mistake. So maybe she *was* dead. Maybe it had been an automobile accident. That would be a hell of an irony. Maybe she was hit by a speeding truck on Lower Broadway, on her way home from the World Trade Center.

'Hey, Jodie,' he said.

She smiled. There was communication. So she *was* dead. Only a dead person could hear another dead person speak, surely. But he had to know.

'Where are we?' he asked.

'St Vincent's,' she said.

Saint *Peter* he had heard of. He was the guy at the gates. He had seen pictures. Well, not really pictures, but cartoons, at least. He was an old guy in a robe, with a beard. He stood at a lectern and asked questions about why you should be let in. But he didn't remember Saint Peter asking him any questions. Maybe that came later. Maybe you had to go out again, and then try to get back in.

But who was St Vincent? Maybe he was the guy who ran the place you stayed while you were waiting for Saint Peter's questions. Like the boot camp part. Maybe old Vincent ran the Fort Dix equivalent. Well, that would be no problem. He'd murdered boot camp. Easiest time he'd ever done. He could do it again. But he was annoyed about it. He'd finished up a major, for God's sake. He'd been a star. He had medals. Why the hell should he do boot camp all over again?

And why was Jodie here? She was supposed to be alive. He realized his left hand was clenching. He was intensely irritated. He'd saved her life, because he loved her. So why was she dead now? What the hell was going on? He tried to struggle upright. Something was tying him down. What the hell? He was going to get some answers or he was going to knock some heads together.

'Take it easy,' Jodie said to him.

'I want to see Saint Vincent,' he said. 'And I want to see him right now. Tell him to get his sorry ass in this room inside five minutes or I'm going to be seriously pissed off.'

She looked at him and nodded.

'OK,' she said.

Then she looked away and stood up. She disappeared from his sight and he lay back down. This wasn't any kind of a boot camp. It was too quiet, and the pillows were soft.

Looking back, it should have been a shock. But it wasn't. The room just swam into focus and he saw the decor and the shiny equipment and he thought *hospital*. He changed from being dead to being alive with the same little mental shrug a busy man gives when he realizes he's wrong about what day it is.

The room was bright with sun. He moved his head and saw he had a window. Jodie was sitting in a chair next to it, reading. He kept his breathing low and watched her. Her hair was washed and shiny. It fell past her shoulders, and she was twirling a strand

536

between her finger and thumb. She was wearing a yellow sleeveless dress. Her shoulders were brown with summer. He could see the little knobs of bone on top. Her arms were long and lean. Her legs were crossed. She was wearing tan penny loafers that matched the dress. Her ankles glowed brown in the sun.

'Hey, Jodie,' he said.

She turned her head and looked at him. Searched his face for something and when she found it she smiled.

'Hey yourself,' she said. She dropped the book and stood up. Walked three paces and bent and kissed him gently on the lips.

'St Vincent's,' he said. 'You told me, but I was confused.'

She nodded.

'You were full of morphine,' she said. 'They were pumping it in like crazy. Your bloodstream would have kept all the addicts in New York happy.'

He nodded. Glanced at the sun in the window. It looked like afternoon.

'What day is it?'

'It's July. You've been out three weeks.'

'Christ, I ought to feel hungry.'

She moved around the foot of the bed and came up on his left. Laid her hand on his forearm. It was turned palm up and there were tubes running into the veins of his elbow.

'They've been feeding you,' she said. 'I made sure you got what you like. You know, lots of glucose and saline.'

He nodded.

'Can't beat saline,' he said.

She went quiet.

'What?' he asked.

'Do you remember?'

He nodded again.

'Everything,' he said.

She swallowed.

'I don't know what to say,' she whispered. 'You took a bullet for me.'

'My fault,' he said. 'I was too slow, is all. I was supposed to trick him and get him first. But apparently I survived it. So don't say anything. I mean it. Don't ever mention it.'

'But I have to say thank you,' she whispered.

'Maybe I should say thank you,' he said. 'Feels good to know somebody worth taking a bullet for.'

She nodded, but not because she was agreeing. It was just random physical motion designed to stop her crying.

'So how am I?' he asked.

She paused for a long moment.

'I'll get the doctor,' she said quietly. 'He can tell you better than me.'

She went out and a guy in a white coat came in. Reacher smiled. It was the guy the Army had sent to finish him off at the end of his parade. He was a small wide hairy man who could have found work wrestling.

'You know anything about computers?' he asked.

Reacher shrugged and started worrying this was a coded lead-in to bad news about a brain injury, impairment, loss of memory, loss of function.

'Computers?' he said. 'Not really.'

'OK, try this,' the doctor said. 'Imagine a big Cray supercomputer humming away. We feed it everything we know about human physiology and everything we know about gunshot wounds and then we ask it to design us a male person best equipped to survive a thirty-eight in the chest. Suppose it hums away for a week. What does it come up with?'

Reacher shrugged again. 'I don't know.'

'A picture of you, my friend,' the doctor said. 'That's what. The damn bullet didn't even make it *into* your chest. Your pectoral muscle is so thick and so dense it stopped it dead. Like a three-inch kevlar vest. It popped out the other side of the muscle wall and smashed a rib, but it went no farther.'

'So why was I out three weeks?' Reacher asked immediately. 'Not for a muscle wound or a broken rib, that's for damn sure. Is my head OK?'

The doctor did a weird thing. He clapped his hands and punched the air. Then he stepped closer, beaming all over his face.

'I was worried about it,' he said. 'Real worried about it. Bad wound. I would have figured it for a nail gun, until they told me it was shotgun debris from manufactured furniture. It penetrated your skull and was about an eighth of an inch into your brain. Frontal lobe, my friend, bad place to have a nail. If I had to have a nail in my skull, the frontal lobe would definitely not be my first choice. But if I had to see a nail in anybody *else's* frontal lobe I'd pick yours, I guess, because you've got a skull thicker than Neanderthal man's. Anybody normal, that nail would have been all the way in, and that would have been thank you and good night.'

'So am I OK?' Reacher asked again.

'You just saved us ten thousand dollars in tests,' the doctor said happily. 'I told you the news about the chest, and what did you do? Analytically? You compared it with your own internal database, realized it wasn't a very serious wound, realized it couldn't have needed three weeks of coma, remembered your other injury, put two and two together and asked the question you asked. Immediately. No hesitation. Fast, logical thinking, assembly of pertinent information, rapid conclusion, lucid questioning of the source of a possible answer. Nothing wrong with your head, my friend. Take that as a professional opinion.'

Reacher nodded slowly. 'So when can I get out of here?'

The doctor took the medical chart off the foot of the bed. There was a mass of paper clipped to a metal board. He riffled through it. 'Well, your health is excellent in general, but we better watch you a while. Couple more days, maybe.'

'Nuts to that,' Reacher said. 'I'm leaving tonight.'

The doctor nodded. 'Well, see how you feel in an hour.'

He stepped close and stretched up to a valve on the bottom of one of the IV bags. Clicked it a notch and tapped a tube with his finger. Watched carefully and nodded and walked back out of the room. He passed Jodie in the doorway. She was walking in with a guy in a seersucker jacket. He was about fifty, pale, short grey hair. Reacher watched him and thought *a buck gets ten this is the Pentagon guy*.

'Reacher, this is General Mead,' Jodie said.

'Department of the Army,' Reacher said.

The guy in the jacket looked at him, surprised. 'Have we met?'

Reacher shook his head. 'No, but I knew one of you would be sniffing around, soon as I was up and running.'

Mead smiled. 'We've been practically camped out here. To put it bluntly, we'd like you to keep quiet about the Carl Allen situation.'

'Not a chance,' Reacher said.

Mead smiled again and waited. He was enough of an Army bureaucrat to know the steps. Leon used to say *something for nothing, that's a foreign language.*

'The Hobies,' Reacher said. 'Fly them down to DC first class, put them up in a five-star hotel, show them their boy's name on the Wall and make sure there's a shitload of brass in full dress uniform saluting like crazy the whole time they're doing it. Then I'll keep quiet.'

Mead nodded.

'It'll be done,' he said. He got up unbidden and went back outside. Jodie sat down on the foot of the bed.

'Tell me about the police,' Reacher said. 'Have I got questions to answer?'

She shook her head.

'Allen was a cop killer,' she said. 'You stick around NYPD territory and you'll never get another ticket in your life. It was self-defence, everybody's cool.'

'What about my gun? It was stolen.'

'No, it was Allen's gun. You wrestled it away from him. Roomful of witnesses saw you do it.'

He nodded slowly. Saw the spray of blood and brains all over again as he shot him. A pretty good shot, he thought. Dark room, stress, a nail in his head, a .38 slug in his chest, bull's-eye. Pretty damn close to the perfect shot. Then he saw the hook again, up at Jodie's face, hard steel against the honey of her skin.

'You OK?' he asked her.

'I'm fine,' she said.

'You sure? No bad dreams?'

541

'No bad dreams. I'm a big girl now.'

He nodded again. Recalled their first night together. A big girl. Seemed like a million years ago.

'But are *you* OK?' she asked him back.

'The doctor thinks so. He called me Neanderthal man.'

'No, seriously.'

'How do I look?'

'I'll show you,' she said.

She ducked away to the bathroom and came back with the mirror from the wall. It was a round thing, framed in plastic. She propped it on his legs and he steadied it with his right hand and looked. He still had a fearsome tan. Blue eyes. White teeth. His head had been shaved. The hair had grown back an eighth of an inch. On the left of his face was a peppering of scars. The nail hole in his forehead was lost among the debris of a long and violent life. He could make it out because it was redder and newer than the rest, but it was no bigger than the mark half an inch away where his brother Joe had caught him with a shard of glass in some long-forgotten childhood dispute over nothing, in the same exact year Hobie's Huey went down. He tilted the mirror and saw broad strapping over his chest, snowy white against the tan. He figured he had lost maybe thirty pounds. Back to 220, his normal weight. He handed the mirror back to Jodie and tried to sit up. He was suddenly dizzy.

'I want to get out of here,' he said.

'You sure?' she asked.

He nodded. He was sure, but he felt very sleepy. He put his head back on the pillow, just temporarily. He was warm and the pillow was soft. His head weighed a ton and his neck muscles were powerless to move it. The room was darkening. He swivelled his eyes upward and saw the IV bags hanging in the far distance above him. He saw the valve the doctor had adjusted. He had clicked it. He remembered the plastic sound. There was writing on the IV bag. The writing was upside down. He focused on it. Concentrated hard. The writing was green. It said *morphine*.

'Shit,' he whispered, and the room spun away into total darkness.

When he opened his eyes again, the sun had moved backward. It was earlier in the day. Morning, not afternoon. Jodie was sitting in her chair by the window, reading. The same book. She was half an inch further through it. Her dress was blue, not yellow.

'It's tomorrow,' he said.

She closed the book and stood up. Stepped over and bent and kissed his lips. He kissed her back and clamped his teeth and pulled the IV needles out of his arm and dropped them over the side of the bed. They started a steady drip on to the floor. He hauled himself upright against the pillows and smoothed a hand over his bristly scalp.

'How do you feel?' she asked.

He sat still in the bed and concentrated on a slow survey up his body, starting with his toes and ending with the top of his head.

'Fine,' he said.

'There are people here to see you,' she said. 'They heard you'd come around.'

He nodded and stretched. He could feel the chest wound. It was on the left. There was weakness there. He reached up with his left hand to the IV stand. It was a vertical stainless-steel bar with a spiral curl at the top where the bags slipped on. He put his hand over the curl and squeezed hard. He felt bruising in his elbow where the needles had been and sensitivity in his chest where the bullet had been, but the steel spiral still flattened from round to oval. He smiled.

'OK, send them in,' he said.

He knew who they were before they got inside. He could tell by the sound. The wheels on the oxygen cart squeaked. The old lady stood aside and let her husband enter first. She was wearing a brand-new dress. He was in the same old blue serge suit. He wheeled the cart past her and paused. He kept hold of the handle with his left hand and drew his right up into a trembling salute. He held it for a long moment and Reacher replied with the same. He threw his best parade-ground move and held it steady, meaning every second of it. Then he snapped it down and the old guy wheeled the cart slowly towards him with his wife fussing behind.

They were changed people. Still old, still feeble, but serene. Knowing your son is dead is better than not knowing, he guessed. He tracked back to Newman's windowless lab in Hawaii and recalled Allen's casket with Victor Hobie's skeleton in it. Victor Hobie's old bones. He remembered them pretty well. They were distinctive. The smooth arch of the brow, the high round cranium. The even white teeth. The long, clean limbs. It was a noble skeleton.

'He was a hero, you know.'

The old man nodded.

'He did his duty.'

'Much more than that,' Reacher replied. 'I read his record. I talked with General DeWitt. He was a brave flyer who did more than his duty. He saved a lot of

544

lives with his courage. If he'd lived, he'd have three stars now. He'd be General Victor Truman Hobie, with a big command somewhere, or a big job in the Pentagon.'

It was what they needed to hear, but it was still true. The old woman put her thin, pale hand over her husband's and they sat in silence, eyes moist and focused eleven thousand miles away. They were telling themselves stories of what might have been. The past stretched away straight and uncomplicated and now it was neatly amputated by a noble combat death, leaving only honest dreams ahead of it. They were recounting those dreams for the first time, because now they were legitimate. Those dreams were fortifying them just like the oxygen hissing in and out of the bottle in time with the old man's ragged breathing.

'I can die happy now,' he said.

Reacher shook his head.

'Not yet you can't,' he said. 'You have to go see the Wall. His name will be there. I want you to bring me a photograph of it.'

The old man nodded and his wife smiled a watery smile.

'Miss Garber told us you might be living over in Garrison,' she said. 'You might be our neighbour.'

Reacher nodded.

'It's possible,' he said.

'Miss Garber is a fine young woman.'

'Yes, ma'am, she is.'

'Stop your nonsense,' the old man said to her. Then they told him they couldn't stay, because their neighbour had driven them down and had to get back. Reacher watched them all the way out to the corridor. Soon as they were gone, Jodie came in, smiling.

'The doctor says you can leave.'

'So can you drive me? Did you get a new car yet?'

She shook her head. 'Just a rental. No time for shopping. Hertz brought me a Mercury. It's got satellite navigation.'

He stretched his arms above his head and flexed his shoulders. They felt OK. Surprisingly good. His ribs were fine. No pain.

'I need clothes,' he said. 'I guess those old ones got ruined.'

She nodded. 'Nurses sliced them off with scissors.'

'You were here for that?'

'I've been here all the time,' she said. 'I'm living in a room down the hall.'

'What about work?'

'Leave of absence,' she said. 'I told them, agree or I quit.'

She ducked down to a laminate cupboard and came out with a stack of clothes. New jeans, new shirt, new jacket, new socks and shorts, all folded and piled together, his old shoes squared on top, Army-style.

'They're nothing special,' she said. 'I didn't want to take too much time out. I wanted to be with you when you woke up.'

'You sat around here for three weeks?'

'Felt like three years,' she said. 'You were all scrunched up. Comatose. You looked awful. In a real bad way.'

'This satellite thing,' he said. 'Does it have Garrison on it?'

'You going up there?'

He shrugged.

'I guess. I need to take it easy, right? Country air might do me good.'

Then he looked away from her.

'Maybe you could stay with me a while, you know, help me recover.'

He threw back the sheet and slid his feet to the floor. Stood up, slow and unsteady, and started to dress, while she held his elbow to keep him from falling.

THE END

Choose your next Jack Reacher novel

The Reacher books can be read in any order, but here they are in the order in which they were written:

KILLING FLOOR

Jack Reacher gets off a bus in a small town in Georgia. And is thrown into the county jail, for a murder he didn't commit.

DIE TRYING

Reacher is locked in a van with a woman claiming to be FBI. And ferried right across America into a brand new country.

TRIPWIRE

Reacher is digging swimming pools in Key West when a detective comes round asking questions. Then the detective turns up dead.

THE VISITOR

Two naked women found dead in a bath filled with paint. Both victims of a man just like Reacher.

ECHO BURNING

In the heat of Texas, Reacher meets a young woman whose husband is in jail. When he is released, he will kill her.

WITHOUT FAIL

A Washington woman asks Reacher for help. Her job? Protecting the Vice-President.

PERSUADER

A kidnapping in Boston. A cop dies. Has Reacher lost his sense of right and wrong?

THE ENEMY

Back in Reacher's army days, a general is found dead on his watch.

ONE SHOT

A lone sniper shoots five people dead in a heartland city. But the accused guy says, 'Get Reacher'.

THE HARD WAY

A coffee on a busy New York street leads to a shoot-out
three thousand miles away in the Norfolk countryside.

BAD LUCK AND TROUBLE

One of Reacher's buddies has shown up dead in the California
desert, and Reacher must put his old army unit back together.

NOTHING TO LOSE

Reacher crosses the line between a town called
Hope and one named Despair.

GONE TOMORROW

On the New York subway, Reacher counts
down the twelve tell-tale signs of a suicide bomber.

61 HOURS

In freezing South Dakota, Reacher hitches
a lift on a bus heading for trouble.

WORTH DYING FOR

Reacher runs into a clan that's terrifying the Nebraska locals,
but it's the unsolved case of a missing child that he can't let go.

THE AFFAIR

Six months before the events in *Killing Floor*, Major Jack Reacher of the
US Military Police goes undercover in Mississippi, to investigate a murder.

A WANTED MAN

A busted nose makes it difficult for Reacher to hitch a ride. When he's
finally picked up by three strangers, it's clear they are hiding something . . .

NEVER GO BACK

When Reacher returns to his old Virginia headquarters he
is accused of a sixteen-year-old homicide.

PERSONAL

Someone has taken a shot at the French president. Only one man could
have done it – and Reacher is the one man who can find him.

MAKE ME

At a remote railroad stop on the prairie, Jack Reacher finds a town full of
silent, watchful people, and descends into the heart of darkness.

NIGHT SCHOOL

Reacher back in his army days, but not in uniform. In Hamburg he teams up with Frances Neagley to confront a terrifying new enemy.

NO MIDDLE NAME

Published in one volume for the first time, and including a brand-new adventure, here are all the pulse-pounding Jack Reacher short stories.

THE MIDNIGHT LINE

Reacher tracks a female officer's class ring back to its owner in the deserted wilds of Wyoming, on a raw quest for simple justice.

PAST TENSE

Deep in the New England woods, Reacher spots a sign to the town where his father was born, while two young Canadians are stranded at a remote, sinister motel . . .

BLUE MOON

On a Greyhound bus, Reacher rescues an old man from a mugger. Elsewhere in the city, two rival criminal gangs are competing for control – will Reacher be able to stop bad things happening?

THE SENTINEL

Reacher works with a local IT nerd to save a small town being held to ransom by a cyber-ware attack.

BETTER OFF DEAD

In an Arizona border town Reacher teams up with an FBI agent in a desperate search for her missing twin brother, with explosive results.

NO PLAN B

In Colorado, Reacher is the sole witness to a murder. The trail leads him to a private prison in Mississippi. And he knows that getting to the truth is worth doing time for.

THE SECRET

Military investigator Jack Reacher, recently demoted, is called to investigate a series of mysterious deaths. The catch? He must work as part of an inter-agency task force.

Alternatively, you can find a list of the books in the order of events in Reacher's life, at www.deadgoodbooks.co.uk/ReacherBooks

Now read on for an extract from
the new Reacher adventure

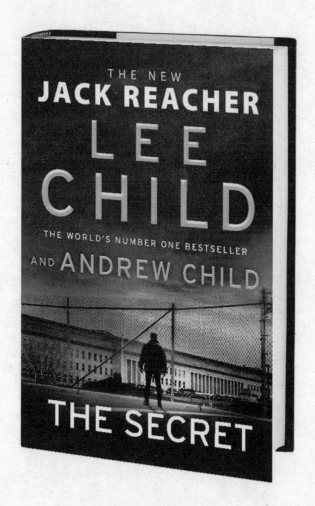

ONE

Keith Bridgeman was alone in his room when he closed his eyes. The morning medical rounds were over. Lunch had been delivered and eaten and cleared away. Other people's visitors had clattered along the corridor in search of relatives and friends. A janitor had swept and mopped and hauled off the day's trash. And finally a little peace had descended on the ward.

Bridgeman had been in the hospital for a month. Long enough to grow used to its rhythms and routines. He knew it was time for the afternoon lull. A break from getting poked and prodded and being made to get up and move around and stretch. No one was going to bother him for another three hours, minimum. So he could read. Watch TV. Listen to music. Gaze out of the window at the sliver of lake that was visible between the next pair of skyscrapers.

Or he could take a nap.

Bridgeman was sixty-two years old. He was in rough shape. That was clear. He could debate the cause – the kind of work he had devoted his life to, the stress he had suffered, the cigarettes and alcohol he had consumed – but he couldn't deny the effect. A heart attack so massive that no one had expected him to survive.

Defying odds that great is tiring work. He chose the nap.

These days he always chose the nap.

*

Bridgeman woke up after only an hour. He was no longer alone. Two other people were in the room with him. Both were women. Maybe in their late twenties. They were the same height. The same slim build. One was on the left side of his bed, nearer to the door. The other was level with her on the right, nearer to the window. They were standing completely still. In silence. Staring at him. Their hair was pulled back, smooth and dark and tight. Their faces were expressionless like mannequins' and their skin shone in the harsh artificial light as if it was moulded from plastic.

The women were wearing white coats over hospital scrubs. The coats were the correct length. They had all the necessary pockets and badges and tags. The scrubs were the right shade of blue. But the women weren't medics. Bridgeman was sure about that. His sixth sense told him so. It told him they shouldn't be there. That they were trouble. He scanned each of them in turn. Their hands were empty. Their clothes were not bulging. There was no sign of guns or knives. No sign of any hospital equipment they could use as weapons. But Bridgeman still wasn't happy. He was in danger. He knew it. He could feel it as keenly as a gazelle that had been ambushed by a pair of lions.

Bridgeman glanced at his left leg. The call button was where the nurse had left it, lying on the sheet between his thigh and the safety rail. His hand darted toward it. It was a fluid movement. Smooth. Fast. But the woman was faster. She snatched the button then dropped it, leaving it dangling on its wire, almost to the floor, well out of Bridgeman's reach.

Bridgeman felt his heart quiver and tremble in his chest. He heard an electronic *beep*. It came from a piece of equipment on a stand near the head of the bed. It had a screen with a number in the centre of the top half and two jagged lines that zigzagged across the full width of the lower half. The first line showed his pulse. It was spiking wildly. Its peaks were surging closer together like they were chasing one another. The number showed his heart rate. It was climbing. Fast. The *beep*s grew louder. More frequent. Then the sound became continuous. Insistent. Impossible to ignore. The number stopped rising. It began to flash. It changed direction. And it kept going down until it reached 00. The lines flattened out. First at the left of the screen and then all the way across until both were perfectly horizontal. The display was inert. Lifeless. Except for the desperate electronic howl.

It told of total cardiac failure.

But only for a moment.

The second woman had grabbed Bridgeman's right wrist when the alarm began to shriek. She had yanked a square blue clip off the tip of his index finger and attached it to her own. The screen flashed twice. Then the sound cut out. The heart rate started to climb. The two lines began to tick their way from left to right. None of the values were quite the same as Bridgeman's. The woman was younger. Fitter. Healthier. Calmer. But the readings were close enough. Not too high. Not too low. Nothing to trigger another alarm.

Bridgeman clutched his chest with both hands. Sweat was prickling out across his forehead and his scalp. His skin felt clammy. He had to make an effort to breathe.

The woman with the clip on her finger lowered herself into the visitor's chair next to the window. The woman on the left of the bed waited a moment then looked at Bridgeman and said, 'We apologize. We didn't mean to startle you. We're not here to hurt you. We just need to talk.'

Bridgeman said nothing.

The woman said, 'We have two questions. That's all. Answer them honestly and you'll never see us again. I promise.'

Bridgeman didn't respond.

The woman saw him glancing past her, toward the door. She shook her head. 'If you're hoping the cavalry's going to come, you're out of luck. Those clips slip off people's fingers all the time. And what do they do? Stick them right back on. Anyone at the nurses' station who heard the alarm will figure that's what you did. So. First question, OK?'

Bridgeman's mouth was dry. He did his best to moisten his lips then took a deep breath. But not to answer questions. To call for help the old-fashioned way.

The woman read his play. She put a finger to her lips and took something out of her coat pocket. A photograph. She held it out for Bridgeman to take. It showed a gloved hand holding a copy of the *Tribune* next to a window. Bridgeman could read the date on the newspaper. Tuesday, 7 April 1992. It was that day's edition. Then he saw two figures through the glass. A woman and a child. A little girl. Even though they were facing away from the camera Bridgeman had no doubt who they were. Or where they were. It was his daughter and granddaughter. In the home he had bought them in Evanston, after his wife died.

The woman took hold of Bridgeman's arm and felt for his pulse. It was fast and weak. She said, 'Come on now. Calm down. Think of your family. We don't want to hurt them. Or you. We just need you to understand how serious this situation is. We only have two questions, but they're important. The sooner you answer, the sooner we're out of here. Ready?'

Bridgeman nodded and slumped back against his pillow.

'First question. You're meeting with a journalist the day after tomorrow. Where is the information you're planning to give her?'

'How do you know about—'

'Don't waste time. Answer the question.'

'OK. Look. There is no information. We're just going to chat.'

'No credible journalist is going to believe a whistleblower without ironclad proof. Where is it?'

'Whistleblower? That's not what this is. The reporter's from a little weekly rag in Akron, Ohio. Where I was born. The story's about my heart attack. My recovery. It's a miracle, according to the doctors. People back home want to read about it. They say I'm an inspiration.'

'Heart attack? That's what you're going with? When you're sitting on a much bigger story?'

'What bigger story?'

The woman leaned in closer. 'Keith, we know what you did. What you all did. Twenty-three years ago. December 1969.'

'December '69? How do you know . . .? Who are you?'

'We'll come to who we are. Right now you need to tell me what information you're planning to give this reporter from Akron.'

'No information. I'm going to tell her about my recovery. That's all. I will never talk about December '69. Why we were there. What we were doing. What happened. Not to anyone. I swore I wouldn't and I keep my word. My wife never even knew.'

'So you don't have any documents or notes hidden in this room?'

'Of course not.'

'Then you won't mind if I take a look around.'

The woman didn't wait for an answer. She started with the locker next to the bed. She opened the door and rummaged through Bridgeman's spare pyjamas and books and magazines. She moved on to a leather duffel on the floor near the door. It held a set of clothes. Nothing else. Next she checked the bathroom. Nothing significant there, either. So she moved to the centre of the room and put her hands on her hips. 'Only one place left to check. The bed.'

Bridgeman didn't move.

'Do it for your daughter. And your granddaughter. Come on. I'll be quick.'

Bridgeman felt his pulse start to speed up again. He closed his eyes for a moment. Took a breath. Willed himself to relax. Then pushed back the sheet, swung his legs over the side of the mattress, and slid down on to his feet. He looked at the woman in the chair. 'Can I at least sit? I'm older than you. I have one foot in the grave.'

The woman held up her finger with the clip attached.

'Sorry. The cable's too short for me to move. You want to sit, use the windowsill.'

Bridgeman turned and looked at the windowsill. Considered sitting on it. But taking orders from one of the women was bad enough so he settled on leaning against it. He watched as the other woman finished her search of the bed. Again she came up empty.

'Believe me now?' Bridgeman said.

The woman took a piece of paper out of her pocket and handed it to Bridgeman. There was a list of names. Six of them, handwritten in shaky, spidery script. Bridgeman's was one of them. He recognized all the other five. Varinder Singh. Geoffrey Brown. Michael Rymer. Charlie Adam. Neville Pritchard. And beneath the final name there was a symbol. A question mark.

The woman said, 'A name is missing. Who is it?'

Bridgeman's heart was no longer racing. Now it felt like it was full of sludge. Like it didn't have the strength to force his blood into his arteries. He couldn't answer. It would mean breaking his oath. He had sworn to never reveal a single detail. They all had, twenty-three years before, when it became clear what they had done. And the missing name belonged to the flakiest of the group. Better for everyone if it remained off the list.

The woman handed Bridgeman another photograph. Another shot of his daughter and granddaughter, on foot this time, halfway across a crosswalk. The picture had been taken through a car windshield.

Bridgeman was channelling all his energy into trying to breathe. It was only a name that the woman wanted. What harm could come from telling her? Plenty, he knew.

The woman said, 'Bonus question. What happens tomorrow? Or the next day? Is the driver drunk? Do his brakes fail?'

Bridgeman said, 'Buck. The missing name. It's Owen Buck.'

The woman shook her head. 'Buck's dead. He died of cancer a month ago. Right after he wrote that list. So his isn't the name I need. He said there was an eighth name.

He didn't know what it was. But he was certain one of you others do.'

Bridgeman didn't answer. He was struggling to make sense of the information. Buck's conscience must have gotten the better of him. He was always mumbling about doing something stupid. But that didn't explain why he told this woman there was an extra name. Maybe his mind had gone. Maybe whatever cancer drugs they gave him had fried his brain.

The woman said, 'Maybe the driver will be distracted? Maybe he'll be asleep at the wheel?'

'Maybe there is another name.' Bridgeman closed his eyes. 'Maybe someone knows what it is. One of the others might. But not me. I don't think one exists.'

The woman said, 'Maybe there'll be enough of your granddaughter left to bury. Maybe there won't.'

Bridgeman was struggling for air. 'Don't. Please. I don't know. I swear. I gave you Buck's name. I didn't know he's dead. I've been sick. I've been in here. No one told me. So if I knew of some other name I'd tell you it, too. But I don't. So I can't.'

'You can. You don't have to say it. You can do what Owen Buck did. Write it down. He gave me six names. You only need to give me one.'

She pulled a pen from her coat pocket and held it out. Bridgeman stared at it for a moment. Then he took it and added *Owen Buck* to the top of the list.

He said, 'That's the only name I know. I swear.'

The woman said, 'Have you ever seen a child's coffin, Keith? Because if you haven't I don't think anything can really prepare you for how tiny it will seem. Especially when it's next to the full-size one your daughter will be in.'

Bridgeman's knees started to shake. He looked like he was ready to collapse.

The woman's voice softened. 'Come on. One name. Two lives saved. What are you waiting for?'

Bridgeman's body sagged. 'Buck was wrong. There isn't another name. Not that I know of. I was there three years. I never heard of anyone else getting brought on board.'

The woman stared at Bridgeman for ten long seconds, then shrugged. She took the pen and the paper and slid them back into her pocket. 'I guess we're done here.' She stretched out and touched Bridgeman's forehead. 'Wait a minute. You feel awful. Let me open the window. Fresh air will perk you up. I don't want to leave you like this.'

Bridgeman said, 'You can't. The windows don't open in this hospital.'

'This one does.' The woman leaned past Bridgeman, pushed down on the handle, and the window swung out on a broad arc. Then she scrabbled under the collar of her scrubs and pulled a fine chain up and over her head. The key to the window was hanging from it. 'Here.' She dropped the chain into the breast pocket of Bridgeman's pyjama top. 'A present. Something to remember us by, because you're never going to see us again. As promised. There's just one last thing before we go. You asked who we are.' The woman stood a little straighter. 'My name is Roberta Sanson.'

The woman with the finger clip climbed out of her chair. 'And I'm her sister. Veronica Sanson. Our father was Morgan Sanson. It's important you know that.'

Morgan Sanson. The name was an echo from the past. An unwelcome one. Four syllables he had hoped to never hear again. It took a fraction of a second for the significance to hit him then Bridgeman pushed off from the wall. He tried to dodge around Roberta Sanson but he never stood a chance. He was too frail. The space was too cramped. And the sisters were too highly motivated. Roberta shifted sideways and blocked his path. Then she grabbed his shoulders with both hands and drove him back until he was pressed against the sill. She checked that he was lined up with the open window. Veronica bent down and took hold of his legs, just above the ankles. She straightened and Roberta pushed. Bridgeman kicked. He twisted and thrashed. Roberta and Veronica pushed one more time. Two more times, to make sure there was no room for error. Then they let gravity do the rest.

TWO

J ack Reacher had never been to the Rock Island Arsenal in Illinois before, but he was the second Military Police investigator to be sent there within a fortnight. The first visit was in response to a report of missing M16s, which proved to be false. Reacher was the last to join his unit, following his demotion from major to captain, so he had been allocated a less interesting allegation. Inventory tampering.

The sergeant who had filed the complaint met Reacher at the main entrance. There were maybe ten years between them. They were about the same height, six foot five, but where Reacher was heavy and broad the older man was skinny and pinched with pale skin and thin, delicate features. He couldn't have been more than 180 pounds. That would be sixty pounds lighter. His uniform hung off his shoulders a little, causing Reacher to worry about the guy's health.

Once the usual courtesies were taken care of the sergeant led the way to Firing Range E, near the base's western perimeter. He locked the heavy steel door behind them and continued to a loading bench that jutted out from the rear wall. Six M16s were lying on it, neatly lined up, muzzles facing away, grips to the right. The weapons weren't new. They had spent plenty of time in the field. That was clear. But they were well maintained. Recently cleaned. Not neglected or damaged. There were no obvi-ous red flags. No visible indication that anything was wrong with them.

Reacher picked up the second rifle from the left. He checked that the chamber was empty, inspected it for defects, then slid a magazine into place. He stepped across to the mouth of the range. Selected single-fire mode. Took a breath. Held it. Waited for the next beat of his heart to subside and pulled the trigger. A hundred yards down range the red star on the target figure's helmet imploded. Reacher lowered the gun and glanced at the sergeant. The guy's face betrayed nothing. No surprise. No disappoint-ment. Reacher fired five more times. Rapidly. Sharp *crack*s rebounded off the walls. Spent cartridges rattled on to the cement floor. A neat 'T' shape was hammered into the figure's chest. It was textbook shooting. There was no sign of any problem with the gun. And still no response from the sergeant.

Reacher pointed to the magazine. 'How many?'

The sergeant said, 'Sixteen.'

'Vietnam?'

'Three tours. No misfires. If it's not broke . . .'

Reacher slid the fire selector to its lowest position. Full auto. The model was old, from before the switch to three-shot bursts. He aimed at the target's centre mass and increased the pressure on the trigger. The green plastic torso should have been shredded. The ten remaining bul-lets should have torn through it in less than a second. But nothing happened. Because the trigger wouldn't move. Reacher changed back to single-shot mode and lined up on the target's face. The crude contour representing its nose split in half under the impact. Reacher toggled to full auto. Again, nothing happened. Which left no doubt. The trigger would not move in that position.

He said, 'They all like this?'

The sergeant nodded. 'All of them. The whole case.'

Reacher crossed to the bench and set the gun down. He removed the magazine, cleared the chamber, pushed out the takedown pins, separated the lower receiver, and examined its interior contours. Then he held it out toward the sergeant and said, 'The trigger pocket's the wrong size. It won't accept the auto-sear. And there are only two trigger pinholes. There should be three.'

The sergeant said, 'Correct.'

'This isn't military spec. Someone's switched out the original with a civilian version. It makes the gun semi-auto only.'

'Can't see any other explanation.'

'Where did these come from?'

The sergeant shrugged. 'Admin error. They were supposed to be sent for destruction but two crates got mixed up and these wound up here by mistake.'

Reacher looked down at the guns on the bench. 'These would be considered end-of-life?'

The sergeant shrugged again. 'I wouldn't say so. Ask me, the condition's acceptable for weapons that would generally be held in reserve. Nothing stood out when the crate was opened. Only when a malfunction was reported. Then I stripped the first one down. Saw the problem right away. Just like you did.'

'Who decides which weapons get destroyed?'

'A dedicated team. It's a special procedure. Temporary. Lasted a year, so far. Result of Desert Storm. The war was a great opportunity for units to re-equip. Assets that are designated surplus as a result come back from the Gulf and get sent here for evaluation. Firearms are our responsibility. We test them and give them a category. Green: fully serviceable, to be retained. Amber: marginally serviceable, to be sold or allocated to civilian gun safety programmes. Doesn't apply to fully automatic weapons, obviously. And Red: unserviceable, to be destroyed.'

'You got sent a Red crate when you should have gotten a Green one?'

'Correct.'

Reacher paused for a moment. The account was plausible. There wasn't a kind of equipment the army owned that hadn't been sent to the wrong place, some time or other. Which was usually totally innocent. Like the sergeant said, an admin error. But Reacher was wondering if there could be a broader connection. Something to do with the recent report of stolen M16s. Someone could designate good weapons as unserviceable, fill their crates with the right weight of whatever trash came to hand, send that to the crusher or the furnace, and sell the guns on the black market. Officially the weapons would no longer exist, so no one would be looking for them. It was a feasible method. A loophole someone needed to close. But it wasn't what had happened here. Reacher had read the report. The inspection was unannounced. A full crack-of-dawn shock-and-awe operation. And it had been thorough. All the weapons crates on the entire base had been opened. All had the correct number of weapons inside. Not so much as a pocketknife was missing.

Not so much as a *complete* pocketknife . . .

Reacher said, 'When did these guns get delivered to you in error?'

The sergeant looked away while he did the math, then said, 'Fifteen days ago. And I know what you're going to ask me next. You're not going to like the answer.'

'What am I going to ask?'

'How you can trace which unit owned these weapons in the Gulf. Before they were sent back.'

'Why would I want to know that?'

'So you can figure out who's stealing the lower receivers. Someone is stealing them, right? And selling them. So that gangbangers or whoever can make their AR15s fully automatic. The Gulf's the perfect place to swap parts out. Officially every last paperclip is tracked. But in reality? Different units have different systems. A few have switched to computers. Most are still paper based. Paper gets lost. It gets wet. It gets ripped. Digits get transposed. People have handwriting that's impossible to read. Long story short, you'd have a better chance of selling bikinis at a Mormon convention than tracking that crate.'

'You don't think I have a future as a swimwear salesman?'

The sergeant blinked. 'Sir?'

Reacher said, 'No matter. I don't care who had these guns in the Gulf. Because that's not where the parts were stolen.'

Roberta and Veronica Sanson heard the impact all the way from the street outside. They heard the first of the screams over the background grumble of traffic. Then the cardiac monitor at the head of the bed started to howl again. Its lines had slumped back down to the horizontal. Its display read 00. No heart activity. Only this time the machine was correct. At least as far as Keith Bridgeman was concerned.

Roberta turned left into the corridor and made her way to the hospital's central elevator bank. Veronica went right and looped around to the emergency staircase. Roberta reached the first floor before her sister. She strolled through the reception area, past the café and the store that sold balloons and flowers, and continued out of the main exit. She walked a block west then ducked into a phone booth. She pulled on a pair of latex gloves and called American Airlines. She asked for information about their routes and schedules. Next she called United. Then TWA. She weighed up the options. Then she tossed the gloves in a trash can and made her way to the public parking lot in the centre of the next block.

The sergeant led the way to a storeroom that was tacked on to the side of a large, squat building near the centre of the site. The wind had picked up while they were at the range which made it hard for him to heave the metal door all the way open, and after Reacher had gone through the guy struggled to close it again without getting blown over. He finally wrestled it into place then locked it. Inside, the space was square, eighteen feet by eighteen. The floor was bare concrete. So was the ceiling. It was held up by metal girders that were coated with some kind of knobby fire-retardant material and flanked by strip lights in protective cages. There was a phone mounted by the door and a set of shelves against each wall. They were made of heavy-duty steel, painted grey. Each had a stencilled sign attached – Intake, Green, Amber, Red – and a clipboard with a sheaf of papers hanging from its right-hand upright. There were no windows and the air was heavy with the smell of oil and solvents.

The shelves held crates of weapons. Short at the top, long at the bottom. There were fourteen crates on the Red shelves. Reacher pulled one of the long ones out on to the floor and cracked it open. He lifted out an M16. It was in much worse shape than the one he had fired earlier. That was for sure. He field-stripped it, checked its lower receiver, and shook his head.

He said, 'It's original.'

The sergeant opened another crate and examined one of its rifles. It was also pretty scuffed and scraped. He said, 'This one's the same.'

Each crate had a number stencilled on the side. Reacher took the Red clipboard off its hook and turned to the last sheet. It showed that the crate he'd picked had been signed off by someone with the initials UE. The crate the sergeant had chosen had been initialled by DS. Reacher could only see one other set: LH. He picked a crate with a corresponding number, removed the lower receiver from one of the guns inside it, and held the part up for the sergeant to see.

The sergeant said, 'Jackpot.'

Reacher said, 'LH signed off on this. Who's LH?'

'Sergeant Hall. In charge of the inspection team.'

'Sergeant Hall's a woman.'

'Yes. Sergeant Lisa Hall. How—'

'UE and DS are men?'

'Yes. But—'

'There are no other women on the team?'

'No. But I still—'

Reacher held up his hand. 'Fifteen days ago you received a Red crate by mistake. Fourteen days ago we received a report that M16s had been stolen from this facility. We checked. They hadn't.'

'I heard about the raid. I don't see the connection.'

'The report was anonymous, but the voice was female. I read the file.'

'I still don't—'

'Sergeant Hall realized a Red crate was missing the day after it got mishandled. She knew it could be traced back to her so she made a bogus accusation. A serious one. Stolen weapons. The investigators came running, just like she knew they would. They opened all the crates, including hers. They were looking for M16s. Complete ones. That's what they found, so they closed the case. No crime detected. Then if the missing receivers came to light, Hall had just been cleared of theft. She was hoping an investigator would make the same jump you did. That the doctored weapons arrived that way, from the Gulf.'

'No. I know Lisa Hall. She wouldn't do something like that.'

'Let's make sure. Where is she today?'

'Don't know, sir.'

'Then find out.'

'Sir.' The sergeant shuffled across to the phone on the wall. Thin clouds of dust puffed up around his feet. He dialled slowly, made the enquiry, and when he was done he said, 'Not on duty, sir.'

Reacher said, 'OK. So where's her billet?'

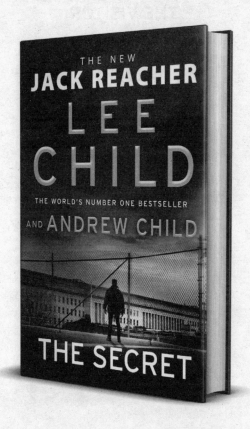

Another close shave for Reacher in
THE VISITOR

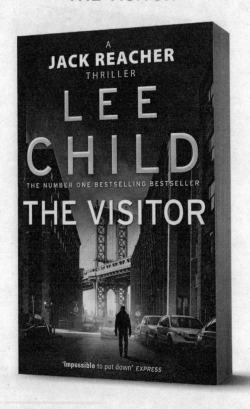

Two women are found dead in their own homes,
naked, in a bath full of paint.
Apparent victims of an army man. A loner, a smart
guy with a score to settle, a ruthless vigilante.
A man just like Jack Reacher.

AVAILABLE IN PAPERBACK,
EBOOK AND AUDIOBOOK

Reacher faces a terrifying
new enemy in
GONE TOMORROW

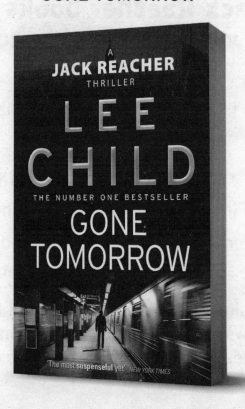

Suicide bombers are easy to spot.
There are twelve tell-tale signs to look for.
Reacher is on the New York subway,
with a woman ticking all twelve boxes.

AVAILABLE IN PAPERBACK,
EBOOK AND AUDIOBOOK

Find out more about the Jack Reacher books at www.JackReacher.com

- Take the book selector quiz
- Enter competitions
- Read and listen to extracts
- Find out more about the authors
- Discover Reacher coffee, music and more . . .

PLUS sign up for the monthly Jack Reacher newsletter to get all the latest news delivered direct to your inbox.

dead good

Looking for more gripping must-reads?

Head over to Dead Good –
the home of killer crime books,
TV and film.

Whether you're on the hunt for an intriguing
mystery, an action-packed thriller
or a creepy psychological drama,
we're here to keep you in the loop.

Get recommendations and reviews from
crime fans, grab discounted books at bargain
prices and enter exclusive giveaways
for the chance to read brand-new releases
before they hit the shelves.

Sign up for the free newsletter:
www.deadgoodbooks.co.uk/newsletter

For up-to-the-minute news about Lee & Andrew Child find us on Facebook

f /JackReacherOfficial

f /LeeChildOfficial

and discover Jack Reacher books on Twitter

🐦 /LeeChildReacher